The shuttle was a disaster area. Across the aisle the far hull had been blown in, leaving a ragged-edged hole a meter or more across. Strands of twisted and blackened metal curled inward from the gap like frozen ribbons; bits and pieces of plastic, cloth, and glass littered everything she could see. The twin seats that had been by the hole had been ripped from their bracings and were nowhere to be seen.

The twin seats that Layn and Raines had been sitting in.

Oh, God. For a moment Jin gazed in horror at the ruined struts. The mission commanders were gone, gone totally from the shuttle . . . from thirty or forty kilometers up.

Reaching up with a hand that was streaked with blood, she groped for her safety harness release. It was jammed; gritting her teeth, she put servo-motor strength into her squeeze and got it free. Shakily, she climbed to her feet, stumbling off-balance on the canted floor.

It was only then that she saw what had happened to Sun.

Jin stared at him for a long minute. *This isn't real,* she told herself wildly, striving to believe it. If she believed it hard enough, maybe it wouldn't have happened . . . *This isn't real. This is our first mission—just our first mission. This can't happen. Not now. Oh, God, please not now.*

TIMOTHY ZAHN

COBRA BARGAIN

BAEN
BOOKS

COBRA BARGAIN

This is a work of fiction. All the characters and events portrayed in this book are fictional, and any resemblance to real people or incidents is purely coincidental.

A Baen Books Original

Baen Publishing Enterprises
260 Fifth Avenue
New York, N.Y. 10001

First printing, February 1988

ISBN: 0-671-65383-0

Cover art by Vincent Di Fate

Printed in the United States of America

Distributed by
SIMON & SCHUSTER
1230 Avenue of the Americas
New York, N.Y. 10020

TIMOTHY ZAHN

COBRA BARGAIN

Chapter 1

"Governor Moreau?"

Deep in personal combat with the official bafflegab staring out at him from his reader, Governor Corwin Jame Moreau switched mental gears with an effort and turned his attention to his intercom. It made for a pleasant change; Thena MiGraw's face was a lot nicer to look at than Directorate papers. "Yes, Thena?"

"Sir, Justin is here. Shall I have him wait a few minutes?"

Corwin grimaced. *Shall I have him wait.* Translation: should she give Corwin a few minutes to prepare himself. Typically perceptive of Thena . . . but Corwin had already stalled this confrontation off a couple of days, and if he wasn't ready now, he never would be. "No, go ahead and send him in," he instructed her.

"Yes, sir."

Corwin took a deep breath, straightening himself in his chair and reaching over to shut off the reader. A moment later the door opened and Justin Moreau strode briskly into the room.

1

Strode briskly; but to Corwin's experienced eye the subtle beginnings of Cobra Syndrome were already starting to show in his brother's movements. The ceramic laminae coating Justin's bones, the implanted weaponry, servos, and joint strengtheners—after twenty-eight years his body was beginning to react to all of it, precipitating the arthritis and anemia that would, a decade or two from now, bring his life to a premature end. Corwin winced in sympathetic pain, wishing for the millionth time that there was something he could do to alter the inevitable. But there wasn't. Like his father before him, Justin had chosen this path willingly.

And like the late Jonny Moreau, he had also chosen to accept his fate with quiet dignity, keeping his pain to himself whenever possible and quietly deflecting any offers of sympathy. In Corwin's opinion, it was a counterproductive approach, serving mainly to increase the Moreau family's collective sense of frustration and helplessness. But he understood his brother well enough to know they had to grant him his choice of how to face the long and painful path ahead.

"Justin," Corwin nodded in greeting, reaching across the desk to offer his brother his hand. "You're looking good. How are you feeling?"

"Pretty good," Justin said. "Actually, I suspect that at the moment you're suffering more from Cobra Syndrome than I am."

Corwin felt his lip twist. "Caught the debate on the pub/info net last night, I see."

Justin made a disgusted sound in the back of his throat. "All of it I could stomach, anyway. Which wasn't very much. Is Priesly as much of a phrijpicker in private as he is in public?"

"I almost wish he was. I'd actually be happier if he and the rest of the Jects were simply the frothing idiots they look like on the net—if they were we'd have found their strings years ago." Corwin sighed. "No, unfortunately Priesly is as sharp as he is gantua-headed, and now that he's finally hammered the Jects into a real political force he sees himself as holding the balance of power in both the Council and Directorate. That's heavy stuff for someone who considers himself an outcast, and he sometimes goes a little overboard."

"Does he?" Justin asked bluntly. "Hold the balance of power, I mean?"

Corwin shrugged. "I don't know," he admitted. "With his pack of sore losers trying to stir up a full-fledged crisis none of the Syndics or Governors seem quite sure of how to handle him. If Priesly offers them a deal that would henceforth keep him quiet . . ." He shook his head. "It's conceivable they might go for it."

"We still need the Cobras," Justin interjected with some heat. "Need them more than ever, in fact. With Esquiline and the other New Worlds expanding like crazy, they need a steady supply of Cobras. Not to mention the need to keep a credible Cobra force here in case some group of Trofts decide to—"

"Easy, brother," Corwin cut him off, hands held palm outward. "You're preaching to the converted, remember?"

"Sorry," Justin growled. "Priesly's pack has a way of getting under my skin. I wish someone had realized sooner that the Jects were a political powder keg waiting for a flicker to come along. *That* should have been obvious as soon as we found out about Cobra Syndrome."

"Hindsight is wonderful, isn't it?" Corwin said dryly. "What would *you* have done, then?"

"Given them the regular nanocomputer and made them full Cobras in the first place," Justin growled. "It's just a waste of time, energy, and expensive equipment to have them running around with bone laminae and servos their computer won't let them use."

Corwin cocked an eyebrow. He'd heard variants of that argument before, but never from Justin. "You don't really mean that."

"Why not?" Justin countered. "Okay, so the training

period uncovered psychological problems the pre-screening had missed. So what? Most of the glitches weren't all that severe; given time, they'd probably have worked things out eventually by themselves."

"And what about the harder cases?" Corwin asked. "Would you really have taken the risk of turning potentially unstable Cobras loose on the general population?"

"We could have handled that," Justin said doggedly. "They could have been assigned out of the way somewhere—permanent spine leopard hunting duty, maybe, or the really tricky cases could have been sent to Caelian. If they didn't work out their problems, eventually they'd have done something stupid and gotten themselves killed."

"And if they weren't so cooperative?" Corwin asked quietly. "If they decided instead that they were being dumped on and went after revenge?"

Some of the energy went out of Justin's face. "Yeah," he sighed. "And then it would be Challinor all over again."

A shiver went up Corwin's back. Tors Challinor's attempted treason had occurred well over half a century ago, before he'd even been born . . . but he remembered the stories his parents had told him about that time. Remembered them as vividly as if he'd been there himself. Jonny had made sure of that; the incident had carried some vital truths, and he hadn't wanted them to ever get lost. "Challinor, or worse," he told Justin soberly. "Remember that this time it wouldn't have been basically stable Cobras pushed by idiot bureaucracy to take matters into their own hands. It would have been flawed Cobras, and a hell of a lot more of them." He took a deep breath, willing the memories away. "Agreed, Priesly is a nuisance; but at least as a Ject all he can go for is political power."

"I suppose you're right," Justin sighed. "It's just that . . . never mind. As long as we're on the subject, though—" Digging into his tunic pocket, he pulled a magcard out and tossed it onto the desk. "Here's our latest proposal for how to close the remaining gaps in the prelim psych tests. I figured as long as I was coming over here anyway I'd give you an advance copy."

Corwin took the magcard, trying not to grimace. A perfectly reasonable thing for Justin to do, and under normal circumstances nothing for anyone to complain about. But things in the Council and Directorate weren't exactly normal at the moment. *Advance notice.* Corwin could just hear what Priesly and his allies would say about this. "Thanks," he told Justin, placing the magcard over by his reader. "Though I may not get time to look at it until after the rest of the Council get their copies, anyway."

Justin's forehead furrowed slightly. "Oh? Well, it's hardly going to make a big splash, I'm afraid. We're projecting to go from a seven-percent post-surgery rejection rate to maybe a four, four and a half percent rate."

Corwin nodded heavily. "About what we expected. No chance of getting things any tighter?"

Justin shook his head. "The psych people aren't even sure we can get it this tight. The problem is that having Cobra gear implanted in people sometimes . . . changes them."

"I know. It's better than nothing, I suppose."

For a moment there was silence. Corwin's gaze drifted out his window, to the Capitalia skyline. That skyline had changed a lot in the twenty-six years since he'd struck out on his own into the maze that was Cobra Worlds politics. Unfortunately, other things had changed even more than the skyline. Lately he found himself spending a lot of time staring out that window, trying to recapture the sense of challenge and excitement he'd once felt about his profession. But the bootstrapping seldom worked. Somewhere along the line, pushed perhaps by Priesly's public bitterness, Cobra Worlds politics had taken on a hard edge Corwin had never before experienced. In many ways it had soured the game for him—turned both his victories and defeats a uniform bittersweet gray—and made the governorship a form of combat instead of a means for aiding the progress of his worlds.

It brought to mind thoughts about his father, who had similarly soured on politics late in life, and more and more often these days he found himself fantasizing about chucking the whole business and escaping to Esquiline or one of the other New Worlds.

But he couldn't, and he knew it. As long as the Jects' sour grapes were threatening the foundation of the Cobra Worlds' security and survival, someone had to stay and fight. And he'd long ago realized that he was one of those someones.

Across the desk from him Justin shifted slightly in his chair, breaking the train of Corwin's musings. "I assume you had a specific reason for asking me here?" he probed gently.

Corwin took a deep breath and braced himself. "Yes, I did. I heard from Coordinator Maung Kha three days ago about Jin's application to the Academy. He was . . ." He hesitated, trying one last time to find a painless way to say this.

"Summarily rejecting it?" Justin offered.

Corwin gave up. "She never had a chance," he said bluntly, forcing himself to look his brother straight in the eye. "You should have realized that right from the start and not let her file it."

Justin didn't flinch. "You mean there's no reason to try and change an unfair policy simply because it *is* policy?"

"Come on, Justin—you *teach* out there, for heaven's sake. You know how traditions hang on. Especially military traditions."

"I also know that those traditions started back in the Old Dominion of Man," Justin countered. "We haven't exactly been noted for blindly adopting their methods in anything else. Why should the military be immune?"

Corwin sighed. Various combinations of Moreau family members had hashed through all this in one form or another dozens of times over the past few years, ever since Justin's youngest daughter had first decided she wanted to follow in her father's Cobra footsteps. Like Justin's father before him . . . and Corwin was well aware that, for the Moreaus at least, family tradition wasn't something to be treated lightly.

Unfortunately, most of the others on the Council didn't see it that way. "Military tradition is always particularly hidebound," he told Justin. "You know it, I know it, the worlds know it. It comes of having conservative old people like you at the top running things."

Justin ignored the attempt at levity. "But Jin would be a *good* Cobra, possibly even a great Cobra—and that's not just my opinion. I've given her the standard screening tests—"

"You've *what*?" Corwin cut him off, aghast. "Justin—damn it all, you know better than that. Those tests are *exclusively* for the use of the Academy."

"Spare me the lecture, please. The point is that she scored in the top five percent of the acceptance range. She's better equipped, mentally and emotionally, than ninety-five percent of the people we've accepted."

"Even granting all that," Corwin sighed, "the point remains that she's a woman, and women have never been Cobras."

"Up till *now* they haven't—"

"Governor!" Thena MiGraw's voice on the intercom cut him off. "There's a man coming—"

And behind Justin the door slammed open and a stranger leaped into the office.

"Destroy the Cobras!" he shrieked.

Corwin froze, the sheer unexpectedness of it holding him in place for those first crucial seconds. The intruder took a few rapid steps into the room, arms waving, raving just short of incomprehensibility. Out of the corner of his eye Corwin saw that Justin had dropped out of his chair, spinning on his heels into a crouch facing the intruder. "All right, hold it!" the Cobra snapped. His hands were up, the little fingers with their implanted lasers tracking the man.

But if the other heard Justin's command, he ignored it. "The Cobras are the destruction of freedom and liberty," he screamed, taking yet another step toward Corwin. "They must be *destroyed!*" His right hand swung in a wide circle toward Corwin's face and then dipped into his tunic pocket—

And Justin's outstretched fingers spat needles of light directly into his chest.

The man shrieked, an oddly gurgling sound. His knees buckled, slamming him to the floor. With an effort, Corwin shook off his stunned paralysis and jabbed at the intercom. "Thena! Security and a med team, fast."

"Already called them, Governor," she said, her own voice trembling with shock.

Justin had stepped to the intruder's side and knelt down beside him. "Alive?" Corwin asked, holding his breath as his brother's fingers touched the other's neck.

"Yeah. At least for the moment. Any idea what the hell that was all about?"

"None. Let's let Security sort it out." Corwin took a deep breath, let it out carefully. "Glad you were here. Thanks."

"No charge. Let's find out what kind of gun he was carrying . . ." Justin reached into the intruder's tunic pocket . . . and an odd expression settled onto his face. "Hell," he said, very softly.

"What?" Corwin snapped, getting to his feet.

Still kneeling beside the wounded man, Justin gazed down at him. "He's unarmed."

Chapter 2

Cari Moreau slouched back in her lounge chair, a seventeen-year-old's version of a martyr's expression plastered across her face. "Aw, come on, Jin," she complained. *"Again?"*

Jasmine Moreau—"Jin" to her family and everyone else she could persuade to use the nickname—gazed at her younger cousin with a combination of patience, affection, and rock-solidness. "Again," she said firmly. "You want to pass this test or don't you?"

Cari sighed theatrically. "Oh, all *right.* Slavemaker. *Misk'rhe'ha solf owp'smeaf, pierec'eay'kartoh—*"

"That's *'khartoh,'* " Jin interrupted. "Kh-sound, not k. And the initial 'p' in *'pierec'eay'khartoh'* is aspirated." She demonstrated. "The difference between p-sounds in 'pin' and 'spin.' "

"I don't hear any difference," Cari grumbled. "And I'll bet Ms. Halverson won't, either."

"Maybe *she* won't, no," Jin agreed. "But if you ever

9

plan to use your catertalk on any Trofts, you'd better be sure to get it right."

"So who says I'm planning to use it on any Trofts?" Cari grumbled. "Any Trofts *I* run into are gonna understand Anglic."

"You don't know that," Jin shook her head. "Traders or demesne representatives assigned to the Worlds will, sure. But who says you're never going to wind up somewhere out in space with only Trofts who snargled off in *their* language lessons, too?"

That got her a snort from her cousin. "That's easy for *you* to say. *You're* gonna be the Cobra zipping around out there, not me. Of *course* you're gonna need to know catertalk and Qasaman and all."

Jin felt a lump rise to her throat. Of all her relatives, Cari was the only one who was truly enthusiastic about her Cobra ambitions . . . and the only one who took for granted that she would achieve them. On that latter point even Jin's father had trouble, and Jin could remember times when only a long private talk with Cari had kept those hopes and dreams alive . . .

And with a jolt she realized that the younger girl had neatly deflected the conversation into a right angle. "Never mind what *I'm* going to need," she growled with mock irritation. "At the moment it's *you* who needs to know this stuff, because *you're* the one who's going to be tested on it tomorrow. Again—and remember the asperated-p in *pierec'eay'khartoh* this time. You pronounce it the wrong way to a Troft and he's either going to fall over laughing or else challenge you to a duel."

Cari perked up a bit. "Why?—is it something dirty the way I said it?" she asked eagerly.

"Never mind," Jin told her. The error was, in fact, a fairly innocuous one, but she had no intention of telling her cousin that. She could remember back three years to when she'd been seventeen herself, and a slight hint of wickedness might help spice up a course Cari clearly considered to be deathly dull. "Let's try it again," she said. "From the top."

Cari took a deep breath and closed her eyes. "*Misk'-rhe—*"

Across the room the phone warbled. "I'll get it," Cari interrupted herself, bounding with clear relief out of her chair and racing toward the instrument. ". . . Hello? . . . Oh, hi, Fay. Jin!—it's your sister."

Jin unfolded her legs from beneath her and walked over to Cari's side. Three steps from the phone screen the expression on Fay's face suddenly registered, and she took the remaining distance in two quick strides. "What's wrong?" she asked.

"Thena MiGraw just called from Uncle Corwin's office," Fay said grimly. "There was some kind of crazy incident there a few minutes ago, and Dad wound up shooting someone."

Beside Jin, Cari gasped. "He *what*?" Jin asked. "Did he kill him?"

"No idea yet. The guy's been rushed to the hospital, and Dad and Uncle Corwin are there now. Thena said she'd call again and let us know if and when they learned anything."

Jin licked suddenly dry lips. "Which hospital are they at?"

Fay shook her head. "She said specifically *not* to go there. Uncle Corwin told her he didn't want anybody else underfoot while they sorted this out."

Jin gritted her teeth. Understandable, but she didn't have to like it. "Did she say how Dad was doing? Or give any other details?"

Fay shrugged uncomfortably. "Dad was pretty shaken up, I guess, but he wasn't falling apart. If there were any other details Thena wasn't giving them out."

Even through the surreal numbness in Jin's mind, she felt a brief flicker of pride. No, of course her father wouldn't fall apart. A Cobra who'd survived both Qasaman missions wouldn't break over something like this. Besides which, she would bet large sums that whatever had happened had been the other guy's fault. "Have you talked to Gwena yet?"

Fay shook her head. "I was hoping to have more details before I did that. She's got all she needs on her mind already, and I'd hate for her to drop everything and fly in unnecessarily."

"Better let her decide how necessary it is," Jin advised. "They can always reschedule her thesis defense, and she'll be pretty hurt if she has to learn about this from the net. Anything on the net yet, speaking of which?"

"This early? Shouldn't be. Anyway, I just wanted you to know what had happened, make sure you were here when Dad gets home."

"Yeah, thanks," Jin nodded. "I'll come now."

"Okay. See you soon." Fay's face vanished from the screen.

Beside Jin, Cari took a shuddering breath. "I'd better call Mom and Dad," she said. "They'll want to know about this."

"Thena's probably already done that," Jin told her, eyes focused on the empty phone screen. Something was nagging, premonition-like, at the back of her mind . . . Reaching out, she tapped the phone's numberpad, keying it into Capitalia's major public/info net. *Search/ proper name: Moreau, Justin,* she instructed it.

"What are you doing?" Cari asked. "Fay said there wouldn't be anything on it yet."

Jin clenched her teeth. "Fay was wrong. Take a look."

There was no sign on the driveway leading to the squat, square building nestled back from the street a few blocks from Capitalia's main business district. Not that a sign would have made much difference; the small plaque beside the windowless front door proclaiming the place to be the Kennet MacDonald Memorial Center would mean little to the average Capitalian citizen.

To the city's Cobra population, the name meant a great deal more. As did the building itself.

The door was locked, but Jin knew the code. The center's softly lit social areas were largely deserted, she noted as she padded quietly past them, with only a relative handful of Cobras sitting together in twos or threes. Attendance had been dwindling, she knew, ever since Priesly and his loud-faced Jects had started harping on what they liked to call "Cobra elitism." Gazing across the empty chairs and tables, Jin's mind flashed back to her childhood, to the hours she'd spent here with her father and the other Cobras. The men who were the true heroes of the Cobra Worlds.

And now those men avoided the center, hesitant to add fuel to Priesly's fires by congregating together. For that alone, Jin thought bitterly, she could wish the Jects to drown in their own saliva.

Her father was where she'd expected to find him: downstairs, alone, in the large practice area the Cobras had dubbed the Danger Room.

For a few minutes she stood above him in the observation gallery, watching and remembering. The target robots the room's computer controlled weren't especially smart, but they were fast and numerous. As a child, Jin had also thought their low-power lasers were dangerous, and she could still remember the terror she'd felt watching from up here as her father went head-to-head against them. In actuality, as she'd finally learned years later, the robots' lasers were dangerous only to a Cobra's pride; but that knowledge couldn't entirely suppress her adrenaline-fueled gut reaction as she watched her father fight.

It wasn't exactly an even fight, for one thing. Arrayed against Justin at any given time were between four and seven of the target robots, all taking pot shots at him, often with little concern for their own welfare. Cover in the Danger Room had been deliberately kept to a minimum, leaving the Cobra no choice but to keep moving if he was to survive.

And Justin kept moving. Superbly, to Jin's admittedly biased way of thinking. Using walls, floor, and ceiling as backstops, his computer-driven servos had him bouncing all around the room, flashes of light flickering almost continuously from the little fingers of both hands as his metalwork lasers combined with his optical-enhancement targeting system to make impossible midair hits on his attackers. Half a dozen times the observation gallery's windows vibrated as reflections from one or the other of Justin's sonic weapons hit them, and once the brilliant spear of his antiarmor laser flashed out from the heel of his left leg to take out a persistent enemy right through the low covering wall it was hiding behind. Jin found herself gritting her teeth as she watched, hands clenched into fists at her sides as her body half crouched in sympathetic readiness. *Someday*, the thought came dimly through her tension, *that could be me in there. Will be me in there.*

At last the lopsided duel was over; and it was with mild surprise that Jin discovered she'd been watching for less than five minutes. Taking a deep breath, she blew at the drop of sweat on the tip of her nose and tapped on the window.

Below, her father looked up, surprise creasing his face as he saw her. *Can I come down?* she hand-signed to him.

Sure, he signed back. *Main door.*

She took the stairway down, and by the time she pushed open the heavy door he had a towel wrapped around his neck and was dabbing at his face with it. "Hi, Jin," he greeted her, coming forward for a quick hug. His expression, she noted, was the flat-neutral one he always used when he was trying to bury some strong emotion. "This is a surprise."

"Thena called an hour ago and said you were on your

way home from the hospital," she explained. "When you didn't show up, I decided to come and find you."

He grunted. "I hope you didn't drive all over Capitalia looking for me."

"Of course not. Where else would you be?"

"Visiting my past?" He glanced around the room.

"Working out tension," she corrected him. "Come on, Dad—I know you better than *that*."

He gave her a half-hearted smile, the mask sliding from his face as he did so to reveal the hidden ache behind it. "You do indeed, my little Jasmine," he said quietly. "You always have."

She put her hand on his arm. "It's a mess, isn't it?"

He nodded. "Yeah. How are you and your sisters holding up?"

"Oh, we're doing all right. The real question is how are *you* doing?"

He shrugged. "As well as can be expected. Better, after this," he added, waving a hand to take in the Danger Room. "How much did Thena tell you?"

"The condensed version only. What happened, Dad?"

His eyes held hers for a minute, then slipped away to look around the room. "It was the stupidest slop-headed thing you've ever seen," he sighed. "On *my* part, I mean. This guy—Baram Monse, the hospital ID'd him—just burst in and started yelling and cursing—anti-Cobra stuff, mainly. I tried stunning him, but he was moving and I turned too slowly to get the sonic lined up properly." He shook his head. "Anyway, he reached into his pocket and I figured he was going for a weapon. It was too late to physically jump him . . . so I used my lasers."

Across the room a maintenance robot trundled in through an access door and began picking up one of the "dead" target robots. "And he didn't have a gun?" Jin ventured at last.

"You got it," Justin said, a touch of bitterness seeping into his tone. "No gun, no spray, not even a tangler reel. Just a simple, harmless, unarmed crank. And I shot him."

Jin looked past him at the maintenance robot. "Was it a setup?" she asked.

From the corner of her eye she caught her father's frown. "What do you mean?" he asked carefully.

"Was Monse trying to goad you or Uncle Corwin into attacking him? Trying to make you look bad?" She turned back to face him. "I don't know if you've seen the net yet, but an absolute flood of condemnation hit the thing practically from the minute Monse was taken off to the hospital. That wasn't reaction—those people had their rhetoric primed and ready to go."

Justin hissed through his teeth. "The thought *has* crossed my mind, I'll admit. And you haven't even heard the best part yet: the fact that Monse is going to live despite taking a pair of setting-two fingertip laser blasts square in the center of his chest. Want to hazard a guess as to how he managed that?"

She frowned. Body armor was the obvious answer . . . but it was clear from her father's tone that it was something more interesting than that. Monse would have needed *some* kind of protection, though—at short range, a twin laser burst at number-two setting would have been perfectly adequate to cut through bones the thickness of ribs or breastbone and take out the lungs or heart beneath them.

Adequate, at least, to cut through normal bones . . . "The same reason Winward lived?" she asked hesitantly.

Justin nodded. "You got it."

A shiver went up Jin's spine. Michael Winward, shot in the chest by a projectile gun during the first Qasaman mission twenty-eight years ago . . . surviving that attack solely because the bullet was deflected by the ceramic laminae coating his breastbone and ribcage. "A Ject," she murmured. "That little phrijpicker Monse is a lousy *Ject*."

"Bull's-eye," Justin sighed. "Unfortunately, that doesn't change the fact that he was unarmed when I shot him."

"Why not?" Jin demanded. "It means I was right—that the whole thing was a setup—*and* it means that Priesly is behind it."

"Whoa, girl," Justin said, putting a hand on each of her shoulders. "What may look obvious to you or me or Corwin isn't necessarily provable."

"But—"

"And until and unless we *can* prove any such connection," he continued warningly, "I'll thank you to keep your allegations to yourself. At this stage it would hurt us far more than it would hurt Priesly."

Jin closed her eyes briefly, fighting back sudden tears. "But why? Why is he picking on you?"

Justin stepped to her side, slipping his arm tightly around her shoulders. Even full-grown, she was a few centimeters shorter than he was—the ideal height, she'd always felt, to nestle in under his arm. "Priesly's not after me in particular," Justin sighed. "I doubt he's even especially after Corwin, except as he's an obstacle that's in Priesly's way. No, what really after is nothing less than the elimination of Cobras from the Cobra Worlds."

Jin licked her lips and hugged him a little closer. She'd heard all the rumors, arguments, and speculations . . . but to hear it said in such a straightforward, cold-blooded way by someone in a position to know the truth sent a chill up her back. "That's insane," she whispered. "Totally insane. How does he expect Esquiline to expand without Cobras leading the way into the wilderness?—Esquiline or the other New Worlds? Not to mention the Caelian Remnant—what's he going to do, just throw them to the peledari and let them get eaten alive?"

She felt his sigh against her side. "Jin, as you grow older you're going to run into a surprising number of otherwise intelligent people who get themselves trapped into some single-rail goal or point of view and never get out of it. Caelian is a perfect example—the people still living there have been fighting that crazy ecology for so long they can't break the habit long enough to back out and accept resettlement somewhere else. Some of the Jects—not all, certainly, but some—are equally single-minded. They wanted to be Cobras—wanted it very badly, most of them—but were deemed unfit, for one reason or another . . . and the love they had has been twisted into hatred. Hatred that demands revenge."

"No matter what the consequences are for the rest of the Cobra Worlds?"

He shrugged. "Apparently not. I don't know—maybe some of them genuinely think the need for Cobras has passed, that everything the Cobras do can be done more efficiently by ordinary men with machines or enhancement exoskeletons. And I'll even admit that some of Priesly's complaints may not be entirely un-reasonable—maybe we *have* picked up a little too much elitist attitude than is good for us."

A maintenance robot passed them, heading toward another of the target robots. Jin's eyes followed it, came to rest on the target . . . and somewhere in the back of her mind a synapse clicked, and for the first time in her life she suddenly realized what those hulking machines she'd been watching all these years really were. "My God," she whispered. "They're Trofts. Those target robots are supposed to be *Trofts*."

"Don't be silly," Justin said; and his voice made her look sharply up at him. On his face—

The expression was blank. Like someone playing poker . . . or someone denying all knowledge of a secret he wasn't allowed to divulge. "I just meant— " she began awkwardly.

"Of course it's not a Troft," Justin cut her off. "Look at the shape, the size and contours. It's nothing but a generic practice target." But even as she looked at him his face seemed to harden a fraction. "Besides, the

Trofts are our trading partners and political allies," he
said. "Our friends, Jin, not our enemies. There's no
reason for us to know how to fight them."

"Of course not," she said, trying hard to match his
same neutral tone as she belatedly caught on. No,
certainly the robots didn't look much like Trofts . . .
but the shape and positioning of their target areas were
too accurate to be accidental. "And I don't suppose anyone really wants to be reminded that they were once
our enemies," she added with a touch of bitterness. "Or
that it was the Cobras who kept that war from even
starting."

He squeezed her shoulders. "The Cobras remember," he said quietly. "And so do the Trofts. That's
what really matters . . . and that's why we'll find a way
to stop Priesly and his lunatic gang." He took a deep
breath. "Come on; let's go home."

Chapter 3

Tamris Chandler, Governor-General of the Cobra Worlds, had come into politics from a successful legal career, and Corwin had noted more than once at Council and Directorate meetings that Chandler seemed to relish his occasional opportunities to play at being prosecuting attorney. He was doing so now . . . but for once, he didn't seem to be enjoying it very much.

"I hope you realize," he said, glaring out from Corwin's phone screen, "how much of a mess your brother has gotten all of us into."

"I understand the mess, sir," Corwin said, keeping a tight rein on his temper. "I contend, however, the assumption that it's Justin's fault."

Chandler waved aside the objection. "Motivational guilt aside, it was he who fired on an unarmed man."

"Who was technically trespassing in my office and threatening me—"

"Threatening *you*?" Chandler cut in, raising his eyebrows. "Did he say anything specifically that applied to you?"

Corwin sighed. "No, sir, not specifically. But he *was* vehemently denouncing the Cobras, and my pro-Cobra views are well known. It may not technically be assault, but any jury would agree that I had cause to fear for my safety."

Chandler glared a moment longer. Then his lip twitched and he shrugged. "It'll never reach a jury, of course—we both know that. And just between us, I think your scenario here is probably correct. Priesly's had you in his sights ever since he joined the Directorate, and to get both you and the Cobras in trouble with a single move is just the sort of sophistication I'd expect from him."

Corwin gritted his teeth against the sarcastic retort that wanted to come out. Sniping at Chandler's thinly disguised admiration of Priesly the Bastard would feel good, but Corwin needed the governor-general's support too much to risk that. "So we both agree the Monse affair was deliberately staged," he said instead. "The question remains, what is the Directorate going to do about it?"

Chandler's eyes drifted away from Corwin's gaze. "Frankly, Moreau, I'm not sure there's anything we *can* do about it," he said slowly. "If you can prove—not allege, *prove*—that Monse came in there trying to goad your brother into opening fire, and if you can *prove* that Priesly was involved in it, then we'll have something we can hook onto. Otherwise—" He shrugged. "I'm afraid he's got too much of a power base for us to throw unsubstantiated accusations at him. You've seen what his people are doing to your brother on the net— he'd flay all the rest of us, too, if we moved against him at this stage."

Or in other words, the governor-general was going to react to this blatant power bid by simply ignoring it. By letting Priesly play out his gambit and hoping he wouldn't bother Chandler himself in the process. "I see," Corwin said, not trying to hide his bitterness. "I presume that if I *am* able to get some of this proof before the Directorate meeting tomorrow that you'll be more supportive of my position?"

"Of course," Chandler said immediately. "But bear in mind that, whatever happens, we won't be spending a lot of time on this incident. There are more important matters awaiting our discussion."

Corwin took a deep breath. *Translation: he'll do what he can to cut Priesly's tirade to a minimum.* It was, he supposed, better than nothing. "Understood, sir."

"Well. If that's all . . . ?"

"Yes, sir. Goodnight, sir."

The screen blanked. Corwin leaned back in his chair, stretching muscles aching with tension and fatigue. That was it: he'd talked to all the members of the Directorate that he had a chance of bringing onto his side in this. Should he move on to the Council and the lower-ranking syndics there? He glanced at his watch, saw to his mild shock that it was already after ten. Far too late to call anyone else now. No wonder, in retrospect, that Chandler had been a little on the frosty side.

A motion off to his side caught his eye, and he looked up as Thena MiGraw put a steaming cup of cahve on his desk. "You about finished for the night?" she asked.

"I don't know if *I* am, but *you* sure should be," he told her tiredly. "Seems to me I told you to go home a couple of hours ago."

She shrugged. "There was some busywork I had to do, anyway," she said, seating herself with her usual grace in a chair at the corner of the desk.

"Besides which, you thought I might need some moral support?"

"That and maybe some help screening out crank calls," she said. "I see that wasn't necessary."

Corwin lifted the cup she'd brought him, savoring for a moment the delicate aroma of the cahve. "The Moreau name's been an important one on Aventine for a long time," he reminded her, taking a sip. "Maybe even the more predatory of the newswriters figure the family's earned a little respect."

"And maybe a little rest, too?" Thena suggested quietly.

Corwin gazed at her, eyes tracing her delicate features and slender figure. A pang of melancholy and loss touched his heart, a pang that seemed to be coming more and more often these days. *I should have married*, he thought tiredly. *Should have had a family.*

He shook off the thought with an effort. There had been good and proper reasons behind his decision all those years ago, and none of those reasons had changed. His father's long immersion in Cobra Worlds' politics had nearly destroyed his mother, and he had sworn that he would never do such a thing to any other human being. Even if he could find a woman who was willing to put up with that kind of life . . .

Again, he forced his mind away from that often-traveled and futile path of thought. "The Moreaus have never been famous for resting when there was work to be done," he told Thena. "Besides, I can rest *next* year. You ought to get on home, though."

"Perhaps in a few minutes." Thena nodded at the phone. "How did the calls go?"

"About as expected. Everyone's a little uncertain of how to handle it, at least from the perspective of practical politics. My guess is that for the time being they'll all keep their heads down and wait for more information."

"Giving Priesly free rein to plant his version in their minds tomorrow." She snorted gently. "Uncommonly nice timing for him, having all this happen just before a full Directorate meeting."

Corwin nodded. "Yeah, I noticed that myself. As did, I'm sure, the other governors. Unfortunately, it doesn't exactly count as evidence."

"Unless you can use it to find a connecting thread—"

She broke off, head cocked in concentration. "Was that a knock?"

Frowning, Corwin hunched forward and keyed his intercom to a security camera view of the outer corridor. "If it's a newswriter—" Thena began ominously.

"It's Jin," Corwin sighed, tapping the intercom and door release. Probably the last person he felt up to facing at the moment . . . "Jin? Door's unlocked—come on in."

"You want me to leave?" Thena asked as he switched the intercom off.

"Not really," he admitted, "but it'd probably be better if you did."

A faint smile flickered across Thena's face as she stood up. "I understand. I'll be in the outer office if you need me." Touching him on the shoulder as she passed, she headed toward the door.

"Uncle Corwin?"

"Come in," Corwin called, waving to the girl—*no; she's a young woman now*—standing in the doorway.

Jin did so, exchanging quiet greetings with Thena as the two women passed each other at the doorway. "Sit down," Corwin invited, gesturing to the chair Thena had just vacated. "How's your dad doing?"

"About as you'd expect," she said, sinking into the chair. "Uncle Joshua came over a while ago and they spent a lot of time talking about other problems the family's had in the past."

Corwin nodded. "I remember similar trips down memory lane. Pretty depressing to listen to?"

She pursed her lips. "A little."

"Try not to let it bother you. It's one of the methods we Moreaus have traditionally used to remind ourselves that things usually wind up working out for the best."

Jin took a deep breath. "Dad told me my application for the Cobra Academy's been rejected."

Corwin's jaw tightened; with a conscious effort he relaxed it. "Did he explain why?" he asked.

She shook her head. "We didn't really discuss it—he had other things on his mind. That's one reason I came to see you."

"Yeah. Well . . . to put it bluntly, you were rejected because you're a woman."

He hadn't really expected her to looked surprised, and she didn't. "That's illegal, you know," she said calmly. "I've studied the Academy's charter, the official Cobra Statement of Purpose, and even the original Dominion of Man documents. There's nothing in any of them that specifically excludes women from the Cobras."

"Of course there isn't," he sighed. "There isn't anything that excludes women from the governorship, either, but you'll notice that there aren't very many women who make it to that office. It's a matter of tradition."

"Whose tradition?" Jin countered. "Neither of those unspoken rules started with the Cobra Worlds. We inherited them from the Old Dominion of Man."

"Sure," he nodded. "But these things take time to change. You have to remember that we're barely two generations removed from the Dominion and its influence."

"It took less than *one* generation for us to give the Cobras their double vote," she pointed out.

"That was different. Tors Challinor's attempted rebellion forced an immediate political acknowledgment of the Cobras' physical power. Your case, unfortunately, doesn't have that kind of urgency to it."

For a long moment Jin just looked at him. "You're not going to fight the Council for me on this, are you?" she asked at last.

He spread his hands helplessly. "It's not a matter of fighting them, Jin. The whole weight of military history is against you. Women just haven't as a rule been welcomed into special military forces. Not *official* military forces, anyway," he corrected himself. "There've always been women rebels and guerrilla fighters, but I

don't think that argument'll go over very well on either
the Council or the Academy."

"You have a lot of influence, though. The Moreau
name alone—"

"May still have some force out among Aventine's
people," he grunted, "but the aura doesn't carry over
into the upper echelons. It never did, really—in many
ways your grandfather was a more popular figure than I
am, and even in his time we had to fight and scrap and
trade for everything we got."

Jin licked her lips. "Uncle Corwin . . . I have to get
into the Academy. I *have* to. It's Dad's last chance to
have one of the family carry on the Cobra tradition.
Now, more than ever, he needs that to hang onto."

Corwin closed his eyes briefly. "Jin, look . . . I know
how much that tradition means to Justin. Every time
one of you girls was born—" He broke off. "The point is
that the universe doesn't always work the way we want
it to. If he and your mother had had a son—"

"But they didn't," Jin interrupted with a vehemence
that startled him. "They *didn't*; and Mom's gone, and
I'm Dad's last chance. His *last chance*—don't you
understand?"

"Jin—" Corwin stopped, mind searching uselessly for
something to say . . . and as he hesitated, he found his
eyes probing the face of the young woman before him.

There was a lot of Justin in her face, in her features
and her expressions. But as he thought back over the
twenty years since her birth he found he could see even
more of her father in her manner and personality. How
much of that, he wondered vaguely, was due to genes
alone and how much was due to the fact that Justin had
been her only parent since she was nine years old?
Thoughts of Justin sent a new kaleidoscope of images
flurrying past his mind's eye: Justin fresh out of the
Cobra Academy, excited by the upcoming mission to
what was then the totally mysterious world of Qasama;
an older and more sober Justin at his wedding to Aimee

Partae, telling Corwin and Joshua about the son he would have someday to carry on the Moreau family's Cobra tradition; Justin and his three daughters, fifteen years later, at Aimee's funeral . . .

With an effort, he forced his thoughts back to the present. Jin was still sitting before him, the intensity of purpose in her expression balanced by a self-control rarely found among twenty-year-olds. One of the primary factors looked for in all Cobra applicants, he remembered distantly . . . "Look, Jin," he sighed. "Odds are very high that there's nothing at all I can do to influence the Academy's decision. But . . . I'll do what I can."

A ghost of a smile brushed Jin's lips. "Thank you," she said quietly. "I wouldn't be asking you to do this if it weren't for Dad."

He looked her straight in the eye. "Yes, you would," he said. "Don't try to con an old politician, girl."

She had the grace to blush. "You're right," she admitted "I *want* to be a Cobra, Uncle Corwin. More than anything else I've ever wanted."

"I know," he said softly. "Well. You'd better get back home. Tell your father . . . just tell him hi for me, and that I'll be in touch on this thing."

"Okay. Goodnight . . . and thank you."

"Sure."

She left and Corwin sighed to himself. *Your basic chicken-egg problem,* he thought. *Which came first: her desire to be a Cobra, or her love for her father?*

And did it really make any difference?

Thena reappeared in the doorway. "Everything all right?" she asked.

"Oh, sure," he growled. "I've just promised to take a running leap at a stone wall, that's all. How do I get myself into these things?"

She smiled. "Must be because you love your family."

He tried to glare at her, just on general principles,

but it was too much effort. "Must be," he admitted,
returning her smile. "Go on, get out of here."

"If you're sure . . . ?"

"I am. I'm only going to be a few more minutes
myself."

"Okay. See you in the morning."

He waited until he heard the outer door close behind
her. Then, with a sigh, he leaned back to his reader,
keying for the government info net and his own private
correlation program. Somewhere, somehow, there had
to be a connection between Baram Monse and Governor Harper Priesly.

And he was going to find it.

Chapter 4

The Directorate meeting started at ten sharp the next morning . . . and it was as bad as Corwin had expected.

Priesly was in fine form, his tirade all the more impressive for being brief. A less gifted politician might have overdone it and wound up boring his audience, but Priesly avoided that trap with ease. In front of the entire Council, where the sheer number of members lent itself to the generation and manipulation of emotional/political winds, the longer-winded speeches were often effective; in front of the nine-member Directorate such ploys were dangerous, not to mention occasionally coming off as downright silly. But Corwin had hoped Priesly would try anyway and hang himself in the process.

He should have known better.

". . . and I therefore feel that this body has the *duty* to reexamine the entire concept of elitism that the Cobras and the Cobra Academy represent," Priesly concluded. "Not only for the sake of the people of Aventine and the other worlds, but even for the Cobras themselves. Before another tragedy like this one occurs. Thank you."

He sat down. Corwin glanced around the table, noting the expressions of the others with the frustration he was feeling more and more these days. They were falling into the standard and predictable pattern: Rolf Atterberry of Palatine firmly on Priesly's side, Fenris Vartanson of Caelian—himself a Cobra—and Governor Emeritus Lizabet Telek just as firmly against him, the others leaning one way or the other but not yet willing to commit themselves.

At the head of the table Governor-General Chandler cleared his throat. "Mr. Moreau: any rebuttal?"

Or in other words, had Corwin found any positive link between Priesly and Monse. "Not specifically, sir," he said, getting briefly to his feet. "I would, though, like to remind the other members of this body of the testimony Justin and I have already put on record . . . and also to remind them that my brother has spoken here many times in the past in his capacity as an instructor of the Cobra Academy. A position, I'll mention, that requires him to submit to frequent psychological, physical, and emotional testing."

"If I may just insert here, sir," Priesly put in smoothly, "I have no quarrel at all with Cobra Justin Moreau. I agree with Governor Moreau that he is an outstanding and completely stable member of the Aventinian community. It is, in fact, the very fact that such a fine example of Cobra screening could still attack an unarmed man that worries me so."

Chandler grunted. "Mr. Moreau . . . ?"

"No further comments, sir," Corwin said, and sat back down. Priesly had taken a chance with that interruption, he knew, and with a little luck it would wind up working against him. The thrust of his arguments, serious though they were, were still a far cry from the result he and Monse had almost certainly been trying

for. If Monse had succeeded in triggering the combat
reflexes programmed into Justin's implanted nanocomputer, Priesly would have had a far stronger bogy to
wave in front of both the Directorate and the populace
as a whole.

Across the table, Ezer Gavin stirred. "May I ask, Mr.
Chandler, what Cobra Moreau's status is at the moment? I presume he's been suspended from his Academy duties?"

"He has," Chandler nodded. "The investigation is
proceeding—much of it at this point into Mr. Monse's
background, I may add."

Corwin glanced at Priesly, read no reaction there.
Hardly surprising—he already knew that whatever
Priesly's connection was with Monse, it was well buried.

"I'd like to also point out, if I may," Lizabet Telek
spoke up with an air of impatience, "that for all the fuss
we're generating—both here and on the nets," she
added with a glance at Priesly, "this Monse character
wasn't killed or even seriously injured."

"If he hadn't had that ceramic laminae on his bones
he would have been," Atterberry put in.

"If he hadn't been trespassing in the first place he
wouldn't have been hurt at all," Telek retorted. "Mr.
Governor-General, could we possibly move on to some
other topic? This whole discussion is turning my
stomach."

"As it happens, we do have another topic to tackle
today—one which is far more serious," Chandler nodded. "All further discussion on the Monse case to be
tabled until further investigations are complete . . .
now, then." He tapped a button next to his reader; a
moment later the door across the room opened and a
dress-uniformed Cobra ushered a thin academic type
into the chamber. "Mr. Pash Barynson, of the Qasaman
Monitor Center," Chandler introduced the newcomer
as he walked over to the guest chair at the governor-
general's left. "He's here to brief us on a disturbing

pattern that may or may not be—Well, I'll let him sort it all out for you. Mr. Barynson . . . ?"

"Thank you, Governor-General Chandler," Barynson said with a self-conscious bob of his head. Setting a handful of magcards down on the table, he picked one up and inserted it into his reader. "Governors; governors emeritus," he said, glancing around at them all, "I'm going to admit right up front that I'm rather . . . uncomfortable, shall we say, about being here. As Mr. Chandler has just indicated, there are hints of a pattern emerging on Qasama that we don't like. On the other hand, what that pattern really means—or even if it really exists—are questions we still can't answer."

Well, that's *certainly clear*, Corwin thought. He glanced across the table at Telek, saw a sour expression flicker across her face. As a former academician herself, Corwin knew, she had even less patience with flowery fence-straddling than he did. "Suppose you elaborate and let us judge," she invited.

That got her a frown from Chandler, but Barynson didn't seem insulted. "Of course, Governor Emeritus," he nodded. "First, since all of you may not be familiar with the background here—" he glanced at Priesly— "I'd like to briefly run through the basics for you.

"As most of you know, in 2454 the Council had a series of six spy satellites placed into high orbit over the world of Qasama for the purpose of monitoring their technological and societal development following the introduction of Aventinian spine leopards into their ecological structure. In the twenty years since then the program has met with only limited success. We've noted that the village system has expanded beyond the so-called Fertile Crescent region, indicating either that the Qasamans' cultural paranoia has eased somewhat or that they've given up on keeping their long-range communications immune from interception. We've spotted evidence of some improvement in their aircraft and ground vehicles, as well as various minor changes you've had full reports on over the years. Nothing, so far, that would give us any reason to believe the Qasaman threat vis-a-vis the Cobra Worlds has in any way changed for the worse."

He cleared his throat and tapped a button on the reader. A series of perhaps fifty dates and times appeared on Corwin's reader—the earliest nearly thirty months ago, he noted, the most recent only three weeks old—under the heading *Satellite Downtimes*. A quick scan of the numbers showed that, for each downtime listed, the affected satellite had lost between three and twelve hours of its record. "As you can see," Barynson continued, "over the last thirty months we've lost something on the order of four hundred hours of data covering various parts of Qasama. Up until recently we didn't think too much about it—"

"Why not?" Urbanic Bailar of the newly colonized world Esquiline cut in. "I was under the impression that the main duty of your Monitor Center was to keep the planet under constant surveillance. I wasn't aware that leaving twelve-hour gaps qualified as *constant*."

"I understand your concern," Barynson said soothingly, "but I assure you that Esquiline was—is—in no danger whatsoever. Even if the Qasamans knew your world's location—which they don't—there's simply no way they could create an attack fleet without our knowing it. Remember that they lost all their interstellar capability shortly after they reached Qasama—they'd be starting from literal step zero." Something flicked across his eyes, too fast for Corwin to read. "No, none of us are in any immediate danger from the Qasamans—that much we're certain of."

"Well, I for one don't see what the fuss is," Atterberry snorted. "Self-repairing machinery like satellites are *supposed* to fail occasionally, aren't they?"

"Yes, but not this often," Governor Emeritus David Nguyen put in.

"Both of you are correct, actually," Barynson nodded, licking briefly at his lips. "Which is why we hadn't paid the gaps any real attention. However, a week ago one of our people, more on a hunch than anything else, tried running location and vector correlations on them. It turned out—well, here, you can see for yourselves," he said, pushing another series of keys.

A map of the Fertile Crescent region of Qasama, home to virtually all the humans on that world, appeared on Corwin's reader. A series of colored ovals and arrows had been superimposed on the landscape.

"Interesting," Telek growled. "How many of these gaps are missing that same chunk of the Crescent's western arm?"

"Thirty-seven of the fifty-two," Barynson said. "All but two of the others—"

"Lose some of the territory directly to the east of that section," Priesly interrupted him.

Corwin felt something cold crawl up his back. "You have any small-scales of that place?" he asked.

A slightly grainy picture replaced the map. "This is a photo taken three years ago, before the rash of malfunctions," Barynson said. "For those familiar with the Qasaman landscape, the city in the left-center of the picture is Azras; the one northeast of it, near top-center, is Purma."

Involuntarily, Corwin glanced up at Telek, to find her eyes likewise on him. *Purma*—the city where the Qasamans had tried their damnedest to kill three members of Telek's original spy mission . . . one of those three being Justin.

"Now *here*—" the photo changed "—is that same area as of the last satellite collection two weeks ago."

Azras and Purma were essentially unchanged. But in the center of the screen— "What's that thing in the middle?" Gavin asked.

"It appears to be a large compound or encampment or something." Barynson took a deep breath. "And from all indications, it's not only encircled by the standard Qasaman defensive wall, but is also completely covered on top."

Protected from overhead surveillance . . . "And those areas on either side of it?" Corwin asked.

"Those could have been blanked out by accident," Barynson said carefully. "But if they're not . . . we think it significant that east—parallel to the planet's rotation—is the obvious direction for practice in firing large, long-range rockets."

There was a long moment of silence. "Are you telling us," Bailar said at last, "that that covered compound is the center of a Qasaman missile base?"

Barynson nodded grimly. "The probability seems high that the Qasamans are attempting to rediscover space travel. And that they may be succeeding."

Chapter 5

For a long minute there was silence in the room. Then Atterberry stirred. "Well," he said to no one in particular, "so much for *that* one."

"So much for that one *what*?" Telek growled at him.

"That attempt to keep the Qasamans down," Atterberry amplified. "Trying to break their intersocial cooperation by tricking the mojos off the people and onto spine leopards—the whole Moreau Proposal, in other words."

"Who says it's been a failure?" Corwin put in, not bothering to keep the annoyance out of his voice. He and his family had sweat blood over that proposal . . . and in the process had saved the Cobra Worlds a long and costly and possibly losing war. "All we have here is an inference from a possible assumption based on questionable data. With that underground communications system of theirs we have no way of really knowing what's going on down there."

"All right," Atterberry snorted. "Let's hear *your* idea of what that compound is for, then."

"There could be hundreds of explanations," Corwin shot back. "Ninety percent of which would have nothing to do with any spaceward expansion."

"Such as a new test facility for the air-to-air missiles they've already got, for instance," Telek said. "Or longer-range ones for use against each other."

Chandler cleared his throat. "I think you're both missing the point," he said. "Whatever they're doing down there, the fact is that *if* Dr. Barynson and his colleagues are correct about the satellite malfunctions, then we're already talking a serious threat. Am I correct, Dr. Barynson, in the assumption that those satellites aren't easily knocked out?"

"Without our realizing that they *had* been deliberately hit?" Barynson nodded. "Most definitely. That's one of the reasons we were so slow to notice the pattern of the downtimes, in fact—with no obvious physical damage anywhere, there was no reason to assume the Qasamans were responsible."

"Have we established the Qasamans *were* responsible?" Vartanson spoke up. "You haven't yet suggested a mechanism for this purported sabotage, Doctor, and until you do I don't see how this can be treated as anything but an admittedly odd coincidence."

Barynson scratched at his cheek. "That's the dilemma we're in, all right, Governor," he admitted. "As I said, there hasn't been any obvious physical damage to any of the satellites. We've checked into some of the other possibilities—high-powered lasers blinding the lenses from the surface, for example—but so far none of the simulations give us the right kind of damage profile."

"How about ionizing radiation?" Vartanson persisted. "And I don't necessarily mean radiation from Qasama."

"Solar flares?" Barynson shrugged. "It's certainly one possibility. But if we assume random flares or ionosphere shifts we're still left with the question of why only that one area was so often left unmonitored."

"It seems to me," Nguyen spoke up quietly, "that we

could argue about this forever without getting anywhere. Mr. Moreau is correct: we have insufficient data for any solid conclusions. The only way we're going to get the kind of information we need will be to go back down there."

"In other words, send in another spy mission," Atterberry said with undisguised distaste. "The last one we sent in—"

"Wound up buying us nearly thirty years of peace," Telek put in tartly.

"Postponing a war that's going to have to be fought anyway, you mean—"

"Who said it's going to have to be fought?" Telek snapped. "For all we know, that compound has nothing to do with us—it could just as well be part of the preparations for an all-out internecine war that'll blow the Qasamans back to a pre-metal culture."

"I hope," Priesly said quietly, "that you aren't as eager for that result as you sound."

Telek's jaw tightened visibly. "I don't particularly want to see the Qasamans destroy themselves, no," she growled. "But if it comes down to a choice between them and us, I want *us* to be the ones who survive."

Chandler cleared his throat. "It should be obvious that, whatever reservations we might have, Mr. Nguyen is correct. Another mission to Qasama is called for, and the sooner we get it underway, the sooner we'll find out what's going on." He tapped a key on his reader, and the telephoto on Corwin's reader was replaced by a list of nine names. "Given the experience of the first Qasaman mission," Chandler continued, "it would appear to make more sense to start primarily with new Cobra recruits than to try and retrain older frontier-duty Cobras for the different kind of action they might face on Qasama. I've taken the liberty of running a preliminary sort-through of the latest acceptance list; these are the names that fell out."

"Sorted how?" Gavin asked.

"Particular emotional stability, ability to mix well and comfortably socially—that sort of thing," Chandler replied. "It's just a preliminary sorting, of course."

Vartanson straightened up from his reader. "How many Cobras were you planning to send on the mission?" he asked Chandler.

"The initial plan is calling for one experienced Cobra and four fresh recruits—"

"You can't have them," Vartanson said flatly.

All eyes turned to the Cobra. "What in the worlds are you talking about?" Bailar asked, frowning.

Vartanson gestured at his reader. "Six of these recruits are from Caelian. We need them back there."

Chandler took a deep breath. "Mr. Vartanson . . . I understand the close community feeling the people of Caelian have—"

"There are barely three thousand of us left, Mr. Chandler," Vartanson said, his tone icy. "Twenty-five hundred civilians, five hundred Cobras—all of us fighting for our lives against Hell's Own Blender. We can't afford to let you take even one of those Cobras away from us . . . and you're not going to."

An uncomfortable silence filled the room. Caelian was a dead-end world, in every sense of the word—a planet abandoned after years of struggle against its incredibly fluid ecology had bought the colonists nothing but a stalemate. Most of the population, when offered transport to the new world of Esquiline a quarter-century ago, had jumped at the chance . . . but for a small fraction of that populace, the mindless Caelian ecology had taken on the status of a powerful and almost sentient enemy, and to run from that enemy had seemed to them to be an acceptance of defeat and dishonor. Corwin had visited Caelian once since that remnant had dug in for the battle, and had come away with the uncomfortable picture of the people of Hell's Blender as rafters on a raging river. Drifting away not only from the rest of the Cobra Worlds community, but possibly even from their own basic humanity.

All of which made Vartanson a very wild card indeed . . . and a man no one else in the Directorate ever really liked to cross.

Not even the governor-general. "I understand," Chandler said again to Vartanson. Soothingly. "Actually, I think that even if we don't find another good candidate, these three new Cobras plus the experienced one ought to be adequate for the mission's needs."

Corwin took a deep breath. "Perhaps," he said carefully, "we ought to see this lack of a fifth Cobra not as a problem but as an opportunity. A chance to throw the Qasamans a curve."

He looked over to see Telek's eyes on him. "You mean like that switch your brothers pulled back on the first mission?" she asked. "Good idea, that—may even have saved the entire mission."

Silently, Corwin blessed her. She couldn't know what he was about to propose, but by reminding the others of how well that other scheme had worked out she'd weakened the automatic resistance his enemies would almost certainly come up with. "Something like that," he nodded, unconsciously bracing himself. "I'd like to suggest that we create, solely for this mission, the first woman Cobra. Now, before you voice any objections—"

"A *woman* Cobra?" Atterberry snorted. "Oh, for— Moreau, that is the most *ridiculous* idea I've ever heard."

"Why?" Corwin countered. "Just because it hasn't ever been done?"

"Why do you suppose it *has* never been done?" Priesly put in. "Because there are good reasons for it, that's why."

Corwin looked over at Chandler. "Mr. Chandler?"

There was a slightly sour look on Chandler's face, but he nodded. "You may continue," he said.

"Thank you." Corwin's gaze swept the table, settled on Priesly and Atterberry as the two most hostile-looking.

"One reason that the idea of women Cobras sounds so outlandish is that the Old Dominion of Man had a fairly strong patriarchal orientation. Women simply weren't considered for elite military troops—though I'll point out that during the Troft War there were a large number of female resistance fighters on both Adirondack and Silvern."

"We all know our history," Nguyen put in gruffly. "Get to the point."

"The point is that even what little we know of Qasaman society paints it as even more patriarchal than the Dominion was," Corwin told him. "If the thought of female warriors strikes *you* as ridiculous, think of how they'll see it."

"In other words," Telek said slowly, "they're not likely to even *consider* the possibility that a woman along on the mission could be a demon warrior."

"A demon *what*?" Priesly frowned.

"It's the Qasaman term for Cobras," Chandler told him.

"Appropriate," Priesly grunted.

Vartanson threw him a cold look. "Being borderline demonic is often part of our job," he said icily.

Priesly's lip twitched, and he turned abruptly back to Corwin. "Your assumption, of course, is that the mission will be caught," he said. "Isn't that being a little pessimistic?"

"It's called being prepared," Corwin said tartly. "But assuming they *won't* get caught brings me to my second point: we want people who can fit in well enough with the Qasamans to poke around for answers without being immediately branded as foreigners. Correct?" He looked at Chandler. "Can you tell me, Mr. Chandler, how many of the Cobra candidates on your list can speak Qasaman?"

"All of them," the governor-general said stiffly. "Give me a little credit, Mr. Moreau—Qasaman may not be an especially popular language course to take, but there's a reasonable pool of proficient people out there to choose from."

"Especially since most young men with Cobra ambitions try and learn it," Gavin pointed out.

"I understand that," Corwin nodded. "How many of this pool can speak it without an Aventinian accent?"

Chandler's brow darkened. "Everyone who learns a foreign language speaks with an accent," he growled.

Corwin looked him straight in the eye. "I know someone who doesn't," he said flatly. "My niece, Jasmine Moreau."

"Ah—well, there it is, everyone," Atterberry put in sardonically. "*That's* what all this is about—just another blatant grab for power by the Moreau family."

"How does this qualify as a grab for power?" Corwin snorted. "By sending my niece out to possibly get herself killed?"

"Enough." Chandler hadn't raised his voice, but something in his tone sliced cleanly through the burgeoning argument. "I've worked up a preliminary cost analysis for the proposed Qasaman mission—we'll take a short recess now for you to examine it. Mr. Moreau, I'd like to see you in my office, if I may."

"You realize, I presume, what you're asking the Directorate to do," Chandler said, gaze locked on Corwin's face. "Not to mention what you're asking me, personally, to do."

Corwin forced himself to meet the other's gaze. "I'm doing nothing but trying to give this mission of yours a better chance of success."

Chandler's lip twitched. "So it's 'my' mission now, is it?"

"Isn't it?" Corwin countered. "You clearly set it up privately, without the assistance or even the knowledge of the Academy board. Not to mention the knowledge of the Directorate itself."

Chandler's expression didn't change. "You have any proof of that?"

"If Justin had known this was in the works, he would have told me about it."

"That's hardly proof. I could have sworn all of the Academy directors to secrecy."

Corwin didn't answer, and after a moment Chandler sighed. "Let's be honest, here, shall we, Moreau? Logic and social goals notwithstanding, the real reason you want your niece in the Cobras is because your brother wants her there."

"She wants it herself, too," Corwin told him. "And, yes, I'll admit that there's part of me that wants to keep the family tradition alive. That doesn't negate the reasons I gave the Directorate a few minutes ago."

"No, but it muddies the politics considerably," Chandler grunted. "Okay, then—run the scenario. Tell me how the votes would fall if we went back and called a showdown."

"Telek and I would vote yes," Corwin said slowly. "Priesly and Atterberry would of course vote no, whether they agreed with me or not. Vartanson and Bailar . . . probably yes. Vartanson because if women were allowed in, it would effectively double Caelian's pool of Cobra candidates; Bailar because the Qasamans are only a few light-years from Esquiline's doorstep and he'll be more concerned with the logic of Jin's case than in history. With Vartanson's double vote, that would give me five votes."

"Which means you need one more vote for a clear majority," Chandler said. "Mine, for instance."

Corwin looked him square in the eye. "Yours was always the only vote I really needed."

For a moment Chandler gazed back at him in silence. "Politics goes in cycles," he said at last. "If the governor-general's office has more power now than it has had in the past, I make no apologies for it." He pursed his lips, slowly shook his head. "But you're wrong if you think I can push this through on my own, against all opposition. Priesly alone would be too much to buck."

Corwin turned away from him, eyes drifting to the governor-general's floor-to-ceiling window and the panoramic view of Capitalia that it opened onto. In his mind's eye, he could see Jin's face, last night, as she pleaded with him . . . could see Justin's expression at the hospital as the enormity of what he'd inadvertently done slowly became apparent. *What price power?* he thought dimly to himself. *What use is this office, anyway, if it's not to do what needs to be done?* "All right, then," he said slowly. "If Priesly needs incentive, I'll give it to him." He turned back to Chandler. "We'll let Jin into the Cobras, ostensibly for the reasons I listed as to her usefulness on a Qasaman spy mission. But we'll also bill it as a grand experiment into whether or not women can successfully be integrated into the entire Cobra program. If it doesn't work—if the experiment's a failure—" he took a deep breath "—then I'll resign my governorship."

It was perhaps the first time he'd ever seen genuine shock on Chandler's face. "You'll—*what?*" the other all but sputtered. "Moreau, that's—it's *crazy.*"

"It's what I want to do," Corwin told him evenly. "I know what Jin's capable of. She'll handle the job, and she'll handle it well."

"That's practically irrelevant. Whatever happens, Priesly will claim the experiment was a failure, just to get you out. You know that."

"He'll *try* to claim that, certainly," Corwin nodded. "Whether or not the claim sticks will depend on how Jin does, won't it?"

Chandler pursed his lips, his eyes searching Corwin's face. "It'll need the approval of the entire Council, of course."

"We all have our supporters and allies there," Corwin said. "Between yours, mine, and Priesly's, we ought to have enough. Especially if we use the secrecy of the

Qasaman mission to keep the experiment on closed-access. Less of a possibility for political flak from the general populace that way."

A lopsided smile creased Chandler's face. "You're getting cynical in your old age."

Corwin looked back out the window again. "No," he said with a sigh. "Just getting political."

And wondered why that should sound so like a curse in his ears.

Chapter 6

Late spring in Syzra District, Jin had once heard, was the most enjoyable time of the year in that particular part of Aventine . . . if you happened to be a duck. Supposedly, for the better part of three months straight, the sky over Syzra was either heavily overcast or pouring its guts out in torrents of cold rain.

But if those stories were true, this day was a pleasant exception. The rising sun, peeking through the dense forest surrounding them at a distance on three sides, shone clear and bright through a sky that had only a few high cirrus clouds to add counterpoint to its brilliant blue. What wind there was came in short, mild gusts; and the air temperature, while chilly, was more bracing than uncomfortable. It was the kind of day Jin had always loved.

And she felt absolutely terrible. Squinting her eyes slightly against the sunlight, she clenched her fists at her sides, tried to stand as tall as the three young men to her right, and fought hard to keep from throwing up.

"All right, recruits, let's bend your ears forward," the man standing facing them bellowed, and Jin clamped down a little more on her rebellious gastrointestinal tract. Instructor Mistra Layn's voice, unusually rich in deep tones, wasn't helping things a bit. *So much for my celebrated cast-iron gut,* she thought wryly to herself, remembering the warnings everyone had given her about the normal physiological reaction to Cobra surgery. Clearly, she'd been too quick to dismiss them; now all she could hope for was that the reaction was as short-term as they'd all said it would be.

"You already know," Layn continued, "that we've been selected for a special mission to Qasama. So I won't bore you with that harangue again. What you're probably wondering instead is why we're out here in the middle of nowhere instead of at one of the main Academy centers. Well?"

It took a second for Jin to realize that he was asking them a question. It took a few seconds longer to realize that none of her fellow trainees were going to respond. "Sir?" she said tentatively.

A flicker of something crossed Layn's face, but his voice was neutral enough. "Trainee Moreau?"

"Sir, are we here because the mission will involve travel through forested areas of Qasama?"

Layn cocked an eyebrow and threw a leisurely look behind him. "Why, yes—there *is* forest here, isn't there? There's forest at the training center in Pindaric District, too, as I recall. So why aren't we there instead of here?"

Jin gritted her teeth. "I don't know, sir."

The young man at Jin's right stirred. "Sir?"

"Trainee Sun?"

"Sir, the Pindaric center concentrates on teaching new Cobras how to hunt and kill spine leopards," Mander Sun said. "Our mission won't involve hunting so much as it will evasion and simply staying alive."

"Don't the Cobras at Pindaric need to learn how to stay alive?" Layn countered.

Her eyes locked on Layn, Jin couldn't see if Sun flushed. But from the tone of his voice she rather thought he had. "The methods of training for attack versus defense are entirely different, sir," he said. "More than that, they would be *obviously* different to the other trainees there. I understood this *was* supposed to be a secret mission."

For a long moment Layn merely looked at Sun. "More or less correct, Trainee Sun. The secrecy part, that is. But who says attack and defense training are different?"

"My grandfather, sir. He was Coordinator of the Academy for twenty years."

"Does that give you the right to stiff-neck your instructor?" Layn said coldly.

This time there was no doubt that Sun flushed. "No, sir," he said stiffly.

"Glad to hear it." Layn let his gaze drift to all four of them. "Because I have no intention of going to Qasama without the absolute best people available backing me up. If I don't think one or more of you measures up, I can and will bounce you—and I don't much care whether it's on the first day of training or while you're being wheeled in to have your nanocomputers implanted. All of you got that?"

Jin swallowed, suddenly conscious of the neck-wrap computer nestling up under her jaw. If she failed her training—was deemed unsuitable, for whatever reason—the nanocomputer that would eventually be implanted beneath her brain would be a mere shadow of the true Cobra computer, disconnecting all of her newly acquired weaponry and severely limiting the power available to the servos augmenting her muscles. She would be, in short, a Ject.

"All right, then," Layn said. "Now. I know you're all eager to find out just what those aching bodies of yours can do. For the moment, actually, that's not a hell of a lot. Those computers around your necks will give you limited servos and no weapons whatsoever. In four days—assuming adequate progress—you'll be given new neckwraps that let you activate your optical and auditory enhancers. After that, over a period of about four weeks, you'll get the use of your fingertip lasers, the lasers plus enhancers, the sonic weapons and arcthrower, the antiarmor laser alone, antiarmor plus everything else, and finally your preprogrammed reflexes. The purpose, you'll note, is to give you the best possible chance of learning to use your new bodies without killing yourselves or anyone else in the process."

"Question, sir?" the trainee at the far end of the line spoke up tentatively.

"Trainee Hariman?"

"Sir, I was under the impression that the normal training period was six to eight weeks, not four."

"Weren't you told this wasn't going to be normal training?" Layn countered.

"Ah, yes, sir, I was. It just seemed to me . . . a little quick, that's all. Especially with the new weapons being introduced with this group."

Layn cocked an eyebrow. "What new weapons are those, Trainee?"

"Ah . . . I was under the impression, sir, that the Council had approved the use of short-range voltage generators for use through the arcthrower circuits."

"You're referring, I take it, to the so-called stunguns? You're well informed, Trainee Hariman."

"Much of the weapons debate has been public knowledge, sir."

"So it has. As it happens, though, that won't be a consideration. For the simple reason that none of you will be participating in that experiment. The Council decided you were going to be experimental enough as it was—" Layn's eyes flicked to Jin "—and there was no need to give you untried equipment as well."

"Yes, sir," Hariman said. "That doesn't explain how

we're going to learn how to be Cobras in four weeks instead of six, sir."

"You questioning your ability as a trainee, or my ability as an instructor?"

"Uh . . . neither, sir."

"Good. Did you say something a moment ago, Trainee Todor?"

"Sir?" The trainee standing between Hariman and Sun sounded startled.

"The question was simple enough, Trainee. Did you say something to Trainee Sun while I was explaining why you hadn't had stun-guns installed?"

"Uh . . . it was nothing, sir."

"Repeat it."

"I, uh . . ." Todor audibly took a breath. "I was just thinking that, as far as extra weaponry was concerned . . . uh, that Trainee Moreau could be easily implanted with a pair of turret guns."

Layn's expression didn't change, but it seemed to Jin that his eyes flicked briefly to her breasts before rising to her face. "Trainee Moreau? Any comment?"

A truly scathing retort had already come to mind, but it seemed better not to use it. At least not here and now. "No, sir," she said.

"No. Well, then, I've got one." Layn's eyes flicked to the other three trainees . . . and abruptly his face hardened. "It's pretty clear that none of you is exactly thrilled at having a woman in the unit. Now, you've all heard the Council's reasons as to why they think this is worth trying, so I won't hash that over again. But I will say this.

"To tell you the absolute truth, I don't much like it either. Special military units have always been men-only, from the Dominion of Man's old Alpha Command all the way on up to the Cobras. I don't like breaking tradition like this; I especially don't like the idea that this is a test to see if the Cobras should be opened up in the future to more women. In fact, I'll go so far as to say that I hope Trainee Moreau will fail. *But.*" His gaze hardened even more. "*If* she fails, she is going to do it *on her own.* Understood? Specifically, she is *not* going to fail because you or I or anyone else pushed her harder than she should have been pushed. Considerations of fairness aside, I don't want anyone claiming that the test was unfair. You got all that?"

There were three murmurs. "I asked if you got all that," Layn snapped.

"Yes, sir," the others said in unison.

"Good." Layn took a deep breath. "All right, then, let's get to work. That tree over there—" he pointed to their right "—is about three kilometers away. You've got six minutes to get there."

Sun moved first, stepping behind Todor and Hariman to take the lead. Jin was right behind him, the other two trainees falling in belatedly after her. *Pace yourself, girl,* she warned herself, trying as best she could to let the servo motors in her legs do most of the work. Around her, the thudding of the others' footsteps filled her ears, almost drowning out the faint whine from above . . .

Abruptly, the sound clicked with her consciousness, and she glanced up, eyes searching the sky. There it was, just coming into sight over the treetops to her right: a Troft-built aircar, bearing toward the complex that was serving as their training center. She twisted her head further around, seeking out Layn, but if the instructor was surprised by the craft's arrival it didn't show in his stance. *Probably someone here to observe from the Directorate,* she decided, shifting her attention back to the race.

To her annoyance, she found that while she'd let the aircar's presence distract her both Todor and Hariman had managed to pass her by. *It's okay,* she reminded herself, picking up her speed a little. *They're more concerned with making sure they don't come in last than they are with pacing themselves. That'll probably work against them.* Todor, she noted, was already breathing harder than he should—either hyperventilating or else not letting his servos take as much of the load as he ought to. Either way, he should find himself in trouble before the run was over.

Involuntarily, Jin's jaw clenched. She didn't like having to play tactical games like this, least of all against the men who were going to be her teammates on Qasama. But she didn't have much choice in the matter. Layn had put it very clearly: her performance here on the training field was going to determine not only whether or not she herself became a full Cobra, but also whether or not any other woman in the Cobra Worlds would ever have that same chance.

She'd never before been much of a one to fight for universal causes; but whether she liked it or not, she was smack square in the middle of this one. In the middle, with nothing but her own stamina and determination going for her.

And—maybe—the legacy of the Moreau family. *Pace yourself,* she repeated over and over to herself, using the words as a running cadence. *Pace yourself . . .*

She was second, behind only Sun, when they at last reached the tree.

The Troft lying on his couch by the aircar's starboard window stirred as the four trainees far below reached the tree. [The second-place human,] he said, his high-pitched catertalk almost swallowed up by the whine of the aircar's thrusters. [It was a female?]

Beside Corwin, Governor-General Chandler harrumphed. "You're very perceptive," he said reluctantly, throwing a glare in Corwin's direction.

"It's just an experiment," Priesly added sourly. "Pushed through by certain elements in our government—"

[Of the four, she is the best,] the Troft said.

Priesly's eyes narrowed. "Why do you say that?" he demanded.

The Troft's arm membranes flexed, then relaxed back against his upper arms. [Our approach, she was the only one who noticed it,] he explained. [Her face, it sought out the sound and confirmed our identity as non-hostile before resuming her running. That sort of alertness, it is a preferred attribute for a Cobra warrior?]

"It is indeed," Chandler admitted. "Well. At any rate, now that you've seen the trainees—at least from a distance—we'll be heading over to the special camp where this proposed mission is being headquartered. You'll be able to examine all the Qasaman data there, see why it is we think there's something happening that we ought to investigate."

The Troft seemed to consider that. [This information, you would not be giving it to me without need. What is it you want?]

Chandler took a deep breath. "In a nutshell: transport. We can use one of our own starships to get the team from here to Qasama, of course, but we haven't yet got a safe way for them to get from orbit to ground. We would like to borrow a Troft military shuttle for that purpose."

"We don't want to land a full starship," Priesly put in. "Not only because of the danger of detection—"

[A vehicle with a stardrive, you do not want it to fall into Qasaman hands,] Speaker One cut him off. [My intelligence, do not insult it, Governor Priesly.]

Priesly shut up, a pained look on his face, and for a moment Corwin could almost feel sorry for him. There'd been no anger in Speaker One's comment—merely a desire to save time—but Priesly hadn't dealt with this particular representative of the Tlos'khin'fahi demesne long enough to know his personality. Speaker One had been an interdemesne trader before being given the Cobra Worlds liaison post four years ago, and Corwin had long since noted that such Trofts had an almost supernatural control over their tempers. Not surprising, given the loose and often combative relationships that existed between the hundreds of demesnes that made up the Troft Assemblage. A trader who got into verbal fights with his customers every third time he was out of his home demesne wouldn't be a trader for long.

"Governor Priesly meant no harm, Speaker One," Chandler spoke up into the conversational void, looking pleased himself at Priesly's discomfiture. "The tactical reasons for borrowing such a landing craft are of course obvious. The financial reasons, I imagine, are also obvious to you."

[Such a shuttle, you cannot afford to buy.]

Chandler nodded. "That's it exactly. Though we're in far better shape now than we were thirty years ago when this whole Qasaman mess began, even now our budget will only support the cost of the mission itself—that is, the personnel, basic equipment, and specialized training. You'll remember we're still paying off the last full starship we bought from you; we can't afford to buy a shuttle, too."

[The Tlos'khin'fahi demesne, why should it lend you this craft? We are far from Qasama, with little at stake should they escape their world.]

Translation: the bargaining had begun. "We don't necessarily want the Tlos'khin'fahi demesne itself to provide the shuttle," Corwin put in before Chandler could answer. "However, as our main trading partner, the health of our economy should be of some concern to you . . . and if our buying a shuttle would hurt that economy, it would have at least a minor effect on you."

[The Baliu'ckha'spmi demesne, would it not have more of a reason to provide you a shuttle?]

Chandler threw a glance at Corwin. "Probably," he conceded. "The problem is that . . . the Baliu'ckha'spmi demesne might infer the wrong thing from such a request."

[You refer to the trade by which you obtained the New Worlds?]

"Basically," Chandler said heavily. "The agreement

was that we would neutralize the Qasaman threat for them, after all. If they decide this means that Qasama wasn't properly neutralized . . . well, we don't really want to open that can of snakes."

The Troft's arm membranes fluttered again as he sorted through the idiom. [The reason for bringing me out here in secret, it is also because of this concern?]

"You don't miss much," Chandler admitted. "Yes, we didn't want any word of this leaking out to other de-mesne representatives if we could possibly avoid it."

For a moment Speaker One was silent. The aircar began a leisurely turn, and Corwin glanced out the window. Below them, nestled in an artificial clearing, was the small logging complex that had been temporar-ily taken over by the Cobra Academy for the special training course. [The question, I will bring it to my demesne-lord's attention,] Speaker One said as the aircar dipped toward a scarred landing square near the main building's entrance. [Some sort of trade, it will of course be necessary.]

"Of course," Chandler nodded, sounding relieved. "We'll be happy to consider any request he suggests."

[My demesne-lord, he will also remember that the original pacification plan was created by the late Gover-nor Jonny Moreau,] the Troft continued. [If I could inform him that one of Governor Jonny Moreau's line would be planning this mission as well, it would give more weight to my arguments.]

Chandler threw Corwin a surprised look. "Why?" he asked.

[Continuity in the affairs of war, it is as valued as in the affairs of business,] the Troft said—rather coolly, Corwin thought. [Such a thing, Governor-General Chan-dler, it is possible?]

Chandler took a deep breath. From the expression on his face, he was clearly envisioning the political flap were he to reinstate Justin to the Academy while still under a cloud from the Monse shooting . . . "I'm afraid,

Speaker One," Priesly spoke up tartly, "the Moreau family is no longer directly involved with such military planning—"

"Fortunately, that won't be a problem," Corwin interrupted him. "The human female you saw in the clearing a few minutes ago—the one you thought was the best of the trainees? She is Jasmine Moreau, daughter of Cobra Justin Moreau and Governor Jonny Moreau's granddaughter."

Priesly sputtered; Chandler cut him off with a hand signal. "Will that be adequate, Speaker One?" the governor-general asked.

There was a slight bump as the aircar touched down. [It will indeed,] the Troft said. [Your data, I will now be pleased to study it.]

Chandler exhaled quietly. "Certainly. Follow me."

Chapter 7

"All right, Cobras, move it out," Mistra Layn growled. "Remember this is a forest—watch your feet *and* your heads."

Keying her auditory enhancers up a notch, Jin fell into her usual leftguard position in the loose diamond formation around Layn and crossed with the others under the trees at the edge of the clearing. It was an operation they'd practiced several times in the past few days: walking through the fenced-off part of the forest around their camp, using their optical and auditory enhancers to try and spot the various animal-cue simulators and moving-head targets the instructors had planted around them. Spotting a squawker or target first earned the trainee a point; nailing it cleanly with fingertip lasers before the group got within the animal's theoretical attack range was worth two more points.

It was just one more of the silly competitions Layn was continually using to pit his trainees against each other. One more needless opportunity, Jin thought bitterly, for the other three trainees to hate her.

It was hardly her fault that she was better than they were at these games. It was certainly not her fault that they couldn't accept that.

Her innocence in the matter was cold comfort, though, and thinking about it brought an ache to her throat. She hadn't expected instant acceptance by the others—she'd known full well that Uncle Corwin's lectures about military traditions hadn't merely been scare tactics. But she had thought that by now, eleven days into the training, some of the hostility would surely have faded away.

But it hadn't. Oh, they were polite enough to her— Layn's big speech the first day of training about letting her fail on her own had been backed up by action, and both he and the others were clearly bending over backwards to avoid any kind of overtly prejudicial behavior. But the whispered comments and secret smiles were still there, lurking most outwardly in the quiet times when the trainees were alone.

Or rather, when Jin was alone. The other three spent a lot of that time together.

It hurt. In many ways, it hurt worse than the worst physical aftereffects of her surgery. She'd always been something of a misfit as she was growing up—either too quiet or too aggressive for the other girls and even most of the boys her age. Only with her family had she ever felt truly at home, truly accepted. With her family, and to a lesser extent with the Cobra friends of her father's . . .

A faint chirping from ahead penetrated her brooding. A tarbine squawker, she identified it, head automatically turning back and forth to pinpoint the sound. There?—*there*. Activating her optical sensors' targeting capability, she locked onto the small black cube nestled in the crook of a branch and fired her right fingertip laser.

A needle of light lanced out, and the box abruptly stopped chirping.

"A tarbine?" Sun called softly to her from the rear point of the diamond.

"Yeah," she said over her shoulder.

"Why'd you kill it?" Layn asked from the center. "Tarbines aren't dangerous."

"No, sir," she said, recognizing that she'd made the right decision and that Layn simply wanted her to explain it for the others. "But where tarbines are, there's a good chance you'll find mojos, too."

"With their accompanying spine leopards or krisjaws," Layn nodded. "Right. Besides which . . . ? Anyone?"

"Their chirping might mask the sound of something more dangerous?" Todor hazarded from in front of Layn.

"Good enough," the instructor grunted. "Enough conversation. Look sharp."

And a bare second later, the exercise abruptly ceased to be routine. Dead ahead, the bushes suddenly parted and a huge cat-like animal stepped out to face them.

A spine leopard.

It's impossible, a small fraction of Jin's mind insisted. The fence surrounding this part of the forest was five meters high, a theoretically impossible barrier even for a spine leopard.

And then the animal snarled, and theory was abruptly forgotten as four sets of fingertip lasers flashed out to converge on the spine leopard's head.

Uselessly, of course, and Jin silently cursed herself for letting her reflexes waste precious time that way. The decentralized spine leopard nervous system was functionally invulnerable to the kind of localized damage the fingertip lasers could inflict. The only known way of dealing with the animals was to get in a clean shot with the antiarmor laser running lengthwise down her left calf—

She was actually starting to shift her weight onto her right foot when the crucial fact caught up with her conscious mind: the trainees' current neckwrap computers didn't allow the antiarmor laser to be activated.

The others' fingertip lasers were still slicing uselessly

at the spine leopard, leaving blackened tracks in the fur where they passed. And the look that was growing in the creature's eyes . . . "Stop it!" Jin snapped. "Can't you see you're just making it mad?"

"Then what the hell do you want—?" Todor barked back.

"Try your disruptors!" Sun cut him off. An instant later a backwash of half audible, half felt sound washed over Jin as the others obeyed, playing tight cones of ultrasound over the spine leopard. *Another waste of time*, Jin thought tightly. Sonic weapons could throw the predators off-balance, but only temporarily; and like the fingertip lasers, their use seemed to enrage the beasts. As soon as this one got its balance back—

And then it struck her. Layn, fully equipped with both antiarmor laser *and* the nanocomputer needed to use it, had yet to fire a shot.

Another test. Of course—and with that all the pieces fell together. A single spine leopard, captured and released into the enclosure, to see if their first response would be to scatter or to continue their assigned mission of protecting Layn. Doubtless the Cobra already had his antiarmor laser target-locked on the animal, ready to fire the second it looked like things were getting out of control.

Phrijpicker mousfin, she snarled mentally at him. It was a particularly stupid trick—under target-lock or not, spine leopards were far too dangerous to fool around with this way, especially on inexperienced trainees. Somehow, they had to stop the thing before it shrugged off the effects of the sonics and charged. And maybe wound up killing someone.

And whatever they were going to do, they had better do it fast, The spine leopard was rolling its weight slightly from side to side now, the spines along its forelegs beginning to bristle outward—a sign that it was starting to feel endangered. Which would make it that much more vicious when it finally attacked . . .

Her eyes flicked around the area, came to rest on the cyprene trees and the thick gluevines running up many of their trunks . . . and a small chapter of family history bobbed to the surface. "Sun!" she snapped, leaping with servo-enhanced strength into the lower branches of a gluevine-wrapped tree midway from her to the spine leopard. Her muscles tensed, but the sudden motion didn't trigger an attack. "Cut the gluevine at the base of the tree," she called back over her shoulder as she got her own lasers going on the top part of the nearest vine. "Rip it free of the trunk—*don't* touch the cut end."

Sun moved to obey, and three seconds later a five-meter section of gluevine hung free in Jin's hand. Glancing down, she saw that the spine leopard was still holding its ground . . . but even as she watched, it leaned back on its back haunches. Preparing to spring . . .

"Hariman—split the vine lengthwise," Sun called. "Moreau?—I've got this end. You ready?"

Which meant he'd figured out what she had in mind. "Ready," she called back, clenching her teeth in anticipation. "Hariman?"

Her answer was a burst of laser fire that cracked the gluevine's thick outer coating, letting the incredibly sticky stuff inside ooze out. "Go!" Sun snapped; and Jin leaped.

Her target was another cyprene just beyond where the spine leopard was coiling itself for its spring. A spring that would carry it to Todor, still doggedly playing his sonic over the predator . . . and as time seemed to slow down for her, Jin saw for the first time that, in moving over to cut the gluevine, Hariman had unwittingly put himself directly in the line of fire between Layn and the spine leopard. Which meant that if this didn't work, either Hariman or Todor would probably die.

The outer twigs of her target tree scratched at her face and hands as she came in through them . . . and with all her strength she hurled the vine to the ground.

Directly across the spine leopard's back.

The creature screamed, a blood-chilling sound Jin had never before heard one make. It almost made her miss grabbing the cyprene's trunk; as it was, she tore a gash in the back of her left hand scrambling for a grip. Twisting around, heart thudding in her ears, she looked down.

The spine leopard went ahead and leaped anyway . . . but even as its feet left the ground, Sun tugged on his end of the gluevine with Cobra servo strength, and an instant later the predator was flying past Todor on a tightly curved course. It landed on its feet, gluevine still draped solidly across its back, foreleg spines spread out in full defensive position—

And twisted to face Sun.

"Stick the vine somewhere and get out of there!" Jin shouted to him.

Sun needed no prompting. In a single motion, he jammed the cut end of the gluevine against the tree he'd cut it from and leaped straight up into the cyprene's branches. Barely pausing to catch his balance, he changed direction and pushed off toward Jin's tree, half a second ahead of the now leashed spine leopard's own leap toward his ankles.

He caught the trunk just above her, sending a rain of twigs and leaves down around her head. "Now what?" he muttered.

"I assume Layn's eventually going to laser it," she told him . . . but the Cobra was still standing there with Todor and Hariman, watching with them as the spine leopard thrashed about trying to free itself from the gluevine. Todor took a step toward the animal, and it paused in its efforts to make a short leap and slash with its front claws.

"Doesn't seem interested in doing so, does he?" Sun grunted as Todor made a hasty leap back. "Maybe they're going to tranq it and use it on the next batch of trainees."

So Sun had tracked the same line of thought she had. "Pretty damn fool game, if you ask me," she growled to him. "They could at least have waited until we had our antiarmor lasers activated."

"So maybe they want us to be creative."

Jin twisted up her head to look at him. "Meaning. . . ?"

"Well . . . how long do you suppose it could live with its pseudospine broken?"

She looked down at the animal. Already it had worried a few centimeters of the gluevine free, sacrificing a narrow line of its fur in the process. Left on its own another minute of two . . . "What say we find out," she suggested grimly.

"Sounds good. You take the rear, I'll take just back of the head. On three; one, two, *three.*"

And Jin pushed off from the tree, arcing into the air as high as she dared. Sun's leap paralleled hers . . . and as they passed the top of their arcs and started down—

"No!" Layn bellowed; but it was far too late. Jin hit the spine leopard full in the back, keeping her knees stiff until the last second in order to transfer as much impact to the spine leopard's body as she could. Sun hit a fraction of a second behind her, and she both heard and felt the twin *cracks*—

"No, damn it, *no!*" Layn yelled again, leaping belatedly forward to kneel down at the limp spine leopard's side . . . but this time Jin could hear a strange note of resignation in his voice. "*Damn* it all—"

The look on his face when he got to his feet effectively silenced any comments Jin might have had. But Sun wasn't so reticent. "Is there a problem, sir?" he asked blandly. "You *did* want us to kill it, didn't you?"

Layn impaled him with a laser-strength glare. "You were merely supposed to get me clear of it," he bit out. "Not—" He took a deep breath. "For your information, *trainee*, you two idiots have just broken the central mobility transmain of an extremely *expensive* robot. I trust you're satisfied."

Sun's jaw fell, and Jin felt her eyes go wide as she looked down at the spine leopard. "I suppose that explains," she heard herself say, "why you didn't laser it."

Layn looked like he was ready to chew rocks. "Return to your quarters, all of you," he snarled. "Evening classes are as usual; you're free until then. Get out of my sight."

The tap on her door was gentle, almost diffident. "Yes?" Jin called, looking up from her reader.

"It's me, Mander Sun," a familiar voice answered. "Can I come in?"

"Sure," Jin called back, frowning as she keyed the door open.

He looked almost shy as he stepped hesitantly a couple of paces into the room. "It occurred to me that someone ought to check up on that cut you got out there this afternoon," he said.

She looked down with a little surprise at the heal-quick bandage on her left hand. "Oh, no problem. The cut wasn't deep, just a little messy."

"Ah," he nodded. "Well, then . . . sorry to have bothered you . . ." He hesitated, looking a little lost.

Jin licked her lips. *Say something!* she told herself as her mind went perversely blank. "Uh—by the way," she managed as he started to turn back toward the door, "do you think Layn's going to make trouble for us because of what we did to that robot?"

"He'd better not try," Sun said, turning back again. "If they're going to drop pop tests like that on us, they'd better not complain when we don't do what they expect." He hesitated just a fraction. "That was, uh . . . a pretty good trick you came up with out there, incidentally. The thing with the gluevine."

She shrugged. "Wasn't all that original, really," she admitted. "My grandfather did something similar once against a berserk gantua. And as long as we're handing out compliments, you were pretty fast on the uptake yourself."

"I didn't have much choice," he said wryly. "It didn't look at the time like you were going to have a chance to explain it to anyone."

"Stupid robot," she muttered, shaking her head. "Almost a shame we didn't figure that part out. Layn would probably have had a stroke if one of us had gone up and petted the thing."

Sun grinned. "I think he came close enough to a stroke as it was." His grin changed into a tight, almost embarrassed smile. "You know, Moreau—Jin . . . I have to admit that I didn't think much at the beginning of having you in the squad. Not for the tradition reasons Layn trotted out, but because none of the women I've ever known has had the kind of—oh, I don't know; the killer instinct, I guess, that a warrior has to have."

Jin shrugged, forcing herself to meet his gaze. "You might be surprised," she said. "Besides, a lot of what Cobras do these days is more like patrol officer work than full-fledged war, certainly in the more settled areas of the Worlds."

"Hold it right there," Sun growled in mock annoyance, holding his hands up palm-outward. "I don't mind having *you* here, but I'm not getting drawn into any theoretical discussions on the merits of women in the Cobras, thank you. Not with a test on surveillance techniques breathing down our necks." He glanced at his watch. "Like in half an hour. Phrij—and I still need to study for it some more."

"Me, too," Jin licked her lips. "Thanks for coming by, Mander. I—uh—"

"Mandy," he said, pulling open the door. "That's what everyone else calls me. See you in class."

"Right. Bye."

For a long minute after he was gone she stared at the closed door, not entirely sure whether or not to trust the warm glow beginning to form deep within her. Could her long isolation from the group really be ending? As quickly and easily as that? Just because she'd unwittingly helped give their rough and demanding instructor something of a black eye?

Abruptly, she smiled. Of course it could. If there was one military tradition that superseded every other, it was the "us versus them" feeling of trainees toward everyone else . . . and *especially* toward instructors. In helping Sun ruin Layn's robot spine leopard, she'd suddenly become one of the "us."

Or at least, she warned herself, *I've got my foot in the door*. But for now, at least, that was enough. The first barrier, her father had often reminded her, was always the hardest to break.

For just a moment she frowned as an odd thought flickered across her mind. Surely Layn hadn't *deliberately* let her destroy that robot . . . had he? No—of course not. The very idea was absurd. He'd already said he didn't *want* her to succeed.

And speaking of succeeding . . . Turning back to her reader, she keyed for a fast scan of the lessons on surveillance methods. As Sun had pointed out, there was a test breathing down their necks.

Chapter 8

The reminder clock on his desk pinged, and Corwin looked up at it with mild surprise. Somehow, while he hadn't been looking, the afternoon had disappeared. It was four fifty, and in just forty minutes the celebration was scheduled to start over at Justin's house. The celebration for his daughter's graduation from the Cobra Academy.

For a moment Corwin gazed unseeingly at the clock, his mind jumping back almost thirty years to the similar celebration his parents had thrown for Justin himself. It had been a strained evening, with everyone trying to ignore the fact that the new Cobra and his twin brother would he heading off in a few days to the mysterious world of Qasama, possibly never to return.

And now it would be Jin who'd be going off in a week. To the same world. Under almost identical circumstances.

To try and fix the same problem.

Corwin could remember a time, far back in the dim haze of his youth, when it had seemed to him that if you fixed a problem right the first time it would stay fixed. When he believed there were problems that *could* be permanently fixed.

The memories made him feel very old.

"Corwin?"

With a jolt, he brought himself back to the real world. "Yes, Thena, what is it?"

"The governor-general's on the line. Says it's important."

Corwin flicked another glance at his clock. "He always does," he growled. "Oh, all right." He stabbed at the proper button, and Thena's image was replaced by Chandler's. "Yes?"

Chandler's face looked like he'd been chewing on something not quite ripe. "I've got some bad news for you, Moreau," he said without preamble. "I have here on my desk a petition calling for your brother Justin to be confined until the matter of the Monse shooting can be definitively cleared up. It's been endorsed by seventy-one members of the Cobra Worlds Council."

Corwin felt his face go rigid. Seventy-one members was something like sixty percent—an utterly incredible number. "That's ridiculous," he said. "The whole thing—"

"The whole thing," Chandler cut him off grimly, "has been pulling far more net space than any seven-week-old issue has any right to be getting. In case you haven't noticed, the public rumblings over the whole mess never completely vanished; and in the past week or so they've started getting louder again."

Corwin gritted his teeth hard enough to hurt. Preoccupied with arrangements and details for the Qasama mission, he hadn't had time to keep up with the ebb and flow of Aventinian public opinion. But then why hadn't Justin or Joshua or someone else pointed it out to him—?

Because they hadn't wanted him to worry, of course. And so, while he'd been busy looking the other way, Priesly's gang had been busy weaving an encirclement.

But maybe it still wasn't too late to fight back. A petition, even one from the Cobra Worlds Council, wasn't legally binding on the governor-general's actions. If he could get Chandler on his side . . . or at least onto neutral . . . "Since you're calling me about it," he said carefully, "do I presume you intend to comply with their demand?"

Chandler's eyes flashed. "It's hardly a *demand*, Moreau—I can ignore the thing entirely if I choose to do so. The question really boils down to whether or not you're worth bucking this kind of public opinion for."

"Or in other words, why risk political fallout over a governor who's on his way out anyway?" Corwin asked softly.

Chandler at least had the grace to look uncomfortable. "It's not like that," he muttered. "Whatever happens with your niece on Qasama doesn't change the fact that you *are* at present a full Aventinian governor."

"True," Corwin nodded. "Not to mention the possibility that Jin may actually do so well out there that I won't have to resign in the first place."

"I suppose that's possible," Chandler conceded. "Hardly likely, though."

Corwin shrugged. Despite his words, it was clear from Chandler's manner that he felt awkward about writing Corwin off without cause. It gave Corwin a psychological lever—a weak one, but the best he was likely to get. "I presume you'll be ordering Justin into house arrest, then?" he asked. "Surely there's no need to put him in an actual prison."

Chandler's eyes bored into his. "It might be enough to satisfy them," he said evenly. "Suppose someone suggests that he's potentially a threat to the community and ought to be somewhere more secure?"

"You could counter by asking this person where the hell he thinks would be a safe place to incarcerate a Cobra who doesn't want to stay put," Corwin told him. "Or point out the obvious fact that Justin's not a danger to anyone who isn't threatening him. Alternatively, if this person's on the Directorate and privy to such information, you could just point out that the use of that Troft shuttle for the Qasaman mission might be in jeopardy if Speaker One finds out you've locked up a Moreau."

Chandler's eyebrows lifted a fraction. "I find it hard to believe you and the Tlossies are that friendly."

"Of course we aren't," Corwin shook his head. "But you'll recall this unnamed someone of yours *was* on the aircar when Speaker One asked that a Moreau help plan the Qasama mission. Reminding him of that ought to make him a little cautious about pushing too hard for public incarceration."

Chandler snorted, gently. "Perhaps. Perhaps." He took a deep breath. "All right. House arrest it is, with as little publicity as we can get away with."

"Thank you, sir." Corwin hesitated. "If I could ask one more favor, though . . . we're having the graduation party for Jin this evening. Could you postpone the order until tomorrow morning? It would make things a lot easier on all of us."

"I hardly think Justin's going to sneak off and leave the planet," Chandler said, almost offhandedly. Having already made up his mind to buck Priesly on one point, bucking him on another one as well apparently didn't cost any extra effort. "The house arrest will officially begin tomorrow morning at eight, then. You realize, of course, that Priesly is likely to consider this a favor you owe him. Whether you look at it that way or not."

"I've already put my career on his block over Jin's Cobra appointment," Corwin said coldly. "If Priesly thinks he can squeeze blood out of me beyond that, he's going to be sorely disappointed."

"I suppose." Chandler sighed. "Though I wouldn't underestimate his skills at manipulating the nets if I were you. Resigning quietly from a governorship and resigning in public disgrace are two very different ends. I think he'd take a great deal of pleasure in the chance to drag the Moreau name out for the gantuas to walk on."

Corwin felt his stomach tighten. The Moreau name. It was a noble part of the Cobra Worlds' young history, one of the few names virtually everyone on Aventine had grown up knowing. Protecting it had been a deciding factor in his father's fight against the Challinor rebellion so many years ago, and his subsequent work in reshaping Aventinian politics; and it was one of the few gifts of real value Corwin himself had to give to his nieces and—if he ever had any—to his own children. The thought of Priesly with his grubby hands on it . . . "If he tries it, he'll be sorry," he told Chandler softly. "Call it a threat, or call it a statement of fact; but make sure he understands."

Chandler nodded. "I'll try. I just wanted *you* to understand what we were dealing with here. Anyway . . . I expect I ought to let you go. You'll of course want to tell your brother about this tonight."

"I will," Corwin sighed. "Goodnight, sir . . . and thank you."

The governor-general threw him a grim smile and vanished from the screen.

For a long moment Corwin just sat there, staring blankly at the empty screen. So Priesly hadn't been content with merely embarrassing Corwin's family; instead, he was out for real blood. *Well, if it's a fight he wants,* he thought bitterly, *it's a fight he's going to get.* And Corwin had been in politics considerably longer than Priesly had. Somehow, he'd find a way to turn all this back on the Ject.

Somehow.

Taking a deep breath, he pushed the thought back as far as he could and got to his feet. He was going to a party, after all, and ought to at least try to project an image of happiness. Whether he felt that way or not.

The red streaks of sunset were fading into the early-evening darkness of the springtime Capitalia sky as Jin drove up to the curb and stepped out onto the walk. For a moment she just stood there in the dusk, gazing at the house and wondering why the home of her childhood should look so different to her now. Surely it wasn't just that she'd been away for four weeks—she'd been away that long many times before. No, the house hadn't changed; it was she who was different. The home of her childhood . . . but she was no longer a child. She was an adult.

An adult; and a Cobra.

Almost automatically, she keyed through a series of settings on her optical enhancers as she walked up toward the house, spotting things about the building and grounds that she'd never known before. The infrared setting showed what seemed to be a minor heat leak in the corner by her bedroom—no wonder that room had always felt colder than the rest of the house in the winter. Telescopic enhancement showed that the allegedly permanent siding was beginning to crack near the guttering; and a telescopic/light-amplified study of a hole in the tall sideyard borlash tree won her a glimpse of bright animal eyes hiding there. Memories of the past, thoughts of the future—all of it mingled together with the reality of the present. The reality that, against all odds, she'd achieved her life's ambition.

She was a Cobra.

The sound of a decelerating car behind her registered on her consciousness and she turned, expecting to see one of her uncles driving up.

It was Mander Sun.

"Hey! Jin!" he called, leaning his head out the window. "Hold up a minute."

She retraced her steps and crossed the street as he pulled to a halt against the opposite curb. "What is it?" she asked, belatedly noticing the hard set of his mouth. "Is anything wrong?"

"I don't know." His eyes probed her face. "Maybe it's just rumors . . . look, I heard something this afternoon from a friend of my dad's who does datawork for the Directorate. Do you know why you were approved for the Academy?"

The obvious reasons—the official reasons—came to Jin's mind, faded unsaid. "I know what I was told. What did *you* hear?"

"That it was a quiet deal," he growled. "That your uncle—the governor—put himself on the line for you. If this mission succeeds he gets to keep his position. Otherwise . . . he has to resign."

Jin felt her mouth go dry. The memory of that horrible night so many weeks ago flashed back to mind: the night her father had shot Monse . . . the night she'd gone and pleaded with Uncle Corwin to get her—somehow—into the Cobras. "No," she whispered. "No. He wouldn't do that. Politics is his *life*."

Sun shrugged helplessly. "I don't know if it's true or not, Jin. I just thought . . . well, that maybe you didn't know. And that maybe you should."

"Why?—so that I can be more nervous about the mission than I already am?" she snarled, the numbness suddenly flashing into anger.

"No," Sun said quietly. "So that you could hear it from a friend. And so I could tell you that the rest of the team is behind you."

She opened her mouth, closed it again as the anger vanished. "So that . . . what?"

He held her gaze. "I talked to Rafe and Peter before coming over here," he said. "We all agreed that you were a good teammate who didn't deserve this kind of extra pack on her shoulders." He snorted gently. "We also agreed that anyone who would pull a scummy move like that on Governor Moreau was a full-blooded phrijpicker, and that a guy like that might arrange to leak the the word to you just before we left—little extra squeeze value, you know. And like I said . . . I thought you'd do better to hear it from friends."

She looked back toward the house so that he wouldn't see the moisture in her eyes. It was true, of course—in retrospect it had to have been something like that. *Oh, Uncle Corwin* . . . "Yes," she said. "I . . . yes. Thank you."

A tentative hand touched hers where it rested on the car. "We'll do it, Jin," Sun said. "All of us together— we'll do such a bang-up job on Qasama that they'll be lucky if they don't have to give us a full-city parade *and* canonize Governor Moreau in the bargain."

Jin blinked the tears back and tried a smile. "You're right," she said, squeezing his hand briefly. "We'll make them sorry they tried to pick on a Moreau."

"And even sorrier that they tried to use a Sun to do it," Sun added with grim pride in his voice. "Anyway. I've got to get moving—my family's waiting for me. You going to be okay?"

"Sure," she nodded. "Mandy . . . thanks." -

"No charge. Partner." Reluctantly, she thought, he pulled his hand away from hers. "Well. Look, you take care of yourself—try not to get into any trouble—and I'll see you at the starfield in a week."

"Right. Bye."

"Bye."

She watched until his car turned a corner and vanished from sight. Then, taking a deep breath, she straightened her shoulders and started back toward the house. Not all the nuances of this mess were clear to her, but one of them was clear enough. The family didn't intend for her to know about Uncle Corwin's bargain; and so, as far as they were concerned, she wouldn't. She'd never had any formal acting experience, but she'd grown up with two older sisters and had long since learned how to bend the truth with a straight face.

Or even with a smiling face. She was going to a party, after all, and ought to at least try to project an image of excitement. Whether she felt that way or not.

Chapter 9

The new Cobras had a week of liberty before they were due to leave. For Jin, at least, the week went by very quickly.

". . . and whatever you do, listen to Layn, okay?" Justin told his daughter as they walked arm in arm up the long ramp leading to the *Southern Cross*'s entryway. "I know he's a pain in the butt as an instructor, but he's a smart tactician and a crackling fighter. Stick with him and you'll be all right."

"Okay, Dad," Jin nodded. "Hey, don't worry—we'll be fine."

Justin looked down at his daughter's face as, for a brief second, an intense feeling of deja vu washed over him. "Qasama is the last place in the world to be overconfident about, Jin," he said quietly. "Everything about the planet is dangerous, from the krisjaws and spine leopards to the mojos to the Qasaman people.

They're all dangerous, and they all hate you. Especially you."

Jin squeezed him a little tighter. "Don't worry, Dad, I know what I'm getting into."

"No, you don't. No one ever does. You have to—well, never mind." He took a deep breath, fighting back the urge to lecture her. "Just be careful, and come back safely. Okay?"

"Good advice," she said solemnly. "*You* be careful, too, huh? At least *I'll* be with a group of Cobras and other competent people. *You'll* be stuck here with Priesly and his mob."

And under Priesly's trumped-up house arrest . . . Justin's jaw tightened momentarily with a freshly renewed awareness of the two guards standing a few paces behind them. "Yeah, well, it's not all *that* bad," he told his daughter, forcing a smile. "As long as Corwin's in there fighting for me Priesly hasn't got a chance of making this thing stick."

Something passed, too quickly to identify, across Jin's face. "Yeah," she said. "Yeah. Well . . . walk me up the ramp?"

He did. At the entryway they exchanged one last hug . . . and as Jin's arms tightened, Cobra-strong, around him, Justin's vision blurred with moisture. A quarter century of hope and frustration was finally over. His child had succeeded him as a Cobra.

A triple tone sounded from the entryway. "I'd better get inside," Jin said into his chest. "I'll see you in a few weeks, Dad. Take care of yourself, okay?"

"Sure." Reluctantly, he released her and took half a step back. She smiled at him, blinking back tears of her own, then turned to wave one last time down the ramp to where her sisters and cousins were waiting for the *Southern Cross*'s takeoff.

Then she was gone, and Justine found himself walking away from the ship. *She'll be all right*, he thought over and over to himself. *She'll be all right. Really she will. She's my daughter—she has to come through it all right.*

And for the first time he truly knew how his own parents must have felt on that day, so long ago, when he and Joshua had themselves lifted off for Qasama. The realization brought a half-bitter smile to his lips.

Whether there was justice in the universe he didn't know. But there did appear to be a certain symmetry.

Chapter 10

It was a two-week trip to Qasama; two weeks that went by very quickly. It was, for one thing, the first time the new Cobras had had a chance to interact with each other on anything approaching a social level. With each other, and also with the two men who would actually be leading the mission.

They were, to her mind, a study in contrasts. Both were top experts at Aventine's Qasama Monitor Center, but at that point all similarity ended. Pash Barynson was middle-aged and thin and short, a few centimeters shorter even than Jin, with sparse black hair and an excruciatingly academic manner that was so stiff that it bordered on caricature. His associate, Como Raines, was almost exactly the opposite, in both manner and appearance. Tall and chubby, aged somewhere in his mid-thirties, he had red-blond hair, a perpetual smile, and an outgoing manner that enabled him to become friends with everyone on board almost before the *Southern Cross* had cleared Aventine's atmosphere.

It was an unlikely pairing, and it took Jin nearly a week to realize that the mission's planners hadn't simply pulled their names out of the grab-bag. Raines, with his easy friendliness, would presumably be the main contact man with the Qasamans, while Barynson's job would be to stay in the background and analyze the data as Raines and the others pulled it in.

From the briefings, too, it was quickly clear that Barynson was the man in charge.

"We'll be making our approach along here—from the uninhabited west—making our landing about here," Barynson said, leaning over the photomap and jabbing a finger at a section of forest. "Timing the touchdown for about an hour before dawn, local time. The nearest of the villages bordering the Fertile Crescent area are about fifteen kilometers to the east and southeast—" he touched each in turn "—with what looks to be lumbering operations to the northeast here on the river at about the same distance. You'll note that the site is—theoretically, at least—a fair compromise between distance and seclusion. Whether it'll turn out that way in practice, of course, we won't know until we get there."

"Any idea what kind of undergrowth we'll have to go through?" Todor asked.

"Unfortunately, no," Barynson admitted. "Most of the data we've got on Qasaman forests comes from far to the east of this site, and infrared studies indicate that the canopy here, at any rate, is different in composition from that area."

"Of course," Raines put in, "if travel turns out to be impractical, we can always take the shuttle up to treetop height and move it closer to the villages."

"Only if things are pretty *damn* difficult," Layn muttered. "We have only the Trofts' word for it that the Qasaman observation systems won't be able to track our approach. The more we move the shuttle around, the higher the risk we'll be spotted."

"Agreed," Barynson nodded. "Though the more immediate danger will probably be the Qasaman fauna. I hope you Cobras will be up to the challenge."

"We're ready," Layn told him. "My men—people— know what they're doing."

Baryson's eyes flicked to Jin, turned quickly away. "Yes, I'm sure they do," he said, almost as if he believed it. "Well, anyway . . . we'll all be equipped with the best simulations of Qasaman clothing that the Center's analysis of telephotos could provide. The landing is timed so that we can get through the forest in daylight and reach one of these villages by nightfall. That'll give us the chance to make a close check of our clothing and get a first approximation of the culture before we have to tackle Azras and the main Fertile Crescent civilization. So; questions?"

Jin glanced across the table, caught Sun's eye. The other shrugged fractionally, echoing Jin's own thoughts: there wasn't a lot of point in asking questions to which there were as yet no answers.

"Very well, then." Barynson threw a look around the table. "We have three days left before planetfall, and for those three days I want all of you to do your best to become Qasamans. You'll wear our ersatz Qasaman clothing, eat our nearest approximations to the food the Qasamans were eating thirty years ago, and—most important of all—speak only Qasaman among yourselves. That rule is absolute—you aren't to speak Anglic to *anyone*, not even to one of the *Southern Cross*'s crew. If any of them talks to you, you aren't to understand them. Is that clear?"

"Isn't that carrying things just a little far?" Hariman asked with a frown.

"The Qasmans had ample opportunity to study Anglic the last time we were here," Jin put in quietly. "Some of them were even able to force-learn it well enough to speak it. If they suspect us, they might throw one of those people at us."

"Right," Barynson nodded, looking impressed despite himself. "The old trick of getting a spy to speak in his native language. I'd just as soon none of us falls for it."

"We understand," Sun said in Qasaman. "We demon warriors, at least, won't fall for it."

"I hope not." Barynson looked him straight in the eye. "Because if you ever do, you'll probably wind up earning your pay the hard way."

Qasama was a dark mass against the stars, a fuzzy new-moon sliver of light at one edge showing the dawn line, as the shuttle fell free of the *Southern Cross* and began its leisurely drift toward the world below. Gazing down through the tiny porthole to her left, Jin licked dry lips and tried to quiet her thudding heart. *Almost there,* she told herself. *Almost there.* Her first mission as a Cobra—a goal she'd dreamed about and fantasized about for probably half her life. And now, with it almost close enough to taste, she could feel nothing but quiet terror.

So much, she thought half bitterly, *for the heroic Cobra warrior.*

"You ever fly before this trip?" Sun, sitting on the aisle seat next to her, asked quietly.

"Aircraft, sure, but never any spacecraft," Jin told him, thankfully turning her attention away from the porthole. "Hardly ever into enemy territory, either."

He chuckled, a sound that almost masked the nervousness she could see around his eyes. "We'll do fine," he assured her. "Parades and canonization, remember?"

A smile broke of its own accord through her tension. "Sure." Reaching across the armrest, she took his hand. It was almost as cold as her own.

"Hitting atmosphere," she heard the pilot say from the red-lit cockpit at the front of the passenger compartment. "Injection angle . . . right on the mark."

Jin gritted her teeth. She understood all the reasons

behind coming in as far as they could on an unpowered glide approach—the light from a ship's gravity lifts was extremely visible, especially against a night sky—but the eerie silence from the engines wasn't helping her nervousness a bit. Looking back out the porthole, she tried not to imagine the planet rushing up to hit them—

"Uh-oh," the pilot muttered.

"What?" Barynson snapped from the seat beside him.

"A radar scan just went over us."

Jin's mouth went a little drier, and Sun's grip on her hand tightened. "But they can't pick us up, can they?" Barynson asked. "The Trofts told us—"

"No, no, we're okay," the pilot assured him. "I was just surprised they're scanning this far from the Fertile Crescent, that's all."

"They're paranoid," Layn muttered from the seat across the narrow aisle from Sun. "So what else is new?"

But they aren't supposed to be that way any more, Jin thought morosely. *They were supposed to lose that when we got the mojos off their shoulders.* That had been the whole point of seeding the planet with Aventinian spine leopards thirty years ago, after all. If it hadn't worked—

She shook her head to clear it. If it hadn't worked, they would find out soon enough. There wasn't any point in worrying about it until then.

"Parades and canonization," Sun murmured, misreading her thoughts. It helped, anyway, and she threw him a grateful smile.

The minutes dragged on. An oddly distant scream of air against the shuttle's hull increased and then faded, and slowly all but the brightest of the stars overhead began to be swallowed up by the thickening atmosphere around them. Straining upward against her restraints, Jin could make out the gross details of the ground beneath them now, and in the distance the horizon had lost all of its curve. Five minutes, she estimated—ten at the most—and they would be down. Setting her nanocomputer's clock circuit, she leaned back in her seat, closed her eyes, took a deep breath—

And through the closed lids she still saw the right-hand side of the passenger compartment abruptly blaze up like a fireball, and a smashing wall of thunder slammed her against her seat and into total blackness.

Chapter 11

The pain came first. Not localized pain, not even particularly bad at first; more like a vague and unpleasant realization that somewhere in the darkness something was hurting. Hurting a *lot* . . .

A large part of her didn't care. The blackness was quiet and uncomplicated, and it would have been pleasant to stay hidden there forever. But the pain was a continual nagging at the roots of the nothingness, and even as she was forced to accept and notice its existence she found herself being forced slowly up out of the blackness. Grudgingly, resentfully, she passed through the black, to a dark gray, to a lighter gray—

And with a gasp as the pain suddenly sharpened and focused itself into arms, chest, and knee, she came fully awake.

She was in an awkward and thoroughly uncomfortable position, half-sitting and half-lying on her left side, the safety harness digging painfully into her chest and upper thighs. Blinking the wetness—*blood*? she wondered vaguely—from her eyes, she looked around the tilted and darkened interior of the shuttle. Nothing could be seen clearly; only after several seconds of straining her eyes did it occur to her befuddled mind to key in her optical enhancers.

The sight made her gasp.

The shuttle was a disaster area. Across the aisle the far hull had been literally blown in, leaving a ragged-edged hole a meter or more across. Strands of twisted and blackened metal curled inward from the gap like frozen ribbons; bits and pieces of plastic, cloth, and glass littered everything she could see. The twin seats that had been by the hole had been ripped from their bracings and were nowhere to be seen.

The twin seats that Layn and Raines had been sitting in.

Oh, God. For a moment Jin gazed in horror at the ruined struts where the seats had been. They were gone, gone totally from the shuttle . . . from thirty or forty kilometers up.

Somewhere, someone groaned. "Peter?" she croaked. Todor and Hariman had been in the seats just behind the missing men . . . "Peter?" she tried again. "Rafe?"

There was no answer. Reaching up with a hand that was streaked with blood, she groped for her safety harness release. It was jammed; gritting her teeth, she put servo-motor strength into her squeeze and got it free. Shakily, she climbed to her feet, stumbling off-balance on the canted floor. She grabbed onto what was left of her seat's emergency crashbag to steady herself, jamming her left knee against the bulkhead in the process. A dazzling burst of pain stabbed through the joint, jolting her further out of her fogginess. Shaking her head—sparking more pain—she raised her eyes to look over the seat back to where Todor and Hariman should be.

It was only then that she saw what had happened to Sun.

She gasped, her stomach suddenly wanting to be

sick. The explosion had apparently sent shrapnel into his crashbag, tearing through the tough plastic and leaving him defenseless against the impact of the shuttle's final crash. Still strapped to his seat, blood staining his landing coveralls where the harness had dug into his skin, his head lolled against his chest at an impossible angle.

He was very clearly dead.

Jin stared at him for a long minute. *This isn't real,* she told herself wildly, striving to believe it. If she believed it hard enough, maybe it wouldn't have happened . . . *This isn't real. This is our first mission—just our first mission. This can't happen. Not now. Oh, God, please not now.*

The scene began to swim before her eyes, and as it did so a red border appeared superimposed across her optically enhanced vision. The sensors built into her Cobra gear, warning her of approaching unconsciousness. *Who cares?* she thought savagely at the red border. *He's dead—so are Layn and Raines and who knows who else. What do I need to be conscious for?*

And as if in answer, the groan came again.

The sound tore her eyes away from Sun's broken body. Clawing her way past him, she stumbled out into the littered aisle, eyes focusing with an effort on the seats where Hariman and Todor dangled limply in their harnesses. One look at Hariman was all she could handle—it was clear he'd died in the explosion, even more violently and terribly than Sun. But Todor, beside him in the aisle seat, was still alive, twitching like a child in a nightmare.

Jin was there in seconds, pausing only to grab the emergency medical kit from the passenger compartment's front bulkhead. Kneeling down beside him, ignoring the pain from her injured knee, she got to work.

But it was quickly clear that both the kit's equipment and her own first-aid training were hopelessly inadequate. Surface-wound treatment would be of no use against the massive internal bleeding the sensors registered from Todor's chest; anti-shock drugs would do nothing against the severe concussion that was already squeezing Todor's brain against the ceramic-reinforced bones of his skull.

But Jin wouldn't—couldn't—give up. Sweating, swearing, she worked over him, trying everything she could think of.

"Jin."

The husky whisper startled her so badly she dropped the hypospray she'd been loading. "Peter?" she asked, looking up at his face. "Can you hear me?"

"Don't waste . . . time . . ." He coughed, a wracking sound that brought blood to his lips.

"Don't try to talk," Jin told him, fighting hard to keep the horror out of her voice. "Just try and relax. Please."

"No . . . use . . ." he whispered. "Go . . . get out . . . of here . . . someone . . . coming. Has to . . . be some . . . one . . ."

"Peter, please stop talking," she begged him. "The others—Mandy and Rafe—they're all dead. I've got to keep you alive—"

"No . . . chance. Hurt too . . . badly. The mish . . . mission, Jin . . . you got . . . got to . . ." He coughed again, weaker this time. "Get out . . . get to . . . some . . . where hid . . . hidden."

His voice faded into silence, and for a moment she continued to kneel beside him, torn between conflicting commitments. He was right, of course, and the more her brain unfroze itself from the shock the more she realized how tight the deadline facing her really was. The shuttle had been deliberately shot down . . . and whoever had done the job would eventually come by to examine his handiwork.

But to run now would be to leave Todor here. Alone. To die.

"I can't go, Peter," she said, the last word turning midway into a sob. "I *can't.*"

There was no answer . . . and even as she watched helplessly, the twitching in his limbs ceased. She waited another moment, then reached over and touched fingertips to his neck.

He was dead.

Carefully, Jin withdrew her hand and took a long, shuddering breath, blinking back tears. A soft glow from Todor's fingertip lasers caught her eye: the new self-destruct system incorporated into their gear had activated itself, shunting current from the arcthrower capacitors inward onto the nanocomputer and servo systems. Automatically destroying his electronics and weaponry beyond any hope of reconstruction should the Qasamans find and examine his body.

No. Not *if* the Qasamans found him; *when* they found him. Closing her eyes and mind to the carnage around her, Jin tried to think. It had been—how long since the crash? She checked her clock circuit, set just before the initial explosion.

Nearly seventy minutes had passed since then.

Jin gritted her teeth. *Seventy minutes?* God—it was worse than she'd realized. The aircraft the Qasamans would have scrambled to check out their target practice could be overhead at any minute, and the last thing she was ready for was a fight. Clutching at Todor's seat, she pulled herself to her feet and made her way forward.

The cockpit was in worse shape even than the passenger compartment, having apparently survived the explosion only to take the full brunt of what must have been a hellish crash landing. One look dashed any hope she might have had of calling the *Southern Cross* for advice or help—the shuttle's radio and laser communicator would have been mangled beyond repair.

Which meant that unless and until the *Southern Cross* figured out on its own that something was wrong, she was going to be on her own. Totally.

Barynson and the pilot—she realized with a distant twinge of guilt that she'd never even known that latter's

full name—were both dead, of course, crushed beyond
the protective capabilities of harness and crashbag. She
barely gave them a second look, her mind increasingly
frantic with the need to get out as quickly as possible.
Behind Barynson's chair—thrown from its rack by the
impact—was what was left of the team's "contact pack,"
containing aerial maps, close-range scanning equipment,
trade goods, and base communicator. Scooping it up,
Jin headed aft to the rear of the passenger compartment
where the rest of the gear was stored. Her survival pack
seemed to be as intact as any of the others; grabbing
Sun's pack as well for insurance, she stepped to the exit
hatch and yanked on the emergency release handle.

Nothing happened.

"Damn," she snarled, tension coming out in a snap of
fury. Swiveling on her right foot, she swung her left leg
around and sent a searing burst of antiarmor laser fire
into the buckled metal.

The action gained her purple afterimage blobs in
front of her eyes and a hundred tiny sizzleburns from
molten metal droplets, but not much more. *All right*,
she grimaced to herself as she blinked away the sudden
tears. *Enough of the hysterics, girl. Calm down and try
thinking for a change.* Studying the warped door, she
located the most likely sticking points and sent antiarmor shots into them. Then, wincing as she took her full
weight onto her weak left knee, she gave the center of
the panel a kick. It popped open about a centimeter.
More kicks and a handful of additional shots from the
antiarmor laser forced it open enough for her to finally
squeeze outside.

They'd been scheduled to land an hour before local
sunrise, and with the extra delay the forest had grown
bright enough for her to shut off her light-amps. Leaning on the hatch, she managed to close it more or less
shut again. Then, taking a deep breath of surprisingly
aromatic air, she looked around her.

The shuttle looked even worse on the outside than it

had on the inside. Every hullplate seemed to be warped
in some way, with the nose of the ship so crumpled as
to be almost unrecognizable. All the protruding sensors
and most of the radar-absorbing overlay were gone, too,
torn away in a criss-cross pattern that looked as if a
thousand spine leopards had tried to claw it to death.
The reason for the pattern wasn't hard to find: for a
hundred meters back along the shuttle's approach the
trees had been torn and shattered by the doomed craft's
mad rush to the ground.

Gritting her teeth, she took a quick look upward. The
blue-tinged sky was still clear, but that wouldn't last
long . . . and when they came, that torn-up path through
the trees would be a guidepost they couldn't miss.
Keying her auditory enhancers, she stood still and listened for the sound of approaching engines.

And heard instead a faint and all-too-familiar purring
growl.

Slowly, careful not to make any sudden moves, she
eased her packs to the ground and turned around. It
was a spine leopard, all right, under cover of a bush
barely ten meters away.

Stalking her.

For a moment Jin locked gazes with the creature,
feeling eerily as if she were meeting the species for the
first time. Physically, it looked exactly like those she'd
trained against on Aventine . . . and yet, there was
something in its face, especially about the eyes, that
was unlike anything she'd ever seen in a spine leopard
before. A strange, almost preternatural alertness and
intelligence, perhaps? Licking dry lips, she broke her
eyes away from the gaze, raising them to focus on the
silver-blue bird perched on the spine leopard's back.

A mojo, without a doubt. It matched all the descrip-
tions, fitted all the stories she'd heard from her father
and his fellow Cobras . . . and it was clear that none of
them had done the birds proper credit. Hawklike, with
oversized feet and wickedly curved talons, the mojo

was as perfect a hunting bird as she'd ever seen. And in
its eyes . . .

In the eyes was the same alertness she'd already seen
in its companion spine leopard.

Again Jin licked her lips. Standing before her was
living proof that the plan her father had worked out all
those years ago had actually worked, at least to some
degree, and under other circumstances she should probably have taken some time to observe the interaction.
But time was in short supply just now, and academic
curiosity low on her priorities list. Two twitches of her
eyes put targeting locks on both creatures' heads. Easing onto her right foot, she swung her left leg up—

And as the mojo shrieked and shot into the sky, the
spine leopard sprang.

The first blast from her antiarmor laser caught the
predator square in the face, vaporizing most of its head.
But even as Jin turned her attention toward the sky the
mojo struck.

Her computerized reflexes took over as the optical
sensors implanted in the skin around her eyes registered the airborne threat, throwing her sideways in a
flat dive. But the action came a fraction of a second too
late. The hooked talons caught her left cheek and shoulder as the bird shot past, burning lines of fire across the
skin. Jin gasped in pain and anger as she fought against
the entangling undergrowth, her eyes searching franti-
cally to locate her attacker. There it was—coming around
for a second diving pass. Praying that her targeting lock
hadn't been disengaged by that roll, she triggered her
fingertip lasers.

Her arms moved of their own accord, the implanted
servos swinging them up at the nanocomputer's direction, and the bird's shimmering plumage lit up as the
lasers struck it. The mojo gave one final shriek, and its
blackened remains fell past Jin's head and slammed
harmlessly to the ground.

For a moment she just knelt there among the vines

and dead leaves, gasping for breath, her whole body trembling with reaction and adrenaline shock. The scratches across her face burned like fire, adding to the aches and throbs of her other injuries. Up until now she'd been too preoccupied with other things to pay much attention to herself; now, it was clearly time to take inventory.

It wasn't encouraging. Her back and neck ached, and a little experimentation showed both were beginning to stiffen up. Her chest was bruised where the safety harness had dug into the skin during the crash, and her left elbow had the tenderness of a joint that had been partially dislocated and then popped back into place. Her left knee was the worst; she didn't know what exactly had happened to it, but it hurt fiercely. "At least," she said aloud, "I don't have to worry about broken bones. I suppose that's something."

The sound of her voice seemed to help her morale. "Okay, then," she continued, getting to her feet. "First step is to get out of here and find civilization. Fine. So. . ." She glanced up at the sky, keying her auditory enhancers again as she did so. No sounds of aircraft; no sounds of predators. The sun was . . . there. "Okay, so that's east. If we crashed anywhere near our landing site, that's the direction we want to go."

And if the shuttle had instead overshot the Fertile Crescent . . . ? Firmly, she put that thought out of her mind. If she was going the wrong direction, the next village would be roughly a thousand kilometers of forest away. Collecting her three packs, she settled them as comfortably as she could around her shoulders and, taking a deep breath, fixed her direction and headed off into the forest.

Chapter 12

It started easily enough, as forest travel went. Within a few meters of the crash site she ran into a patch of mutually interlocking fern-like plants that lasted most of the first kilometer, giving her the feeling of wading through knee-deep water; and she'd barely left the ferns behind when she found herself having to use fingertip lasers to cut through a maze of tree-clinging vines that reminded her of Aventinian gluevines with five-centimeter thorns. But physical obstacles were the least of her worries, and even as she used lasers and servo strength to good advantage against the forest's best efforts, she tried to keep as much of her attention as possible on the subtle sounds filtering in through her audio enhancers.

The first attack came, in retrospect, right where she should have expected it: at the spot where the forest undergrowth abruptly vanished into a wide path of trampled earth bearing northwest. The path of a bololin herd . . . and where there were bololins, there were bound to be krisjaws, too.

She didn't identify the attacker as a krisjaw at first, of course. It wasn't until after the brief battle was over, and she was able to turn over the laser-blackened corpse and get a clear look at the wavy, flame-shaped canines that she could positively identify the beast. Vicious, cunning, and dangerous was how krisjaws has been described to her; and even with only this one interaction to go on she could well understand why the first generation of humans to reach Qasama had done their damnedest to try and wipe the things out. Wrapping a field bandage from her kit around the gash the predator's claws had torn in her left forearm, she continued on her way. Krisjaws were as nasty as Layn had warned, but now that she knew what to listen for she should be able to avoid being sneaked up on. If the forest didn't get any worse, she decided, she should be able to get through all right.

The forest, unfortunately, got worse.

The line of trampled undergrowth marking the bololins' route turned out to be nearly three kilometers wide, and within that cleared area an astonishing number of ground animals and their ecological hangers-on had set up shop. Insects buzzed around her in large numbers, attracted perhaps by the blood from her injuries. Most of them were merely annoying, but at least one large type was equipped with stingers and showed little compunction about using them. It was as she was swatting at a group of those that she found out that krisjaws weren't Qasama's only predator species.

This kind—vaguely monkey-like except for their six clawed limbs—hunted in packs, and it cost her another clawing before she found the best way to deal with them. Her omnidirectional sonic, designed originally to foul up nearby electronic gear, turned out to be equally effective in disrupting the monkeys' intergroup communication, and the arcthrower with its thundering flash of current scattered them yipping back into the cover of the surrounding trees.

Unfortunately, the sonic had an unexpected side effect, that of attracting a species of gliding lizard that, like the monkeys, launched their attacks in groups from the trees above her. Smaller and less dangerous than the larger predators, they were also too stupid to be frightened by the arcthrower's flash. She wound up having to kill all of them, collecting several small needle-toothed bites in the process.

It seemed like forever before she finally reached the road cutting across her path.

Captain Rivero Koja gazed down at the high-resolution photo on his viewing screen, a cold hand clenched around his heart. The line of destruction through the Qasaman forest could mean only one thing. "Hell," he said softly.

For a long moment the *Southern Cross*'s bridge was silent, save for the quiet clicking of keys from the scanner chief's station. "What happened?" Koja asked at last.

First Officer LuCass shrugged helplessly. "Impossible to tell, sir," he said. "Some malfunction, perhaps, that knocked them too far off their glide path—"

"Or else maybe someone shot them down?" Koja snapped, his simmering frustration and helplessness boiling out as anger.

"The Trofts claimed that wouldn't happen," LuCass reminded him.

"Yeah. Right." Koja took a deep breath, fought the rage back down to a cold anger. If only the *Southern Cross* had been overhead when the shuttle went down, instead of in their own orbit half a world away. If only they'd *been* there; had seen the crash as it happened, instead of finding out about it an hour afterward . . .

And if they had, it wouldn't have made any difference. None at all. Even if the *Southern Cross* had the capability of landing down there—which it didn't—they would still have been too late to save anyone. A crash like that would have killed everyone on board on impact.

Koja closed his eyes briefly. *At least*, he thought, *it would have been quick*. It wasn't much consolation.

"I'll be damned," the scanner chief muttered abruptly into his thoughts. "Captain, you'd better take a look at this."

Koja turned back to his display. A closer view of the crash site had replaced the first photo on his display. "Lovely," he growled.

"Maybe it is," the chief said, picking up his lightpen. A circle appeared briefly in the photo's lower right-hand corner. "Take a look and tell me if I'm seeing what I think I am."

It was an animal—that much was obvious even to Koja's relatively untrained eye. A quadruped, with the build of a hunting feline, lying prone on the leafy ground cover in the clearing the shuttle's passage had torn through the tree canopy. "A spine leopard?" he hazarded.

"That's what I thought, too," the other nodded. "Notice anything unusual about its head?"

Frowning, Koja leaned closer. The head . . .

Was gone. "Must have gotten caught in the crash," he said, feeling suddenly queasy. If something *out*side the shuttle had been torn up that badly . . .

"Maybe, maybe not," the chief muttered, an odd note in his voice. "Let me see if I can get us in a little closer—"

A new, tighter photo replaced the one on the display, the normal atmospheric blurring fading away as the computer worked to clean up the image. The spine leopard's head . . .

"Oh, my God," LuCass whispered from his side. "Captain—that's not crash damage."

Koja nodded, the cold hand on his heart tightening

its grip. Not crash damage; laser damage. *Cobra* laser damage.

Someone had survived the crash.

"Complete scan," Koja ordered the scanner chief through dry lips. "We've got to find him."

"I've already done a check of the area we can penetrate—"

"Then do it again," Koja snapped.

"Yes, sir." The chief got busy.

LuCass took a step closer to Koja's chair. "What are we going to do if we *do* locate him?" he asked softly. "There isn't any place down there we could possibly set this monster down."

"Even if there was, I doubt the Qasamans would sit back and let us do it." Koja clenched his teeth until they ached. He'd asked the Directorate—*begged* the Directorate—to rent a second shuttle from the Trofts as an emergency backup. But no; the damned governor-general had deemed it an expensive and unnecessary luxury and vetoed the request. "Any chance we could get some food and medical supplies down to him? It would at least give him a fighting chance."

LuCass was already typing on Koja's computer keyboard. "Let's see what we've got on board . . . well, we could foam some ablator onto a mini cargo pod. A parachute . . . yes, we could rig a chute. Pressure sensor to tell it when to pop . . . ? Hmm. Nothing . . . wait a second, we could put it on a simple timer and have it pop at a prefigured time. Looks feasible, Captain."

"At which point the question arises of where to send it so that he can actually find it." Koja looked over at the scanner chief. "Anything?"

The other shook his head. "No, sir. The canopy's just too thick for short-wave or infrared penetration. His only shot at civilization is to the east, though—we could try dropping the supplies where the road ahead of him intersects an eastward path." He hesitated. "Of course, there's no guarantee he's lucid," he added. "He could be going in *any* direction, in that case, or even walking around in circles. Or his brain could be functioning fine but his body too badly injured to get all the way to the road."

"In either case he's dead," Koja said tightly. "He may be dead even if he *does* get to a village—the Qasaman leaders are hardly going to keep the shuttle crash an official secret." He looked at LuCass. "Get a crew busy on that pod," he ordered. "Include a tight-beam split-freq radio with the other supplies. We'll have a spot picked out to aim for by the time you're ready."

"Yes, sir." LuCass turned back to his own board, keyed the intercom, and began issuing orders.

Exhaling in a silent sigh, Koja looked back at the dead spine leopard still on his display. *And it's all just so much wasted effort,* he thought blackly. Because as long as the Cobra was alone in enemy territory the time clock would be ticking down toward zero. Eventually, the Qasamans would identify him; or else a wandering krisjaw or spine leopard would find him; or else something completely unknown would get him.

Qasama was a deathtrap . . . and the only people who had any chance at all of pulling him out of it were back on Aventine. Eight days and forty-five light-years away.

Eight days. Koja cringed, trying desperately to find a closer alternative. The New Worlds, perhaps—Esquiline and the other fledgling colonies—or even the nearby Troft demesne of Baliu'ckha'spmi. But Esquiline would have no spacecraft capable of making groundfall, either; and with neither an official credit authorization nor a supply of trade goods on board, trying to deal through an unfamiliar Troft bureaucracy for the rent of another shuttle could take literally months.

Eight days. A minimum of fourteen days for the round trip, even if the faster *Dewdrop* was available. Add the time needed to choose and equip a search and rescue team, and it could easily be twenty days before they could even begin to look for him.

And with or without a supply pod, twenty days alone on Qasama was a death sentence. Pure and simple.

But that didn't mean they had to give up without a fight . . . and if the fight in this case consisted of hoping for a miracle, then so be it. The fact that one of the Cobras had survived the crash was a miracle in and of itself; perhaps the angel in charge of this area would be feeling generous.

Eventually, they would find out. In the meantime. . .

Reaching to his keyboard, Koja began plotting out the route and fueling stops for a least-time course back to Aventine. It had been his experience that miracles, when they happened, tended to favor those who had laid the proper groundwork for them.

Chapter 13

Jin stood at the road for a long time, trying to figure out what to do next.

It was, at any rate, confirmation that the shuttle had indeed crashed to the west of the Fertile Crescent. Roads always led to civilization; all she had to do was follow it.

The question was, which way?

For a moment the landscape seemed to swim before her eyes, and the red warning border appeared superimposed on the scenery. She twisted her head, sending a jolt of pain through the stiffness in her neck. There had been no fewer than five such warnings in the past half hour, a sure sign that she was losing it. Combat fatigue, shock from her injuries, some slow poison in the animal bites and scratches she'd suffered—it didn't much matter the cause. What mattered now was finding somewhere safe to collapse before she did so on her feet.

So . . . which way?

Blinking hard against a sudden moisture in her eyes, she studied the road. Two lanes wide, probably, paved with some kind of black rocktop—hardly a major thoroughfare. Running almost due north-south, at least at this point, it was probably one of the connecting roads between the small forest villages west and northwest of the major Fertile Crescent city of Azras. The maps in her pack showed those villages to be anywhere from ten to fifteen kilometers apart. A trivial distance for a Cobra in good condition, but her present condition was anything but good.

The red circle appeared around her vision again. Biting hard on her lower lip, she again managed to force it away.

Thoughts of the maps had reminded her of something. Something important . . . Concentrating hard, she tried to force her brain awake enough to think of what it might be. Her packs—that was it. Her packs, with their Aventinian maps and packaged survival food and Qasaman clothing—

Qasaman clothing.

With an effort, Jin keyed her auditory enhancers. Nothing but insect and bird twitterings. Stepping off the road, she walked back to the line of trees and dropped her packs to the ground behind a bush that seemed to be half leaves and half thorns. Locating her personal pack among the three, she fumbled the catches open and pulled out a set of Qasaman clothing.

Changing clothes was an ordeal. Between the oozing cuts on her arms and face and the ache and throbbing of her crash injuries, every movement seemed to have its own distinctive pain. But with the pain came a slight clearing of her mind, and when she was done she even had the presence of mind to stuff her torn Aventinian garb away and to push all three packs into at least marginal concealment under the thorn bush. A minute later she was trudging along the road, heading north for no particular reason.

She never heard the car's approach. The voices, when they called to her, seemed to come from a great distance, echoing out of a wavering mist that filled her ears as much as it did her eyes.

"—matter with you? Huh?"

Bringing her feet to a halt, she tried to turn around, but she'd made it only halfway when a pair of hands suddenly were gripping her shoulders. "—God in heaven, Master Sammon! Look at her face—!"

"Get her into the car," a second, calmer voice cut the first off. "Ende—give him a hand."

And in a dizzying flurry Jin was picked up by shoulders and thighs and carried bouncing to a dimly seen red box shape. . . .

The air sensor strapped to his right wrist beeped twice, and Daulo Sammon raised it close to his face, rubbing some of the dust off his goggles for a better view. The readout confirmed what his lungs and the beep had already told him: that the air in this part of the mine was beginning to get stale. Raising his other wrist, Daulo consulted his watch. Officially, the workers had fifteen minutes to go before their shift was over. If he had the air exchangers started now, running them for perhaps three minutes . . .

Not worth it. "Foreman?" he called into his headset microphone. "This is Daulo Sammon. The shift is hereby declared over; you may begin moving the men back to the shaft now."

"Yes, Master Sammon," the other's voice came back, hissing with static from the ore veins' metallic interference. Daulo strained his ears, but if the foreman was pleased or surprised by such uncommon leniency, his voice didn't show it. "All workers, begin moving back to the central core."

Daulo clicked his headset off the general frequency and turned back himself, his light throwing sharp shadows across the crisscrossing of shoring that half covered

the rough tunnel walls. His grandfather had expected
the mine to play out in his own lifetime, and had
neglected its safety accordingly, and it had taken Daulo's
father nearly ten years to reverse the deterioration that
had ensued. *Will it all be gone before it becomes mine?*
Daulo wondered, sweeping his light across the star-
sparkling rock peeking out between the bracings. A
small part of his mind rather hoped it would; the thought
of being responsible for all the lives that toiled daily
down here had always made him a little uneasy. He'd
seen his grandfather neglect that responsibility, and
had seen what the burden had done to his father. To
have that weight on his own shoulders . . .

But if the mine went, then so did the Sammon family's wealth and prestige . . . and very likely its place in
the village, as well. Without the mine, only lumber
processing would remain as a major industry, and it was
for certain the Sammon family wouldn't be involved in
that.

And as for the dangers of the mine, outside Milika's
wall the miners would have to risk the krisjaws and
razorarms and all the rest of Qasama's deadly animal
life. Behind his filter mask, Daulo's lip twisted as the
old proverb came to mind: on Qasama there were no
safe places, only choices between dangerous ones.

He reached the central shaft a few minutes later to
find a growing line of men waiting for their turns at the
mine's three elevators. Bypassing them, he stepped to
the car that was currently loading and motioned the
men already in it to get off. They did so, making the
sign of respect as they passed him. Stepping into the
elevator, Daulo slid the gate closed and punched for
the top.

The ride up was a long one—though not as long as
the trip the opposite direction always seemed—and as
the car shook around him he pulled off headset, goggles, and mask and gingerly rubbed the bridge of his
nose. A hot shower was what was needed now—a shower,

followed by a good meal. No; the meal would be third—after the shower he would presumably be summoned by his father for a report on his trip down the mine. That was all right; he would have time to organize his observations and conclusions while he scrubbed the mine's grit and chill from his body.

The sudden stream of light as the car reached ground level made Daulo blink. Shifting the equipment around in his hands, he surreptitiously wiped away the sudden tears as the operators outside opened the gates and stepped back, making the sign of respect as they did so. Daulo stepped out, nodding at the mine chief as the latter also made the sign of respect. "I trust, Master Sammon," the chief said, "that your inspection found nothing wanting?"

"Your service to my father seems adequate," Daulo told him, keeping his face and voice neutral. He had, in fact, found things down there to be excellent, but he had no intention of saying so on the spur of the moment. Aside from the danger of swelling the mine chief's ego with unnecessary public praise, Daulo's father had always warned him against rendering hasty judgments. "I shall report to my father what I have seen."

The other bowed. Passing him, Daulo walked out from under the elevator canopy and headed past the storage and preparation buildings toward the access road where Walare was waiting with his car.

"Master Sammon," Walare said, making the sign of respect as Daulo came up to him. Daulo climbed in, and a moment later Walare was guiding the car off the mine grounds and onto Milika's public streets.

"What news is there?" Daulo asked as they turned toward the center of town and the Sammon family house.

"Public news or private?" Walare asked.

"Private, of course," Daulo said. "Though you can skip past the backlife gossip."

In the car's mirror, Walare's eyes were briefly surrounded by smile lines. "Ah, how times have changed," he said with mock sadness. "I remember a time—no more than three years ago—when the backlife news was the first thing you would ask for—"

"The news, Walare; the news?" Daulo interrupted with equally mock exasperation. He'd known Walare ever since the two were boys; and while the public relationship between driver and Sammon family heir were rigidly defined, in the privacy of Daulo's car things could be considerably freer. "You can reminisce about the lost golden age later."

Walare chuckled. "Actually, it's been a very quiet day. The Yithtra family trucks are mobilizing—someone there must have found a rich section of forest. Perhaps because of that, the mayor's trying again to talk your father into supporting his efforts to have the top of the wall rebuilt."

"Waste of money and effort," Daulo snorted, glancing behind him. Part of the village wall was visible past the village's buildings, the forest-like paintings on the lower part in sharp contrast with the stark metal mesh extension atop it. "The razorarms can't get over what we've got now."

Walare shrugged. "Mayors exist largely to make noise. What else is there for him to make noise about these days?"

Daulo grinned tightly. "Besides our trouble with the Yithtra family, you mean?"

"What can he say about that that he hasn't already said?"

"Not much," Daulo admitted. There were times he wished the competition between his family and the Yithtra family didn't exist; but it was a fact of life, and disliking it didn't change that. "Anything else?"

"Your brother Perto brought in that shipment of spare motor parts from Azras," Walare said, his voice abruptly taking on a grim tone. "Along with a passenger: an injured woman they found on the road."

Daulo sat up a bit straighter. "A woman? Who?"

"No one at the house recognized her."

"Identification?"

"None." Walare hesitated. "Perhaps it was lost in . . . the trouble she had."

Daulo frowned. "What sort of trouble?"

Walare took a deep breath. "According to the driver who helped bring her in, she'd been clawed at least once by a krisjaw . . . as well as clawed by a baelcra and bitten by one or more monota."

Daulo felt his stomach tighten. "God above," he muttered. "And she was still alive?"

"She was when they brought her to the house," Walare said. "Though who knows how long she'll stay that way?"

"God alone," Daulo sighed.

Chapter 14

They reached the house a few minutes later, Walare guiding the car expertly through the filigreed doors and over to the wide garage nestled behind a pair of fruit trees in one corner of the large central courtyard. Stomach tightening against what he knew would be a horrible sight, Daulo headed for the women's section of the house.

Only to discover that his worst fears had been for nothing.

"Is that the worst of it?" he asked, frowning across the room at the woman on the bed. Surrounded by three other women and a doctor, with a blanket pulled up to her neck, it was nevertheless clear that the injured woman wasn't the horribly mauled victim he'd expected to find. There was a bad set of scratches on her cheek, visible beneath the healing salve that had been applied, and a rather worse set on her arm that was still being treated. But aside from that . . .

From her seat across the bed Daulo's mother glanced

up at him. "Please stay back," Ivria Sammon said softly. "The dust on your clothing—"

"I understand," Daulo nodded. His eyes searched the visible wounds again, then settled for the first time on her face. About his age, he judged, with the soft-looking skin of someone who had spent little time out in the sun and wind. His eyes drifted down her left arm, past the wounds, to her hand.

No ring of marriage.

He frowned, looking at her face again. No mistake— she was at least as old as he was. And still unmarried—?

"She must have come from a far way," Ivria said quietly, almost as if to herself. "See her face, the way her features are formed."

Daulo glanced at his mother, then back at the mysterious woman again. Yes; now that he was looking for it he could see it, too. There was a strangeness in the face, a trace of the exotic that he'd never seen before. "Perhaps she's from one of the cities to the north," he suggested. "Or even from somewhere in the Eastern Arm."

"Perhaps," the doctor grunted. "She certainly hasn't built up much resistance to monote bites."

"Is that what the problem is?" Daulo asked.

The doctor nodded. "On the arms and hands—here, and here," he added, pointing them out. "It looks like she had to fend them off with her bare hands."

"After her ammunition ran out?" Daulo suggested. She surely hadn't fended off that krisjaw with her bare hands, after all.

"Perhaps," the doctor said. "Though if she had a gun it was gone by the time she was found. As was the holster."

Daulo gnawed at his inner cheek, glancing around the room. A pile of clothing had been tossed into the corner; keeping well back from the bed, he stepped over to it. The injured woman's clothes, of course—the bloodstains alone would have attested to that, even without the odd feel of the cloth that branded it as from someplace far away. And the doctor was right: there *was* no holster with the ensemble. Nor any markings on the belt where one might once have hung.

"Maybe she had some companions," he suggested, dropping the clothing back on the floor. That would certainly make more sense than a single woman wandering alone out in the forest. "Was any effort made to see if there were others in the area where she was found?"

It was Ivria who answered. "Not at the time, but I believe Perto has now gone back to continue the search."

Stepping to the room's intercom, Daulo keyed the private family circuit. "This is Daulo Sammon," he identified himself to the servant who answered. "Has Perto returned from the forest?"

"One moment, Master Sammon," the voice answered. ". . . He is not answering."

Daulo nodded. Out of the house, away from all the Sammon family holdings in Milika, Perto would be out of touch with the buried fiber-optic communications network which was the only safe way to send messages in Milika. "Leave a message for him to contact me as soon as possible," he instructed the other.

"Yes, Master Sammon."

Daulo keyed the intercom off and turned back for one last look at the woman. *Where could she be from?* he wondered. *And why is she here?* There were no answers as yet . . . but that lack would eventually be corrected. For the moment the important fact was that the Sammon family had matters under control. Whether this mysterious woman represented a totally neutral happenstance, or a chance opportunity granted them by God, or part of some strange plot by one of their rivals, the Sammons were now in position to use her presence to their own advantage.

Which reminded him, he still had to clean up before

his meeting with his father. Opening the door quietly, he slipped out of the room.

"Come in," the familiar grating voice came from the opposite side of the carved door; and, steeling himself, Daulo opened the door and went in.

He could still remember a time, not all that long ago, when he'd been absolutely terrified of his father. Terrified not so much by Kruin Sammon's strength and stature, nor even by the man's cold voice and piercing black eyes; but by the fact that Kruin Sammon *was*, to all intents and purposes, the Sammon family. His was the power that ran this immense house and the mine and nearly a third of the village; his the influence that stretched beyond Milika to touch the nearby villages and logging camps and even the city of Azras, whose people normally treated villagers like themselves with barely concealed contempt. Kruin Sammon was *power* . . . and even after the fear of that power had abated somewhat, Daulo had never forgotten the emotions it had aroused in him.

It was only much later that he had realized it was probably a lesson his father had deliberately set for him to learn.

"Ah; Daulo," the older man nodded from his cushion-like throne in solemn greeting to his eldest son. "I trust your trip down the mine went well?"

"Yes, my father," Daulo said, making the sign of respect as he stepped to the cushion before Kruin's low work table and seated himself before it. "The necessity for extra shoring is keeping progress slow in the new tunnel, but not as slow as we feared it would."

"And the job is being done properly?"

"It appeared to be, yes, at least to the best of my knowledge."

"The job is being done properly?" Kruin repeated.

Daulo fought to keep his emotions from his face and voice. That had been a thoughtless qualification—if there

was one thing his father hated, it was equivocation.
"Yes, my father. The shoring was being done properly."

"Good," Kruin nodded, picking up a stylus from the
table and making note on a pad. "And the workers?"

"Content. In my presence, at any rate."

"The mine chief?"

Daulo thought back to the other's face as he'd left the
elevator. "Impressed by his own importance," he said.
"Eager that others know of it, as well."

That brought a faint smile to Kruin's lips. "He is all of
that," he agreed. "But he's also capable and conscien-
tious, and the combination is one that can be put up
with." Tossing the stylus back on the table, he leaned
back against the cushions and gazed at his son. "And
now: what is your impression of our visitor?"

"Our—? Oh. The woman." Daulo frowned. "There
are things about her I don't understand. For one thing,
she's well within marriageable age and yet is unmarried—"

"Or is widowed," Kruin put in.

"Oh. True, she could be a widow. She's also not from
anywhere around here—her clothing is made of a cloth
I'm unfamiliar with, and the doctor said she had a low
tolerance to monote bites."

"And what of her rather dramatic entrance to Milika?
—found alone on the road after some unspecified accident or such?"

Daulo shrugged. "I've heard of people getting stranded
on roads before, my father. And even of surviving krisjaw
attacks."

The elder Sammon smiled. "Very good—you antici-
pated my next question. But have you ever heard of
someone who was close enough to a krisjaw to be
clawed *and* still survived the experience?"

"There are cases," Daulo said, a small part of his
mind wondering why he was being so stubborn. He
certainly had no reason to take the mysterious woman's
part in this debate. "If she had one or more armed

companions during the attack one could have shot the creature off of her, even at that late moment."

Kruin nodded, lips tightening together. "Yes, there's that possibility. Unfortunately, it leads immediately to another question: these alleged defenders of hers seem to have vanished, djinn-like, into thin air. Why?"

Daulo thought about it for a long minute, painfully aware that his father must have already thought all this through and was merely testing him to see if he came up with similar answers. "There are only three possibilities," he said at last. "They are dead, incapacitated, or in hiding."

"I agree," Kruin said. "If they are dead or incapacitated, Perto will find them—I've sent him to search the road now for just that purpose. If they are hiding . . . again, why?"

"Afraid, or part of a plot," Daulo said promptly. "If afraid, they will reveal themselves once their companion is proved to have come to no harm. If part of a plot—" he hesitated "—then the woman is here either to infiltrate and spy on our house or else to distract our attention from her companions' task."

Kruin took a deep breath, his eyes focused somewhere beyond Daulo's face. "Yes. Unfortunately, that is my reasoning, as well. Have you any thoughts as to who would plot against us?"

The snort escaped Daulo's lips before he could stop it. "Need we look farther than the Yithtra family?"

"It could be that obvious," Kruin shrugged. "And yet, I generally credit Yithtra with more subtlety than that. And more intelligence, too—with a new shipment of lumber due in, he'll have more than enough legitimate work to keep him occupied. Why launch a plot to discredit us at the same time?"

"Perhaps that's how he expects us to think," Daulo suggested.

"Perhaps. Still, it would be good to remember that

there are others on Qasama who might find profit in stirring up mischief in Western Arm villages."

Daulo nodded thoughtfully. Yes; and foremost among them were the enemies of Mayor Capparis of Azras. Capparis's unlikely friendship with the Sammon family—and the easy access that relationship gave the mayor to the mine's output—had been a thorn in the side of Capparis's enemies for a long time. Perhaps one of them was finally going to try and break the Sammon family's power, to replace them with someone more malleable.

Especially with that strange self-contained Mangus operation east of Azras gobbling up so much of the mine's output lately. Azras and the other cities in the Western Arm were enough of a headache to Milika and its fellow villages; Mangus and its slimy purchasing agents were as bad in their way as all the cities combined. If someone in Azras thought Mangus's mineral needs would go still higher—and thought that someone other than the Sammon family should profit by those needs . . . "What shall we do, then, my father?" he asked. "Send this woman out of our house, perhaps allow her to recuperate in the mayor's house?"

Kruin was silent a moment before answering. "No," he said at last. "If our enemies believe we consider her harmless, it gives us a slight advantage in this game. No, we will keep her here, at least for now. If Perto fails to find any companions for her—well, by then we may be able to question her directly about how she survived her journey."

And if that story was patently false . . . ? "I understand. Shall I assign a guard to her recovery room?"

"No, we don't want to be that obvious. As long as she's ill and confined to the women's section the normal contingent of guards there will be adequate. You will alert them to be prepared for possible trouble from her, of course."

"Yes, my father. And once she's recovered?"

Kruin smiled. "Why, then, as a proper and dutiful host, it will be your responsibility to act as escort to her."

And to learn just what she's up to. "Yes, my father," Daulo nodded. The elder Sammon's posture indicated the audience was at an end; getting to his feet, Daulo made the sign of respect and bowed. "I will attend to the guards, and then await Perto's return."

"Goodbye, my eldest son," Kruin said with an acknowledging nod. "Make me proud of you."

"I will." *As long as breath is in me,* Daulo added silently.

Pulling open the heavy door, he slipped quietly out of the chamber.

Chapter 15

The first thing Jin noticed as she drifted back to consciousness was that something furry was tickling the underside of her chin. The second thing she noticed was that she didn't seem to hurt anywhere.

She opened her eyes to slits, squinting against the light streaming in from somewhere to her right and trying to orient herself. If her memory was correct— and there might be some doubt about that—it had been past noon when she finally made it through the forest and found the road. Could it still be afternoon on that same day? No, she felt far too rested for that. Besides which . . . Gently, she tried turning her neck. Still a little stiff, but not nearly as bad as it had been. At least a day had passed, then, probably more.

And she'd been unconscious through the whole thing. Naturally unconscious? Or had she been deliberately drugged?

Drugged *and* interrogated?

From her right came the squeak of wood on wood. Keeping her movements small, Jin turned her head. Seated in a heavy looking chair beside the window was a young girl, perhaps seven or eight years old, seated crosslegged with an open book across her lap. "Hello," Jin croaked.

The girl looked up, startled. "Hello," she said, closing her book and laying it on the floor beside her chair. "I didn't realize you were awake. How are you feeling?"

Jin forced some moisture into her mouth. "Pretty good," she said, the words coming out better this time. "Hungry, though. How long was I asleep?"

"Oh, a long time—almost five days—though you were awake and feverish for part of—"

"Five *days*?" Jin felt her mouth fall open in astonishment . . . and then the rest of the girl's comment caught up with her. "I was feverish, you said?" she asked carefully. "I hope I didn't say or do anything too outlandish."

"Oh, no, though my aunt said you're very strong."

Jin grimaced. "Yes, I've been told that." She just hoped her Cobra-enhanced strength hadn't hurt anyone . . . or given her away. "Did anyone—I'm sorry; what is your name?"

The girl looked stricken. "Oh—forgive me." She ducked her head, raising her right hand to touch bunched fingers to her forehead. "I am Gissella; second daughter of Namid Sammon, younger brother of Kruin Sammon."

Jin tried the hand gesture, watching Gissella's face closely as she did so. If she botched the maneuver the younger girl didn't seem to notice. "I am Jasmine," Jin introduced herself. "Third daughter of Justin Alventin."

"Honored," Gissella nodded, getting to her feet and walking around the foot of the bed. "Excuse me, but I was to let my Aunt Ivria know if you awakened in your right mind."

She stepped to the door and what looked like an

intercom set into the wall next to it, and as she got her connection and delivered her news Jin took a quick inventory of her injuries.

It was astonishing. The deep gashes on arm and cheek were already covered with pink skin, and the deep bruises left across her chest by the shuttle safety harness were completely gone. Her left knee and elbow were still tender, but even they were in better shape than she would have expected from the way they'd felt right after the crash. Either the injuries had been more transient than she'd thought at the time, or else—

No. No *or else* about it. Qasaman medicine was as advanced as that of the Cobra Worlds, pure and simple. Possibly more so.

Gissella finished her conversation and stepped to a wardrobe cabinet on the opposite side of the door. "They'll be here shortly," she said, withdrawing a pale blue outfit and holding it out for Jin's approval. "Aunt Ivria suggested you might like to get dressed before they arrive."

"Yes, I would," Jin nodded, pulling back the furry blanket and swinging her legs out of bed.

The material, she quickly discovered, was markedly different from that of the best-guess Qasaman clothing the team had landed with, but the design was similar. Still, Jin took no chances, feigning trouble with her left arm in order to let Gissella do as much of the actual fastening and arranging as possible. Fortunately, there were no major surprises. *Which means I ought to be able to dress myself adequately from now on,* Jin thought as she straightened the hem of the short robe/tunic. *At least until they switch styles on me.* Trying to relax, she listened for the others to arrive.

She didn't have to wait very long. Within a few minutes her enhanced hearing picked up the sound of three sets of footsteps approaching. Taking a deep breath, she faced the door . . . and a moment later the panel swung open to reveal two women and a man.

The first woman was the one in charge of the party—
that much was abundantly clear from both her rich
clothing and her almost regal bearing. She was a woman,
Jin recognized instinctively, who commanded the respect of those around her and would demand nothing
less from a stranger in her household. The second woman
was in sharp contrast: young and plainly dressed, with
the air of one whose role was to go unnoticed about her
duties. *A servant,* Jin thought to herself. *Or a slave.*
And the man—

His eyes were captivating. Literally; it took Jin a long
second to free her gaze from those dark traps and give
the rest of him a quick once-over. He was young—her
age, perhaps a year or two younger—but with the same
regal air as the older woman. And some of the same
features, as well. *Related?* she wondered. Very possibly.

The older woman stopped a meter away from Jin and
ducked her head a few degrees in an abbreviated bow.
"In the name of the Sammon family," she said in a
cool, controlled voice, "I bid you greeting and welcome."

Something expectant in her face . . . on impulse, Jin
repeated the fingertips-to-forehead gesture Gissella had
already shown her. It seemed to work. "Thank you,"
she told the older woman. "I am honored by your
hospitality." The verbal response wasn't the prescribed
one—that much was quickly apparent from the others'
faces. But they seemed surprised, rather than outraged,
and Jin crossed her mental fingers that the story she'd
concocted would cover these slips well enough. "I am
Jasmine, daughter of Justin Alventin."

"I am Ivria Sammon," the older woman identified
herself. "Wife of Kruin Sammon and mother of his
heirs." She gestured to the youth, now standing beside
her. "Daulo, first son and heir of Kruin Sammon."

"I am honored by your hospitality," Jin repeated,
again touching fingers to forehead.

Daulo nodded in return. "Your customs and manners mark you as a stranger to this part of Qasama," Ivria continued, eyes holding unblinkingly on her. "Where is your home, Jasmine Alventin?"

"I have spent time in many different places," Jin said, working hard at controlling her face and voice. This was the stickiest part; no matter what she said now, the lie could be eventually run to ground if they were persistent enough. Given that, her best chance lay with one of the half-dozen cities dotting the western curve of the Crescent, where the higher population density should make any investigation at least a little harder. "My current home is in the city of Sollas."

For a single, awful moment she thought she'd made a mistake, that perhaps something unknown had happened to Sollas in the years following her father's first visit to Qasama. The hard look that flicked across Ivria's face—

"A city dweller," Daulo said sourly.

"City dweller or not, she is our guest now," Ivria replied, and Jin started breathing again. Whatever they had against cities, at least it wasn't something that immediately branded her as an offworlder. "Tell me, Jasmine Alventin, what has brought you to Milika?"

"Is that where I am, then?" Jin asked. "Milika? I didn't know where it was I was brought—the accident that wrecked our car . . ." She shivered involuntarily as images from the shuttle wreck rose unbidden before her eyes.

"Where did this accident happen?" Ivria asked. "On the road from Shaga?"

Jin waved her hands helplessly. "I don't really know *where* we were. My companions—my brother Mander and two others—were searching the forest for insects to take back to their laboratory."

"You were in the forest on foot?" Daulo put in.

"No," Jin told him. "Mander studies insects, trying

to learn their secrets and put them to use. He has—or had; I suppose it's ruined now—a specially built car that can maneuver between trees and through a forest's undergrowth. I was just along for the trip—I wanted to see how he worked." She let a note of puzzlement creep into voice and face. "But I'm sure he knows much more about where the accident happened. Can't you just ask *him* about it when he awakens?"

Ivria and Daulo exchanged glances. "Your companions are not here, Jasmine Alventin," Daulo said. "You were alone when my brother found you on the road."

Jin stared at him a long moment, letting her mouth sag in what she hoped was a reasonable semblance of shock. "Not . . . but they were *there*. With me. We—we all walked to the road together—Mander killed a krisjaw that attacked me—no, they *have* to be here."

"I'm sorry," Ivria said gently. "Do you remember if they were still with you when you reached the road?"

"Of course they were," Jin said, letting her voice drift toward the frantic. "They were still with me when I was carried into the truck. Surely they saw—it was your brother, Daulo, who found us? Didn't he *see* them?"

Daulo's cheek twitched. "Jasmine Alventin . . . you were suffering the effects of several monote bites when Perto found you. Hallucinations are sometimes among these effects. My brother wouldn't have left your companions if they'd been anywhere nearby—you must believe that. And after you were safe here he took several men and went back to do an even more thorough search, covering both the road and the forest areas flanking them, all the way back to Shaga."

Thorough enough to find the packs I hid? Jin's stomach tightened; and immediately relaxed. No, of course the packs were still hidden. If anyone had found them she'd have awakened in a maximum-security prison . . . if she'd been allowed to awaken at all. "Oh, Mander," she whispered. "But then . . . where is he?"

"He may still be alive," Daulo said, his voice steady with forced optimism. "We can send more people to look for him."

Slowly, Jin shook her head, gazing past Daulo into space. "No. Five days . . . If he's not out by now . . . he's not coming out, is he?"

Daulo took a deep breath. "I'll send more searchers, anyway," he said quietly. "Look . . . you've had a bad time, and I doubt that you're fully recovered. Why don't you have a warm bath and something to eat and then rest for a few more hours."

Jin closed her eyes briefly. "Yes. Thank you. I'm . . . sorry. Sorry for everything."

"It's our honor and our pleasure to offer you our hospitality," Ivria said. "Is there someone elsewhere on Qasama to whom a message should be sent?"

Jin shook her head. "No. My family is . . . gone. My brother was all I had left."

"We grieve with you," Ivria said softly. For a moment she was silent; then, she made a gesture and the young Qasaman woman behind her stepped forward. "This is Asya; she will be your servant for as long as you are under our roof. Command her as you will."

"Thank you," Jin nodded. The thought of having a private servant grated against her sensibilities—especially a servant whose manner seemed more fitting to a slave— but it would undoubtedly be out of character to refuse.

"When you feel up to joining us, let Asya know, and she'll find me," Daulo added. "It will be my privilege to be your guide and escort while you are in Milika."

"I will be most honored," Jin said, trying to ignore the warning bells clanging in the back of her mind. First a live-in servant, then the owner's son to walk her around the place. Common hospitality . . . or the first indications of suspicion?

But for the next couple of days, at least, it hardly mattered. Until her elbow and knee were fully functional again, she had little choice but to stay in Milika and recuperate; and if the Sammons wanted to keep her under a microscope, she could handle that. "I look forward to seeing your house and village," she added.

And for a second the compassion seemed to leave Daulo's eyes. "Yes," he said, almost stiffly. "I'm sure you do."

Chapter 16

It turned out to be surprisingly easy for Jin to get used to having a servant around.

The exception was the bath. Jin hadn't had company in the bathroom during baths since she was ten, and to have someone standing quietly ready with cloth, soap, and towel was both strange and not a little discomfiting. The hot water itself felt wonderfully good—and the bathroom more luxurious than any she'd ever seen, let alone been in—but she nevertheless cut the operation as short as she reasonably could.

Once past that, though, things improved considerably. Asya ordered her a large dinner, setting it out at a small window seat table overlooking a magnificently landscaped courtyard. *Sort of like the way your family fusses over you when you're sick*, Jin decided as Asya seated her and began serving. *Or like having an obedient little sister available to boss around.* That role she remembered all too well.

The food itself wasn't as strange-tasting as she'd feared

it would be, and she astonished herself by eating everything Asya had had sent up. The trauma of the crash and trek through the forest, combined with five days of fasting, had given her more appetite than she'd realized.

And apparently more fatigue, too. She'd barely finished the meal when she began to feel sleep tugging again at her eyelids. Leaving Asya to clean up, she made her way back to her bed and got undressed. *I wonder,* the thought occurred to her as she slid under the furry blanket, *if the food might have been drugged.*

But if it had there was nothing she could do about it. As long as she was in Milika and the Sammon household, she was in their power. Best to look as innocent and guileless as possible . . . and concentrate on getting her strength back.

When she awoke again, the room was dark, with only a bare hint of light coming in around heavy curtains covering the room's window. "Asya?" she whispered, keying her optical enhancers to light-amplification. There was no response, and a quick visual survey of the room showed she was alone. Activating her auditory enhancers, she picked up the sounds of slow breathing from the doorway leading to the bathroom/dressing area, and Jin remembered now noticing that one of the couches there had seemed to be of a daybed design. Sliding out of bed, she padded to the doorway and looked in.

Asya was there, all right, snuggled under a blanket on the daybed, oblivious to the world. For a long moment Jin stood watching her, pondering what she should do . . . and as she stood there, it suddenly occurred to her that of the four members of the Sammon household she'd seen so far, none of them had been accompanied by a mojo. Or had worn clothing adapted to carrying one.

She frowned into the darkness. Had the plan, then, worked? Had they truly succeeded in splitting the Qasamans away from their bodyguard birds? *If so, that might explain their reaction to my telling them I was from Sollas,* she realized. *General hostility between villages and cities may have begun.*

Unfortunately, it could just as easily be that Ivria and Daulo had left their mojos behind when they came to see her, for whatever reason. She needed to find out for sure . . . and the sooner the better.

Gnawing thoughtfully at her lip, she looked back at the door where her visitors had entered that afternoon. Somehow, she doubted that Daulo's offer of hospitality had included midnight tours; but on the other hand, no one had suggested that she was a prisoner here, either. Stepping back over to the wardrobe, she located the clothing she'd worn earlier and quietly put it on. Then, senses fully alert, she opened the door and stepped out.

She was in the approximate center of a long hallway, its dim indirect lighting bright enough for her to see without the aid of her enhancers. Halfway to the end in either direction were archways that led off opposite to the courtyard, perhaps to larger suites than hers. The decor was elaborate, with delicate tracings and filigrees of gold and purple everywhere.

All this she noted only peripherally. Her primary attention was on the end of the hallway, and the pair of uniformed men standing there.

Each with the silver-blue plumage of a mojo glinting on his shoulder.

For a second Jin hesitated; but it was too late to back out now. The guards had seen her, and while she didn't yet seem to have provoked anything but mild interest in them, ducking back into her room could hardly fail to pique their interest. The other direction . . . ? But a glance behind her showed another pair of men standing at that end of the hall, too. Gritting her teeth, she turned back and started down the corridor, walking as casually as she could manage.

The guards watched her approach, one of them taking a step away from the far wall as she neared them.

"Greetings to you, Jasmine Alventin," he said, touching his fingers to his forehead. "We stand at your service. Where do you go at this time of the evening?"

"I woke up a short while ago," Jin told him, "and as I couldn't fall back asleep I thought a walk would help."

If that sounded odd to the guard it didn't show in his expression. "Few in the household are still awake," he said, glancing down the hall and making a quick series of hand signals. Jin looked around the corner, saw that the hallway bent around to that direction, probably following the perimeter of the courtyard she could see from her window. At the far end of that hallway were another pair of guards, one of them signaling to someone around the corner from him. These guards, too, came equipped with mojos. "I'll see if there is any of the Sammon family who can receive you," Jin's guard explained.

"That's really not necessary—" Jin started to say.

But it was too late. The guard in the distance was already gesturing back their way. "There is a light on in Kruin Sammon's private office," Jin's guard informed her. "The guard down there will escort you."

"That's really not necessary," Jin protested, heart loud in her ears. If this was the same Kruin Sammon who'd already been identified as patriarch of this family— "I don't want to cause unnecessary trouble."

"Kruin Sammon will wish to be informed that you need entertainment," the guard admonished gently; and Jin swallowed any further argument. The guards clearly had orders concerning her . . . and again, a sudden backing out at this stage would attract the wrong kind of attention.

"Thank you," she told him through stiff lips. Forcing herself to walk steadily, she started down the long hallway ahead toward the men and mojos waiting there. . .

Kruin Sammon leaned back into his cushions, a mixture of irritation and deep thought on his face. "How far did you go?"

"All the way down the road to Shaga, and then out to Tabris," Daulo told him. "We found absolutely nothing. No car, no bodies, no marks where a car might have bololined its way into the forest."

Kruin sighed and nodded. "So. Your conclusion?"

Daulo hesitated a second. "She's lying," he said reluctantly. "She faked the accident, perhaps deliberately inflicting her injuries on herself, in order to gain entrance to our house."

"I find no grounds to argue with you," Kruin agreed. "But it still seems so much effort for so little gain. Surely there are many simpler paths that would have gained her the same end."

Daulo pursed his lips. That was the same knot that had steadfastly refused to come apart for him, as well. "I know, my father. But who knows what convoluted scheme our enemies may have come up with? Perhaps they wish us to spend so much time trying to unravel her secrets that we fail to anticipate their main thrust."

"True. I take it, then, that you would counsel against my sending word to Azras and asking Mayor Capparis to contact the authorities in Sollas?"

"Since it seems clear enough already that she's a plant," Daulo said, "I don't see that it would gain us very much. It would merely confirm that she lied about her home, and in the meantime might alert her friends that we suspect her."

"Yes." For a moment Kruin was silent. Then, with a sigh, he shook his head. "I feel my age tugging at me, my son. In days gone by I would have relished the challenge of such a battle of wits as this. Now, all I can see before me is the danger this woman represents to my family and house."

Daulo licked his lips. Seldom in his life had he been given this kind of unobstructed view into his father's soul, and it was both embarrassing and a little unnerving. "It's the duty of a family leader to consider the well-being of his household," he said, a little stiffly.

Kruin smiled. "And as such you see your own future. Does the thought of so much responsibility frighten you?"

Daulo was saved from the need to answer such an awkward question by a soft ping from Kruin's low desk. "Enter," the elder Sammon said into the inlaid speaker.

Daulo turned to look as the door behind him opened. Two of the guards from the women's wing entered; and sandwiched in between them—

"Jasmine Alventin," Kruin said calmly, as if her presence was no surprise at all. "You are awake late."

"Forgive me if I've overstepped the bounds of your hospitality," the woman said, matching Kruin's tone as she made the sign of respect in that odd way of hers. "I awoke and thought I would walk about until I felt ready to sleep again."

"There are few entertainments available in Milika at night, I'm afraid," Kruin told her. "Unlike, I presume, the larger cities you're accustomed to. Shall I call for food or drink for you?"

"No, thank you," she shook her head. If the reference to her claimed home city startled her, Daulo couldn't see any sign of it in her face. "I'm embarrassed enough already for disrupting your work—please don't let me be any further trouble."

Daulo finally got his tongue unstuck. "Perhaps you'd like to continue your walk out in the courtyard," he suggested. "My father and I are finished here, and I'd be honored to accompany you."

He watched her face closely, saw the brief surprise flicker across her eyes. "Why—I would also be honored," she said. "But only if it's truly no trouble for you."

"None at all," he said, getting to his feet. He'd rather expected her to make some excuse to turn him down—if she was prowling around on some nefarious errand, she'd hardly want to have the Sammon family heir along to watch. But now that he'd made the offer, he couldn't back out. "It *will* have to be a short tour, though," he added.

"That would be fine," she agreed. "I'm not especially sleepy, but I realize I'm not fully recovered yet."

Daulo turned back to his father. "With your permission . . . ?"

"Certainly," Kruin nodded. "Don't be too late; I want you to be at the mine with the first diggers in the morning."

"Yes, my father," Daulo bowed, making the sign of respect. Turning back, he caught the guards' eyes. "You may return to your posts," he told them. "Come," he added to Jasmine, gesturing toward the door. "I'll show you our courtyard. And as we walk you can tell me how our home differs from yours."

Chapter 17

Great, Jin groused at herself as they left Kruin's chambers and headed down the hall toward an ornate stairway. *Just great. A moonlight walk with the local top man's son, discussing a home town you've never been to. Terrific way to start a mission, girl.*

Though as the initial panic began to fade she realized it wasn't quite as bad as it sounded. She'd studied hundreds of satellite photos of Qasaman cities; more importantly, she'd seen all the tapes that had been made at ground level through her Uncle Joshua's extra "eyes" when he and her father were in Sollas thirty years ago. Whatever had changed since then, she at least wouldn't have to build her story up from ground level.

Though it would certainly be safer to steer the conversation away from Sollas entirely . . . and perhaps, in the process, get started on her own research.

Twisting her head as they walked, she looked back at the departing guards and forced a small shiver. "Is something wrong?" Daulo asked.

"Oh, no," she assured him, taking a deep breath. "Just . . . the mojos. They scare me a little."

Daulo glanced back himself. "Mojos are available," he said tartly. "Or would you prefer we not protect our household as best we can?"

"No, I didn't mean that," she shook her head. "I understand why you need them, this deep in the forest and all. I'm just not used to having dangerous animals that close to me."

Daulo snorted. "Those bololin herds you let trample through Sollas don't qualify as dangerous?"

"The more intelligent among us stay as far back from them as possible," she retorted.

"Which makes Mayor Capparis and his people doubly stupid, I suppose?"

Jin's mouth went a little dry. Who in blazes was Mayor Capparis? Someone she should be expected to know? "How do you mean?" she asked cautiously.

"I mean because he has a mojo *and* also participates with his people in the bololin shootings when they come through," Daulo ground out. "Or doesn't Azras even count as a city, being down here at the end of the Eastern Arm with us provincials?"

Jin began to breathe again. Azras was a name she knew: the Fertile Crescent city just southeast of here, fifty kilometers or so southwest of the mysterious roofed compound she was here to take a look at.

And with that useful tidbit of information in hand it would be wise to back off a little. "Forgive me," she said to Daulo. "I didn't mean to sound overbearing or prejudiced."

"It's all right," he muttered, sounding a bit embarrassed. They reached the bottom of the staircase and he steered her toward a large double door. "I shouldn't have reacted so strongly, either. I just get tired of the cities and their infernal harping on the mojo question. Maybe in Sollas they're more trouble and danger than they're worth, but you don't have to worry about razorarms and krisjaws there, either."

"Of course," Jin murmured. So in at least some of the cities the mojo presence had gone from practically universal to practically nonexistent over the past thirty years. How much had that trend affected the villages? "Do you mostly just take them along when you go outside, then?" she asked.

The double door leading outside, she noted, wasn't guarded like the hallways upstairs had been. Daulo pulled it open himself, giving her a somewhat odd look as he did so. "People who choose to own mojos carry them however and wherever they choose," he said. "Some only outside the walls, others at all times. Do all the people of Sollas have this same fascination for birds?"

Jin stepped out into the darkness of the courtyard, thankful that the gloom hid her blush. "Sorry—I didn't mean to bore you. I was merely curious. As I said, I haven't had much experience with them."

Daulo said nothing for a moment, and Jin took advantage of the silence to look around her. The courtyard, impressive enough when seen from an upper window, was even more so at ground level. Fruit trees, bushes, and small sculptures were visible in the dim light of small glowing globes set into a second-floor overhang. Off to the right, she could hear what sounded like the steady splashing of water from a small fountain, and the light breeze carried with it the scents of several different kinds of flowers. "It's beautiful," she murmured, almost unconsciously.

"My great-grandfather created it when he built the house," Daulo said, and there was no mistaking the pride in his voice. "My grandfather and father have changed it somewhat, but there's still much of the ancient Qasama in it. Does your house have anything like this?"

"Our house is but one of several facing onto a common courtyard," Jin said, remembering the tapes she'd studied. "It's not as large as this one, though. Certainly not as lovely."

The words were hardly out of her mouth when a faint scream abruptly wafted through the night air.

Jin jerked, thoughts snapping back to Aventine and the forest where her team had fought against spine leopards—

"It's all right," Daulo said into her ear, and she suddenly realized he'd moved close to her. "Just a rogue razorarm trying to get over the wall, that's all."

"That's *all?*" Jin asked, fighting to calm her stomach. The thought of a spine leopard running loose in the sleeping village . . . "Shouldn't we do something?"

"It's all right, Jasmine Alventin," Daulo repeated. "The mesh is high enough to keep it out. It'll either eventually give up or else get its paws or quills stuck, in which case the night guardians will kill it."

The scream came again, sounding angrier this time. "Shouldn't we at least go and make sure things are under control?" she persisted. "I've seen what—razorarms—can do when they get crazy."

Daulo hissed between his teeth. "Oh, all right. From the sound it *is* in our section of town. You can wait here; I'll be back in a few minutes." Stepping away from her, he headed across the courtyard toward a long outbuilding nestled in one corner.

"Wait a minute," Jin called after him. "I want to go with you."

He threw an odd look over his shoulder. "Don't be absurd," he snorted, disappearing into the outbuilding through a side door. A few seconds passed; and then, with a gentle hum, a large door in the building's front swung up. A low-slung vehicle emerged, gliding across the drive with the utter silence only a very advanced electrical motor could provide. A second door, richly filigreed, opened to provide exit from the courtyard.

And a second later Jin was alone.

Well, that's just terrific, she fumed, glaring at the courtyard door as it swung closed again. *What does he think I am, some useless bit of—?*

Of course he does, she reminded herself with a grimace. *Severely paternalistic society, remember? You knew that coming in. So relax, girl, and try and take it easy, okay?*

Easier advice to give than to take. The whole idea of being a secondary citizen, even temporarily, rankled more than she ever would have imagined it could. But if she was going to maintain her cover, she had no choice but to stay within that character.

Or at least to not get caught stepping outside of it. . . .

The sounds of activity were growing louder, now, centering somewhere toward the west. Keying in her optical enhancers, Jin made a careful sweep of both the courtyard and the windows and doors looking out onto it. No one was visible. Trotting to the western edge of the courtyard, she did a second sweep, this time adding in her infrared sensors as well. Same result: she was alone and unobserved. Gritting her teeth, she looked at the three-story wall towering above her, made a quick estimate of its height, and jumped.

She was, if anything, a bit long on her guess, and a second later she found herself gazing down from midair at the roof of the Sammon house. Fortunately, Daulo's great-grandfather had gone in heavily for ornamental stonework when he'd built the place, and it was no effort to find hand and foot grips as her upward momentum peaked and she started the downward trip. Taking care not to make noise, she clambered up and across the slightly slanted roof to its peak. From that vantage point she could see across much of the village; and there, perhaps a kilometer away to the west, was the wall.

It looked about as she would have expected it, given the pictures brought back from Qasaman villages further north and east. The main part was a three-meter height of tough ceramic, hard and thick enough to withstand a charging bololin, with its inner surface painted to blend in with the forest just beyond it. Unlike the others she'd seen, however, this one had a bonus: an extension of some kind of metal mesh that added another two meters to its original height.

Midway up that fence, holding on with all four feet, was the spine leopard she'd heard.

Jin chewed at her lip. Below the animal, moving around in a purposeful manner, were a handful of figures armed with large handguns. She strained, but even with optical enhancers at full magnification, she couldn't tell if Daulo was among them. *Probably not*, she assured herself. *He couldn't have gotten there that fast.*

And even as she watched, a car pulled up beside the wall and Daulo got out.

For a few seconds he and the men already there conversed. Then, two of the men set up ladders and climbed to the top of the main wall, staying well to either side of the spine leopard. Below them, Daulo and one other raised their guns in two-handed marksman's grips. Apparently they were hoping to kill the predator and grab the carcass before it fell to the ground outside.

Idiots, Jin thought, heart pounding in her ears. If stray bullets or ricochets didn't get the men up there, there was a good chance the spine leopard's death throes would. With their decentralized nervous systems spine leopards weren't easy to kill, certainly not quickly.

The multiple flashes from the guns were like sunglints off rippling water in her enhanced vision. She bit at her lip . . . and by the time the quickfire stutter of the shots reached her it was all over. Before the spine leopard had even sagged completely against the mesh the men on the wall were in front of it, hands poked through to grip the animal's forelegs. Two more men— Jin hadn't even noticed them get up on the wall—grabbed the top of the mesh and pulled themselves up and over to the spine leopard's side. Another second and they'd each taken a hind leg in one hand; hanging onto the mesh with the other hand, they heaved the carcass over the top to flop onto the ground inside the wall.

Carefully, Jin let her breath out, an odd shiver running up her back as the two men climbed the mesh again to safety. Of course these people knew what they were doing—they'd had a whole generation, after all, to figure out how to deal with the spine leopard legacy the Cobra Worlds had given them. There was little need for her to worry about the Qasamans on that account.

Which meant she could concentrate all of her worrying on herself.

Daulo was getting back into his car now. Carefully, Jin retraced her steps to the edge of the roof. With her leg servos and ceramic-coated bones there to take the impact, the fastest way down would be to simply drop straight back into the courtyard. But the noise of the impact might be loud enough for someone to hear, and after seeing that display of firepower she wasn't in the mood to risk drawing unwelcome attention. Licking her lips, she hooked her fingers into servo-strength talons and started the long climb down the stonework.

She'd decreased the distance by nearly a full story by the time her auditory enhancers picked up the hum of the outer door opening. Clenching her teeth, she let go and dropped the rest of the way to the ground. By the time Daulo came looking for her she was seated on a low bench beneath a fragrant tree, waiting for him.

"Are you all right?" she asked.

"Oh, sure," he nodded. "It was just a razorarm stuck in the wall. We got it without any trouble."

"Good," Jin told him, standing up. "Well, then, I suppose—"

She broke off abruptly as the courtyard did a mild *tilt* around her. "Are you all right?" Daulo asked sharply, stepping to her side and taking her arm.

"Sudden flash of dizziness," Jin said, swallowing hard. Even with her servos doing most of the work, her rooftop sightseeing trip had apparently taken more out of her than she'd realized. "I guess I'm not as recovered as I thought I was."

"Shall I call for a litter?"

"No, no, I'll be all right," she assured him. "Thank you very much for bringing me out here—I hope I didn't take up too much of your time."

"It was my pleasure, Jasmine Alventin. Come on, now . . ."

He insisted on walking her all the way back to her suite, despite her protestations that she really *was* all right. Once there, he also wanted to awaken Asya, and it took the best part of Jin's verbal skills and several minutes of whispered debate out in the hall before she convinced him that she would make it from doorway to bed without further assistance.

For a long time after his footsteps had faded down the hall she stared at the ceiling above her bed, listening to the pounding of her heart and thinking about those quickfire weapons. For a while there she'd actually started to relax in the comfort and luxury of the Sammon house . . . but that warm feeling was gone now. *The entire planet of Qasama is one big fat enemy camp*, Layn had told them again and again.

Now, for the first time, she really believed it.

Chapter 18

She awoke to the delicate aroma of hot food, and opened her eyes to find a truly massive breakfast set out by the window seat. "Asya?" she called, climbing out of bed and padding over to the table.

"I am here, mistress," Asya said, appearing from the other room and touching her fingertips to her forehead. "How may I serve you?"

"Are we expecting company for breakfast?" Jin asked her, indicating the size of the meal.

"It was sent up on the order of Master Daulo Sammon," Asya told her. "Perhaps he felt you were in need of extra nourishment, after your illness. May I remind you that your meal yesterday was as large as this?"

"My meal yesterday followed a five-day fast," Jin growled, staring in dismay at the spread. "How am I supposed to eat all this?"

"I am sorry if you are displeased," Asya said, moving toward the intercom. "If you'd like, I can have it removed and a smaller portion brought up."

"No, that's okay," Jin sighed. She'd been taught since childhood not to waste food, and the sinking feeling that she was about to do exactly that was sending reflexive guilt feelings rippling through her stomach. But there was nothing that could be done about it now. Sitting down, she took a deep breath and dug in.

She managed to make a considerable dent in the meal before finally calling it quits. Along the way she noticed something that hadn't registered the day before: each variety of food, whether served cold or hot, remained at its original temperature throughout the course of the meal. A classy trick; and her eventual conclusion that there were miniature heat pumps or microwave systems built into each of the serving dishes didn't detract a bit from its charm.

Charming or not, though, it was also a sobering reminder of something she still had a dangerous tendency to forget: that for all their colorful customs and cultural differences, the Qasamans were emphatically *not* a primitive society.

"What would you do next, mistress?" Asya asked when Jin finally pushed herself away from the table.

"I'd like you to choose an outfit for me," Jin told her, still uncertain as to how all the clothing in her closet went together. "Then I'd like to walk around Milika for awhile, if that would be all right."

"Of course, mistress. Master Daulo Sammon suggested that you might want to do that; he left instructions that I was to call him when you were ready to go out."

Jin swallowed. The busy heir again taking valuable time out of his schedule to play escort for a simple accident victim . . . "I would be honored," she said between stiff lips.

It turned out that Daulo was still out on some unspecified family business when Asya called for him. Jin tried suggesting that Asya escort her instead, but whoever was on the other end of the intercom politely informed her she would wait for Daulo.

The wait turned out to be nearly an hour. Jin chafed at the delay, but there was really nothing she could do about it if she was to stay in character. Finally, though, Daulo appeared, and the two of them headed out into the bustle of Milika.

The tour proved well worth the wait. Towns and villages on Aventine and the other Cobra Worlds, Jin had long ago learned, basically grew on their own, with no more attention given to design and structure than was absolutely necessary. Milika, clearly planned in detail from the ground up, was a striking contrast to that laissez-faire attitude. What was even more impressive was the fact that whoever had done the planning had actually put some intelligence into the job.

The village was basically a giant circle, some two and a half kilometers across, with five major roads radiating like spokes between an inner traffic circle and a much larger outer circular drive. Inside the Small Ring Road was a well-groomed public park called the Inner Green; circling the village between the Great Ring Road and the wall, Daulo informed her, was a larger belt of parkland called the Outer Green.

"The Greens were designed to be public lands, common meeting and recreational places for the five families who founded Milika," Daulo told her as they passed through the crowds of pedestrians on the Small Ring Road and crossed over onto the Inner Green. "Like your home in the city, most of the minor family members and workers live in group houses bordering on small common courtyards, and this allows them more space than they would otherwise have."

"A good idea," Jin nodded. "The children especially must like it."

Daulo smiled. "They do indeed. Specific play areas have been built for them—there, and over there. There are others on the Outer Green, as well." He waved around at the residential areas outside the park. "Originally, you see, each of the five wedge-shaped main sections of the village was to be the property of one family. Over the years, unfortunately, three of the founding families have become split or diluted; these three," he added, indicating the directions. "Only the Sammon family and the Yithtra family remain as sole possessors of their sections."

Jin nodded. Something bitter in his voice . . . "It sounds like you would prefer there to be only one such family," she commented without thinking.

"Would that be your choice, as well?" he countered.

She looked at him, startled by the question, to find his face had become a neutral mask. "The way your village chooses to live is hardly my business," she told him, choosing her words carefully. What kind of local politics had she stumbled into? "If it were all up to me, I would choose peace and harmony between all peoples."

He eyed her in silence another moment before turning away. "Peace isn't always possible," he said tightly. "There are always some whose primary goal is the destruction of others."

Jin licked her lips. *Don't say it, girl,* she warned herself. "Is that the Sammon family's goal?" she asked softly.

He sent her a razor-edged look. "If you believe such a thing—" He broke off, looking annoyed with himself. "No, that is *not* our goal," he ground out. "There's far too much petty conflict between us—and I, for one, am tired of wasting my energy that way. Our true enemy lies out there, Jasmine Alventin; not in the cities or across village greens." He pointed at the sky.

The true enemy: us. Me. Jin swallowed. "Yes," she murmured. "There are no real enemies here."

Daulo took a deep breath. "Come," he said, starting back across the Small Ring Road. "I'll take you to the main marketplace in our section of the village. After that, perhaps you'd like to see the Outer Green and our lake."

The marketplace was situated along one edge of the Sammon family's wedge, its placement clearly designed to get business from both its own section and the one across the spoke-road from it. It was also the most familiar thing Jin had yet found in Milika, an almost direct photocopy of the marketplaces her uncle had visited thirty years earlier. A maze of small booths where everything from food and animal pelts to building services and small electronic devices were available, the marketplace was crowded and noisy and just barely on the civilized side of pandemonium. Jin had never understood how anyone could actually shop in such a madhouse day after day without going insane; now that she was actually here, she understood it even less.

And as they made their way through the crowds she kept an eye out for mojos.

They were there, all right, silvery-blue hunting birds riding patiently on the special epaulet/perches she'd seen in the Qasaman films. Thirty years ago, virtually every adult had been accompanied by one of the birds; here and now, a quick estimate put the proportion with mojos no higher than twenty-five percent. *So in the cities the mojos have largely disappeared,* she decided, remembering her conversation with Daulo the previous night, *while in the villages they're still a major force. Is that the "mojo question" Daulo mentioned?*

And was the mojo question one of the driving forces behind the village-city hostility she kept hearing about? If Qasama's city-based leaders had finally decided that having mojos around was dangerous, it would make sense for them to press the whole planet to get rid of them.

Except that the villages couldn't do that. Whatever the long-term effects caused by mojos, it was an undeniable fact that they made uncommonly good bodyguards . . . and people out in the Qasaman forest definitely needed all the protection they could get. Jin could attest to that personally.

So what it seemed to boil down to was that the Moreau Proposal to seed Qasama with spine leopards had indeed undermined the universal cooperation the Cobra Worlds had found so frightening . . . at a price of making the world even more dangerous for its inhabitants.

There are always some whose primary goal is the destruction of all others, Daulo had said. Had the Cobra Worlds been guilty of that kind of arrogance? The thought made her stomach churn.

Someone nearby was calling for a Jasmine Alventin . . . *Oof—that's me*, she realized abruptly. "I'm sorry, Daulo Sammon—what did you say?" she asked, feeling her cheeks redden with embarrassed anger at the slip.

"I asked if there was anything you'd like to buy," Daulo repeated. "You lost everything in that car wreck, after all."

Another test? Jin wondered, feeling her pulse pick up its pace. She had no idea what a normal Qasaman woman might have been carrying into the forest on a bug-hunting expedition. *No, he's probably just being polite*, she reminded herself. *Don't get paranoid, girl . . . but don't get sloppy, either.* "No, thank you," she told him. "I had nothing of real importance except clothing; if I may take some of the clothing your family has lent me when I go, I will be sufficiently in your debt."

Daulo nodded. "Well, if something should occur to you, don't hesitate to let me know. Since you mention it, have you given any thought to when you might wish to leave?"

Jin shrugged. "I don't wish to impose on your hospitality any longer than necessary," she said. "I could leave today, if I'm becoming a burden."

Something flicked across his face. "If that's what you'd like, it can be arranged, of course," he said. "You're certainly no burden, though. And I'd counsel, moreover, that you stay until you're fully recovered from your ordeal."

"There's that," she admitted. "I'd hate to collapse somewhere between Azras and Sollas—to find assistance elsewhere as caring as the Sammon family has been would be too much to ask."

He snorted. "You've been taught the fine art of flattery, I see." Still, the statement seemed to please him.

"Not really—just the fine art of truth," she countered lightly. *Except for the grand lie I'm currently feeding you about myself.* The thought brought heat to her cheeks; quickly, she looked around for something to change the subject. Beyond the market to the northwest was an oddly shaped building. "What's that?" she asked, indicating it.

"Just the housing for the mine elevators," he told her. "It's not very attractive, I'm afraid, but my father decided it had to be replaced too often to justify proper ornamentation."

"Oh, that's right—your father mentioned a mine last night," Jin nodded. "What kind of mine is it?"

Daulo threw her a very odd look. "You don't know?"

Jin felt sweat breaking out on her forehead. "No. Should I?"

"I'd have thought that anyone planning a trip would at least have learned something about the area to be visited," he said, a bit huffily.

"My brother Mander did all the studying," she improvised. "He always took care of . . . the details." Unbidden, Mander Sun's face rose before her eyes. A face she'd never see again . . .

"You cared a great deal for your brother, didn't you?" he asked, his tone a little softer.

"Yes," she whispered, moisture blurring her vision. "I cared very much for Mander."

For a moment they stood there in silence as the bustling marketplace crowds broke like noisy surf around them. "What's past cannot be changed," Daulo said at last, reaching down to briefly squeeze her hand. "Come; let me show you our lake."

Given the overall size of Milika, Jin had envisioned the "lake" as a medium-sized duck pond sandwiched between road and houses; and it was a shock, therefore, to find a rippling body of water fully three-quarters of a kilometer long cutting across the Sammon section of Milika. "It's . . . big," she managed to say as they stood on the spoke-road bridge arching over the water.

Daulo chuckled. "It is that," he agreed. "You'll notice it goes under the Great Ring Road over there and extends a way into the Outer Green. It's the source of all the water used in Milika, not to mention the obvious recreational benefits."

"Where does the water come from?" Jin asked. "I haven't seen any rivers or creeks anywhere."

"No, it's fed by an underwater spring. Or possibly an underwater river, tributary perhaps of the Somilarai River that passes north of here. No one really knows for sure."

Jin nodded. "How important, if I may ask, is a nearby source of water to the operation of your mine?"

Looking at the lake, she could still feel his eyes on her. "Not particularly," he said. "The mining itself doesn't use any, and the refining process is purely catalytic. Why do you ask?"

She hesitated; but it was too late to back out now. "Earlier, you mentioned people who sought others' downfall," she said carefully. "Now I see that, along with the mine, your part of Milika also controls the village's water supply. Your family indeed has great power . . . and that sort of power often inspires others to envy."

She counted ten heartbeats before he spoke again. "Why are you interested in the Sammon family?" he asked. "Or in Milika, for that matter?"

It was a fair question. She'd already learned about all she really needed to about Qasama's village culture, and would at any rate be moving on within a day or two to scout out the cities. The political wranglings of a small village buried out in the forest ought to be low on her priority list. And yet . . . "I don't know," she said honestly. "Perhaps it's out of gratitude for your help; perhaps because I'm growing to feel a friendship for your family. For whatever reason, I care about you, and if there's any way I can help you I want to do so."

She wasn't sure just what reaction she was expecting—acceptance, gratitude, even suspicion. But the snort of derision that exploded behind her ear took her completely by surprise. "*You* help *us?*" he said scornfully. "Wonderful. A woman with no family?—just what help do you propose to give?"

Jin felt her cheeks burning. *Count to ten, girl,* she ordered herself, clamping down hard on her tongue. *You're sliding way out of character.* "I'm sorry," she said humbly through clenched teeth. "I didn't mean it that way. I just thought—well, even though my family's gone, I *do* have friends."

"*City* friends?" he asked pointedly.

"Well . . . yes."

"Uh-huh." Daulo snorted again, gently, then sighed. "Let's just forget it, Jasmine Alventin. I appreciate the gesture, but we both know that's all it is."

"I . . . suppose we do."

"All right. Come, I'll take you across to the Outer Green."

Gritting her teeth, she lowered her eyes like a good little Qasaman woman ought to and followed Daulo across the bridge.

Chapter 19

The courtyard outside Daulo's suite was dark, his late supper over and the dishes cleared away; and with the stillness and privacy came thoughts of Jasmine Alventin.

He didn't want to think about her. In fact, he'd gone to great pains to immerse himself in work over the past few hours in order to *avoid* thinking about her. He'd ended their walking tour of Milika early in the afternoon, professing concern over her weakened condition, and gone directly back to the mine to watch the work on the shoring. After that, he'd come back to the house and spent a couple of hours poring over the stacks of paperwork that the mine seemed to generate in the same volume as its waste tailings. Now, having postponed eating so that he wouldn't have to face her over a common family meal, he'd hoped the fullness of his stomach would conspire with the pace of the day to bring sleep upon him.

But it hadn't worked that way. Even while his body slumped on its cushions, numbed with food and fatigue, his mind raced ahead like a crazed bololin. With, of course, only one topic at its forefront.

Jasmine Alventin.

As a young boy the fable of the Gordian Knot had always been one of his favorites; as a young man one of his chief delights was the solving of problems that, like the Knot, had driven other men to despair. Jasmine Alventin was truly such a problem, a Gordian Knot in human guise.

Unfortunately, it was a Knot that refused to unravel.

With a sigh, he rolled off his cushions and got to his feet. He'd been putting this off for almost a day now, hoping in his pride that he could get a grip on this phantom without artificial assistance. But it wasn't working that way . . . and if there were even a slight chance that Jasmine Alventin was a danger to the Sammon family, it was his duty to do whatever was necessary to protect his household.

His private drug cabinet was built into the wall as part of his bathroom vanity, a reinforced drawer with a lock strong enough to discourage even the most persistent of children. It had been barely a year now since his acceptance into this part of adult society, and he still felt a twinge of reflex nervousness every time he opened the drawer. It would pass with time, he'd been told.

For a long moment he gazed in at the contents, considering which would be the best one to use. The four red-labeled ones—the different types of mental stimulants—drew his eye temptingly, but he left them where they were. As a general rule, the stronger the drug, the stronger the reaction afterward would be, and he had no particular desire to suffer a night of hellish dreams or to spend the coming day flat on his back with vertigo. Instead, he selected a simple self-hypnotic which would help him organize the known facts into a rational order. With luck, his own mind would be able to take it from there. If not . . . well, he would still have the mental stimulants in reserve.

Returning to his cushions, he emptied the capsule into his incense burner and lit it. The smoke rose into the air, at first thin and fragrant, then increasingly heavy and oily smelling. And as it enveloped him, he took one more try at untying the Gordian Knot that was Jasmine Alventin.

Jasmine Alventin. A mysterious young woman, survivor of an "accident" which no one had witnessed and which therefore no one could confirm. A suspiciously timed arrival at Milika, coincident with a flurry of activity by the Yithtra family's lumber business and fresh metals orders from the Mangus operation. Her speech that of a city-educated business mediator, yet her manners more befitting some ignorant outcast from polite society. And the things she *said* in that cultured voice—

Even with the artificial calmness of the hypnotic wrapped like a smoky cocoon around him, Daulo still gave muttered vent to his feelings about this one. *I want to go with you,* she'd said—as if going out in the dead of night to take care of a razorarm was the sort of thing women did all the time. *Let me help you*—totally laughable coming from a lone woman with neither family nor estate. It was as if she lived in her own private world. A private world with its own private rules.

And yet she couldn't be dismissed simply as that sort of feeblebrained scatterhead. Every time he'd tried to do so she'd casually done or said something that painted an exact opposite side of her. A half-dozen examples came to mind, the most obvious being her casual understanding of the consequences of having Milika's lake on Sammon family territory. Even more disturbing, she had a distinct talent for deflecting questions that she didn't want to answer . . . and a talent like that required intelligence.

So what was she? Innocent victim as she claimed? Or agent sent in by someone to cause trouble? The facts fell almost visually into neat organization in front of Daulo's eyes . . . without doing any good at all. The

Knot remained tightly tied; and the only fresh conclusion he could find at all was that, totally against both his will and his common sense, he was growing to like her.

Ridiculous. He snorted, the sudden change in his steady respiration pattern bringing on a short fit of coughing. It was ridiculous—totally, completely ridiculous. Without position, she was at the very least beneath his own social status; at the very worst, she might be coldly using him to try and destroy everything he held dear.

And yet, even as he gazed mentally at the list of points against her, he had to admit there was still something about her that he found irresistible.

Just what I needed, he groused silently. *Something else about Jasmine Alventin that won't unknot.* So what could it be? Not her features or body; they were pleasant enough, but he'd seen far better without this kind of threat to his emotional equilibrium. It certainly wasn't her upbringing; she couldn't even make a simple sign of respect properly.

"Good evening, Daulo."

Startled, Daulo twisted around on his cushions, blinking through the haze to see his father walk quietly between the hanging curtain dividers. "Oh—my father," he said, starting to get up.

Kruin stopped him with a gesture. "You weren't at your customary place at evening meal tonight," he said, pulling a cushion toward his son and sinking cross-legged onto it. "I came to see if there were some trouble." He sniffed at the air. "A hypnotic, my son? I'd have thought that after a full day a sleep-inducer would be more appropriate."

Daulo looked at his father sharply, the last remnants of the hypnotic's effects evaporating from his mind. He'd hoped he could rid himself of this obsession with Jasmine Alventin before anyone else noticed. "I've been rather . . . preoccupied today," he said cautiously. "I didn't feel up to a common meal with the rest of the family."

"You may feel worse tomorrow," Kruin warned, waving a finger through one last tendril of smoke and watching it curl around in the eddy breezes thus created. "Even these mild drugs usually have unpleasant side effects." His eyes shifted back from the smoke to Daulo's face. "Jasmine Alventin asked about you."

A grimace passed across Daulo's face before he could stifle it. "I trust her recovery is proceeding properly?"

"It seems to be. She's a very unusual woman, wouldn't you say?"

Daulo sighed, quietly admitting defeat. "I don't know *what* to think about her, my father," he confessed. "All I know is that I'm . . . in danger of losing my objectivity with her." He waved at the incense burner. "I've been trying to put my thoughts in order."

"And did you?"

"I'm . . . not sure."

For a long moment Kruin was silent. "Do you know why you're living in this house, my son? Amid this luxury and prestige?"

Here it comes, Daulo thought, stomach tightening within him. *A stern reminder of where the family's wealth comes from—and the reminder that it's my duty to defend it.* "It's because you, your father, and his father before him have toiled and sweated in the mine," he said.

To his surprise, the elder Sammon shook his head. "No. The mine has made things easier, certainly, but that's not where our true power lies. It lies here—" he indicated his eyes "—and here—" he touched his forehead. "Material wealth is all very good, but no man keeps such wealth unless he can learn how to read the people around him. To know which are his friends and which his enemies . . . and to sense the moment when some of those loyalties change. Do you understand?"

Daulo swallowed. "I think so."

"Good. So, then: tell me what form this lack of objectivity takes."

Daulo waved his hands helplessly. "I don't know. She's just so . . . different. Somehow. There's a . . . perhaps it's some kind of mental strength to her, something I've never before seen in a woman."

Kruin nodded thoughtfully. "Almost a if she were a man instead of a woman?"

"Yes. That's—" Daulo broke off abruptly as a horrible thought occurred to him. "You aren't suggesting—?"

"No, no, of course not," Kruin hastened to assure him. "The doctor examined her when she was brought in, remember? No, she's a woman, all right. But perhaps not one from a normal Qasaman culture."

Daulo thought that over. It *would* go a long ways toward explaining some of the oddities he'd observed in her. "But I thought everyone on Qasama lived in the Great Arc. And besides, she claimed to be from Sollas."

"*We* don't live strictly inside the Great Arc," Kruin shrugged. "Only a short ways outside it, true, but outside nonetheless. Who's to say that others don't live even further? As to her claimed city, it's possible that she was afraid to tell us her true home. For reasons I can't guess at," he added as Daulo opened his mouth to ask.

"An interesting theory," Daulo admitted. "I'm not sure how it would stand up to Occam's Razor, however."

"Perhaps an additional bit of new information would save it from that blade," Kruin said. "I've been thinking about the accident Jasmine Alventin claimed to have been in, and it occurred to me that if it happened near Tabris someone there might have either heard the crash or found one of her companions."

"She couldn't possibly have come that far," Daulo objected. "Besides, we checked all the way along that road."

"I know," Kruin nodded. "And I trust your findings. But in such a case as this I thought extra confirmation might be a good idea, so I sent a message there this morning. Someone *did* hear a sound like a large and violent crash . . . but not near the road or village. It was far to the north, several kilometers away at the least. In deep forest."

Daulo felt his mouth go dry. Several kilometers due north of Tabris would put the accident anywhere from five to ten kilometers from the place where Perto had found her on the road. The suggestion that she might have made it from Tabris proper—a full twenty kilometers of forest road—had been ludicrous enough, but *this*—"She couldn't have survived such a trek," he said flatly. "I don't care *how* many companions she started out with, she couldn't have made it."

"I'm afraid that would be my assessment, as well," Kruin nodded reluctantly. "Especially through the heightened activity the bololin migration a few days ago probably stirred up. But even if we allow God one miracle to get her out alive, there's an even worse impossibility staring at us: that of getting a car so far into the forest in the first place."

Daulo licked his lips. This one, unfortunately, was obvious. "So it wasn't a car that crashed. It was an aircraft."

"It's beginning to look that way," Kruin agreed heavily.

Which meant she'd lied to them. Pure and simple; no conceivable misinterpretation about it. Anger and shame welled up within Daulo's stomach, the emotions fighting each other for supremacy. The Sammon family had saved her life and taken her in, and she'd repaid their hospitality by lying to them . . . and by playing *him* for a fool.

Kruin's voice cut into his private turmoil. "There are many reasons why she might lie about that," he said gently. "Not all of them having anything to do with you or our family. So my question for you, my son, is this: is she, in your judgment, an enemy of ours?"

"My judgment doesn't seem to be worth a great deal at this point," Daulo retorted, tasting bitterness.

"Do you question *my* judgment in asking for yours?" Kruin asked, his tone suddenly cold. "You will answer my question, Daulo Sammon."

Daulo swallowed hard. "Forgive me, my father—I didn't mean impertinence. It was just that—"

"Don't make excuses, Daulo Sammon. I wish an answer to my question."

"Yes, my father." Daulo took a deep breath, trying desperately to sort it all out. Facts, emotions, impressions . . . "No," he said at last. "No, I don't believe she came here for the purpose of harming us. I don't know why I think that, but I do."

"It's as I said," Kruin said, his cold manner giving way again to a gentler tone. "The Sammon family survives because we have the ability to read others' purposes. I've tried since childhood to nurture that talent in you; the future will show whether I've succeeded." Moving with grace, he got to his feet. "At the meal tonight Jasmine Alventin announced that it was her belief she'd recovered sufficiently from her injuries to return to her home. She'll be leaving tomorrow morning."

Daulo stared up at him. "She's leaving *tomorrow?* Then why all this fuss about whether or not we can trust her?"

Kruin gazed down at him. "The fuss," he said coolly, "was over whether or not it would be wise to let her out of our sight and control."

Daulo clenched his teeth. "Yes, of course. I'm sorry."

A faint smile touched Kruin's lips. "I told her we would give her transportation as far as Azras. If you'd like, you may accompany her there."

"Thank you, my father," Daulo said steadily. "It would also give me the opportunity to discuss future purchases with some of our buyers there."

"Of course," Kruin nodded, and Daulo thought he

saw approval on the elder Sammon's face. "I'll leave you to your sleep, then. Goodnight, my son."

"Goodnight, my father."

And that's that, Daulo thought when he was once again alone. *Tomorrow she'll be gone, and that'll be the end of it. She'll return to whatever mysterious village she really comes from, and I'll never see her again.* There was some hurt in that; perhaps even a little bit of anger. But he had to admit his primary reaction was relief.

If a Gordian Knot couldn't be unraveled, after all, the next best thing was to send it out of sight.

Chapter 20

An hour, Daulo had thought as he and Jasmine drove off down the winding forest road toward Azras. *We'll have one more hour together, and then I'll never see her again.*

But he was wrong. They were on the road together considerably less than an hour.

"This is insane," he fumed as the gatekeepers swung the heavy north gate of Shaga village closed behind them and he let the car coast to a halt at the side of the road. "There's nothing here you can possibly want."

"How do you know?" she countered, fumbling for a moment before she was able to get the door open. "I thank you for the ride, Daulo Sammon—"

"Would you for one minute listen to me?" he snarled, getting out on his side to glare at her across the car roof. "You're a stranger in this part of Qasama, Jasmine Alventin—you've admitted that yourself. I *assure* you that Shaga is no closer to your home than Milika was."

"Sure it is—ten kilometers closer," she retorted.

It was a long time since anyone had talked to Daulo like that, and for a moment he was speechless. Jasmine took advantage of the pause to retrieve from the back seat the small shoulder bag Daulo's mother had given her. "All right, fine," Daulo managed at last as she closed the door and slipped the bag's strap over her shoulder. "So you're ten kilometers closer to Azras. What does that gain you?—especially since no one here is likely to offer you a free ride even as far as Azras? So enough of this nonsense. Get back in the car."

She gazed across the roof at him . . . and again, it wasn't the kind of look he was accustomed to receiving from a woman. "Look, Daulo Sammon," she said in a quiet voice. "There's something I have to do—by myself—and I have to do it *here*. Please don't ask me any more. Just believe me when I tell you that the less you have to do with me, the better."

Daulo gritted his teeth. "All right, then," he bit out. "If that's how you want it. Goodbye." Feeling his face burning, he got back in the car and started off, continuing on toward the center of the village.

But only for a short way. Unlike Milika, Shaga had been haphazardly constructed, its roads curving and twisting all over the place, and Daulo hadn't gone more than a hundred meters before the woman's image in his mirror disappeared behind a turn in the road. Another hundred meters brought him to a cross road, which he took; and less than two minutes later he'd circled his way back to where he'd dropped her off.

There was no reason why she should suddenly decide to stay in Shaga; which could only mean that it was what she'd intended all along. Either she was planning to double back to Milika by unknown means—and for equally unknown purposes—or else she was meeting someone here. Whichever it turned out to be, he had every intention of keeping track of her while she did it.

But whatever her purpose, it didn't seem to involve the center of town. Even as he drove cautiously to within sight of the north gate he spotted her walking briskly away from him, paralleling the wall. He eased the car forward a bit, taking care to stay well back of her. There were few buildings in this part of Shaga, and while that meant he could keep watch on her from a reasonable distance away, it also meant he would be easier for her to spot.

But she apparently had no inkling that anyone might be watching. She never once looked over her shoulder . . . and as she continued on, Daulo noticed she was angling toward the wall.

Was she going to try and climb out? Ridiculous. It would get her out of Shaga without being seen, perhaps, but then where would she be? *Out on a forest road, that's where,* he thought sourly, *with razorarms and krisjaws all around her. And ten solid kilometers to anywhere safe.*

And yet she clearly *was* headed for the wall. Daulo gnawed at his lip, wondering if perhaps his original assessment had been right, after all. Perhaps she *was* simply a feeblebrained scatterhead.

Right by the wall, now, she paused and glanced around her. Looking for a ladder, probably. Daulo tensed, wondering if she would notice him sitting in this parked car—

And an instant later she was standing on top of the wall.

Daulo gasped. *God above!* No climbing, no running start, no leaping up to grab hold of the top with fingers— she'd simply bent her knees and *jumped.*

To the top of a wall over a meter taller than she was.

She took the anti-razorarm mesh just as casually, grabbing the top with one hand as she jumped to deflect her body into a tight-moving arc that dropped her onto her feet on the other side. An instant later she was gone.

For another five heartbeats Daulo just sat there, dumbfounded. She *was* insane, all right . . . insane, but with an athletic ability that was totally unheard of.

And she's getting away.

With a jerk, Daulo broke his paralysis and swung the car back toward the gate.

She was already out of sight by the time he was back on the road, but with forest hemming them in on both sides there were only two directions she could have gone. And since she'd already turned down a free ride on to Azras . . . Trying to keep an eye on both sides of the road at once, Daulo started back toward Milika.

For several painful minutes he wondered if he'd guessed wrong. With no more than a three-minute head start, there was simply no way she could have gotten this far ahead of him, even at the deliberately slow speed he was making. He was just wondering if he should turn around when he caught a glimpse of someone just around a curve ahead.

It took another few minutes of experimentation to find the speed that would let him get a glimpse of her every couple of minutes but yet not get him too close. It turned out she was every bit as phenomenal a runner as she was a high jumper.

Hang with her, he told himself grimly, teeth clenched with tension at this unaccustomed trick driving. *She can't keep up this kind of pace for very long. Just hang with her.*

She *did* hold the pace, though, and for considerably longer than he would have guessed possible. It was only as they passed the halfway point back to Milika that she began to slow down; and it was pure luck on his part that he happened to get a glimpse of her heading off toward the tree line paralleling the road a dozen meters to the west.

He pulled over quickly, wincing at the sounds of crunching vegetation beneath his wheels as he eased off the road and stopped. But presumably she was making at least as much noise wading through the undergrowth of the forest. At any rate, she didn't turn around, but merely dropped her shoulder bag behind a large thaurnni bush and kept going.

Straight into the forest.

No, was his immediate thought. *She's not really going into the forest. She's cutting through a bit to throw me off her track. Or—*

But even as a part of his brain tried to think up safer alternatives he was digging under the seat for the quickfire pistol holstered there and climbing quietly out of the car. There was only one thing out there that could possibly be worth risking the razorarms and krisjaws for.

Her wrecked aircraft. The aircraft whose existence she'd taken great pains to conceal . . . and which therefore was very probably worth seeing.

Besides which—he was honest enough to admit—his pride wouldn't let him lose track of her now. Taking a deep breath, he cradled the barrel of his gun with his left hand and stepped in under the tree canopy.

Daulo had been out in the raw Qasaman forest before, of course, but never under conditions like this; and it only gradually dawned on him just how different this was. Always before he'd been part of a squad of village hunters, shielded from danger by their guns and experience. Now, however, he was alone. Worse, he was trying to follow another person without being spotted in turn, a chore that took far more concentration than he liked.

And no one knew he was here. Or would even miss him for several hours.

If he was killed, would they ever even find his body?

He fought the growing fear for nearly fifteen minutes . . . and then, all at once, something seemed to snap within him. The sounds of animals and insects buzzing and scurrying all around him mingled with the rapid thud of his heartbeat in his ears, and suddenly it didn't seem quite so important anymore that he, personally, find out what Jasmine Alventin was up to. *This is crazy*, he told himself, wiping sweat from his forehead with the back of a trembling hand. *She wants something from her aircraft?—fine. She can have it.* Whatever it was, it was no longer worth risking his life over—especially when he could have a squad of armed men waiting for her by the time she came back to retrieve her bag. Checking one last time to make sure she wasn't looking back, he turned around—

The purring growl came from off to his left, and his heart skipped a beat as he nearly tripped over his feet spinning around to face it. A razorarm stood there, crouched ready to spring.

It was one thing to face a razorarm caught in a village wall's upper mesh; it was something else entirely to encounter one on its own home ground. Daulo didn't even realize he'd pulled the trigger until the gun abruptly jerked in his hand and a stutter of thunderclaps shattered the quiet of the forest. Dimly, through the gun's roar, he heard the razorarm's purr become a scream—saw the clawed front paws coming at him like twin missiles—

And with a flash like a lightning bolt from God, the razorarm blazed with light and flame.

It slammed into him, flooding his nostrils with the nauseating stench of seared meat and fur. He staggered back, gagging, trying to shove the dead weight off his shoulders and chest—

"Daulo—duck!"

The warning did no good. Daulo's horror-numbed muscles had no chance to react before a flash of silver-blue exploded in his face—

And to the stench was added pain.

Pain like nothing he'd ever felt before—a dozen nails jabbing and twisting and ripping through his flesh. He was aware in a distant way that he was screaming; aware that his efforts to tear his tormentor away merely made the pain worse. One eye was closed against something slapping at it; with the other he saw Jasmine running toward him, the look of an avenging angel on her face. Her hands reached out—*no*, he tried to scream, *don't try to tear it off*—

And then her hands seemed to flicker with light . . . and the claws digging into his face were suddenly stilled.

"Daulo!" Jasmine said tautly, her hands gently yet firmly pulling the tormentor off him. "Oh, my God— are you all right?"

"I'm—yes, I think so," he managed, struggling to regain his dignity in front of this woman. "It—what happened?"

"You tried to shoot a razorarm," she said grimly, holding his hands firmly away from the throbbing in his cheek as she examined the wounds with eyes and fingertips. "It wasn't a complete success."

"It—?" Turning away from her probing fingers, he looked down at the carcass lying limply beside him.

Its head was gone. Burned away.

"God be praised," he sighed. "That lightning bolt was . . ." He paused, an eerie feeling crawling up his back. The second attacker . . . his eyes found where Jasmine had tossed it. The razorarm's mojo, of course. Also burned.

Slowly, he looked back at Jasmine Alventin. Jasmine Alventin, the uncultured woman who'd appeared from nowhere . . . and who'd made it through raw forest alone . . . and whose hands had spat fire deadly enough to kill.

And it all finally fell together.

"God above," he groaned.

And to his everlasting shame, he fainted.

Chapter 21

Daulo wasn't unconscious for more than about ten minutes. It was still plenty of time for Jin to dress his injuries as best she could, move the spine leopard and mojo carcasses away before they could attract scavengers, and call herself every synonym for idiot that she could think of.

The worst part was the knowledge that her detractors had been right. Totally. She simply didn't have what it took to be a Cobra; not the emotional toughness, not even the ability to keep her focus on her mission. Certainly not the basic intelligence.

She looked down at Daulo for a moment, gritting her teeth hard enough to hurt. That was it, then—the mission was scrubbed. An hour after he got home half the planet would be out here looking for her. Nothing left to do now but to strike out into deep forest and wait in the vain hope that she might somehow connect up with the next team the Cobra Worlds sent. Whenever in the distant future that might be.

Not that it mattered. At this point it would be better for everyone concerned if she died here, anyway.

Daulo groaned, and his hands twitched against his chest. Another minute and he'd be fully conscious, and for a moment Jin debated whether or not it would be safe for her to leave him here alone. The road wasn't more than fifteen minutes away, and his injuries wouldn't slow him down all that much. And he *did* have a gun.

Sighing, Jin stayed where she was, giving the area a quick visual sweep. There wasn't much point, after all, in shooting spine leopards and mojos off a man and then turning him loose for the forest to take another crack at.

When she looked down again, his eyes were open. Staring up at her.

For several heartbeats neither spoke. Then Daulo took a shuddering breath. "You're a demon warrior," he croaked. There was no question in his voice.

Nor anything that required a verbal answer. Jin merely nodded once and waited. Daulo's hand went to his cheek, gingerly touched the handkerchief Jin had tied there with a strip of cloth. "How . . . badly am I hurt?"

He was clearly fighting to sound and act natural. "It's not too bad," Jin assured him. "Deep gouges in places, but I don't think there's any major muscle or nerve damage. Probably hurts like blazes, though."

A ghost of a smile touched his lips for a second. "That's for sure," he admitted. "I don't suppose you'd happen to have any painkillers with you."

She shook her head. "There are some near here, though. If you feel up to a little travel we could go get them."

"Where are they?—at your wrecked spacecraft?"

Jin hissed between her teeth. So they *had* found the shuttle, after all. "You're a good actor," she said bitterly. "I would have sworn that none of you knew about the crash. No, the painkiller's in my pack, hidden near the road. Unless your people have grabbed that by now, of course."

She took his arm, preparing to lift him upright, but he stopped her. "Why?" he asked.

"Why what?" she growled. "Why am I here?"

"Why did you save my life?"

"That's a stupid question. Come on—I've got to retrieve those packs before the rest of your army starts beating the bushes for me. You at least owe me a little head start."

Again she started to lift him; again he stopped her. "You don't need a head start," he said, his voice trembling slightly. "No one else knows about you. I followed you in alone."

She stared at him. Truth? Or some kind of test?

Or a ploy to keep her in one place while they encircled her?

It doesn't really matter, she realized wearily. As long as Daulo was alive, the clock was already ticking down. "Well . . ." she said at last. "We still need to go and get you that painkiller. Come on."

She'd expected to have to support him most of the way back, and was mildly surprised that he made it the whole way under his own power. Either the physical shock to his system wasn't as bad as she'd feared or else the boneheaded male arrogance she'd already seen too much of on Qasama *did* have its useful side. They made it back to the road in just over fifteen minutes . . . and there was indeed no army waiting for them.

"So," Daulo said with elaborate casualness after she'd treated his cuts with a disinfectant/analgesic spray and replaced the handkerchief with a proper heal-quick bandage. "I suppose the next question is where we go from here."

"I don't see much of a question," Jin growled. "I'd guess you're going back to Milika to sound the alarm, and I'm going to start running."

He stared silently at her . . . and, oddly enough, behind the tight mask she could see there was a genuine battle of emotions underway. "I see you don't know very much about Qasama, Demon Warrior," he said after a moment.

It was a second before she realized he expected a response. "No, not really," she told him. "Not much more than I learned from you over the past couple of days. That's one of the reasons we came, to find out more."

He licked his lips. "We put a high premium on honor here, Demon Warrior. Honor and the repayment of debts."

And she'd just saved his life . . . Slowly, it dawned on Jin that it might not yet be over. "I see your dilemma," she nodded. "Would it help to tell you I'm not here to make war on Qasama?"

"It might—if I could believe you." He took a deep breath. "Is your spacecraft really wrecked?"

Jin shivered at the memory. "Totally."

"Why were you going back there, then?"

And there was no longer any way out of it. She was going to have to admit, in public, just what an emotional idiot she was being. "I had to leave the wreck in a hurry," she said, the words tearing at her gut. "I thought it would be found right away, and that there would be a manhunt started—" She broke off, blinking angrily at a tear that had appeared in one eye. "Anyway, I left . . . but it seemed to me that if you'd found it the authorities would certainly have checked all nearby villages for strangers. Wouldn't they?"

Daulo nodded silently.

"Well, don't you see?" she snapped suddenly. "You *haven't* found it . . . and I ran off and left my friends there. I can't just . . . I have to—"

"I understand," Daulo said softly, getting to his feet. "Come. We'll go together to bury them."

It took them only a few minutes to get the car off the road and into concealment behind a pair of trees. Then, together, they headed back into the forest.

"How far will we need to go, Demon Warrior?" Daulo asked, peering up at the leafy canopy overhead and trying not to feel like he'd just made a bad mistake.

"Five or six kilometers, I think," the woman told him. "We should be able to get through it a lot faster than I did the first time. Thanks to your people's medical skill."

"It's the kind of skill that comes from living on a hostile world," he ground out. "Of course, it's been considerably more hostile lately—say, in the past twenty or thirty years?"

She didn't answer. "Did you hear me, Demon Warrior?" he demanded. "I said—"

"Stop calling me that," she snapped. "You know my name—use it."

"Do I?" he countered. "Know your name, I mean?"

She sighed. "No, not really. My name is Jasmine Moreau, of the world Aventine. You can also call me Jin."

"Djinn?" he said, startled. All the childhood scare-stories of djinns came flooding back in a rush . . . "Given to you when you became a demon warrior, I assume?"

She glanced a frown over at him. "No. Why?—oh, I see. Huh. You know, I never noticed that before. No, it has nothing to do with the djinns of folklore—it's just pronounced the same. It's a name my father gave me when I was very young."

"Um. Well, then, Jin Moreau, I'd still like an answer to my question—"

"Freeze!"

For a single, awful second he thought he'd pushed her too far and that she'd decided to kill him after all. She dropped onto her side, left leg hooking up beneath her skirt—

There was a brilliant thunderbolt flash, and a smoking krisjaw slammed into the dead leaves.

"You okay?" she asked, rolling to her feet and peering around them.

Daulo found his tongue. "Yes. That's . . . quite a weapon," he managed, blinking at the purple afterimage.

"It comes in handy sometimes. Let's get moving—and if I yell, you hit the ground fast, understand? If there are as many animals out here today as there were my first time through it could be a busy trip."

"There shouldn't be," he shook his head. "You came in right after a major bololin herd went through, and that always stirs up lots of animal activity."

It pleased him to see that that knowledge was completely new to her. "Well, that's relief. In that case it should only take us a couple of hours to get to the shuttle."

"Good," he nodded. "And maybe to pass the time you could explain to me just why your world declared war on ours."

Watching her out of the corner of his eye, he saw her grimace. "We didn't declare war on you," she said quietly. "We were told by others that Qasama was a potential threat. We came to see if that was true."

"What threat?" he scoffed. "A world without even primitive spaceflight capability? How could we possibly be a threat to a world light-years away?—especially one protected by demon warriors?"

She was silent for a moment. "You won't remember it, Daulo, but for much of Qasama's history all of you lived together in a state of extreme noncompetition."

"I know that," he growled. "We aren't ignorant savages who don't keep records, you know."

She actually blushed. "I know. Sorry. Anyway, it seemed odd to us that a human society could be so—well, so cooperative. We tried to find a reason—"

"And while you were looking you became jealous?" Daulo bit out. "Is that it? You envied us the society we'd created, and so you sent these razorarm killing machines in to kill and destroy—"

"Did you know that mojos can control the actions of their owners?"

He stopped in mid-sentence. "What?"

She sighed. "They effect the way their owners think. Cause them to make decisions that benefit the mojo first and the owner only second."

Daulo opened his mouth, closed it again. "That's absurd," he said at last. "They're bodyguards, that's all."

"Really? Does your father have a mojo? I never saw him with one."

"No—"

"How about the head of the Yithtra family? Or any of the major leaders of Milika or Azras."

"Cities like Azras have hardly any mojos at all," he said mechanically, brain spinning. No; it had to be a lie. A lie spun by Aventine's rulers to justify what they'd done to Qasama.

And yet . . . he had to admit that he *had* always sensed a difference in the few mojo owners he knew well. A sort of . . . placidity, perhaps. "It doesn't make sense, though," he said at last.

"Sure it does," she said. "Out in the wild mojos pair up with krisjaws for hunting purposes—hunting and, for the mojos, access to embryo hosts."

"Yes, I know about the native reproduction cycle," Daulo said hastily, obscurely embarrassed at discussing such things with a woman. "That's why cities were designed to let bololin herds charge on through, so that the mojos there could get to the tarbines riding the bololins."

"Right," she nodded. "You could have walled the cities like you did the villages, you know, and kept the bololins out completely. It would have saved a lot of grief all around . . . except that it was in the mojo's best interest to keep the bololins nearby, so that's how you built them. And because they didn't want to risk their own feathers with any more bodyguarding than they could get away with, they made sure you cooperated with each other in every facet of life."

"And so we had no warfare, and no village-city rivalry," Daulo growled. He understood, now . . . and the cold-bloodedness of Aventine's scheme turned his stomach. "So you decided to interfere . . . and with krisjaws all but gone from the Great Arc, you had to give the mojos somewhere else to go. So you gave them razorarms."

"Daulo—"

"Have you seen enough of what Qasama has become since then?" he cut her off harshly. "Okay, fine—so perhaps we used to bend our own lives a little to accommodate other creatures. Was that too high a price to pay for peace?"

"Was it?" she countered softly.

The obvious answer came to his lips . . . and faded away unsaid. If what she said was the truth, *had* it really been worth the price? "I don't know," he said at last.

"Neither do I," she whispered.

Chapter 22

They made the trip in just under two hours . . . and for Jin, the whole thing was in sharp contrast with the ordeal a week earlier.

There was no way to tell, of course, how much of the difference was due to the abatement of the bololin coattail effect Daulo had described and how much was due to her own recovery. Certainly there was less fighting; only one other predator besides the krisjaw tried its luck with them, compared with the half-dozen single and multiple attacks she'd had to fight off on her last trip through. On the other hand, with her alertness and concentration again at full capability, it could have been simply that she was spotting potential trouble early enough for evasive methods to be effective.

Ultimately, though, the real reason didn't matter. She'd brought both herself *and* an untrained civilian safely through some of the most dangerous territory Qasama had to offer . . . and it brought a welcome measure of self-confidence back to her bruised ego.

"Here we are," she said, gesturing to the battered hulk of the shuttle as they finally cleared the edge of the interweaving-fern patch and stepped out from the trees into view of the crash site.

Daulo muttered something under his breath, gazing first at the shuttle and then at the long death-scar it had torn into the landscape. "I was never truly sure . . ." His voice trailed off into silence, and he shook his head. "And you *survived* this?"

"I was lucky," she said quietly.

"God was with you," he corrected. He took a deep breath. "Forgive me for doubting your story. Your companions . . . ?"

Jin gritted her teeth. "Inside. This way."

The hatch door was as she'd left it, stuck a couple of centimeters open, and she had to put one foot against the hull to get the necessary leverage to pull it open. *At least,* she thought grimly, *that means none of the larger scavengers have gotten to them. Grateful for small favors, I suppose.* Taking one last clean breath, she braced herself and stepped inside.

The smell wasn't quite as bad as she'd feared it would be. The bodies themselves looked perhaps a bit worse.

"The door wouldn't have kept out insects," Daulo commented from right behind her. His voice sounded only slightly less strained than she felt, and it was clear he was breathing through his mouth. "Are there any shovels on board?"

"There's supposed to be at least one. Let's try back here."

They found it almost at once, in with the emergency shelter equipment. It was sturdy but small, clearly designed for only minor entrenchment work. But Jin had had no intention of digging very deeply anyway, and the extra strength her Cobra servos provided more than made up for the awkwardness of the short handle. Half an hour later, the five graves near the edge of the crash site were ready.

Daulo was waiting for her near the shuttle, and she found that while she'd been digging he'd improvised a stretcher from some piping and seat cushions and had hacked loose five of the expended crashbags to use as body bags. *They might as well be useful for something,* she thought bitterly at the thick plastic as she and Daulo worked the bodies into them. *They sure didn't do much good while we were all alive.*

And a few minutes later she and Daulo stood side by side in front of the graves. "I . . . don't really know a proper burial service," Jin confessed, partly to Daulo, partly to the bodies in their graves before her. "But if its purpose is to remember and mourn . . . that much I can do."

She didn't remember afterward just what she said or how long she spoke; only that her cheeks were wet when she was finished. A quiet goodbye to each in turn; and she was picking up the shovel when Daulo touched her arm. "They were your friends, not mine," he said in a quiet voice. "But if you will permit me . . . ?"

She nodded, and he took a step forward. "In the name of God, the compassionate, the merciful . . ."

He spoke only a few minutes; and yet, in that short time Jin found herself touched deeply. Though the phrasing of the words showed them to be a standard recitation, there was at the same time something in Daulo's delivery that struck her as being intensely personal. Whatever his feelings toward Jin or the Cobra Worlds generally, he clearly felt no animosity toward her dead teammates.

". . . We belong to God, and to Him we return. May your souls find peace."

The litany came to an end, and for a moment they stood together in silence. "Thank you," Jin said softly.

"The dead are enemies of no one," he replied. "Only God can approve or condemn their actions now." He took a deep breath, threw Jin a hesitant glance. "One of them—you called him Mander?"

"Mander Sun, yes," she nodded. "One of my fellow . . . demon warriors."

"Was he truly your brother, as you named him in the story you told my family?"

Jin licked her lips. "In all except blood he was truly my brother. Perhaps the only one I will ever have."

"I understand." Daulo looked back at the graves, then glanced up at the sun. "We'd best be leaving soon. I'll be missed eventually, and if a search finds my car it'll probably find your packs, too."

Jin nodded and again picked up the shovel.

Filling in the graves took only a few more minutes, and when she was done she took the shovel back to the shuttle. "No point in letting it lie around out here and rust," she commented.

"No."

Something in his voice made her turn and look at him. "Something?"

He was frowning at the blast damage in the shuttle's side. "You're certain it couldn't have been an internal malfunction that made this?"

"Reasonably certain," she nodded. "Why?"

"When you expressed your surprise earlier that it hadn't been discovered, I assumed the crash had somehow concealed it. But *this*—" he waved at the shattered trees "—couldn't possibly be missed by any aircraft looking for it."

"I agree. It's *your* world—any ideas why no one's shown up yet?"

He shook his head slowly. "This area is well off normal air routes, which would explain why it hasn't been found by accident. But I don't understand why our defense forces wouldn't follow up on a successful hit."

Jin took a deep breath. She'd wondered long and hard about that same question . . . and had come up with only one reasonable answer. "Unless it wasn't your defense forces that did it in the first place."

Daulo frowned at her. "Who else *could* it have been?"

"I don't know. But there've been some odd things happening here, Daulo. That's why we came, looking for some answers."

"And to change any of them you didn't like?" he said pointedly.

She felt her face warming. "I don't know. I hope not."

He stared at her for several seconds more. "I think," he said at last, "that the rest of this conversation ought to wait until my father can be included."

Jin's mouth went dry. "Wait a minute, Daulo—"

"You have a choice of three paths before you now, Jasmine Moreau." Daulo's face had again become an emotionless mask, his voice hard and almost cold. "You can come with me and accept the decision of my family as to what we should do with you. Or you can refuse to confess your true identity and purpose before my father and leave right now, in which case the alarm will be out all over Qasama by nightfall."

"Assuming you can make it back through the forest alone," Jin pointed out softly.

"Assuming that, yes." A muscle in Daulo's cheek twitched, but otherwise his face didn't change. "Which is of course your third choice: to allow the forest to kill me. Or even to do that job yourself."

Jin let her breath out in a hiss of defeat. "If your father elects to turn me over to the authorities, I won't go passively," she told him. "And if I'm forced to fight, many people will be hurt or killed. Given that, do you still want me to come back to your household?"

"Yes," he said promptly.

And at that, Jin realized, the choice was indeed clear. She could take it or leave it. "All right," she sighed. "Let's get going."

Chapter 23

"My son knew from the beginning that you were different," Kruin Sammon said, staring unblinkingly at Jin as he fingered an emergency ration stick from her pack, spread open on the low table beside him. "I see he erred only in degree."

Jin forced herself to meet the elder Sammon's gaze. There was no point now in continuing to pretend she was a good little submissive Qasaman woman. Her only chance was to persuade them that she was an equal, one with whom bargains could be struck.

Persuading them to make any such bargains, of course, would be something else entirely.

"I'm sorry it was necessary to lie to you," she told him. "You have to realize that at the time I was helpless and feared for my life."

"A demon warrior, helpless?" Kruin snorted. "The history of your attacks on Qasama don't mention such failings."

"I've explained our side of all that—"

"Yes—your side," Kruin cut her off harshly. "You hear from these—these—"

"Trofts," Daulo supplied quietly from his place beside his father's cushions.

"Thank you. You hear from these Troft monsters—who also visited us professing peace, I'll point out—you hear from them that we're dangerous, and without even considering the possibility that they may be wrong you prepare to make war on us. And don't claim it was the fault of others—if my son hasn't yet recognized your name, I do."

"Her name?" Daulo frowned.

Jin licked her lips. "My father's name is Justin Moreau," she said evenly. "His brother's name is Joshua."

Daulo's face went a little pale. "The demon warrior and his shadow," he whispered.

So the ghost stories about her father and uncle hadn't faded with time. Jin fought back a grimace. "You have to understand, Kruin Sammon, that in our judgment the mojos were as much a threat to your people as they were to ours. We were considering your welfare, too, when we made our decision."

"Your kindness has clearly gone unrewarded," Kruin growled, heavily sarcastic. "Perhaps the Shahni will offer you some honor for your actions."

"The option was full warfare," Jin told him quietly. "And don't scoff—there were those who thought that would be necessary. Many among us were terrified of what a planet of people under mojo control could do to us when they escaped the confines of this one world. Do your histories record that it was *your* people who threatened to come out someday and destroy *us*?"

"And *this* is your justification for such a devastating preemptive strike?" Kruin demanded. "A threat made in the heat of self-defense?"

"I'm justifying nothing," Jin said. "I'm trying to show that we didn't act out of hatred or animosity."

"Perhaps we'd have preferred a more heated emotion

to such icy calculation," Kruin retorted. "To send animal predators to fight us instead of doing the job yourselves—"

"But don't you see?" Jin pleaded. "The whole razorarm approach was the only one that would get the mojos away from you without causing any truly permanent damage to your safety and well-being."

"Permanent damage?" Daulo cut in. "What do you think the extra mesh above the wall is for—?"

Kruin stopped him with a gesture. "Explain."

Jin took a deep breath. "Once the majority of razorarms are accompanied by mojos, most of their attacks on people should stop."

"Why?" Kruin snorted. "Because the mojos have fond memories of us?"

"No," Jin shook her head. "Because you can kill the razorarms."

A frown creased Kruin's forehead. "That makes no sense. We can't possibly destroy enough of them to make a difference."

"We don't have to," Daulo said, his voice abruptly thoughtful. "If Jasmine Moreau is right about the mojos, simply having the capability to kill them will be enough."

Kruin cocked an eyebrow at his son. "Explain, Daulo Sammon."

Daulo's eyes were on Jin. "The mojos are intelligent enough to understand the power of our weapons; is that correct?" She nodded, and he turned to face his father. "So then the mojos have a strong interest in making sure there's as little fighting as possible between us and their razorarms."

"And what of the one in the forest this morning?" Kruin scoffed. "It had a mojo, and yet attacked you."

Daulo shook his head. "I've been thinking about that, my father. It didn't attack until I first fired on it."

"Speculation," Kruin shook his head. But the frown remained on his face.

"Remember your history," Jin urged him. "Your own

people told us that the krisjaws, too, were once relatively harmless to the Qasaman people. It was only after the mojos began deserting them for you that they became so dangerous."

Kruin's gaze drifted to the offworld supplies and equipment spread out on his table. "You said the Shahni were aware of the mojos' effect on us. Why then would they have risked their internal harmony by purging the cities of their mojos?"

Jin shook her head. "I don't know. Perhaps the mojos simply deserted the cities more quickly once an alternative came along."

"Or perhaps the cities realized that the main conflict would be not with their own citizens but with those of us in the villages," Daulo muttered.

"Perhaps." Kruin looked hard at Jin. "But whatever the reasons or motivations, what ultimately matters is that the people of Aventine interfered with our society. And in doing so brought hardship and death upon us."

Jin looked him straight in the eye, trying to shake off the feeling that she personally was on trial here. "What matters," she corrected quietly, "is that you were slaves. Would you rather we have left you as you were, less than truly human?"

"It's always possible to claim love as a motive for one's actions," Kruin said, a bitter smile on his face. "Tell me, Jasmine Moreau: if our positions were reversed, would you honestly thank us for doing to you what you have done to us?"

Jin bit at her lip. It would be so easy to lie . . . and so pointless. "At the place in your history where you now live . . . no. I can only hope that future generations will recognize that what we did truly *had* to be done. And will accept that our motives were honorable even if they can't honestly thank us."

Kruin sighed and fell silent, his eyes drifting away from her and to his table. Jin glanced at Daulo, then turned to look out the window. The afternoon shadows were starting to stretch across Milika, and in a short while it would be time for the evening meal.

A perfect time to drug or poison her if they decided she was too dangerous to bargain with . . .

"What is it you want from us?" Kruin cut abruptly into her thoughts.

Jin turned her attention back to him, bracing herself. The question was an inevitable one, and she'd put a great deal of thought into considering just how much she should tell them. But each time she'd turned the problem over in her mind she'd come to the same conclusion: complete honesty was the only way. Whatever trust they had in her now—and she didn't flatter herself that it was much—would evaporate instantly if they ever caught her in another lie. And without their trust she had no chance at all of completing her mission. Or even of staying alive. "First of all," she said, "I have to tell you that for the past thirty years we've been keeping tabs on you through spy satellites orbiting your world."

She braced herself for an explosion, but Kruin merely nodded. "That's hardly a secret. Everyone on Qasama has seen them—dim specks moving across the night sky. It's said that a favorite topic of conversation when the Shahni meet is how we might go about destroying them."

"I can't blame them," Jin admitted. "Well, anyway, it seems that someone's finally come up with a way to do it."

Kruin cocked an eyebrow. "Interesting. I take it you came here to stop that person?"

Jin shook her had. "Actually, no. Our group came to gather information, and that alone. It's not quite as simple as it sounds, you see: the satellites aren't being physically destroyed, just temporarily disabled . . . and we're so far unable to figure out how it's being done."

She described as best she could the gaps that had been made in the satellites' records. "What eventually

tipped them off was the discovery that there was a
definite pattern in the blank regions. Most of them fell
over that roofed complex northeast of Azras."

"You must mean Mangus?" Daulo said.

"Is that what it's called?" Jin frowned. The word
sounded vaguely familiar . . . "Is Mangus someone's
name?"

Daulo shook his head. "It's the ancient root of the
word *mongoose*. I don't know why they call the place
that."

Jin felt her mouth go dry. *Mongoose*. A lengendary
Old Earth animal . . . whose fame lay in their ability to
kill cobras. *I could probably tell you*, she thought morosely, *why they named it that*. "Any idea what exactly
they're doing in there?"

Kruin's eyes were hard on her face; but, surprisingly,
he didn't ask about whatever it was he saw there.
"Electronics research and manufacture," he said. "Quite
a lot of it, apparently, judging by the quantities of
refined metals they buy from us."

"Quantities that seem excessive for that kind of electronics manufacture?" Jin asked.

"How much metal would be excessive?" Kruin countered.
"I'd need to know their output before making any
comparison."

"Well, what exactly do they make? Do you have any
examples here?"

Kruin shook his head. "Their goods go mainly to the
cities."

Or at least that's what they tell the villages, anyway,
Jin thought. "Any way to check on what their output
actually is?"

Kruin and Daulo eyed each other. "We could probably get the appropriate figures for Azras," Kruin told
her. "For the other cities . . . unlikely. It might help if
we knew what it is you're looking for."

Jin took a deep breath. "The analysis group on

Aventine seemed to think Mangus might be a site for missile testing."

Kruin's face went suddenly hard. "Missile testing? What kind of missiles?"

Jin held out her hands, palm upward. "That's one of the things I have to find out. But I can only think of two uses for missiles: as vehicles for space travel . . . or as weapons."

For a long moment Kruin stared at her in silence. "So if it's the first, you'll report that we're again a threat to you?" he said abruptly, his voice harsh. "And the demon warriors will come here again and destroy Mangus as a warning? Whereas if it's merely the cities planning blackmail or open warfare on the villages, you'll all smile and leave us alone?"

Jin met his gaze without flinching. "If all we wanted was to destroy you, we could do it in a hundred different ways. That's not a threat, that's simple reality. You came originally from the Dominion of Man—you must have some memories of the horrible weapons a technological world can create."

Kruin grimaced. "We do," he admitted. "It was one of the reasons our ancestors left."

"All right, then. We aren't going to try and destroy you—whether you believe that or not, it's true. It's also true that we have absolutely no interest in fighting an unnecessary war with you. We don't have the time or money or lives to waste on one, for starters. If Qasama is developing space flight . . . well, we ought to be able to live with that. *If*, that is, we can be reasonably certain that the whole planet isn't going to rise, en masse, and attack us."

Daulo hissed derisively. "Who on Qasama would be foolish enough to lead such a suicidal attack? And who would be foolish enough to follow them?"

Jin shook her head. "I don't know. That's another of the things I have to find out."

"And if Mangus is building missiles for internecine

war?" Kruin persisted. "Will your people, having revived in us this ability to destroy, simply turn their backs on us?"

Jin clenched her teeth. Again there was no point in lying. "It's possible. I hope not, but our leaders *could* decide that way. Bear in mind, though, that with my companions dead I *am* this mission. If my report states that you're not a threat, and that we stand more to gain by establishing political and trade relations with your culture than by letting that culture destroy itself . . ." She shrugged. "Who knows what they'll do? And with my uncle on the Directorate, my voice will at least have a chance to be heard."

"This is your uncle who barely escaped from Qasama with his life?" Kruin reminded her pointedly.

She shook her head. "Different uncle. His brother, Corwin Moreau, is a governor on Aventine."

Kruin frowned. "Your family has such status and power in your world?"

A shiver ran up Jin's back. Her father under house arrest; Uncle Corwin's political power balanced precariously across her own shoulders . . . "For the moment, at least, it does," she sighed. "There are forces trying to change that."

"With the decision dependent on the report you bring back?" Kruin asked.

"More on how I personally do on the mission." Jin shook her head. "But never mind that. I've told you why I'm here, answered all your questions as well as I could. I need to know—now—whether you're going to allow me to complete my mission."

Kruin pursed his lips. "Keeping your identity within our family would be highly dangerous—I'm sure you realize that. If you were discovered by some other means the repercussions would be disastrous. What do you offer in exchange for this risk on our part?"

"What do you suggest?" Jin asked, trying to keep her

voice steady. *I did it*, she thought, not quite sure she believed it. *He's actually bargaining with me.*

Now if only he wanted something she could deliver.

"As you're now well aware," Kruin said, "your plan to split our society into conflicting factions has succeeded only too well. Whatever Mangus turns out to be, you also know that there's already a certain amount of trouble between the cities as a group and the villages as a group. Besides the mojo question, the tension is fueled by the fact that heavy industry is concentrated in the cities, while control of resources lies mainly with the villages."

Jin nodded. It was a classical enough situation, probably played out hundreds of times throughout mankind's early days. Fleetingly, she wished she knew how those various Old Earth cultures had handled it. "I hope you don't want me to try and defuse the situation—"

"Grant me more intelligence than that," Kruin cut her off coldly. "This is *our* world—*our* politics, *our* culture, *our* people—and any advice you as an outlander could give would be less than useless."

Jin swallowed. "Excuse me. Please continue."

Kruin glared at her a moment before continuing. "We're already preparing to stand together against attempts to dominate us—the village leaders in this part of Qasama meet periodically to discuss the situation and coordinate any activities that seem called for. But there are some who see turmoil as a chance for advancement . . . and if there is indeed turmoil in Qasama's immediate future, I want the Sammon family able to face it without such dangerous distractions at our backs."

Jin grimaced. "Distractions such as the Yithtra family across the Inner Green?"

"I see Daulo has told you of them," Kruin growled. "Then you'll understand that their obsession with dragging us down is something that must be dealt with. Now would seem to be a good time to do so."

"Are you asking me to murder one or more of them?"

Jin asked quietly. "Because if you are, I'll tell you right now that I can't do that."

"You're a warrior, aren't you?" Daulo put in.

"Killing in warfare isn't the same as murder," she countered.

"I don't ask you to murder," Kruin shook his head. "I ask merely that you find a way to diminish the Yithtra family's influence in this village. That's the bargain I offer you, Jasmine Moreau: destruction of the Yithtra family's power in exchange for sanctuary in our household."

Jin licked her lips. It ought to be possible, surely, though at the moment she didn't have the vaguest idea how she would pull off such a trick. *But then what happens?* she wondered. *What would that kind of power loss mean in this culture?—loss of homes, maybe, the whole family even turned out of the village? Could it even lead directly to wholesale death, either suicide or murder?*

The moral implications were bad enough . . . but the possible political ramifications were even worse. It would set a clear precedent of Cobra-World meddling in Qasaman affairs, with all that that would mean from both sides' perspectives. The Directorate would probably welcome the idea of rewarding cooperative Qasamans; but from the Qasaman side, Kruin's bargain smacked of high treason. Could she ethically allow herself to be a part of such a thing?

Or did she really have any choice? "I offer you a counter proposal," she said at last. "I won't destroy the Yithtra family's power directly; but I will so enhance your own prestige and standing that they won't dare oppose you."

Kruin gazed at her, his eyes measuring. "And how do you propose to do that?" he asked.

"I don't know," she confessed. "But I'll find a way."

For a long minute the room was silent. Then, taking a deep breath, Kruin nodded gravely. "The bargain is sealed. You, Jasmine Moreau, are now under the protection of my family. Our household is yours; we shield you with our lives."

Jin swallowed. "Thank you, Kruin Sammon. I will betray neither your hospitality nor our bargain."

Kruin nodded again and rose from his cushions, Daulo following suit. "Tomorrow representatives from Mangus will be arriving at Milika to receive a shipment of our metals. You may wish to begin your investigation by observing them."

"I will do so," Jin said.

"And now—" Kruin leaned back down to his desk and touched a button "—it's time for the evening meal. Come, let us join the others."

Jin kept her expression neutral. Drugs or poison at the evening meal . . . "Yes," she agreed. "Let us."

Chapter 24

The insistent warble of his bedside phone snapped Corwin wide awake. *Must be some trouble*, was his first thought, focusing with an effort on his clock. But it wasn't the middle of the night, after all; it was only a little after six and almost time to get up anyway. *Probably just Thena with some latebreaking appointment change or something*, he decided, reaching to the phone and jabbing the instrument on. "Hello?"

But it wasn't Thena's face that appeared on the screen. It was Governor-General Chandler's . . . and it was as grim as Corwin had ever seen the man. "You'd better get over to the starfield right away," he said without preamble. "The *Southern Cross*'ll be landing in about fifteen minutes, and you'll want to see what they've got."

"The *Southern Cross*?" Corwin frowned, a knot starting to form in his stomach. "What's gone wrong?"

"Everything," Chandler snarled. "Just get down here."

Corwin gritted his teeth. "Yes, sir."

The phone screen went black. "Damn," Corwin muttered under his breath. Swinging his legs out of bed, he grabbed his clothes and started pulling them on. There was only one conceivable reason why the *Southern Cross* would be back so soon: the Qasaman mission had met with some kind of disaster.

He paused, half dressed, heart pounding in his throat. A disaster. An emergency, perhaps, requiring swift action . . . and long experience had showed him that committees and councils weren't built for speed.

Most jobs are done, the old couplet came back to him, *by committees of one.*

Gritting his teeth, he reached back to the phone and punched a number.

He arrived at the starfield twenty minutes later to find that Chandler had sealed off one of the conference rooms in the entrypoint building. Two other Directorate members—Telek and Priesly—had arrived before him . . . and one look at their faces told him that the situation was even worse than he'd feared.

He was right.

Captain Koja's report was short, partly because there wasn't much to say and partly because the enhanced telephoto on the wall display behind him said it all anyway. "We elected not to wait and see if he found the survival pod," the captain concluded, "under the assumption that we could serve him better by getting back and sounding the alarm." He looked at Chandler. "That's really all I have, sir. Do you have any questions?"

Chandler asked something and was answered, but Corwin didn't really hear any of it. A horrible shimmer of unreality seemed to have fallen between him and the rest of the room. Between him and the rest of the universe. That last image of Jin as she'd waved to them from the *Southern Cross*'s entryway hovered ghost-like in front of his face . . . in front of the computer-enhanced image of the shuttle's death still displayed on the

conference-room wall. *I sent her there*, the thought
swirled like a bitterly cold tornado through his mind. *I
pushed it through. I forced them to make her a Cobra.
And then I sent her off to Qasama . . . all in the name
of thwarting political enemies.*

In the name of politics.

Someone was calling his name. He looked over to see
Chandler eyeing him. "Yes?"

"I asked if you had any comments or suggestions,"
the governor-general repeated evenly.

For a moment Corwin locked eyes with him. Chandler returned the gaze steadily, without so much as
flinching. It was the statesman look that Corwin had
seen on him so often . . . and always hated. It inevitably
appeared at those times when Chandler wanted to appear above politics, or to disclaim all responsibility for
something he'd had a hand in. *So that's how it's going
to be here, too, is it?* Corwin thought silently toward
that look. *Not going to accept any more responsibility
than you absolutely have to? Well, we'll just see about
that.*

But first there was a question he had to ask. Shifting
his eyes to Koja, he took a deep breath. "Captain, is
there . . . ?" He licked his lips and tried again. "Is there
any indication as to . . . which of the Cobras might
have survived?"

A muscle in Koja's cheek twitched. "I'm sorry, Governor, but there isn't," he said, almost gently. "We've
gone over the data a hundred times in the past eight
days. There just isn't any way to tell."

Corwin nodded, feeling the others' eyes on him.
"Then it *could* be Jin who's still alive down there,
couldn't it?"

Koja shrugged fractionally. "It could be her, yes.
Could be *all* the Cobras, for all we can tell."

No false hope, Corwin warned himself. But the ad-
monition wasn't serious, and he knew it. Without hope,
he could already feel his mind turning inward again,

away from the wave of guilt threatening to overwhelm him. But *with* hope . . . that same wave could be turned outward. Turned outward to claim vengeance for what had happened to his niece. Alive or dead, he owed her that much. "For the moment," he said, looking back at Chandler, "we can skip over any recriminations as to why the *Southern Cross* wasn't carrying any emergency equipment for just such a disaster as this. Right now our first priority is to get a rescue team together and out to Qasama as quickly as possible. What steps have you taken toward that end?"

"I've spoken to Coordinator Maung Kha," Chandler replied. "The Academy directors are gong to assemble a list for us."

"Which will be ready when?" Corwin asked.

Priesly shifted in his seat. "You want it fast or you want it good?" he asked Corwin.

"We want it both," Telek snapped before Corwin could respond.

"I'm sure you do, Governor—" Priesly began.

"Mr. Chandler," Telek cut him off, "do I assume I've been included in this council of war because of my first-hand expertise on Qasaman matters? Fine. Then kindly pay attention to that expertise when I tell you that Moreau's right. If you want your Cobra back alive, minutes could literally count. The Qasamans are fast and smart, and once they make their move they don't leave a whole hell of a lot of room to maneuver in."

"I understand," Chandler said with clearly forced patience. "But as Governor Priesly points out, to do the job properly takes a certain amount of time."

"That depends on how far into complicated channels you insist on dragging the process," Corwin told him.

"Channels exist for a reason," Priesly growled. "The Academy has the computers and lists you'd need to find the best people for the job. Unless you'd rather just toss some ragtag collection of Cobras together on your own?"

"I won't have to," Corwin said calmly. "It's already being done."

All eyes turned to him. "What's that supposed to mean?" Chandler asked cautiously.

"It means that before I left home this morning I called Justin and told him something had gone wrong with the mission."

"You *what*?" Priesly snarled. "Moreau—"

"Shut up," Chandler cut him off. "And . . . ?"

"And I told him to organize a rescue mission," Corwin said calmly. "He should have a list ready in an hour or so."

For a long moment the room was filled with a brittle silence. "You've overstepped your bounds rather badly," Chandler said at last. "I could have you removed from office for that."

"I realize that," Corwin nodded. "One other thing: Justin will also be leading the team."

Priesly's mouth fell open. "Justin Moreau is under house arrest," he bit out. "In case you've forgotten, there are charges of assault pending against him."

"Then those charges will have to be summarily dropped, won't they?"

"Oh, of course," Priesly snarled. "What, you expect us to just roll over—?"

"Justin's been to Qasama," Corwin said, his gaze on Chandler. "He's seen the Qasamans up close, both in combat and non-combat situations. There's no one else anywhere in the Worlds who has those same qualifications."

"There were forty-eight Cobras who participated in the second Qasaman mission," Chandler pointed out. His face was a mask, but Corwin could sense the anger behind it . . . and perhaps a growing resignation, as well. "One of them could lead the mission."

"Except that none of them have anything near Justin's experience with Qasaman society," Telek shook her head. "He's right, Mr. Chandler. The best choice for team leader is someone from our first spy mission. And there's only one other person young enough even to be considered."

"Well, let's get him, then," Priesly demanded.

Telek turned glacial eyes on him. "Help yourself. His name's Joshua Moreau."

A second silence fell over the room. "I don't have to let you get away with this, you know," Chandler told Corwin at last, very softly. "I can ignore your brother's unauthorized recommendations and take those of the Academy directors instead. And Mr. Priesly's correct—we *can* get someone else to lead the mission."

"And can you also hear what the people of Aventine will say," Corwin returned, just as softly, "when they learn that their leaders wasted time wrangling over fine details. And then settled for second best."

"That's blackmail," Priesly snapped.

Corwin looked him straight in the eye. "That's politics," he corrected. Getting to his feet, he looked back at Chandler. "If we're done here, sir, I'll be going to my office—Justin'll be contacting me there when he's finished. I'm sure he'll want to personally organize the team as the members arrive in the Capitalia; can I assume you'll have his release papers filed by noon or so?"

Chandler gritted his teeth. "It can be managed. I suppose you'll want a full pardon?"

"That or a formal dropping of the charges. Whichever you and Mr. Priesly decide to work out."

He started for the door, but Chandler stopped him. "You realize, of course," the governor-general said darkly, "that as of right now you've taken this entire rescue mission onto your own head. If it fails—for any reason—it'll be *you* who bears the brunt of that failure."

"I understand," Corwin said between tight lips. "I also understand that if it succeeds Mr. Priesly and his associates will do their best to make sure I get as little of the credit as possible."

"You understand politics very well," Telek murmured. "I'm almost sorry for you."

Corwin looked at her. "Fortunately, I understand family loyalty, too. And know which one's more important."

He nodded to Chandler and left.

Corwin had seen Justin's organizational skills many times in the past; but even so he was astonished by the speed with which his brother got the rescue team assembled in Capitalia. By eight that evening—barely fifteen hours after the *Southern Cross* had reentered Aventine's system—the *Dewdrop* was loaded and ready to lift.

"You sure you've got everything you'll need?" Corwin asked as he and Justin stood together a little way from the *Dewdrop,* watching the last load of equipment disappear into the cargo hatch.

"We'll make do," Justin replied, his voice glacially calm.

Corwin threw him a sideways glance. For a man who'd just lost a daughter—either dead or captive— Justin was far too calm, and it was making Corwin more than a little nervous. Whatever the other was feeling about his daughter's fate, it wasn't healthy to keep it bottled up forever. Somehow, it was going to have to come out . . . and if Justin was saving up the anger to dump on the Qasamans, it would be a very bloody purging indeed.

"Something?" Justin asked, his eyes still on the loading.

Corwin pursed his lips. "Just wondering about your people," he improvised. "You put the list together pretty quickly—you still sure they're the ones you want?"

"You've seen the profiles," Justin said. "Four vets of the last Qasaman mission, eight young but experienced Cobras with impressive spine leopard hunting records."

"But without any military training," Corwin pointed out.

"We've got six days to change that," his brother reminded him.

"Yeah." Corwin took a deep breath; but Justin got in the next word.

"I don't think I thanked you yet for getting Chandler to let me off those trumped-up charges," he said calmly.

"No problem," Corwin shrugged. "They didn't have a lot of choice, actually."

Justin nodded, agreement or simple acknowledgment. "I also appreciate what you've done in putting your neck on this fresh block for me. If I'd had to sit around for the next two weeks . . . it would've been pretty hard. At least this way there's something I can do."

"Yeah. Well . . . I expect you know that if Jin's—if she didn't make it, I mean . . . that extracting vengeance from the Qasamans isn't going to help any."

"That depends on what happened to her, doesn't it?" Justin countered. "If she died in the crash . . . well, I'll hold the Trofts partly to blame for that. They're the ones who claimed their shuttle would get through the Qasamans' detectors. But if Jin was captured—" His face hardened. "Teaching the Qasamans a lesson won't bring Jin back, no. But it might prevent someone else's child from dying at their hands."

Corwin bit at his lip. "Just remember that you have two other daughters," he reminded Justin quietly. "Make sure you come back to them, all right?"

Justin nodded solemnly, and his lip twitched in a faint smile. "Don't worry, Corwin; the Qasamans won't even know what hit them." Across the way, the *Dewdrop*'s cargo hatch swung shut with a muffled thud. "Well, that's it—time to go. Hold the fort here, okay?"

He gave Corwin a brief, almost perfunctory hug, and a moment later had vanished up the ramp into the *Dewdrop*'s main entryway.

They won't even know what hit them. Justin's statement echoed through his mind . . . and standing there alone, Corwin shivered at the lie in those words. Justin would make sure the Qasamans knew what had hit them, all right. What had hit them, and why.

And he wondered if he'd now sent his brother to die on Qasama. Just as he'd done his niece.

Chapter 25

Jin had never been one to make snap judgments of people. But in the case of Radig Nardin she was severely tempted to make an exception.

"Overbearing sort, isn't he?" she murmured to Daulo as they stood a short distance from where Nardin was loudly supervising the loading of his metals.

"Yes," Daulo said tightly. His eyes and most of his attention, she saw, were on Nardin; his arms, at his sides, were rigid.

Jin licked her lips. The tension in the air around them seemed almost thick enough to cast a shadow, and her stomach was beginning to tighten in sympathetic reaction. Whatever it was that was happening here, things seemed to be rapidly building up to a head, and she found herself easing away from Daulo just in case she suddenly needed room to maneuver. Nardin's two drivers and aides were somewhere off to the side . . . there. Nowhere near cover, should Nardin decide to pick a fight—

197

"Stop!" Daulo snapped.

Jin whipped her eyes back to Nardin. Almost leisurely, he turned around to face them, his hand raised in striking pose above one of the sweating Sammon workers. His gaze flicked measuringly across Daulo's clothing, returned to his face. "You tolerate insubordinate attitudes in your workers, Master Sammon?" he called.

"If and when such insubordination is seen," Daulo said evenly, "it will be punished. And *I* will do the punishing."

For a moment the two young men locked eyes. Then, breathing something inaudible, Nardin lowered his arm. Turning his back on Daulo, he stalked a few meters away from the loading area.

Jurisdictional dispute? Jin wondered. Apparently. Or else Nardin just liked going out of his way to irritate people. "You all right?" Jin asked Daulo quietly.

The other took a deep breath, seemed to relax a bit. "Yes," he said, exhaling in a hiss. "Some people just can't handle power this young."

Jin glanced at him, wondering if he noticed the irony of those words coming from a nineteen-year-old heir. "Radig Nardin is high in the Mangus hierarchy?" he asked.

"His father, Obolo Nardin, runs the place."

"Ah. Then Mangus is a family-run operation like yours?"

"Of course." Daulo seemed puzzled that she'd even have to ask such a question.

Across the way, the last few crates were being loaded onto the trunk. "How often does Mangus need these shipments?" she asked Daulo.

He considered. "About every three weeks. Why?"

She nodded at the truck. "Riding inside a crate might be the simplest way for me to get inside Mangus."

Daulo hissed thoughtfully between his teeth. "Only if

you had time to get out before they locked all the crates away somewhere."

"Do they do that?"

"I don't know—I've never been there. Mangus always sends someone to pick up their shipments."

"Is that normal?"

"It is for Mangus. Though if you're right about what they're doing in there, it makes sense for them not to let villagers in."

The qualifier caught Jin's attention. "Only villagers? Can city people get in?"

"Regularly," Daulo nodded. "Mangus brings in work parties from Azras every two to three weeks for one-week periods. Simple assembly work, I gather."

"I don't understand," Jin frowned. "You mean they import their entire labor force?"

"Not the entire force, no. They have some permanent workers, most of them probably Nardin family members. I assume their assembly work comes in spurts and they'd rather not keep people there when they're not needed."

"Seems inefficient. What if some of those workers take other jobs in the meantime and aren't available when they need them?"

"I don't know. But as I said, it's simple assembly work. Training newcomers wouldn't be hard."

Jin nodded. "Do you know anyone personally who's been in one of the work parties?"

Daulo shook his head. "For city people only, remember? We only know about it through my father's relationship with Mayor Capparis of Azras."

"Right—you've mentioned him before. He keeps you informed on what Azras and the other cities are doing?"

"Somewhat. For a price, of course."

That price being preferential access to the Sammon family mine, no doubt. "Do the rest of Azras's political leaders share in this tradeoff?"

"Some." Daulo shrugged, a bit uncomfortably. "Like everyone else, Mayor Capparis has enemies."

"Um." Jin focused on Nardin's arrogant expression again; and, unbidden, an image popped into her mind. Peter Todor, early in their Cobra training, visibly and eagerly awaiting the moment when Jin would finally give up and quit. The moment when he'd be able to gloat over her defeat. "Is there any reason," she asked carefully, "why Mangus or Mayor Capparis's enemies should resent Milika in particular?"

Daulo frowned at her. "Why would they?"

She braced herself. "Could you be charging more for your goods than they consider fair?"

Daulo's eyes hardened. "We don't overcharge for what we sell," he said coldly. "Our mine produces rare and valuable metals, which we purify to a high degree. They'd be costly no matter who sold them."

"What about the Yithtra family, then?" Jin asked.

"What about them?"

"They sell lumber products, right? Do *they* overcharge the cities?"

Daulo's lip twisted. "No, not really," he admitted. "Actually, most of the lumber business out there bypasses Milika entirely. The Somilarai River, which cuts through the main logging area to the north, passes directly by Azras, so much of the lumber is simply floated downriver to processing areas there. What the Yithtra family has done has been to specialize in exotic types of wood products like rhella paper—things the more wholesale lumbering places can't do properly. You probably saw a few rhella trees on your way in from your ship: short, black-trunked things with diamond-shaped leaves?"

Jin shook her head. "Afraid I was looking more at what might be crouching up there than I was at the trees themselves. These rhellas are rare?"

"Not all that much, but the paper made from the inner pulp is the preferred medium for legal contracts, and that creates a high demand. Writing or printing on fresh rhella paper indents the surface, you see," he added, "and that indentation is permanent. So if the writing is altered in any way, it can be detected instantly."

"Handy," Jin agreed. "Expensive, too, I take it?"

"It's worth the cost. Why are you asking all this?"

Jin nodded toward Nardin. "He has the air about him of someone who's getting all ready to gloat," she said. "I was wondering if he's looking forward to gloating over the villages in general or Milika in particular."

"Well . . ." Daulo hesitated. "I'd have to say that even among Qasama's villages, we're considered somewhat . . . not renegades, exactly, but not quite part of the whole community, either."

"Because you're not tied into the central underground communications network?"

He looked at her in surprise. "How—? Oh, that's right; you learned all about that when you took over that Eastern Arm village your last time through. Yes, that's a large part of it. And even though other villages are now starting to sprout up outside the Great Arc, we were one of the first." He eyed her. "This is all part of your research on us?"

Jin felt her face warming. "Some," she admitted. "It's also related to the problem of Mangus, though."

He was silent for a long moment. Shifting her eyes from the loading dock, Jin looked around her. It was a beautiful day, with gentle breezes coming from the southwest adding contrast to the warmth of the sunlight. The sounds of village activity all around her melded into a pleasant hum; the occasional clinking of chains and cables from the mine entrance nearby added to the voices of the workers.

It was almost a shock to shift her eyes westward and see the wall. The wall, and the metal mesh addition the village had had to erect against the high-jumping spine leopards . . . the spine leopards her people had sent to them.

On the recommendation of her own grandfather.

A sudden shiver of guilt ran up her back. What would Daulo and Kruin think, she wondered bleakly, if they knew her family's role in bringing this burden onto them? *Maybe that's why I was marooned here in the first place*, the thought occurred to her. *Maybe it's part of a divine retribution on my family.*

"You all right?" Daulo asked.

She shook off the train of thought. "Sure. Just . . . thinking about home."

He nodded. "My father and I were wondering last night about what plans your people might be making to get you back."

She shrugged uncomfortably. "They're not likely to be planning anything except my memorial service. The way the crash destroyed the shuttle's transmitters, there wasn't any way I could signal our mother ship; and between that and what they would have seen from orbit they'd have assumed that everyone was dead. So they'll go on back, and everyone will mourn us for awhile, and then the Directorate will start debating what to do next. Maybe in a few months they'll try this again. Maybe it won't be for a couple of years."

"You sound bitter."

Jin blinked away tears. "No, not bitter. Just . . . afraid of how my father's gong to take this. He wanted so much for me to be a Cobra—"

"A what?"

"A Cobra. It's the proper name for what you call a demon warrior. He wanted so much for me to follow in the family tradition . . . and now he'll wonder if he pushed me where I didn't want to go."

"Did he?" Daulo asked quietly.

Oddly enough, Jin felt no resentment at the question. "No. I love him a lot, Daulo, and I might have been willing to become a Cobra just from that love. But, no—I wanted this as much as he did."

Daulo snorted gently. "A warrior woman. Seems almost a contradiction in terms."

"Only by your history. And on our own worlds Cobras are more like civilian peacekeepers than fighters."

"Almost like what the mojos were to us," Daulo pointed out.

Jin considered. "Interesting analogy," she admitted.

He gave a sound that was half snort, half chuckle. "Just think of the sort of peacekeeper force we could have if we combined the two."

"Cobras and mojos?" She shook her head. "No chance. In fact, it's occurred to me more than once that that may be exactly the thought that scared our leaders the most: the idea that your mojos might spread to Aventine, that we might wind up having our Cobras controlled by alien minds."

"But if it would make them less dangerous—"

"The mojos have their own priorities and purposes," Jin reminded him. "I'd just as soon not find out what one might do with a Cobra."

Daulo sighed. "You're probably right," he conceded. "Still—"

"Master Sammon?" a voice called from behind them. They turned, and Jin saw Daulo's chauffeur waving to them from the doorway of the mine's business center. "A call for you. Important, he says."

Daulo nodded and set off at a brisk trot. Jin watched him take the chauffeur's place at the phone, then turned back to watch Nardin. *Mangus. Mongoose.* The name alone gave the lie to all her talk about city versus village warfare. A compound called Mongoose could have only one possible focus, and that was outward from Qasama. In the back of her mind, her conscience twinged: should she continue to let Daulo and his father believe that Mangus was a plot against the villages? Especially since they might withdraw their support from her if they knew the truth?

"Jasmine Alventin!"

She started and twisted around. Daulo was beckoning urgently to her as he opened the car's left-hand rear door; the chauffeur was already in the front seat. Heart thudding in her throat, Jin jogged over to join them. "What is it?" she asked, pulling open the right-hand door and sliding in the back beside Daulo.

"One of our people noticed a Yithtra family truck coming in by the south gate," Daulo said, his voice tight. "It had something like a tree trunk sticking from the back, covered with some kind of cloth so that it couldn't be seen."

Jin frowned. "An unusual tree they don't want anyone to see?"

"That's what our spotter thought. It occurred to me that there's something else of that shape that they might be even more anxious to hide from sight."

Jin's mouth went dry. *A missile?* "That's . . . crazy," she managed. "Where would they have gotten something like that?"

Daulo's eyes flicked to the chauffeur. "Whatever it is, I want to try and get a look at it."

The chauffer sped them down the spoke road to the Small Ring, turning counterclockwise onto it. "The simplest route would be to take the spoke road directly from the south gate to the Small Ring," Daulo muttered. "But in this case . . . I'm going to guess they'll turn instead onto the Great Ring and take it to the Yithtra section, then come down that spoke road to the house. What do you think, Walare?"

"Sounds reasonable, Master Daulo," the chauffeur nodded. "Shall I run that in reverse and see if we can catch them?"

"Right."

Guiding the vehicle expertly through the pedestrian crowds, Walare curved around the Inner Green, passed the spoke road from the south gate, and continued on toward the grand house Daulo had identified some days earlier as that of the Yithtra family. Another spoke road angled off just before it, and Walare turned down it. Jin looked back at the house as they headed away, noting the liveried guards at all the visible entrances—

"There," Daulo snapped, pointing at a small truck far ahead down the spoke road. Jin keyed in her optical enhancers for a look at the truck's three occupants. All three looked oddly tense, but none seemed especially suspicious of the car approaching them. A minute later the two vehicles passed each other, and Daulo and Jin both spun around in their places.

There was indeed something cylindrical poking awkwardly out from between the truck's rear doors; and it was indeed swathed heavily in some kind of silky white cloth. "Follow it," Daulo ordered Walare. "Well, Jasmine Alventin?" he added as the car swung into a tight U-turn.

Jin pursed her lips, trying to estimate the object's length and circumference. "It's not very big, if it's what we think it is," she told him. "Rather obvious, too."

"Point," Daulo admitted. "Especially since they've got regular log carriers they could have used to bring something like that in without it being seen at all. You think perhaps it *is* nothing but a tree trunk brought in to stir us up?"

Jin chewed at her lip. It might be possible to glean something even through all that cloth. "Let me try something," she said. Leaning her head out the side window, she keyed in her optical enhancers' infrared capability.

The reflection/radiation profile was strong and dramatic; and even with the background clutter from the truck and pavement around it, there was no room for doubt. "It's metal," she told Daulo.

He nodded grimly. "I'm sure you realize what this means. The Yithtra family's made a deal with Mangus."

"Or else they stole it. Which could get the whole village in trouble."

Daulo hissed between his teeth. "Trouble from agents seeking to retrieve it?"

Or straightforward retaliation, Jin thought. But there was no point in worrying Daulo with that one. "Basically," she told him. "On the other hand, we've now got a chance to pick up some information without having to go all the way to Mangus for it."

He stared at her. "Are you *serious?* We can't break into the Yithtra family house."

"I didn't think we could," Jin told him tightly. "That's why I'm going to have to do this here and now."

He said something incredulous sounding, but she was too busy thinking to pay attention. There were a dozen ways to take out a vehicle, but all of them would instantly brand her as a demon warrior. To their right, another of Milika's marketplaces stretched alongside the street, teeming with potential witnesses to anything she tried.

Potential witnesses . . . but also potential diversions. "Pull up closer to the truck," she ordered the chauffeur. "In a minute I'll want you to pass it."

"Master Daulo . . . ?" the other asked.

"Do it," Daulo confirmed. "Jin—?"

"I'm going to jump out as you start to pass and get into the truck," she told him, eyes searching across the marketplace booths ahead as she lowered the window. Somewhere out there had to be what she was looking for . . .

There—right beside the street fifty meters ahead: a group of six customers holding an animated discussion beside a vendor of food and drink . . . and four of the six carried mojos on their shoulders. "Pull up," she ordered Walare. "Daulo Sammon, I'll meet you back at the house." From the corner of her eye she saw them closing on the truck ahead; activating her target system, she locked onto the bellies of three of the mojos. Even in the glare of full daylight, she knew, it was going to be a calculated risk to fire even low-power shots from her fingertip lasers. But there wasn't anything she could do about that except cross her fingers and pray that no one noticed them. Walare had them directly behind the truck now, and was starting to pull around; and as the food booth shot past, Jin fired three shots in rapid succession.

It was all she could have hoped for. The birds' screams pierced the air like a triple siren, followed immediately by an equal number of human bellows. Jin got a quick glimpse of the scorched mojos tearing furiously around through the air as everyone nearby scrambled for safety from the birds' unexpected behavior; and as the sudden ruckus audibly spread behind her she wrenched the car door open and flipped her legs out onto the pavement. For a second she held onto the door for balance as her feet caught the stride; then, shoving the door shut, she surged forward. Her timing was perfect: with Walare halfway into his passing maneuver, her side of the car had been directly behind the truck, out of view of any rear-facing mirror. A two-second quick-sprint put her beside the cylinder's bouncing nose; grabbing the edge of one of the open doors, she pulled herself up and through the gap and into the welcome shadows inside the truck.

She took a shuddering breath, acutely aware of the time limit now counting down. In five minutes or less the truck would reach the Yithtra house, and if she didn't get out before then, she might very well have to shoot her way out. Crouching down beside the cylinder, she tore away its silky covering . . . and froze.

The cloth wasn't just cloth. It was light and tight-woven, with cords tied between it and the cylinder.

A parachute.

And the cylinder beneath it was smooth and white, with black scorch marks liberally splattered over its surface. Marks that nevertheless didn't obscure the lettering on the loosely fastened access panel:

TYPE 6-KX TRANSFER CONTAINER: FOR GOVERNMENTAL SHIPPING USE ONLY.

God above, she thought numbly. The Yithtra family hadn't bought or stolen a missile, after all. They'd found something far worse: a goodbye present from the *Southern Cross*.

A present for her.

Chapter 26

For a long second her mind seemed to be on ice, skidding along without control. The pod's existence was bad enough; but its existence in the hands of Qasamans was even worse. The minute the Yithtra family realized what it was they'd found and turned it over to the authorities—

And she had maybe three minutes to figure out a way to stop that. Gritting her teeth, she dug her fingers under the access panel's edge and pried it open.

The contents were no surprise: packaged emergency rations, lightweight blankets, medical packs, a backpack and water carrier—all the things a castaway in hostile territory might need to survive. All of them clearly labeled with Anglic words.

Which meant obscuring the writing on the outside of the pod wouldn't gain her anything. Unless she could also completely destroy the pod's contents . . .

A trickle of sweat ran down her cheek. She jabbed and probed her fingers through the packages, trying desperately to think of something. Her lasers weren't designed for starting this kind of fire, but if they'd sent her some cooking fuel—

Her roving fingers struck something that rustled: a tightly folded piece of paper. Frowning, she dug it out and opened it. The message was short:

Can't get down to you. If you can hang on, we'll be back with help as quickly as we can. We'll listen for your call at local sunrise, noon, sunset, and midnight—if you can't signal, we'll come down and find you.

Courage!

Captain Rivero Koja

Jin bit down hard on her lip. *We'll come down and find you.* In her mind's eye she saw a full Cobra assault force descend on Milika, shooting indiscriminately as they tried to find her . . . Swearing under her breath, she dug into the packages with renewed energy, searching now for the transmitter Koja's note implied had been packed in with the supplies. But either it was buried too deeply among the groceries . . .

Or else the Yithtra workers who'd found and opened the pod had already taken it out.

Damn. It was right there, a few meters away from her in the cab of the truck . . . and yet it might as well be in orbit. For one wild second she had the image of herself blasting through to the cab with her antiarmor laser, using her sonic to stun the cab's occupants and retrieve the transmitter—

And then taking what refuge she could in deep forest. While the Sammon family went up on treason charges.

Angrily, she shook the train of thought from her mind. The transmitter was gone, period. Crumpling Koja's note into her pocket, she jammed the access panel back in place and stepped to the rear doors, grabbing for balance as the truck made a sharp right-hand turn. Between the doors, the Small Ring Road appeared.

Which meant the truck had left the spoke road and would be reaching the gate of the Yithtra house any moment now. Licking her lips, Jin peered through the gap, trying to find something she could use to create a diversion. But nothing obvious presented itself. There were as many pedestrians out there as usual, and once out of the truck she ought to have enough cover to blend into. But there was nothing she could do to cover the jump itself. Clenching her teeth, she got ready; and as the truck abruptly decelerated, she swung down out the rear and dropped to the pavement below. A couple of braking steps brought her to a halt; turning quickly, she started walking down the road away from the Yithtra house.

No shouts of discovery followed her. Behind her, she heard the truck come to a brief halt and then start up again, vanishing behind the background hum of closing gateway doors. Fighting a trembling in her hands, she kept walking.

Eventually, after a wandering route, she reached the Sammon house.

Kruin Sammon laid the crumpled paper down on his desk and looked up at her. "So," he said. "It seems your anonymity is about to come to an end."

Jin nodded. "So it seems," she agreed tightly.

"I don't see why," Daulo objected from his usual place beside his father. "The Yithtra family can't really make trouble for you unless they can offer the Shahni some physical proof. Why can't you simply break into the Yithtra household tonight and destroy or steal the pod?"

Jin shook her head. "It wouldn't work. First of all, there's a fair chance they'll have odds and ends from the pod scattered around throughout the house by then, and there's no guarantee I'd be able to retrieve all of it.

More importantly, the very fact that I got in and out of a guarded house without being caught will be pretty strong evidence that I'm not just an offworlder, but an offworld demon warrior. I don't think we want to cause that kind of panic just yet."

"So the Yithtra family informs the Shihni that an offworlder has landed secretly among us." Kruin's eyes were steady on Jin's face. "And for their patriotism and alertness the Yithtra family gains new prestige. Is this how you help us bring them down?"

A wisp of anger curled like smoke in Jin's throat. "I realize you have your own priorities, Kruin Sammon," she said as calmly as she could, "but it seems to me you'd do better to forget about the Yithtra family earning a pat on the head and concentrate instead on the problems this might cause Milika as a whole."

"The problems it might cause *you*, you mean," Kruin countered. "We of Milika are blameless, Jasmine Moreau, if we are duped by a cunning offworlder into extending our hospitality."

Jin looked hard at him. "Are you abrogating our bargain, then?" she asked softly.

He shook his head. "Not if it can be helped. But if it should become clear that your capture is certain, I will not allow my household to be destroyed in the process." He hesitated. "If that happens . . . I'll at least give you warning."

So that any major firefights will take place away from Sammon territory? Still, it was as much as she could expect under the circumstances . . . and probably more than she would have gotten elsewhere. "I thank you for being honest with me," she said.

"Which is more than you have been with us," the elder Sammon said.

Jin's stomach began to tighten into a knot. "What do you mean?"

"I mean your true name," he said evenly. "And the connection of that name to Mangus."

Jin's eyes flicked to Daulo, feeling a sudden chill in the room. The younger man looked back at her steadily, his face as masked as Kruin's. "I never lied to you," she said, eyes still on Daulo. "To either of you."

"Is the withholding of truth not a lie?" Daulo asked quietly. "You understood the significance of the name *mongoose*, yet didn't share that knowledge."

"If I'd wanted to keep it to myself, why did I tell you at all that we were called Cobras?" she countered. "The fact is that I didn't think it was all that important."

"Not *important*?" Kruin spat. "*Mongoose* is hardly a name of a place seeking only to dominate Qasaman villages. And if Mangus is truly an attempt to fight back at our common enemies, how can the Sammon family help you destroy it?"

"I don't seek to destroy it—"

"More half-truths," Kruin shot back. "Perhaps *you* don't but others will surely follow you."

Jin took a deep breath. *Steady, girl*, she warned herself. *Concentrate, and be rational.* "I've already told you I don't know what my people will do with my report—*and* pointed out that a non-threatening Qasama is perfectly welcome to advance back into space. But if the Shahni are truly bent on attacking us, do you really think they'll do so without the full weight of Qasama behind them? Or to put it another way, won't they demand that both cities and villages supply their full shares of the resources *and* manpower—" her eyes flicked to Daulo "—that a full-scale war requires? Whether you want to or not?"

For a moment Kruin sat in silence, gazing at Jin. She forced herself to return the gaze; and after a moment he shifted on his cushions. "You again try to prove that Mangus threatens us directly. Yet without any proof."

"Whatever proof exists will only be found inside Mangus itself," Jin pointed out, feeling the knots in her stomach starting to unravel again. Whatever his apprehensions, it was clear that Kruin was smart enough to

see that the scenario Jin painted made too much sense
to ignore. "The only way to find out for sure will be to
get inside and take a look for ourselves."

"Ourselves?" A faint and slightly bitter smile touched
Kruin's lips. "How quickly you change between offworlder
and Qasaman, Jasmine Moreau. Or don't you think we
know that once inside Mangus it will be *your* priorities,
not ours, that you will address?"

Jin's hands curled into fists. "You insult me, Kruin
Sammon," she bit out. "I don't play games with people's lives—not those of my own people, not those of
yours. If Mangus threatens *any*one—Aventinian *or*
Qasaman—I want to know about it. *That's* my priority."

For a moment Kruin didn't answer. Then, to her
astonishment, he inclined his head toward her. "I had
assumed you were a warrior, Jasmine Moreau," he said.
"I see I was mistaken."

She blinked. "I don't understand."

"Warriors," he said softly, "don't care about the people they are told to kill."

Jin licked her lips, a cold shiver replacing the fading
indignation in her muscles. She hadn't meant to blast
Kruin that strongly—certainly hadn't meant to imply
that Milika's welfare was truly any of her concern. She
was here for only one purpose, she reminded herself
firmly: to find out if the Cobra Worlds were being
threatened. If it was merely one group of Qasamans
preparing to slaughter another, that was none of her
business.

Except that it was.

And for the first time her conscious mind was forced
to acknowledge that fact. She'd *lived* with these people;
lived with them, eaten their food, accepted their help
and hospitality . . . and there was no way she could
simply turn her back on them and walk away. Kruin
was right; she *was* no warrior.

Which was to say, no Cobra.

A sudden moisture obscured her vision; furiously,

she blinked it away. It didn't really matter—she'd already fouled things up so badly that one more failure wouldn't make much of a difference. "Never mind what I am or am not," she growled. "The only issue here is whether you're still going to help me get into Mangus, or whether I'm going to have to do it all myself."

"I've given you my pledge once," Kruin said coldly. "You insult me to ask again."

"Yes, well, it seems to be a day for insults," Jin said tiredly. All the fight was draining away, leaving nothing but emotional fatigue behind. "Daulo spoke of work parties hired from Azras. Can you ask your friend the mayor to get me into one of them?"

Kruin glanced at his son. "It may be possible," he said. "It could take a week to make the arrangements, though."

"We can't afford that much time," Jin sighed. "I've got to be in and out of Mangus within the next six days."

"Why?" Kruin frowned.

Jin nodded toward Koja's letter on the low desk. "Because that note changes everything. There won't be any six-month debate now as to whether or not another mission should be sent here. Koja will have burned space getting back, and there'll be a rescue team on its way just as soon as it can be scrambled together."

Kruin's lips compressed slightly. "Arriving when?"

"I don't know exactly. I'd guess no more than a week."

Daulo hissed between his teeth. "A *week?*"

"Bad," Kruin agreed calmly. "But not as bad as it might be. With a new supply of metals on its way to Mangus, they should be needing to call in extra workers soon."

"How soon?" Jin asked.

"Within your six-day limit, I'd guess," Kruin said. "I'll send a message to Mayor Capparis this afternoon and ask if a member of my household can be worked into one of the parties."

"Please ask if he can make it two members," Daulo said quietly.

Kruin cocked an eyebrow at his son. "A noble offer, my son, but not well thought out. For what reason—besides curiosity—should I allow you to accompany Jasmine Moreau on this trip?"

"For the reason that she still knows so very little about Qasama," Daulo said. "She could betray herself as an offworlder in a thousand different ways. Or worse, she could fail to understand or even to notice something of vital importance once inside."

Kruin cocked an eye at Jin. "Have you a response?"

"I'll be fine," Jin said stiffly. "I thank you for your offer, Daulo, but I don't need an escort."

"Are his arguments invalid?" Kruin persisted.

"Not necessarily," she admitted. "But the risks outbalance the benefits. Your family is well known here, and probably at least slightly known in Azras. Even with the disguise kit I've got in my pack, there's a good chance he'll be recognized by someone in the work party, or even by Radig Nardin or someone in Mangus itself. At least as much chance, I'd guess, as that I'll be caught in an error." She hesitated; *no, better not say it.*

But Kruin saw through the hesitation. "And . . . ?" he prompted.

Jin clenched her teeth. "And if there *is* trouble . . . I stand a much better chance of getting out alone than if Daulo is with me."

An instant later she wished she'd kept her mouth shut. Daulo sat up stiffly on his cushion, face darkening. "I don't need the protection of a woman," he bit out. "And I *will* go with you into Mangus."

And there was no longer any room for argument, Jin realized with a sinking heart. Logic was fine in its place; but when set against the emotions of threatened manhood, there was only one possible outcome. "In that case," she sighed, "I would be honored to have your company and protection."

It was only much later that it occurred to her that perhaps she'd been guilty of the same kind of nonrational thinking . . . that perhaps the very fact she'd forgotten something as basic to Qasama as the expanded male ego meant that she really *did* know too little about Qasama to tackle Mangus alone.

It wasn't a particularly encouraging thought.

Chapter 27

"I looked up what records we had this afternoon," Daulo's silhouette said from beside Jin, "and it looks like my father's guess was a little pessimistic. It should be only two to three days before Mangus asks Azras to organize a work party."

Jin nodded silently as they passed through the darkened courtyard toward the steady splash of the fountain. It was odd, she thought, how easily a place could start to feel familiar and comfortable. *Too comfortable, maybe*? she wondered with a twinge of uneasiness. Layn had warned them against losing the undercurrent of mild paranoia that every warrior in enemy territory ought to maintain, and she could remember thinking it incredible that anyone in such a position could possibly relax that much. Now, it seemed, she was doing just that.

Which made it all the more urgent she move on to Azras and Mangus as soon as possible.

"You're very quiet," Daulo said.

She pursed her lips. "Just thinking how peaceful it is here," she told him. "Milika in general; your house in particular. I almost wish I could stay."

He snorted gently. "Don't worry too much about it. If you lived here for a few months you'd quickly find out it's not the Eden you seem to think." He paused. "So . . . what are your people likely to do if it turns out you were right? That Mangus is a base for striking back at you?"

Jin shrugged. "It probably depends partly on what *you* do in that case."

He frowned. "What do you mean?"

"Come on, Daulo Sammon, don't play innocent. If Mangus isn't a threat to Milika, you and your father have no reason to help me further. In fact, you have every reason to betray me."

His eyes grew hard. "The Sammon family is a family of honor, Jasmine Moreau," he bit out. "We've sworn protection to you, and we'll stand by that bargain. No matter what."

She sighed. "I know. But we were . . . warned not to get overconfident."

"I understand," Daulo said quietly. "I'm afraid you'll just have to take my word for it."

"I know. But I don't have to like it."

In the darkness, his hand tentatively sought hers. It brought back memories of Mander Sun . . . blinking back tears, she accepted the touch. "We didn't ask to be your enemies, Jin Moreau," Daulo said quietly. "We have enough to fight against right here on Qasama. And we've been fighting against them for long time. Haven't we earned the right to some rest?"

She sighed. Thoughts of Caelian flashed through her mind . . . and thoughts of her father and uncle. "Yes. So has everyone else I know."

For a few minutes they continued to wander around the courtyard in silence, listening to the nighttime sounds of Milika beyond the house. "Is there a meaning to the name *Jin*?" Daulo asked suddenly. "Jasmine, I know, is an Old Earth flower, but the only use of Jin I've ever heard is for the mythological spirit."

She felt a touch of heat in her cheeks. "It was a nickname my father gave me when I was young. He said—at least to me—that it was just a shortened version of Jasmine." She licked her lips. "Maybe that's really all he meant it to be . . . but when I was about eight I found an old Dominion of Man magcard in the city library that listed several thousand common names and their meanings. *Jin* was given as an Old Japanese name that meant 'superexcellent.' "

"Indeed?" Daulo murmured. "A great compliment for your father to give you such a name."

"Maybe too great," Jin admitted. "The listing noted that it was rarely given, precisely because its meaning placed so great a demand on a child."

"And you've been trying to live up to it ever since?"

It was a thought that had often occurred to her. "I don't know. It's possible, I suppose. I remember that for weeks afterward I felt like everyone was looking expectantly at me, waiting for me to do something superexcellent."

"And so here you are on Qasama. Still trying."

She swallowed through a throat that suddenly ached. "I guess so. Or at least trying to make my father proud of me."

It was a long moment before Daulo spoke again. "I understand, perhaps more than you realize. Our families are not so different, Jin Moreau."

A flicker of movement from one of the windows overhead caught Jin's eye, saving her from the need to find a good response to that. "Someone's in your father's office," she said, pointing.

Daulo stiffened, then relaxed. "One of our people—a messenger. Probably bringing Mayor Capparis's reply to my father's message this morning."

"Let's go find out," Jin said, changing direction back

toward the door. Beside her, Daulo seemed to draw back. "If that would be all right with you," she added quickly.

The extra tension vanished as male pride was apparently assuaged. "Certainly. Come with me."

Alone with Jin, Daulo had lost track of time a bit, and it was with mixed embarrassment and guilt that he led her down the empty corridors toward his father's office. Most of the household had retired to their chambers by now, and the corridors echoed oddly to their footsteps as they walked. *I should have returned her to her rooms half an hour ago,* he thought, hoping the heat rising to his cheeks wasn't visible. *Father will probably be angry with me.* For a moment he searched for an excuse to give Jin for changing his mind and getting her upstairs instead, but nothing occurred to him that didn't sound limp or contrived.

The guard at Kruin Sammon's door made the sign of respect as they approached. "Master Sammon," he said. "How may I serve you?"

"The messenger who came to my father—is he still within?" Daulo asked.

"No, he left a moment ago. Do you wish to speak to him?"

Daulo shook his head. "No, I seek to speak to my father."

The guard nodded again and turned to the intercom box. "Master Sammon: Daulo Sammon and Jasmine Alventin are here to see you." An inaudible reply and the other nodded. "You may enter," he said as the door's lock clicked open.

Kruin Sammon was seated at his desk, a stylus in his hand and an oddly intense look on his face. "What is it, my son?" he asked as Daulo closed the door.

"We saw from the courtyard that a messenger had arrived, my father," Daulo said, making the sign of respect. "I thought it might be news from Azras."

Kruin's face seemed to harden a bit more. "Yes, it was. Mayor Capparis has arranged housing for two people, and promises to facilitate your entrance into the work party whenever Mangus announces its formation."

"Good," Daulo said, feeling his eyebrows come together in a frown. His father's expression . . . "Is anything wrong, my father?"

Kruin licked his lips and seemed to take a deep breath. "Come here, Daulo," he sighed.

A hollow feeling settled into Daulo's stomach. Squeezing Jin's hand briefly, he left her side and stepped to his father's desk. "Read this," the elder Sammon said, handing him a piece of paper. His eyes slid away from Daulo's gaze. "I'd intended that it be delivered to you tomorrow morning, an hour before dawn. But now . . ."

Gingerly, Daulo accepted the paper, heart thudding in his ears. To have discomfited his father so . . .

DAULO:

IN MY MESSAGE TO MAYOR CAPPARIS THIS AFTERNOON I ALSO INFORMED HIM THAT THE YITHTRA FAMILY HAS DISCOVERED AN ARTIFACT FROM OFFWORLD. HE HAS INFORMED ME IN TURN THAT MY MESSAGE HAS BEEN FORWARDED TO THE SHAHNI, WHO WILL BE SENDING A FORCE TO QUESTION THE YITHTRA FAMILY AS TO THEIR REASONS FOR NOT INFORMING THEM ABOUT THIS ARTIFACT THEMSELVES.

YOU AND JASMINE MOREAU WILL NEED TO LEAVE AS SOON AS IS PRACTICAL—TOO MANY PEOPLE OUTSIDE OUR HOUSEHOLD HAVE SEEN HER FOR HER TO REMAIN HIDDEN HERE. A CAR HAS BEEN PREPARED FOR YOU, CONTAINING ALL THE SUPPLIES YOU SHOULD NEED FOR A WEEK IN AZRAS. MAYOR CAPPARIS HAS OFFERED YOU THE USE OF HIS GUEST HOME WHILE YOU WAIT FOR MANGUS TO BEGIN ITS HIRING.

BE CAREFUL, MY SON, AND DO NOT TRUST JASMINE MOREAU MORE THAN YOU MUST.

KRUIN SAMMON

Daulo looked from the paper to his father. "Why?" he asked, dimly aware that his heart was thudding in his ears.

"Because it was necessary," Kruin said simply. But the look in his eyes belied the confidence of the words.

"You had no right, my father." Daulo could hear a tremor in his voice; could feel his face growing hot with shame. *The Sammon family is a family of honor*—he'd said those words to Jin not half an hour ago. *We've sworn protection to you* . . . "We had a bargain with Jasmine Moreau. One which she has not broken."

"And which I've not broken, either, Daulo Sammon. You've known you'll need to go to Azras eventually. Now it'll simply be sooner than we'd expected."

"You swore not to betray her—"

"And I have not!" Kruin snapped. "I could have told Mayor Capparis everything about her; but I didn't. I could have kept from you both the knowledge that the Shahni were sending investigators; but I didn't."

"Fancy words do not hide truth," Daulo bit out. "And the truth is that you swore to her the protection of our house. Now you drive her from both our house and our protection."

"Take care, Daulo Sammon," his father warned. "Your words are dangerously lacking in respect."

"My words echo my thoughts," Daulo shot back. "I'm ashamed for my family, my father."

For a long moment the two men stared at each other in silence; and it was almost a shock for Daulo to hear Jin's voice come from close beside him. "May I see the paper?" she asked calmly.

Wordlessly, he handed it to her. *And now the world ends*, the thought came distantly to him. *The vengeance of a demon warrior betrayed.* The memory of the headless corpse of the razorarm she'd killed brought bile into his throat . . .

It seemed a long time before she lowered the note and looked Kruin in the face. "Tell me," she said quietly, "would the Yithtra family have kept the pod secret for long?"

"I doubt it," the elder Sammon said. His voice was even . . . but Daulo could see a trace of his own fears in his father's eyes. "As soon as they've gained all the secrets they can from the pod, they'll alert the Shahni themselves."

"Within the week, you think?"

"Probably sooner," Kruin said.

She looked at Daulo. "You agree?"

He worked moisture back into his mouth. "Yes. Doing that would still gain them favor in the eyes of the Shahni and yet let them have first look at anything of value."

She turned back to Kruin. "I understand," she said. "In other words, as you said, it was inevitable that I would eventually be chased out of Milika anyway."

Daulo suddenly realized he was holding his breath. "You . . . I don't understand. You're not angry?"

She turned back to him . . . and he shrank within himself from the smoldering fire in her eyes. "I said it was inevitable," she ground out, "and that I understood. I *didn't* say I wasn't angry. Your father had no right to do such a thing without consulting me first. We could have left this afternoon and been safely hidden away in Azras by now. As it is, if we wait until dawn we stand a fair chance of being trapped in Milika. By then they'll not only be swarming around Milika, but they'll also have aircraft flying around looking for the wrecked shuttle. *And* they'll have roadblocks set up." She looked at Daulo. "Which means we leave tonight. Now." She seemed to study him. "Or at least *I* have to leave. You can stay if you want to."

Daulo gritted his teeth. Under normal conditions, a supreme insult to suggest he would go back on his word. Under these conditions, it was no more than he deserved. "I said I would go with you, Jasmine Moreau, and I will." He looked at his father. "Have the supplies you mentioned been assembled yet?"

"They're already in the car." Kruin pursed his lips. "Daulo—"

"I'll try and send word when the work party is formed," Daulo interrupted him, not especially in the mood to be polite. "I hope you'll at least be able to stall any investigations into Jasmine Moreau's identity until then."

The elder Sammon sighed. "I will," he promised.

Daulo nodded, feeling a bitterness in his soul. His father's promise . . . a word that had always seemed to him as immutable as the laws of nature. To see that word deliberately broken was to lose a part of himself.

And all of it because of the woman at his side. A woman who was not only not a Sammon, but was in fact an enemy of his world. It made him want to cry . . . or to hate.

Clenching his teeth, he took a deep breath. *We've sworn protection to you*, they'd said to her, *and we'll stand by that bargain. No matter what.* "Come, Jin," he said aloud. "Let's get out of here."

Chapter 28

In the daytime, Jin knew, it took about an hour to drive from Milika to Azras. At night, with Daulo taking it a little easier, it took half again that long, with the result that it was just about midnight when they crossed the Somilarai River and drove on into the city.

"So now what?" Jin asked, peering with some nervousness down the largely deserted streets. The last thing she wanted was for them to be conspicuous.

"We go to the apartment Mayor Capparis is lending us, of course," Daulo said.

"Did he send you the key, or are we going to have to wake up someone?"

"He sent the combination," Daulo told her. "Most temporary homes in Azras use keypad locks. That way all you have to do is change the combination when the occupants leave."

Which was basically the same system the Cobra Worlds used. "Oh," Jin said, feeling a little silly.

They passed the center of town and continued into the eastern part of the city, pulling up at last in front of a large building very reminiscent of the Sammon family house in Milika. Unlike that structure, though, this one had been carved up into apartments which—judging from the size of theirs— weren't appreciably bigger than the two-room suite the Sammon family had given her. In that space were squeezed a tiny foodprep area, a living room, and a bedroom.

A single bedroom.

"Small wonder the city people resent us," Daulo commented, dropping his cases in a corner of the living room and taking a few steps to peer around the corners into each of the rooms. "The average worker in my family's service has a larger home than this."

"Must be lower-class housing," Jin murmured. A hundred ways to approach the issue occurred to her; but there was no point in cat-footing around it. "I see there's just one bed here."

For a long moment he just looked at her—not at her body, she noted, but into her face. "Yes," he said at last. "I really shouldn't have to ask."

"Qasaman women are that pliant?" Jin asked bluntly.

He pursed his lips. "Sometimes I forget how different you are. . . . No, Qasaman women aren't overly pliant; just realistic. They know that women don't function well without men . . . and as the heir to a powerful family, I'm not exactly someone they want to refuse."

A shiver of disgust ran up Jin's back. For just a second the polite veneer around Daulo had cracked, giving her a glimpse of something far less attractive beneath it. Rich, powerful, probably pampered, as well— he'd likely had life pretty much his own way since the day he was born. On Aventine that type almost always grew up into selfish, immature adults. On Qasama, with the pervasive male contempt for women, it would be far worse.

She shook the train of thought away. *It's a different culture,* she reminded herself firmly. *Assumptions and extrapolations may not be valid.* She'd seen his discipline in regards to the family business, after all; some of that must have seeped into his personal life, as well.

But whether it had or not, she had to lay down the ground rules right here and now. "So," she said coolly. "Does that mean you've taken advantage of your family's power to prey on young women who haven't got any choice in the matter?—and, worse, with the underlying hint that you might marry them someday? At least the razorarms are honest with their victims."

Daulo's eyes flashed with anger. "You know *nothing* about us," he spat. "Nothing about us, and even less about me. I don't use women as playthings; nor do I make promises I don't intend to keep. You of all people should know *that*—else why am I here?"

"Then there should be no problem," she said quietly. "Should there."

Slowly, the fire faded from Daulo's eyes. "So now it's you who toy with me," he said at last. "I risk my honor and position for you, and in return you stir up anger in me to drive away all other feelings."

"Was that the reason you agreed to come with me?" she countered. "And as long as you've brought it up, tell me: if I accepted your advances, wouldn't you some day wonder whether I had manipulated you that way?"

Daulo glared at her in silence for a moment. Then he sighed. "Perhaps I would have. But is it any better this way? Perhaps now you're manipulating me through the aura of mystery about you, an aura that might disappear if you showed an ordinary woman's behavior with a man."

Jin shook her head. "I'm not manipulating you, Daulo Sammon. You're helping me for the reasons of rational self-interest that we've already discussed. You're too intelligent to make decisions based on your hormones."

He smiled bitterly. "And so now you make it a point of honor for me to stay away from you. You play your games well, Jasmine Moreau."

"It's not a game—"

"It doesn't matter. The end result is the same." Turning his back on her, he stomped to the bags they'd brought in and began rummaging through them. "You'd best get some sleep; we'll need to rise early for worship." Pulling out a blanket, he strode to the living room couch and began tucking it in.

Worship? she wondered. *They never did that in Milika. Do the proper places only exist in the cities?* She opened her mouth to ask . . . but it didn't seem like a good idea to prolong the conversation. "I understand," she said instead. "Goodnight, Daulo."

He grunted in return. Pursing her lips, Jin turned and went into the bedroom, shutting the door behind her.

For a long minute she sat on the bed, wondering if perhaps she'd played the whole thing wrong. Would it really have been so bad to go ahead and accept his advances?

Yes, of course it would have . . . because she'd have been doing it for the wrong reasons. Perhaps to avoid having to argue the point with him, or to pay back his family for their hospitality, or even to cynically ensure his continued cooperation by bonding him emotionally to her.

Her Cobra gear provided her an arsenal of awesome weapons. She had no intention of adding her body to that list.

Daulo would understand someday, too. She hoped.

Daulo woke her shortly after sunrise, and after taking turns to clean up in the cramped bathroom they left the apartment and set off on foot down the street.

Azras by day was a strikingly different place than it had seemed the night before. Like the cities Jin's Uncle Joshua had seen on his visit to Qasama, the lower parts of Azras's buildings were painted with wild forest-pattern colors that seemed sometimes to throb with movement. Above the colors, the buildings were glistening white, demonstrating the kind of careful maintenance that bespoke either a healthy city budget, a strong civic pride, or both.

It was the people, though, that attracted most of her attention.

They were out in force—perhaps three hundred within sight—all walking the same direction she and Daulo were going. *All of them going to worship?* she wondered. "Where exactly are we going?" she asked Daulo quietly.

"One of the *sajadas* in the city," he told her. "Everyone—even visitors—are expected to go to worship on Friday."

Sajada. The word was familiar; and after a moment it clicked. Daulo had pointed out Milika's *sajada* to her on that first tour of the village, but at the time she'd still been posing as a Qasaman and had been afraid to ask what the place was. But then why had they never gone there . . . ? *Ah—of course.* Presumably this type of worship was a weekly event, and her only other Friday on Qasama had been spent flat on her back recovering from her crash injuries.

Which immediately brought up another problem: she hadn't the foggiest idea of what she was heading into, or how she'd be expected to behave once they got there. "Daulo, I don't know anything about how you worship here," she muttered.

He frowned at her. "What do you mean? Worship is worship."

There were several possible responses to that; she chose what she hoped was the safest one. "True, but form varies widely from place to place."

"I thought you learned everything about us from your father's trip here."

Jin felt sweat breaking out on her forehead. Walking through a crowd of Qasamans was hardly the time to be making even veiled references of this sort. "His hosts didn't show him everything," she murmured tightly. "Would you mind keeping your voice down?"

He threw her a brief glare and fell silent. *No*, she thought morosely, *he hasn't forgiven me yet for last night*. She just hoped his bruised ego would heal before he did something dangerous.

They reached the *sajada* a few minutes later, an impressive white-and-gold building that looked to be a scaled-up version of the one she'd seen in Milika—and now that she thought about it, almost identical with similar structures she'd spotted in the tapes from the previous mission. A conformity which, taken with Daulo's comment about worship being worship, implied a strong religious uniformity all across Qasama. A state-controlled religion, then? Or merely one that was independently pervasive? She made a mental note to bring up the subject if and when Daulo ever calmed down.

Joining the flow of people, they climbed the steps and headed inside.

"Well?" Daulo asked an hour later as they left the *sajada*. "What did you think?"

"It was like nothing I've ever experienced before," Jin told him honestly. "It was . . . very moving."

"Or primitive, in other words?"

His voice was heavy with challenge. "Not at all," she assured him. "Perhaps more emotional than I'm used to, but a worship service that doesn't touch the emotions is pretty much a waste of time."

A little of the stiffness seemed to go out of his back. "Agreed," he nodded.

The crowds heading home seemed to be thinner than they had been on the way into the *sajada*, Jin noticed,

and she asked Daulo about it. "Most of them will have
stayed at the *sajada* with their *heyats*," he told her.

"*Heyats?*"

"Groups of friends and neighbors who meet for further worship," he explained, throwing her an odd look.
"Don't you have anything like that on—at home?" he
amended, glancing around at the scattering of other
pedestrians within earshot.

"Well . . . they're not called *heyats*, anyway," she
said, thinking hard. It was evident the Qasamans took
their religious expression very seriously. If she was
going to win Daulo back as a more or less willing ally
again, she had better find an answer that emphasized
the similarities between Qasaman and Aventinian worship and minimized the differences. "But as you said
earlier, worship is worship," she continued. "Only our
style is different. The intent is certainly the same."

"I understand that. It's the style I'm trying to find
out about."

"But style isn't really what counts . . ." She trailed
off as something ahead caught her attention. "Daulo . . .
how obvious is it that we're not city people?"

They took another three steps before he answered.
"Those *ghaalas* up there, are they what you're worried
about?"

"I don't know that word," she murmured, "but if you
mean those teens leaning against the building, yes,
that's who I mean. Can they tell from our clothing that
we're from a village?"

"Probably," Daulo said calmly. "But don't let it worry
you. They won't bother us." He paused. "And if they
do, let me handle it. Understand?"

"Sure," Jin said. Her heart, already pounding in her
ears, picked up its pace a bit. The scruffy-looking
youths—seven of them, she counted—definitely had
their eyes on her and Daulo.

And were definitely drifting away from the wall onto
the walkway. Moving to block their path.

Chapter 29

A drop of sweat ran down between Jin's shoulderblades. *Cross the street,* she wanted to urge . . . but she knew full well what Daulo's reaction would be. She might as well suggest they turn and run back to the *sajada* for sanctuary.

At least none of the youths blocking the walkway appeared to be armed. That was something, anyway.

"But if you have to fight," she murmured suddenly, "stay as far back from them as you can. Understand?"

He glanced at her; but before he could comment one of the youths swaggered a step forward.

"Hello there, baelcra-keeper," he said conversationally as she and Daulo stopped. "Your own *sajada* burn down last night or something?"

"No," Daulo replied with a touch of ice in his voice. "Though if we're going to mention the *sajada*, you don't seem to be dressed for a visit there."

"Maybe we went earlier," another youth said with a

sly grin. "Maybe you and your woman were too busy *pharpesing* to go then, huh?"

Another word the Troft translation tapes hadn't covered; but Daulo jerked as if he'd been stung. "And who'd know all about *pharpesing* better than *ghaalas* like you?" he snapped.

Insult traded for insult, clearly; but none of the toughs seemed especially disturbed. In fact, to Jin's eye they almost looked pleased by Daulo's reaction. As if they'd been deliberately trying to get him mad.

Which may have been exactly what they'd planned. At seven-to-one odds, picking a fight would be little more than a game to them. And a game with potentially rich rewards, too, if Daulo's clothing also identified his social and financial positions. It might not even take an overt robbery, in fact—depending on how Qasaman law was written, it was possible that if they could get Daulo to throw the first punch, they could claim damages from him. It could explain why the youths hadn't moved to encircle them: they might have to be able to claim afterwards that Daulo hadn't been threatened.

And in that case . . . there might just be something Jin could do to throw salt water on their little scheme.

". . . ought to slink back to your little drip-water village now and tend your *pharpesing* little women, okay?"

Beside her, Jin could feel Daulo trembling. Whatever the incomprehensible slang was they'd been tossing back and forth, he was tottering on the brink of losing control. Gritting her teeth, Jin took a deep breath. This was it—

"All right," she snapped, suddenly stepping forward. "That's just about enough of *that*. Get out of our way."

The toughs' jaws sagged with astonishment, instant proof that she had indeed just kicked the supports out from under their game plan. Picking a seven-to-one fight with a man was one thing; picking the same fight with a woman was something else entirely. Not even a financial settlement would make up for what a fiasco like that would do to their reputations.

"Shut your mouth, woman," the first youth snarled at her, his cheek twitching with obvious uncertainty. "Unless this *fhach*-faced friend of yours prefers hiding behind—"

"I said *get out of our way!*" Jin yelled. Raising her arms, she charged.

The move caught him totally flatfooted, and she'd slammed her shoulder into his ribs before he could even get his hands up to stop her.

It didn't hurt him, of course—she was taking enough of a chance here without exhibiting Cobra strength in the bargain. But the damage to his pride was all she could have hoped for. Snarling something incomprehensible under his breath, he grabbed her arms and thrust her into the grip of two of his companions—

And stepped past her just in time to catch Daulo's fist in his face.

The blow staggered him back. Daulo followed it with a punch to his solar plexus, knocking him to the ground. "Leave him alone!" Jin wailed as the two holding her arms pulled her back out of the way and the other four belatedly moved in to circle Daulo. The hands on her upper arms tightened their grip; crossing her arms across her chest, she reached up with opposite hands to press theirs against her arms.

Pinning them solidly in place.

One down, two out of the fight, she ticked off mentally. Daulo and his opponents were crouched in what seemed to be variants of the same fighting stance, the toughs continuing to circle as if unsure of whether or not they really wanted to take on the man who'd just decked their leader.

And then, almost in unison, they moved in.

Daulo knew enough about street fighting not to let all four reach him at the same time. He took a long stride to his left, flailing a wild punch at the youth on that side to force him back.

He seemed as surprised as anyone when the punch actually connected. Even more so when the youth went down and stayed there.

A second tough got within range and snapped a kick in Daulo's direction. Daulo leaped belatedly out of its way; but his move turned out to be unnecessary. The kick missed by at least twenty centimeters, and even as Daulo stepped forward to throw a countering punch, the youth lost his balance totally and toppled to the walkway.

It was enough for the other two. Backing away, they glanced at each other and at their two companions still holding—and being held against—Jin's arms. Then, turning, they took off down the walkway.

Daulo swung around to face Jin and her warders. "Well?" he demanded.

Jin recognized a cue when she heard it. She released her pressure grip on their hands, senses alert in case they tried something last-ditch foolish.

They didn't. Letting go of her, they sidled past Daulo and ran.

Daulo watched them go. Then, turning back to Jin, he looked her up and down. "You all right?" he asked at last.

She nodded. "You?"

There was a peculiar expression on his face. "Uh-huh. We'd better get out of here, before there are any awkward questions asked."

Jin glanced around. No one was approaching them, but several of the passersby were eyeing them from a healthy distance. "Right."

They'd covered another block before he finally asked the inevitable question. "What did you do to them?"

She shrugged uncomfortably. This could be extremely ticklish . . . "Well, for starters, I was hanging onto the ones who were holding my arms, keeping them out of the fight. The others . . . I gave them each a blast of focused ultrasonic in the head before you hit them."

"Which is why you wanted me to keep back, I suppose. And that knocked them out?"

"No, I didn't want to hit them that hard. I just gave them enough of a jolt to rattle their brains and throw their balance off track."

Walking closely beside him, she could feel his arm begin to tremble. *Uh-oh*, she thought tensely. *Too much for his Qasaman ego to take?* "Daulo? You okay?"

"Oh, sure," he said, a noticeable quaver in his voice. "I was just wondering what their friends are going to say when they hear about this. Seven of them, beaten right into the ground by a villager and a woman."

She frowned up at him . . . and only then realized that the trembling she heard and felt wasn't rage or shame.

It was suppressed laughter.

She fell silent after that . . . which gave Daulo the rest of the way back to their temporary home to try and figure out just why the whole thing was so funny.

On one level, it shouldn't have been—that much he was acutely aware of. For him to have been defended by a *woman* was something that should have him red-faced with shame, not shaking with laughter. Even if she *was* a demon-warrior woman, and even if the alternative *had* been to get himself beaten to blood-pulp.

No, he told himself firmly. *That's not the way to think of it. It's more like a couple of villagers putting one over on a bunch of jerkfaced city ghallas. Or a villager and a villager-by-adoption, anyway.*

The thought startled him. *Villager-by-adoption.* Was he really starting to think of Jin Moreau in such friendly terms? *No—impossible*, he assured himself. She was a temporary ally, temporarily under his protection as a

point of honor. Nothing more. In a few days her rescu-
ers would come, and she'd go, and he'd never see her
again.

And he wondered—though not very hard—why that
thought finally stilled the laughter within him.

"Are all the formalities over for the day?" she asked
as they reached the apartment. "I'd like to change
clothes."

"They're over at least until sundown," Daulo told
her, keying the lock and opening the door. "And that
service is optional."

"Good," she said, stepping inside. "I think it must be
a basic human failing not to be able to come up with
formal clothing as comfortable as day-to-daywear—what's
that light?"

"Phone message," Daulo explained, frowning. Who
might have known to call them here? Walking over to
the instrument, he keyed for the message.

The phone beeped, and a thin strip of paper slid out
from the message slot. "What?" Jin asked.

"It's from Mayor Capparis," Daulo told her, reading
it quickly. "He says Mangus has called for a work
party to be assembled at the city center this Sunday
morning."

"How do they pick the workers?"

Daulo skimmed the paper. "Looks like it's on the
basis of need. Unemployed and poor first, based on city
records—"

"Wait a second," she interrupted him. "Aren't
they even going to try and contact any of the workers
they've had out there before? Ones they've already
trained?"

"Maybe they already have."

"Oh. Right."

"Um. Mayor Capparis recommends we stick to the
marketplaces' second-booths when we pick up city-style
clothing."

Jin nodded. "Good idea. What about those city records, though? How are we going to fake that?"

Daulo shrugged. "Presumably Mayor Capparis will take care of that."

"Um." Jin stepped toward him. "May I see the message?"

He handed the paper over. She gazed at it for what seemed to be an unnecessarily long time. "You having trouble reading it?" he asked at last.

"No," she said slowly. "I was just wondering . . . It's addressed to you. By name."

"Of course it is. So?"

"So doesn't it strike you as odd that those toughs just happened to be hanging around directly between the *sajada* and here?"

He frowned. "I don't see the problem. You're the one who pointed out we were dressed in villagers' clothing. They were just after some fun."

"Maybe." She chewed at her lip, an annoying habit of hers. "But suppose for a moment that there was more to it than that. Suppose that whoever it is who doesn't want villagers snooping around inside Mangus found out we were going to try for one of their work parties."

"That's ridiculous," Daulo snorted. "How would they find out . . ." He trailed off, eyes dropping to the paper still in her hand. "Mayor Capparis wouldn't tell them," he said flatly.

"I'm not suggesting he did," Jin shook her head. "But this message presumably came from his office. Couldn't someone there have found out about it, either before or after it was sent?"

Daulo gritted his teeth. It *wasn't* all that farfetched, unfortunately. If one of the mayor's enemies had gotten wind of the scheme, putting them into the hospital would be a safe and simple way for him to thwart it. "It's possible, I suppose," he admitted aloud to

Jin. "But if you're suggesting we pick up and run, forget it."

"We don't have to run," she said. "Just move. Find somewhere else, where no one—including Mayor Capparis—knows where to find us."

"We still have to show up at the city center," he pointed out.

"True. But there's nothing much we can do about that."

"Then what's the point of hiding now?" he countered. "All it does is buy us a couple of days."

"A couple of days can mean a lot. Among other things, it gives us more time to prepare."

She was right; and down deep he recognized that. But on the surface, his honor had surged once again to the fore. "No," he shook his head. "I'm not running. Not without better proof than that."

She took a deep breath, and he braced himself for an argument. "Then the deal's off," she said bluntly.

He blinked with surprise. "What?"

"I said the deal's off. You might as well head back to Milika right now, because I'm going into Mangus alone."

"That's ridiculous. I'm not letting you do something that—that—" He shut up, realizing with annoyance he was starting to sputter. "Besides, what do we have to worry about? With your powers—"

"My powers are designed to protect *me*," she cut him off. "Not friends or people around me; just me. And if you're not going to cooperate, I can't take the risk of something happening to you."

"Why?" he snarled. "Because my father would call the Shahni down on your head?"

"Because you're my friend," she said quietly.

For a moment he just glared at her, feeling his arguments melt and drain away. "All right," he gritted at last. "I'll offer you a compromise. If you can prove we're under direct attack, I'll agree to anything you say."

She hesitated, then nodded. "Fair enough. Well . . . let's see. I suppose the best way to start would be for you to call up Mayor Capparis's office and leave a message telling him that we're moving to a new place. We won't really be going anywhere," she hastened to add, "but if there's an informant there, he'll get the word out to his fighters. Then we can find a place on the sidelines and watch what happens. If anything."

He clenched his teeth, trying without success to find some grounds on which to object. Then, silently, he stepped to the phone.

Mayor Capparis wasn't in, of course, probably still meeting with one of the *heyats* at his own *sajada*. Leaving the message, he hung up and turned back to Jin. "Okay. Now what?"

"Now we load everything back in the car and drive off as if we're leaving," she told him. "We need to go out and buy some city-style clothes, anyway. First, though, we'll want to find some place near here that would be a plausible hiding place."

"Easy enough," Daulo grunted, stepping over to where he'd laid out his clothing the night before. "We just look for an apartment whose door has no protector."

"Protector?"

"Yes," he said. "The traditional carved medallions every household places near their doors to protect them from the evil eye. Didn't you notice the ones in Milika?"

He had the minor satisfaction of seeing her blush with chagrin. "No, I'm afraid I completely missed them," she admitted. "Well . . . good. That'll make the hunt easier, anyway."

"So what happens once we've found this empty apartment?"

She smiled lopsidedly. "With any luck, sometime tonight it'll be attacked."

And with that she disappeared into the bedroom. *No*, Daulo told himself firmly, *you don't want to know*. Swallowing, he returned to his packing.

Chapter 30

"You're actually going out in public like that?" Daulo asked.

Standing before the apartment's largest mirror, Jin took one last look at herself in her gray night-fighter garb and turned to face him. Seated on the couch, his hand rubbing restless patterns on the end table beside him, Daulo glared back with barely controlled distaste. "If it's the outfit that offends you," she said coolly, "you'd better get used to it. From what you've told me it sounds like Mangus will be hiring mainly men for their work party, and if I'm going to get in it'll have to be disguised as a man."

He growled something under his breath. "This whole thing is ridiculous. Even if someone *was* out to get us, what makes you think they fell for that little game of yours? Suppose, for starters, they haven't noticed that that's our car parked outside the other apartment?"

"I told you one of those toughs was watching when we drove off this morning," she reminded him, pulling her full-face mask from the back of a chair and fitting it on. "You have to make it a *little* hard for them, Daulo— everyone gets suspicious of prizes handed over on silver platters."

"It'll serve you right if they're too stupid to catch your subtleties," he snorted. "Then while you're out there watching an empty apartment, they'll break in here instead."

"That's why you're going to have this," she told him, pulling a small cylinder from her belt and handing it over. "Short-range signaller—flip the top cap back and push the button if you're in trouble. I'm only going to be two blocks away; I can be here before you've stopped insulting each other."

Sighing, he took the device. "I just hope all this is nothing but a fever-trick of your imagination."

"I hope so, too," she admitted, scooping up the pack she'd prepared and settling it onto her shoulders. "But if it isn't, then tonight is the obvious time for them to strike."

"I suppose so. Well, at least we'll know one way or another by morning."

Probably a lot sooner than that, Jin thought. "Right. Well, I'm off. Lock the door behind me, and don't be afraid to signal if you hear anything suspicious. Promise?"

He managed a smile. "Sure. You watch yourself, Jin Moreau."

"I will." Activating her optical enhancers, she cracked open the door and looked outside. No one was in sight. Slipping out, she closed the door behind her and headed off down the street.

She'd been ensconced in her chosen place of conceal-ment, halfway under an outside stairwell, for barely an hour when they showed up: the same seven toughs who'd accosted her and Daulo on the street that morning.

And it was quickly clear they weren't total amateurs at this. Moving silently down the deserted street, tak-

ing advantage of shadows and cover, they approached
the vacant apartment from both directions. Two stopped
at the car, presumably making sure no one was watching from there, before joining the rest at the apartment
door. One crouched over the lock, and after a few
seconds swung it open. Moving quickly, the group filed
inside the darkened apartment.

They probably hadn't even realized yet that the place
was deserted when she caught up with them; and it was
for certain that none of them had a chance to shout
before her disruptor's ultrasound washed over them
from close range, hammering them into instant unconsciousness. They dropped into seven heaps on the floor
and lay still.

Jin nearly wound up joining them. For a long minute
she staggered against the wall, gripping her stomach
and fighting to keep her balance. Layn had warned
them about the dangers of using sonics in such enclosed
spaces; but there had been no other way to silently
disable the toughs without killing them. And questions of ethics apart, with the Shahni now aware that
there was an outworlder on Qasama, leaving laser-ridden
corpses lying around would be about as clever as standing up at the *sajada* and identifying herself as a demon
warrior.

Eventually, the throbbing in her head and gut faded
away, and she set about tying up the would-be assail-
ants with rope from her pack. That accomplished, she
stepped to the door again and scanned the street. Still
no one in sight, and she gave silent thanks that Azras's
night life shut down so early in the evening. With a
little luck, she might get back to the apartment in time
to get at least a few hours' sleep.

Thoughts of the apartment reminded her of Daulo;
Daulo, who still didn't believe they were under deliberate attack. Pulling her signaller from her belt, she
flipped back the lid . . . and paused. True, she could
show him evidence that the toughs had indeed tried it

again, but given the Qasaman sense of personal honor, they might conceivably have launched this second attack entirely on their own. What she needed was some kind of admission from one of them as to who had put them up to this job.

And until she had such a confession, there was no point in dragging Daulo out here. Putting the signaller back, she returned to the unconscious youths. Assuming the one who'd thrown the first challenge this morning was the leader . . . locating him, she hoisted him to her shoulder and carried him across the street to the car. It would have been nice to have a supply of those sophisticated interrogation drugs they were always using in the telvide fictions, but in their absence she would just have to fall back on one of the more traditional methods. And for that, she was going to need a little more privacy.

Starting the car, she headed off through Azras's deserted streets.

The knock on the door jolted Daulo awake, and for a disoriented heartbeat he stared in confusion at the darkened ceiling. Then it clicked. "Coming," he growled, getting stiffly out of the chair where he'd fallen asleep. Jasmine Moreau, returning from her little hide-seek game—and the stupid woman had managed to forget the door's combination. *If this is the kind of people who become Cobras*, he thought sourly as he straightened his tunic and stomped to the door, *we haven't got much to worry about*. The knock came a third time; "I'm coming," he snarled and threw open the door.

Three men stood there: one middle-aged, the other two much younger. Their city-style clothing was all similar; their grim faces were almost identical. "Are you Daulo Sammon of the village Milika?" the middle-aged man asked.

Daulo got his tongue working. "I am," he nodded. "And you?"

"May we come in?"

It wasn't really a question. Daulo stepped aside and the three filed into the room, the last flicking on the light as he passed the switch. "And you are . . . ?" Daulo asked again, squinting as his eyes tried to adjust to the sudden light.

The door was closed with a thud, and when Daulo could see clearly again he found the middle-aged man standing in front of him, holding out a gold-rimmed pendant from around his neck. "I am Moffren Omnathi; representing the Shahni of Qasama."

Daulo felt an icy shiver run up his back. "I am honored," he managed through stiff lips, making the sign of respect. "How may I serve you?"

Omnathi's eyes flicked around the room. "Your father, Kruin Sammon, sent the Shahni a message through Mayor Capparis of the city Azras yesterday. Do you know the content of this message?"

"Ah . . . in a general way, yes," Daulo said, wishing he knew what, if anything, his father had told this man. "He said he was going to inform the Shahni that the Yithtra family had discovered an offworld artifact."

"Essentially correct," Omnathi nodded casually. "Do members of the Yithtra family find such artifacts regularly?"

Daulo frowned. "No, of course not, sir."

"Oh? An unusual event, then?"

"Most certainly."

"An event most people would think worth staying to see?"

Daulo fought to keep his expression neutral as he finally saw the net the other was weaving. "I suppose most people would, yes."

"Yet you chose to come to Azras instead. Why?"

A drop of sweat trickled between Daulo's shoulder-blades. "I had an errand to perform here."

"One that couldn't wait a few days?"

One of Omnathi's companions emerged from the bedroom and stepped to the older man's side. "Yes?" Omnathi asked without taking his eyes off Daulo.

"Nothing but some of his own clothing," the other reported. "Certainly nothing a woman would wear or use."

Omnathi nodded, and Daulo thought he saw a brief flicker of annoyance cross his face. "Thank you," Omnathi told the other. "You see now, Daulo Sammon, that we're aware you didn't come to Azras alone. Where is the woman you brought here?"

Two blocks over, the thought flashed through Daulo's mind, and his stomach tightened with the realization that she could wander back at any time. "I really don't know where she is—"

"Why not?" the older man snapped. "According to Mayor Capparis, your father asked him to get you and an unnamed companion into some sort of work party. Was this woman to be your companion?"

"Of course not," Daulo said, trying for a combination of amusement and insult at the very idea. "I had planned to ask my brother to go to Mangus with me, but decided against it when this other matter came up."

He watched Omnathi, holding his breath, but the mention of Mangus didn't spark any reaction he could see. "You didn't tell Mayor Capparis about your change in plans. For that matter, we were rather surprised to find you here, since you'd told him you were moving elsewhere."

Daulo shrugged. "I thought that Mangus might have a listening ear in Mayor Capparis's office," he said, adopting Jin's theory for lack of anything better to say. "I thought if they were watching for two people instead of one, I might have a better chance of getting in."

Omnathi's forehead creased slightly. "You sound like you're preparing to assault an armed camp. What do you want with Mangus, anyway?"

Daulo hesitated. "I don't believe the place is what it seems," he said.

Omnathi flicked a glance to one of his aides. "Tarri?"

"Mangus is a private manufacturing center about fifty kilometers east of here," the other said promptly. "High-quality electronics, both research and manufacture. Run by the Obolo Nardin family; I believe the last full check by the Shahni was carried out approximately two years ago. No hints then of any unusual activity."

Omnathi nodded and turned back to Daulo. "You have recent evidence to dispute that last?"

Daulo drew himself up a bit. "They refuse to allow villagers in," he said stiffly. "For me, that's adequate reason to be suspicious."

Omnathi's lip twisted. "Hard though it may be for you to understand, city-bred prejudices are often as ridiculous as those of villagers," he growled. "At any rate, you'd do better to save your pride for more important matters—the safety and protection of your world, for example. Tell us what you know about the woman."

"She told me her name was Jasmine Alventin," Daulo said, again wishing he knew what they'd learned from his father. "We found her on the road, injured, and brought her into our house."

"And . . ."

"And she told us she was from Sollas and that she'd been in an accident. That's all."

"Didn't you think it advisable to press for further details?" Omnathi persisted. "Or even to check up on her story?"

"Of course we did," Daulo said, trying to sound offended. "We sent men out to search the roads for her car and companions."

"Did you find them?"

"No." Daulo glanced at the other two men, looked back at Omnathi. "What is this all about, anyway? Is she an escaped criminal or something?"

"She's an offworld invader," Omnathi said bluntly.

Daulo had expected him to ignore or evade the question; the very unexpectedness of the reply startled him almost as much as if he were hearing it for the first time. "She's—*what*?" he breathed. "But . . . that's impossible."

"Why?" Omnathi snapped. "You said yourself the Yithtra family had found an offworld artifact. Didn't it ever occur to you that an offworld artifact might be accompanied by someone to use it?"

"Yes, but . . ." Daulo floundered, hunting desperately for something to say. Jin's words just before she'd left popped back into his mind: *you have to make it a little hard for them, Daulo—everyone gets suspicious of prizes handed over on silver platters.* "But it was Jasmine Alventin who told us it was an offworld artifact in the first place," he said. "Why would she do that if it were hers?"

Omnathi frowned. "What do you mean? Told you how?"

"Well, when I heard there was a truck bringing something unusual into Milika I drove off to take a look," Daulo explained, trying to keep his voice and face under control. "Jasmine Alventin was with me at the time, and at a slow section of the road she suddenly got out of the car and climbed in the back of the truck to see what it was."

Omnathi seemed taken aback. "Your father didn't mention that," he said.

Daulo took a deep breath. "Well, actually . . . I believe I told him it was *I* who looked into the truck."

Omnathi's eyes were steady on him. "You *believe* you told him?"

Daulo licked his lips. "I . . . suppose I wanted to . . . take the credit."

For a long moment the room was silent. Omnathi and the others just looked at him, contempt showing in varying degrees in their expressions. "You told us you didn't know where the woman was," Omnathi said at last. "Why not?"

"Because she left me just after sundown," Daulo

said. "She said she was anxious to get back home and asked me where she could pick up a bus heading north. I took her to the waiting area at the city center and left her there."

"Did you, now." Slowly, Omnathi ran the tip of his tongue along his upper lip, gazing hard at Daulo. Daulo stared back, listening to his heart thudding in his chest. "Tell me," Omnathi said abruptly, "did you actually see her get on any of the buses?"

"Ah . . ." Daulo considered. "No, not really. She *was* walking toward the one for Sollas when I drove away, though."

One of the other men cleared his throat. "Shall I have the bus intercepted?" he asked.

"No," Omnathi said slowly. "No, I think that would be a waste of time. She didn't take that bus. Or any of the others."

Daulo blinked. "I don't understand—"

"Tell me, Daulo Sammon," Omnathi interrupted him. "Where is your car?"

"Uh . . . just outside the building, in the parking area."

Omnathi shook his head. "No. In fact, it's nowhere for six streets around you. We looked for it."

Daulo's heart skipped a beat. He and Jin had left the vehicle parked in plain sight only two blocks away . . . "That's impossible," he managed. "I left it right outsi—"

"Do you have the keys?" Omnathi asked.

No; he'd given them to Jin in case she had some need of the vehicle while she was out. "Of course," he said. "They're on the table over there."

One of the men moved over to look. "No, they're not," he reported, sifting through the personal items Daulo had piled there.

"Find them," Omnathi ordered. "Have you been gone from this apartment since she left, Daulo Sammon?"

"No." Daulo watched as the two men began search- ing the room, feeling the sweat begin to gather on his forehead again. It was all very well to ease them toward the conclusion that Jin had stolen his car, but they weren't going to believe it unless he came up with a plausible mechanism for that theft. "I *was* asleep when you arrived, though—"

"What's this," one of the searchers interrupted him, holding up a small black cylinder.

The signaller Jin had given him.

"I . . . don't know," he said through stiff lips. "It's not mine."

"Be careful with it," Omnathi said sharply, stepping over to the other's side and taking the signaller from him. He studied it for a moment, then carefully lifted the top cap. *Push the button if you're in trouble, and I'll be there*, Jin had said . . .

But Omnathi made no move to do that. "Interesting," he murmured. "Looks like a radio transceiver of some kind—here's the antenna." He looked back at Daulo. "Did you tell her how to work the lock combination on the apartment door?" he asked.

"Uh . . . not directly, no. Though she might have seen me key it."

Omnathi nodded grimly. "I'm sure she did." He hefted the signaller in the palm of his hand. "Do you snore when you sleep, Daulo Sammon?"

The question took Daulo by surprise. "Ah . . . I really don't know. Perhaps a bit."

Omnathi grunted. "Doesn't really matter, I suppose. The sound of a sleeper's breathing is fairly distinctive to someone who knows what to listen for."

"Sir . . . I—"

Omnathi impaled him with a glare. "She planted this on you," he grated. "All she had to do was pretend to get on that bus, then follow you back and wait for you to fall asleep. Then she slipped in, took your keys, and left. Any idea how long you were asleep?"

Daulo shrugged, feeling a little dazed. They were

practically writing his alibi for him. "An hour, perhaps. Maybe longer."

Omnathi muttered something under his breath. "An *hour*. God in heaven."

Daulo licked his lips. "Sir . . . I don't understand any of this. What is Jasmine Alventin's interest in my family?"

"I don't think she has any interest in you whatsoever," the older man sighed. "She's simply been using you: first to help her recover from her spacecraft's crash, and after that to create a diversion."

"A diversion?"

"Yes." Omnathi waved toward the northwest. "Once she realized her discovery was inevitable, she simply took charge of the timetable, letting your father know about the supply pod in Yithtra family hands and perhaps encouraging him to notify the Shahni before they did. Then, while the focus of our attention was on her spacecraft and your village, she persuaded you to bring her here, distracted you further with a feint toward the bus, and proceeded to steal your car." He paused, eying Daulo thoughtfully . . . and when he spoke again his voice had taken on a hard edge. "But innocent victims or not, the Sammon family nevertheless has aided an enemy of Qasama. It's possible that you may yet be punished for that."

Daulo swallowed hard. "Yet we *did* inform the Shahni about the offworld artifact as soon as we knew about it," he reminded the other.

"That may weigh in your favor," Omnathi nodded. "Whether it does or not will depend on how quickly we capture this Jasmine Alventin. And what we learn from her."

He signaled his men, and they headed for the door. There, Omnathi paused and looked back. "Tell me, Daulo Sammon; your father said the woman asked many questions. Did she ask about anything specifically about our culture or technology?"

The question caught Daulo by surprise. "Uh . . . no, not that I can remember. Why?"

"It occurs to me that this penetration of Mangus might originally have been her idea."

"It wasn't," Daulo shook his head. "Getting into Mangus has been something I've wanted to do for a long time."

"Perhaps. Then again, perhaps the idea was yours and the timing hers." For a moment Omnathi gazed thoughtfully at him. "Very well, then. Satisfy your pride as you will, Daulo Sammon. But remember while you do so that your real enemies aren't in Mangus or anywhere else on Qasama."

Daulo bowed and made the sign of respect. "I will, Moffren Omnathi."

They left. Daulo stood where he was for a handful of heartbeats; then, moving carefully on weak knees, he wobbled to the window and peered out at the car's taillights pulling away down the street. An emissary of the Shahni themselves . . . and Daulo had lied through his teeth to him.

For an enemy of Qasama.

He spat an oath into the empty room. *Curse you, Jasmine Moreau,* he thought viciously. *For God's sake, be careful. Please.*

Chapter 31

The tough gasped as the ammonia fumes rose into his
nostrils and he returned abruptly to consciousness. "I'd
suggest you keep quiet," Jin advised him, making her
voice as deep and manly as she comfortably could.

He obeyed . . . but his eyes suddenly came wide
open as he got his first clear look around him. Jin
couldn't really blame him; sitting on the edge of a high
roof, with nothing between him and a long fall but two
thin ropes belaying his trussed wrists and ankles to a
stubby chimney five meters away, he had a perfect
right to be scared. In fact, she rather admired his
self-control in not screaming his head off. "Let's start
with your name, shall we?" she said, squatting down
beside him.

"Hebros Sibbio," he managed, eyes focused on his
lifelines.

"Look at me when I speak to you," Jin ordered. He
did so, eyes almost unwillingly shifting up to her masked

face. "That's better. Now tell me who told you to break into the apartment you hit tonight."

"I . . . no one," he said, his voice cracking slightly.

Jin sighed theatrically. "Perhaps you don't fully understand the situation here, Hebros Sibbio," she said coldly. "Your hairy butt is hanging well past the edge there. All I have to do is cut these two ropes and you'll be off to explain all this to God instead of to me. You think He'll be more lenient with you?" He shuddered and shook his head. "Neither do I," she agreed. "So tell me who put you up to this job."

"I don't know!" he gasped. "As God is my witness, I don't *know*. A man—he didn't give his name—called me up this morning and told me he wanted us to beat up a village man who would be at an apartment at Three-forty-six Kutzko Street."

"And kill him?"

"No! We don't kill—not even villagers. I wouldn't have agreed if that had been the bargain."

"Keep your voice down. What *was* the bargain, then? What payment did he promise you?"

Sibbio shivered again. "There was to be no payment. He promised only not to reveal some of our other . . . activities to the rulers of Azras."

"Illegal activities?"

"Yes. And he named some of them . . ." He trailed off, staring pleadingly at her. "It's the truth—I swear by God's presence it is."

Blackmail, then . . . which unfortunately eliminated the chance of backtracking a payment drop. "Did he tell you the villager's name, or say *why* he wanted him beaten up?"

"No."

For a moment the rooftop was silent as Jin considered. If Sibbio was telling the truth, it meant his mystery caller had at least a passing familiarity with Azras's underworld and its activities. At the same time, paradoxically, that knowledge must be fairly limited for him to have picked such an obviously small-time group as Sibbio's to handle his dirty work.

Unless this was as well organized as Azras's criminal underworld got. She made a mental note to check with Daulo on that one.

Either way, Sibbio was clearly a dead end. "There's a small knife by the chimney over there," she pointed, getting to her feet. "You can roll or otherwise work your way over to it and cut yourself free. Your friends are still at the apartment you broke into; collect them and all of you get out of Azras."

Sibbio's mouth fell open. "Get out . . . but this is our home."

"Too bad," Jin said, letting her voice harden. "Because for the next few days it'll be *my* home, too . . . and if I see you again while I'm here, Hebros Sibbio, you'll be taking that premature trip to see God that we discussed earlier. Understood?"

He nodded up at her, a single nervous motion of his head. Jin didn't especially like threatening the boy, but she liked the thought of him talking to Mangus even less. "Good. Let's both hope I never see you again."

Moving quietly across the roof, she reached the stairwell that she'd brought Sibbio up by and opened the door. He would make it to the knife, eventually, unless he lost his balance first and fell off the roof. As far as she was concerned, it didn't much matter what happened.

Nevertheless, she waited silently at the open door until he was safely away from the roof's edge.

She was two blocks from their apartment, visions of a soft bed hovering siren-like in front of her eyes, when she spotted the two cars parked at the building.

Instantly, she shut off the lights and pulled over to the curb, keying in her optical enhancers' telescopic and light-amp capabilities as she did so. Both cars were empty, but—she flipped briefly to infrared—the tires

and drive shafts were still warm. And though her angle
was bad, it looked very much like the lights in their
apartment were on.

A cold chill ran up her spine. From what she'd seen
of both village and city life, midnight visitors weren't
exactly commonplace on Qasama. Could they be mes-
sengers from Milika, perhaps, bringing news from Daulo's
father?

Or had Mangus hired a back-up set of muscle?

Jin cursed under her breath and started the car forward again. The direct route through the front door was
out, of course—even if it was something as innocuous as
a message from home, there was no plausible excuse
she could think of as to why she, a woman, would be
out alone at night. And if Daulo was in trouble, she had
no intention of walking straight into his attackers' arms,
anyway.

But there were always more indirect routes to be
had . . .

She pulled around the next corner, parking the car a
block away in a handy row of similar vehicles. Keeping
to the shadows, enhanced senses alert for trouble, she
made her way back to the apartment building, arriving
at the side opposite to theirs within a couple of minutes. The building didn't offer much in the way of
handholds, but she didn't have time for a long climb,
anyway. Taking one last look around, she bent her
knees and jumped.

She made it onto the roof without any sound louder
than a slight scraping of shoes on roof tiles. Crossing it,
she squatted down at the edge and scanned the courtyard below for signs of life. There weren't any that she
could see. Not surprisingly; with no access to the courtyard from outside except through the individual apartments, there would be no reason for anyone to watch
the place once they'd established she wasn't hiding
there. Setting her jaw, she eased over the edge, scrab-

bled for handholds that weren't there, and dropped to the ground.

The downside landing wasn't nearly as quiet as the upside one had been, and for what seemed like a long time she crouched motionlessly, auditory enhancers at full power as she waited for some kind of reaction. But the inhabitants of Azras must have had the city dwellers' traditional ability to sleep through noise, and after a minute she rose and loped across the courtyard to the rear of their apartment.

Through the sliding glass door, she could see the diffuse glow of lights from either the foodprep area or living room. Unfortunately, that was *all* she could see—the arrangement of the rooms didn't allow a direct view into the front of the apartment. An ear pressed against the glass yielded nothing. *Into the valley of death, and all that*, she thought grimly; and, pointing her little finger at the door's lock, she fired a burst from her metalwork laser.

The crack and spitting of flash-vaporized metal seemed to thunder in her ears, but there was no reaction from inside. Sliding the door open a crack, Jin slipped inside, closing it behind her. From the living room ahead came the faint scraping of shoes on rug.

She held her breath and keyed her auditory enhancers to full power. The sound of breathing came to her . . . the sound of *one* person breathing.

So all the company's left? Apparently . . . but there was no point in taking chances. Curling her hands to rest her thumbs lightly against the triggers in her third-finger nails, she straightened her little fingers into laser firing position and stepped around the corner.

Daulo, standing at the window, spun around as if he'd been stung. "Jin!" he gasped, seeming to wilt. "God above, you startled me."

"Sorry," she apologized, glancing quickly around. Daulo was indeed alone. "I thought you might be in trouble," she added, dropping her hands back to her sides.

"I am," he sighed, walking unsteadily to the couch and sinking into it. "But you're in more. They know who you are."

"They who?" Jin asked, her heartbeat picking up again. "Mangus?"

"Worse. The Shahni." He hissed between his teeth. "I just had a visit from one Moffren Omnathi and two of his men. They've identified you as the outworlder they're looking for. I managed—maybe—to persuade them that you'd stolen my car and headed north toward Sollas."

Jin took a moment to digest that. She'd known it would happen eventually. But she hadn't expected it quite so soon. "Did you tell them we'd been working together?"

"Do I *look* stupid?" he snorted. "Of course not. I played the total innocent, telling them you were a stranger who'd talked me into bringing you to Azras and then disappeared. Fortunately—I guess—they found that signaller you left, and decided you'd used it to listen for me to go to sleep so you could sneak in and take my car keys."

Jin bet at her lip. "As good a theory as any, I suppose. I just hope they didn't make it up just to make you think they believed you."

"Well, they left, didn't they?"

"Maybe. Did you actually see them go?"

"I saw the car pull away, yes."

"*One* car? Because there were two here when I drove up."

Daulo muttered something under his breath and started to get to his feet. "Should I—?"

"No, don't look out," Jin stopped him. "If they spotted me coming in, it's too late. If they didn't, you don't want to seem unusually suspicious."

Daulo exhaled a ragged breath. "I thought they seemed too willing to believe me. God above. I hoped they were accepting my words because of my family's position."

"More likely they just weren't sure enough to arrest you. Or else backed off in hopes that you'd lead them to me." Jin glanced at the curtained window, wondering what devices the Qasamans might have for looking through cloth and glass. But if they were doing so, again it was already too late. "They didn't have any photos of me, did they?" she asked.

"Not that they showed me," Daulo shook his head. "Though it hardly matters. As my father pointed out, there were plenty of people in Milika who saw you."

"Well enough to provide the investigators with a good description?"

He threw her an odd look. "Using hypnotics? Of course."

Jin gritted her teeth. She should have realized they'd have something like that available—her father's mission had noted the Qasamans' penchant for mind-enhancement drugs. "Yeah, I forgot about those. Well, maybe the disguise paraphernalia in my pack will be enough."

"You're not going to stay in Azras, are you?"

"Not with the alert already out for your car," Jin shook her head. "I'll head out of town, try to find a place off the road to hide the car in. With luck I'll be able to stay with it until the work party is formed on Sunday. Let me take a set of that cheap city clothing we bought—"

"Hold it a second," Daulo interrupted her, eyes narrowing. "You're not still going to try to get in there, are you?"

"Why not? Unless you told our friend Moffren Omnathi that was what we were planning. Oh, my God," she interrupted herself as the name suddenly clicked.

"What?" Daulo asked sharply.

"Moffren." The name tasted sour on her tongue. "Moff. The man who played guide to our first survey mission, thirty years ago. And very nearly nailed it."

She shook her head. "Well, that's the end of the game for you, Daulo. First thing in the morning you find yourself a ride back to Milika and get out of here."

Daulo frowned at her. "Why? Just because the Shahni sent an old enemy of yours to ask me some questions?"

"No—because whatever pits there are in the story you told him, he'll find them," she retorted. "And when he does, he'll act. Fast."

"And you think running back to Milika will keep him from getting to me?"

Jin braced herself. "Of course not. But maybe it'll slow him down enough to let me get into Mangus."

For a long moment his eyes were steady on hers. "So that's what it comes down to, isn't it?" Daulo said at last. "Your mission."

Jin forced her jaw muscles to relax. "Would you have me run somewhere and hide?" she asked.

"Would you have *me* do so?" he countered quietly. "Would you have me go back to my father and tell him I gave up a chance to perhaps uncover a threat to our family because I was afraid?"

"But if they're watching you and you try to go into Mangus—"

"And if they're watching me and I try to run back to Milika?"

Again, they locked gazes. "Daulo, look," Jin sighed at last. "I know this isn't something a woman says to a man on Qasama . . . but I feel responsible for your safety. I talked you and your father into this scheme, after all, and if I can't be right at your side I may not be able to protect you."

"You didn't promise me any protection."

"Not to you, no. I *did* promise it to myself."

To her surprise, he smiled. "And I made a promise to *my*self, Jasmine Moreau: to protect you from your cultural ignorance while in Mangus. I can't do that from Milika."

"But—" Jin took a deep breath, sighed in defeat. She

simply didn't have time to argue the point any further. The longer she lingered here, the more time Moff would have to weave a net around Azras, and she had to get Daulo's car out of town before that happened. "Will you at least think about it? Please?"

He rose from the couch and stepped forward. "I will," he said softly, reaching out to take her hand. "You be careful, all right?"

"I will." She hesitated, looking up at his eyes. *Cultural differences*, she reminded herself distantly. *He might take this wrong*, but for once, she didn't care; the need to hold someone tightly was almost overpowering in its intensity. Leaning toward him, she put her arms around him.

He didn't pull away, nor did he attempt to make the hug into anything else. Perhaps with potential danger all around them, a simple nonsexual contact from a friend was something he needed right now, too.

For a minute they held each other tightly. Then, almost unwillingly, Jin pulled back. "You take care of yourself, too, okay?" she said. "And if you decide to stay . . . don't look for me in the work party."

He nodded, reaching up to stroke her cheek. "I understand. You'd better go now."

Three minutes later, the city clothing Daulo had given her knotted into a bundle on her back, she was back at the car. No one lay in wait near the vehicle; no one jumped out of the shadows or shot at her as she climbed in and drove away. Either the Shahni's people hadn't gotten the Azras part of their operation fully organized yet, or else Moff was growing careless in his old age. Personally, she wouldn't bet much money on the latter.

But for the time being she appeared to have gained a little breathing space, and she was determined to use it to the fullest. A few kilometers south of Azras—an adequate gap between trees in the forest—and she would have a place to hide for the next day and a half.

A little face-shaper gel from her pack, perhaps a wig
and some skin darkening, and she'd be able to walk into
Azras Sunday morning without being recognized. And
after that . . .

But there was no point in trying to think too far
ahead. With Qasama's official government actively in
the game, she had to be ready to play every move by
ear. And hope that her Moreau family heritage counted
for something besides just a name.

Chapter 32

"Like this?" Toral Abram asked, shifting his left foot in front of his right.

"Right," Justin nodded. "Now just uncurl your legs and drop onto your back onto the floor, pulling your knees to your chest as you do so."

The young Cobra obeyed, and a second later was spinning around, belly-up, in an awkward-looking fetal position. "And this is a *military* maneuver?" he asked wryly as he came to a halt.

"Trust me," Justin assured him. "You try that with your antiarmor laser firing and you'll look *very* military."

"If there's anyone left nearby to see you," one of the other Cobras lined up against the walls muttered.

"That *is* the basic idea," Justin nodded as a nervous chuckle swept the room. "Okay, Toral, off the floor. Dario, your turn."

One of the other Cobras took Abram's place in the center of the room and got into ready position. "Ceiling flip," Justin ordered; and a second later the *Dewdrop*

265

shook as the Cobra jumped upward, bounced feet-first off the ceiling, and landed a handful of meters away from his starting point.

"One of these days," a voice at Justin's elbow muttered, "one of you is going to kick a hole in the deck doing that."

"Hello, Wilosha," Justin nodded to the middle-aged man who'd slipped unnoticed into the room. "Just can't get enough of the show, can you?"

"Watching the ship's structural integrity beaten into rubble always gives me a thrill," Second Officer Kal Wilosha retorted. "Haven't you practiced these more violent maneuvers enough?"

"No, but unfortunately we don't have the time to do it right." Justin raised his voice. "Okay, Dario, nice job. Don't forget to keep your hands up when you land so that you'll be able to fire if you need to. Now give the backspin a try."

"Yes, sir."

He did marginally better than Abram had. "Again," Justin ordered. "Remember that your nanocomputer will do a lot of the work on these basic maneuvers if you'll let it. Just get things started, relax, and let your body take it from there."

Dario nodded and set himself for another try. Beside Justin, Wilosha hissed through his teeth. "Problem?" Justin asked him.

"Just . . . wondering."

"What about?" This time Dario did better.

"Oh . . . Cobras." Wilosha waved his hand vaguely. "The nanocomputers, if you insist on specifics. Has it ever occurred to you that no one on the Cobra Worlds really knows anymore just exactly how the things are programmed?"

"I don't let it worry me," Justin told him. "The Academy supervises every step of the nanocomputer manufacture."

"Oh, right. So they supervise a bank of automated

circuitry replicators—what does that prove? Does a list or printout exist anywhere showing *exactly* what the nanocomputers are or are not capable of?"

"What are you worried about, that the Dominion of Man may have planted a program bomb?" Justin asked quietly. The conversation, he noted, was beginning to attract his students' attention.

"No, of course not," Wilosha shook his head. "But there doesn't have to be deliberate malice involved to make something dangerous."

Justin looked at him for a long moment. It would serve the man right to expose him here and now, in front of a roomful of Cobras . . . but it would be a childish trick, and Justin was long past the age for childish tricks. "Cobras, take a break," he called. "Be back in fifteen minutes."

The others filed out without comment or question, and a minute later Justin and Wilosha were alone. "I hope it wasn't something I said," Wilosha commented, his voice almost light but his expression tight and wary.

"Just wanted a little peace and quiet," Justin told him, and threw a punch at the other's face.

Wilosha could never have evaded a serious attempt to hit him, not with Justin's Cobra servos driving the punch. But his reflexes tried their best, throwing his arm up in front of his face . . . and because Justin had his audio enhancers on and knew what to listen for, he caught the faint whine of servos from the other's arm.

"What the hell was *that* all about?" Wilosha snarled, taking a hasty step back toward the wall.

Justin made no move to follow. "Just showing you how easy it is for a Cobra to identify a Ject. Even with the restraints your nanocomputer puts on your servos, they still kick in to that limit when you react as quickly as you just did."

Wilosha's lip twisted. "A great technique, for sure. I can just see you walking down the streets of Capitalia throwing punches at everyone you pass. You could have just asked me, you know."

"Asked you what? I already knew what you were. This was just to prove to you that I knew."

"Of course. You probably had me spotted ever since we lifted, right?"

Justin snorted gently. "No. Only since you started showing up at every other practice with your mouth spitting venom and your eyes looking envious. What conclusion would *you* have come to?"

"I don't envy you," Wilosha snapped. Too quickly. "I come to your workouts to keep an eye on you—nothing more."

"Keep an eye on us for what? What is it about us that you're so afraid of?"

Wilosha took a deep breath. "I don't think this is the right time for a debate, Moreau. So you might as well get your team back in here and continue—"

He broke off as Justin took a long step toward the door, blocking the other's quiet move in that direction. "Actually, Wilosha, I think this is an excellent time for a debate," he told the other coldly. "Or at least for a little chat. There are some things I'd like to know, starting with why the hell you Jects are trying to make a lifelong career out of sour grapes."

For a moment Wilosha glared at him in silence. "You're not more than a couple of years younger than I am," he growled at last. "You must be feeling the first twinges of Cobra Syndrome arthritis. That's what the Lord High decision-makers of the Academy did to us: sentenced us to a premature death, and for nothing. Don't you think that's enough reason for us to be bitter?"

"No," Justin said flatly. "I'm sorry, but it's not. Nobody beat you over the head and forced you to apply to the Academy. You knew the risks going in; and if it didn't work out, then those are the breaks. Life requires certain sacrifices—on everyone's part. And as long as we're on the subject of premature deaths, you might recall all the Cobras who've died a hell of a lot younger than you are fighting spine leopards."

A muscle twitched in Wilosha's cheek. "I'm sorry. But it's not the ones who've died for Aventine that we object to."

"All of us have risked our lives," Justin reminded him. "You can't single out those who happen to have survived to vent your contempt at."

"It's not contempt," Wilosha insisted. "It's an honest and legitimate concern over the problems we see in the whole Cobra system."

Justin felt his stomach muscles tighten. "You sound like Priesly banging his fist over the net."

"So Governor Priesly's done the best job of putting it into words; so what?" Wilosha countered. "The point is still valid: that when you're on the outside looking in you get a different perspective on things. You Cobras see the prestige and physical power and political double vote; while we see the elitism and the arrogance that goes with absolute job security."

Justin favored him with a cold smile. "Absolute job security, hm? That's very interesting . . . especially given that that's exactly what Priesly's gotten out of you and the other Jects."

Wilosha blinked. "What are you talking about? The governorship isn't a permanent position."

"I wasn't talking about the governorship. I was referring to his status as head and chief speaker for a highly vocal political group. Think it through, Wilosha. Aventine can't simply get rid of the Cobras, for reasons you know as well as I do."

"We don't want to get rid of you, just alter your power structure to—"

"Just shut up and listen, will you? So all right; if the Cobras are always going to exist, why shouldn't an organization whose sole purpose in life is to oppose the Cobras do likewise?"

For a moment Wilosha stared at him. "Are you suggesting," he said at last, "that Governor Priesly started this whole movement solely to create a political base for himself?"

Justin shrugged. "You know more about the inner workings of your group than I do. *Is* that how he's using it? You might start by deciding whether or not you were this bitter about being rejected from the Cobra Academy before Priesly told you you ought to be."

"You're twisting the facts," Wilosha growled. But he didn't sound totally convinced. "Through Priesly we threaten your elite status, so of course you try to impugn his motives and activities."

"Perhaps," Justin said quietly. "But *I* didn't send someone charging into *his* office trying to make the Jects look like dangerous homicidal maniacs. Think about it, Wilosha. Do you really want to be on the side of a man who deliberately mangles truth in the name of political power?"

Wilosha snorted. "You're skating pretty close to slander," he said. "Unless you have some proof that that incident happened the way you claim it did. Some proof besides your brother's word, of course."

Justin felt disgust rising like bile in his throat. "Oh, for— " He took a breath, released it through clenched teeth. "Just get out of here, Wilosha. I haven't got time to waste arguing with someone who's already decided to let the party do his thinking for him."

Wilosha's face darkened. "Look, Moreau—"

"I said get out. We've got work to do."

The other opened his mouth, closed it again. Eyes on Justin, he sidled past the Cobra and out the door. The dull metal panel slid closed, and for a moment Justin stared at it, listening to his heartbeat slowly settle down and wondering if the talk had done any good at all. He could almost sympathize with Wilosha; the man was, after all, a would-be Cobra, and a strong sense of loyalty was high on the list of qualities the Academy screened its applicants for.

On the other hand, so were intelligence and integrity
. . . and if he'd knocked even some of the stars out of
Wilosha's eyes, the other might at least start watching
Priesly's moves and words more closely. And if he
found sufficient truth to the idea that Priesly was being
corrupted by his own power . . .

It might help blunt Priesly's power. But it wouldn't
help bring Jin back.

Clenching his teeth, Justin took a ragged breath.
She's alive, he told himself firmly. Just as he had through
the long and sleepless nights of the past four days. *She's
alive, and we're going to get her out of there.*

Stepping up to the door, he slid it open and stepped
out into the corridor. "Cobras!" he bellowed. "Break
time's over. Get back here—we've got a lot of work
ahead of us."

Chapter 33

The crowd milling around the Azras city center was large and noisy, composed mainly of youths and seedy-looking older men. Some, the younger ones especially, seemed to be radiating a combination of impatience and desperation, but in general the mood of the crowd was that of slightly bored normality. At one end, seated at a table, city officials took names of each of the would-be workers, keying them into portable computer terminals where the names were—presumably—ranked according to previous work history, skills, and other pertinent information. Working his way slowly toward the table in what the city dwellers probably considered a neat line, Daulo fought against his own nervousness and tried to look inconspicuous.

"Ah—Master Sammon," a voice came from behind him; and Daulo's heart skipped a beat. As casually as he could, he turned around. "Greetings, Master Moffren Omnathi," he nodded gravely, making the sign of respect and then shifting his eyes to the young man standing at Omnathi's side. "I greet you as well, Master . . . ?"

"I am Miron Akim," the other answered. "If you'd like, I'll be glad to hold your place in line while you and Master Omnathi confer."

Daulo swallowed hard; but before he could say anything, Omnathi had taken his arm and eased him out of line.

"You'll excuse this unorthodox approach, I hope," Omnathi commented quietly as he led Daulo away toward a relatively empty part of the center.

"What's this about?" Daulo demanded. Or rather, tried to demand; to his own ears his voice sounded more guilty than threatening. "I thought we'd settled everything two days ago."

"Yes, so it seemed," Omnathi nodded calmly. "But a couple of things have come up since then that I thought you could possibly help us with."

"Such as?" Daulo asked, stomach tightening.

Omnathi waved a hand at the assembled crowd. "This Mangus place, for instance. Your determination to gatecrash struck me as being rather a waste of time and energy, even given the stiffneck pride often associated with villagers." Daulo snorted; Omnathi ignored him. "So I had my men do a complete file check and confirmed that, as we told you, Mangus is indeed nothing more than a private electronics development center."

"And you'd like me therefore to leave and go home?" Daulo growled.

"Not at all. It occurred to me that perhaps you'd been mistaken about the timing of this gatecrash being your idea . . . and that Jasmine Alventin might still think this work party was the best way to get in."

Daulo's lungs seemed to have forgotten how to breathe. For a half dozen heartbeats the only sound was the dull buzz of the crowd around them, a buzz that seemed distant behind the roar of blood in Daulo's ears. "Understand, please," Omnathi said at last, "that at the

moment I'm not accusing you of anything except un-
knowing cooperation with an enemy of Qasama. I'm
even willing to believe that her prompting may have
been so artfully buried that you honestly think all this
was your idea. But from now on, that's over. You know
now that she's an offworld spy . . . and you'll be expected to behave accordingly."

"All right," Daulo said. "Threat received and understood. So what exactly do you want from me now?"

Omnathi sent a leisurely glance around the crowd.
"If the electronics information in Mangus is truly her
goal, than a little thing like a planetary search isn't
likely to slow her down much. She'll find a way in . . .
and if she does, I want someone there who can identify
her."

"Someone like me, I suppose?" Daulo asked.

"Exactly," Omnathi nodded. "Of course, spotting her
is only the first step. You haven't had any training in
methods of fugitive capture, and it's a little too late to
teach you. Fortunately, I remember that you'd originally planned to have your brother along on this trip."

Daulo glanced at the line behind him. "Which is why
Miron Akim is here, isn't it? To go in with me?"

"And to command you." Omnathi's face hadn't changed
. . . but his voice was suddenly covered with ice. "From
this moment on, Daulo Sammon, you're under the
direct authority of the Shahni."

Daulo swallowed hard. So Jin had been right—the
story he'd worked so hard to spin for Moffren Omnathi
two nights ago had been that much wasted effort. The
Shahni knew enough—or at least suspected enough—
and Miron Akim was their countermove. Placing him
under Shahni authority and Shahni surveillance . . .
"And under their sword, too?" he asked.

Omnathi gave him a long look. "If you aid us in
capturing the Aventinian spy, all other questions concerning your involvement in this will be forgotten. Otherwise . . . as you say, the sword will be waiting." He

glanced over Daulo's shoulder. "You'd better get back into line. Miron Akim will give you any further information you may need."

"You realize this is probably a waste of time," Daulo pointed out, driven by something he didn't quite understand to make one final effort. "She probably won't even show up in Mangus."

"It's our time to waste," Omnathi said calmly. "Farewell, Daulo Sammon."

And with that he turned his back and disappeared into the crowd. Daulo looked after him for a long moment, wondering what to do now. If he simply turned the opposite way and left Azras right now . . .

But of course it wasn't just him under the Shahni's sword. Taking a deep breath, he tried to quiet the thunder of his heartbeat and headed back to the line.

Akim was waiting for him. "Ah—Daulo Sammon," he nodded. "You had a pleasant talk, I take it?"

"Oh, certainly," Daulo said irritably, stepping back into line beside him. The man behind them muttered something about the end of the line; Akim sent the man an icy look and he fell silent.

They reached the table about ten minutes later, and it was only then that Daulo realized that Mayor Capparis himself was overseeing the operation. "Ah!" the mayor beamed at Daulo as he and Akim stepped up to the table. "Daulo Matrolis and his brother Perto. I'm glad you heard about this opportunity."

"I also, Mayor Capparis," Daulo said politely, making the sign of respect. He'd never heard the name *Matrolis* before, but knew a cue when he heard it. So did the man at the computer; he was busy tapping keys before Daulo even had to repeat the name. "Thank you," he nodded when he'd finished. "You can find out over there whether or not you'll be accepted." He pointed to another table at the edge of the city center, near a half dozen parked buses.

"Thank you," Daulo said, making the sign of respect

to both him and the mayor. Akim followed suit, and they headed off through the crowd.

"Daulo and Perto Matrolis, eh?" Akim murmured as they walked. "Do I assume that the files matching those names will show us highly suited for this work party?"

"This whole exercise would be a waste of time if it didn't, wouldn't it?" Daulo returned tartly.

"Agreed. Interesting, too, that you got Mayor Capparis himself to take a hand in this."

"Is it that hard to believe?"

Akim shrugged. "Perhaps not in this part of Qasama. For myself, I find it refreshing to see cooperation between city and village leaders. More often we see you at each other's throats."

"Um." Daulo looked around the buses, estimating their capacity. If they were to be filled completely, it looked like the work party would be something on the order of a hundred-fifty men. *Odd that they'd elect to go through this routine every two weeks*, he thought. *Permanent workers would be a lot easier . . . though perhaps they don't have any long-term housing facilities out there*. His eyes drifted to the area near the table . . . "Uh-oh."

"What is it?" Akim murmured.

"Over there—those men watching the proceedings?" Daulo said, turning his head partly away.

Akim glanced the indicated direction. "That's the group from Mangus," he identified them. "Drivers and a couple of higher officials."

"One of the officials is the director's son, Radig Nardin," Daulo growled. "He knows me."

Akim frowned. "How well?"

"Well enough to identify me," Daulo gritted.

"Is he likely to keep you out if he spots you?"

Daulo thought back to the attacks on him and Jin. "I think so, yes."

"Um." Akim considered. "I suppose I could identify myself to him . . . but that would probably start rumors

floating around Mangus, and I'd just as soon avoid that.
All right. Wait here; I'll go find one of our people and
arrange for a distraction."

"Good." Daulo looked back over—

And felt a shock run straight through his core. In the
center of the group from Mangus, talking earnestly to
Nardin, was a smallish man. Or rather, a smallish figure
wearing a man's clothing. Clothing he recognized . . .

It was Jin Moreau.

God above. The scene seemed to waver before Daulo's
eyes. Right there, in the middle of Azras, with people
all around. If Akim turned to look—if he identified
her—they would both be dead.

But Akim was already gone.

Licking his lips, Daulo tried to still the shaking of his
hands. Whatever Jin's purpose in doing something so
insane, if she would just hurry it up and get *out* of here,
she might still have a chance.

And as he watched, Jin did indeed turn away. Accompanied by Nardin and one of the other men, she
walked to the end of the line of buses—

And got into a car parked there.

Daulo watched the vehicle pull away onto the street;
watched it disappear behind the buildings surrounding
the city center; and was still gazing after it when Akim
returned. "All set," he reported. "Which one is Radig
Nardin?"

"He's gone," Daulo said mechanically. "Drove off a
couple of minutes ago."

"Oh? Well, that solves *that* problem."

Daulo took a deep breath. "I guess so."

Chapter 34

Azras was twenty kilometers north of the section of
forest where Jin had hidden Daulo's car—a healthy run
even for a Cobra, and one that allowed plenty of time
for worrying about what lay ahead. Just one more reason to be thankful that the predawn jog itself was totally
uneventful.

Her timing, for a change, was good, and she arrived
at the city just as the sky to the east was growing light.
Already some of the shopkeepers in the nearest marketplaces were beginning to prepare their booths for
business, and she drifted through the streets pretend-
ing to be on various errands, feeling safer than she had
since landing on Qasama. Disguised in lower-class male
clothing, her hair covered by a carefully trimmed wig
and her features altered slightly with face-shaper gel,
she ought to be totally unrecognizable, especially to
people who thought they had a good picture to go by.

That was the theory, at any rate . . . and as the
morning progressed, it appeared to work in practice.

She bought herself some breakfast—a nice treat after a day of emergency ration bars—and spent an hour wandering around the marketplace, observing the citizens of Azras as they began their new day.

She'd forgotten to ask Daulo when the work party selection would get underway, but when she made her first pass by the city center she saw that timing wasn't going to be critical. The park-like open area was teeming with men, most of them standing in a ragged and snaky line running up to a set of tables at one end. She watched for a few minutes, timing the procedure and estimating how long it would take to process the entire line, and then wandered off. Without Daulo it would be foolish to try and get into the work party in any straightforward way, and there would be little opportunity to try anything less obvious until the workers were ready to move out.

An hour later she returned, to find perhaps thirty minutes' worth of line left. Easing through the milling crowd of those who'd had their turns at the tables and were awaiting the results, she made her way across the center toward where a line of buses were parked along the street. Transport to Mangus, presumably. Also the simplest way for her to penetrate the place, assuming she could find some private hiding place atop, beneath, or inside one of them.

And with most of her attention on the buses, she suddenly found herself walking directly toward Daulo.

Fortunately, he was nearing the front of the line and seemed to have most of his own attention on the tables ahead. *Bless the angel who watches over fools*, Jin thought to herself, shifting her path to give him a wide berth. Beyond him, near the buses, another official-looking table had been set up; beyond that, a group of men were loitering near the vehicles. Together they effectively canceled any chance for approaching the buses from this side. If she swung around to the other side, made her approach from there—

Her thoughts froze in place. One of the men in that group, eyes ranging alertly over the crowd . . .

Was Radig Nardin. Watching, presumably, for Daulo.

For a half dozen heartbeats she just stood there, oblivious to the men milling around her. With Moffren Omnathi and the Shahni occupying her worries lately, she'd almost forgotten Mangus's own attempts to discourage her and Daulo. But Mangus obviously hadn't . . . and having seen Daulo in Milika less than four days ago, there was little chance Nardin would fail to recognize him.

At least, assuming he was able to continue looking . . .

She chewed at her lip, thinking hard. Step close and stun him with her sonic, hoping the others would assume he was ill and rush him away for treatment? But she would have to be practically up against him to deliver that kind of jolt without the others feeling some fringe effects. Use her lasers to set one of the buses on fire? No good; with his rank Nardin wouldn't be one of those fighting the fire. Besides which, any large-scale trouble she caused would more than likely just hold up the loading of the workers without guaranteeing that Nardin wouldn't still be around to watch it.

Unless . . .

She gritted her teeth. It was a borderline crazy idea . . . but if it worked, it would solve both her problems at one crack.

Across the city center, near the rearmost of the line of buses, was a small shedlike building, possibly a public toilet. Jin crossed to it and, positioning herself facing the wall away from the would-be workers, she worked her fingernails under the edges of the face-shaper gel and began tearing it away. It wasn't a pleasant task— the stuff wasn't supposed to be removed except with a special solvent—and her cheeks and chin felt raw by the time she'd finished. The wig and men's clothes she would have to leave as is; but if Nardin had been paying attention during his trip to the Sammon mine it ought to be enough.

In Milika she'd noted evidence of gaps between social classes, and as she walked up to Nardin's group it became quickly apparent that city dwellers worked under a similar set of rules. A lower-class man, wearing the clothing Jin was, would never have tried to barge right up to someone of Nardin's status, a fact that registered clearly in the startled expressions of those around Nardin as she passed between them. She was within arm's reach of the other, in fact, before two of the entourage broke their astonishment enough to step into her path. "Where do you think you're going?" one of them snarled at her.

"To speak to Master Radig Nardin," she said calmly. "I have a message for him."

Nardin turned to glare at her. "Since when do—?"

The words froze on his lips as recognition flashed onto his face, followed immediately by a whole series of startled emotions. "You—what—?"

"I bring a message for your father, Master Nardin," she said into his confusion, touching fingertips to her forehead. "May I approach?"

Nardin glanced at his companions, seemed to pull himself together. "You may. Let her pass," he ordered.

She sensed the shock pass through the others as she slipped between them—apparently they hadn't yet realized that she was in fact a woman. Dimly, she wondered if transvestism was a crime on Qasama, then dismissed the thought. "I bring a message for your father from Kruin Sammon of Milika," she told him. "Will you take me to him?"

Nardin's face had become an unreadable mask. "I remember you," he said. "You were in the village Milika in the company of Kruin Sammon's eldest son. Who are you that he trusts you with messages?"

"My name is Asya Elghani, Master Nardin."

"And your relation to the Sammon family?"

"That of a business professional," Jin said, choosing her words carefully. She had no idea if the service she was about to describe even existed on Qasama; but with the widespread Qasaman use of drugs, there was no reason why it shouldn't. "I'm a messenger, sent as I said to your father, Obolo Nardin."

Nardin cocked an eyebrow, his gaze flicking pointedly over her clothing. "And what is so special about you that you should be trusted with messages of any importance? Aside from the fact that few people would think you so trustworthy?"

Jin ignored the snickers from the others. "What makes me special," she told Nardin, "is that I carry an oral message . . . the contents of which I don't know."

Nardin's eyes narrowed. "Explain."

Jin let a look of barely controlled impatience drift across her face. "The message was given me while I was in a special drug-induced trance," she said. "Only in your father's presence will I be able to return to that trance and deliver the message."

He gazed at her for a long moment, and she mentally crossed her fingers. "How important is this message?" he asked. "Is the timing of its delivery crucial?"

"I have no way of knowing either," Jin told him.

One of the other men stepped close to Nardin. "With your permission, Master Nardin," he murmured, "may I suggest that the timing of this supposed message is extremely suspicious?"

Nardin's eyes stayed on Jin. "Perhaps," he muttered back. "However, if this is a ruse, it does little but buy him some time." Slowly, he nodded. "Very well, then. I'll take you to my father."

Jin bowed. "I'm at your disposal, Master Nardin," she said.

He turned and headed to the rear of the line of buses. Jin followed, sensing a second man join them. A car was parked behind the buses; the other man slid into the driver's seat as Nardin and Jin took the back, and almost before she had her door closed the vehicle swung out into the street and headed east.

Carefully, Jin took a breath, exhaled it with equal care. Once again, it seemed, the pervasive Qasaman disdain of women had worked in her favor. Nardin might have swallowed the same "private message" routine coming from another man, but he almost certainly wouldn't have let a male stranger into his car without some extra protection along. But as a woman, Jin was automatically no threat to him.

Settling back against the seat cushions, she watched the cityscape go past her window and tried to figure out just how best to turn that blind spot to her advantage.

Chapter 35

It was a fifty-kilometer drive from Azras to Mangus, along a road that was clearly newer and in better shape than the highway Jin had jogged alongside earlier that morning. Neither Nardin nor the driver spoke to her throughout the trip, which gave her little to do but study the scenery outside and—more surreptitiously— the two of them.

Neither examination was all that impressive. Nardin rode impassively, eyes flicking to her occasionally but generally staying on the road ahead. The driver, too, seemed stiff and distant, even toward Nardin. Their few exchanges were short and perfunctory, and she could sense none of the easy camaraderie that she'd seen between Daulo and his own driver. *A strict master/servant relationship*, she decided eventually, *without a scrap of friendship or even mutual respect to it*. In retrospect, given her first impression of Nardin four days previously, it wasn't all that unexpected.

The landscape outside wasn't quite as unfriendly, but

it more than made up for that in sheer dullness, consisting mainly of flat tree-dotted plains. Further to the east, she knew, the dense forest that surrounded Milika began again, extending across Qasama to the villages at the opposite end of the Fertile Crescent. But here, at least, the forest had failed to take.

Which meant that there would be far fewer deadly predators between them and Azras, should she and Daulo need to get out of Mangus in a hurry. Fewer beasts, and considerably less cover. All things considered, she would have preferred to take her chances with the predators.

Mangus was visible long before they reached it . . . and the satellite photos hadn't nearly done the place justice. From what she could see of the high black wall surrounding it, the compound appeared to be shaped roughly like a diamond, in sharp contrast to the circular shape of Milika and the villages her father had visited on Qasama. The diamond's long ends seemed to point southeast and northwest—*along the direction of the planet's magnetic field*, she decided, remembering the similarly angled streets in Azras and the other cities. Qasama's migrating bololin herds took their direction from magnetic field lines, and builders either had to deflect the huge beasts around human habitations or else give them as free a passage as possible.

Impressive as the wall was, though, it paled in comparison to the shimmering dome-shaped canopy arching over it.

The Cobra Worlds' satellites hadn't been able to make much of the canopy. It was metal or metal coated; it wasn't solid, but a tightly woven double mesh of some sort whose varying interference patterns actually blocked the probes more effectively than a solid structure would have; and it was almost entirely opaque to every electromagnetic wavelength the satellites were able to work with.

Now, seeing it at ground level, Jin found she couldn't

add much more to that list. It was anchored, she could see, by tall black pylons set into the ground outside the wall, which were in turn held in place by pairs of guy cables. How the canopy was being held up in the center was still a mystery, especially since its slight but visible rippling in the wind showed it to be more akin to fabric than to rigid metal. She was peering toward it, trying to see through the slight gap between its lower edge and the upper part of the wall, when a movement past the wall to her left caught her eye. Keying her optical enhancers to telescopic, she focused on it.

It was a bus. Identical to the ones that had been waiting to bring Daulo and his fellow workers to Mangus . . . except that this one was heading northward on a different road. As was the bus that followed it. And the next. And the next.

"They're going to Purma," Radig Nardin said into her thoughts. Startled, she looked at him, to find him gazing hard at her.

"I see, Master Nardin," she said, remembering to show proper respect. "May I ask who they are?"

His forehead creased a fraction more. "Last week's workers. On their way home."

Jin hesitated. Another question might be out of Qasaman character . . . but, then, she'd already established herself as an anomaly, anyway. "Do you hire from Purma often?"

"Every other week or so," he said. "It alternates with the hiring from Azras."

"I see." Carefully, Jin settled back into her seat, returning her eyes to the wall and dome ahead. So Mangus *did* have enough work to keep what amounted to a full-time force busy. So why didn't they simply go ahead and hire permanent workers, instead of going through all this trouble every week?

They had passed the line of pylons now, and as they neared the end of the road a gateway swung open up in the wall ahead. The only gateway on this side of the compound, she noticed, and built furthermore along the lines of a minor bank vault. Bololin-proof, for certain.

There were half a dozen buildings visible as the car drove through the gateway and into Mangus proper: an office-looking one directly ahead, a residence-type building beyond it, a guard station and garage flanking the road to right and left. But Jin saw them only peripherally. Her full attention was grabbed by the totally unexpected black wall rising off to her right.

It ran, as near as she could tell, between two of the diamond-shape's corners, cutting Mangus into two roughly equilateral triangles. A single gate was set into it at its center, a gate that looked to be just as strong as the one they'd just passed through. *The only way into that section?* she wondered, remembering that there'd been just one gateway into Mangus on the western part of the outer wall.

If so, that implied that Mangus's dark secrets came in two distinct shades. Now if only Radig's father Obolo Nardin kept his office beyond that internal wall . . .

But it wasn't going to be quite that easy. "The administrative center, Master Nardin?" the driver called over his shoulder.

"Yes," Radig said, looking at Jin. "You'll be given—" his eyes flicked down "—more suitable clothing before being brought before my father."

"Thank you, Master Nardin," Jin nodded gravely. Leaning slightly toward the window, she saw that another of the black pylons rose from the top of the interior wall, reaching upward to the center of the overhead canopy. The shield's primary support, clearly, with perhaps medium-strength ribs extending from it to the outside pylons to maintain the dome shape. Simple but effective. "I trust you'll provide me with transportation back to Azras once I've delivered my message," she added to Nardin.

He cocked an eyebrow. "That may depend," he said coolly, "on just what the message is."

*   *   *

They kept her waiting a long time, far longer than it
took her to change into the clothes they'd given her.
Long enough, in fact, that she was beginning to wonder
if they were secretly monitoring her; and if so, when
she as a supposedly busy professional ought to start
looking annoyed at having her time wasted. But eventually someone came, and she was taken down a series
of corridors to Obolo Nardin's throne room.

There was no other way to think of the place. Larger
and far more elaborate than Kruin Sammon's study—
larger even than the big-city mayor's office she'd seen
tapes of—it was clearly designed to intimidate all who
came in. A light breeze continually played across her
face as she was led through and around the maze of
hanging curtains to the center. A quick mental picture
flashed across her mind, a picture of a spider waiting in
the center of his web . . .

"What is your name?" the man on the cushion throne
growled at her.

With an effort, Jin forced the spider image from her
mind. *I'm a Cobra*, she reminded herself. *Spiders aren't
supposed to scare me.* "I am Asya Elghani, Master,"
she said, making the sign of respect and studying his
unnaturally bright eyes. Excessive use of Qasama's mind
drugs? "Are you Obolo Nardin?"

The man's face didn't change . . . but an abrupt
shiver ran up her back. "I am," he said. "What have
you to say to me?"

Jin took a deep breath. This was it. Now if only he
bought her performance. . . . Letting her face go slightly
slack as if entering a hypnotic state, she dropped her
voice an octave. "This is Kruin Sammon," she intoned.
"I know what you are doing here in Mangus, Obolo
Nardin, and I know what you are risking. With that
knowledge I can destroy you . . . but I can also aid you.
You need the resources I possess, as well as the strength
of the western villages whose loyalty I command. I

propose therefore an alliance between us, with the rewards shared equally. I await your reply."

Carefully, Jin brought her eyes back into focus. "Did you receive the entire message, Master Nardin?" she asked in a normal voice again.

Obolo Nardin's eyes were steady on her face. "Indeed I did," he grunted.

"I've already been paid to bring Kruin Sammon a reply, should you wish to send one," she continued, struggling to keep her face and voice impassive. Deep in the back of her mind, alarm bells were beginning to go off. Something here wasn't quite right . . . "However, in that event, I would need time to prepare myself—"

And without warning the scene ahead of her was abruptly rimmed by red.

A jolt of adrenaline surged through her as, reflexively, she held her breath. Suddenly it all clicked: the long delay back at the changing room, the careful scrutiny Obolo Nardin was giving her, the breeze blowing in her face . . . a breeze undoubtedly laden with sleeping drug. They'd considered what to do with her, decided that the message cover was nonsense, and were taking the appropriate action.

At her sides, Jin's hands curled into fists, nails digging into the skin of her palms to ward off the drug's effect. She might be able to stun Obolo with her sonic and get out of here . . . but the hanging curtains could hide a hundred other men, and even now she couldn't afford to give herself away. On the other hand, she couldn't hold her breath forever, either, and she'd probably already inhaled enough of the stuff to put her under before she got too far, anyway. And Obolo was still staring at her. Still waiting . . .

Waiting for her to collapse? *All right*, she decided suddenly. "I—Master Nardin—" she began drunkenly, using the last of her reserve of air; and rolling her eyes up, she collapsed to the floor.

She'd made sure to let her head roll so as to face away from the direction of the sleep breeze, but the stars of her impact had barely cleared away before the air now playing at the back of her head was shut off anyway. Footsteps came slowly around one of the curtains . . . stopped at her side . . . "That was quick," Radig Nardin's voice said. "Even for a woman."

"She's a soft offworlder," Obolo replied contemptuously. "If this is the best our enemies can do, we have little to fear from them."

An iron spike seemed to drive itself up through Jin's stomach. *God above—they know who I am!* But how—?

"Perhaps." A hand pulled at Jin's shoulder, rolling her over on her back. Keeping her eyes closed, she activated her optical enhancers, keying for zero magnification and the lowest light-amp setting. Radig peered at her face a moment, then straightened up again to face his father. "I'll have her body searched for tiny instruments before we confine her."

"As you choose, my son, but I doubt there's any need."

"Her clothing yielded nothing—"

"You're forgetting the crash of her spacecraft," the elder Nardin cut his son off. "She carries no devices because none survived with her."

"Perhaps. Have you decided yet what to do about Daulo Sammon?"

"Why, nothing, of course—his father has offered us a deal," Obolo said, heavily sarcastic. "Didn't you hear his message?"

Radig glanced down at Jin again. "You'll forgive me, my father, if I fail to see any humor in the situation. Or do you consider it impossible that the Sammon family has in fact made an alliance with this spy?"

"Hardly impossible," Obolo grunted. "Unlikely, though."

"Then let me get rid of him," Radig urged. "As long as he's here, he presents a danger to us."

"True. Unfortunately, removing him at this point may be even more dangerous. Tell me, have you identified the man who came into Mangus with him?"

Radig's lip twitched. "Not yet. But he's probably just someone else from that bololin dropping of Milika."

"'Probably' isn't good enough," Obolo said coldly. "The Shahni know the woman is on Qasama, and they know she stayed in the Sammon household while in Milika. This man could well be a Shahni agent assigned to Daulo Sammon, either as protector or as jailer."

"But in either case, why accompany Daulo Sammon *here*?"

"*She* is here, is she not? Whatever she and our enemies know or suspect, it's not impossible she might have shared that knowledge with Kruin Sammon."

"But then allowing an agent of the Shahni—"

"Radig Nardin." Obolo's voice was like the crack of a whip. "Control your fears and *think*. As far as the Shahni are concerned, Mangus is an electronics firm—nothing more. If we behave openly, they'll have no reason to doubt that. If, on the other hand, we make an inflated presentation of plucking Daulo Sammon from among the workers and throwing him outside our wall, will this agent's curiosity not be aroused?"

Radig took a deep breath. "It's still dangerous, my father."

"Of course it is. There's no profit without danger, my son. If your nerve threatens to fail you again, concentrate on that."

"Yes, my father." Radig glowered down at Jin. "And for what potential gain do we risk keeping *this* one alive?"

Obolo snorted. "You consider keeping a *woman* alive to be a risk?"

"She's not a normal woman, my father—she's an agent of the Cobra Worlds. That makes her dangerous."

Abruptly, Jin noticed that the red border was still

around her vision . . . that it was, in fact, getting thicker
. . . as the view itself seemed to be fading away . . .

No! she told herself furiously, trying to fight the
sleep flowing over her mind. *Come on, Jin—hang on.*
But it was too hard to muster the necessary emotion.
And it was so comfortable here on the floor . . .

Her last memory was that of rough hands digging
under her armpits and legs, lifting her up and floating
her away . . .

Chapter 36

". . . The screen in front of each of you will display a brief summary of each of the steps I've just outlined," the instructor concluded his presentation, waving his hand over his podium toward the rows of equipment-laden tables in front of him. "If you have any questions tap the 'help' key; if that still doesn't do it, tap the 'signal' key and someone will come to your work station. Any questions? All right, then. Get to it, and remember that the future of communication on Qasama may depend on you."

Shifting his eyes to the screen attached to the work table, Daulo suppressed a grimace and picked up a circuit board and a handful of components. He hadn't really expected to be given a missile casing and told to load a warhead onto it . . . but assembling telephone circuitry was hardly what he'd hoped for, either. "Not wasting any time getting us to work, are they?" he murmured.

He glanced to the side in time to see Akim's shrug. "They're paying all of us quite well," he pointed out.

Daulo gritted his teeth and plugged the first component into the circuit board. He'd been trying to pique Akim's curiosity about Mangus itself ever since being ushered off the bus, and had yet to make any impression on the man. Akim was on the trail of a female offworlder, and he clearly had no intention in being distracted from that single-minded path. "At least it explains why they don't bother hunting down their previous workers," Daulo commented, trying another approach. "If everything they do here is this simple-minded it's just as easy to teach a new group from the beginning."

Akim glanced up and around, and for a moment Daulo hoped he might argue the point. But he merely nodded. "Inefficient, to some degree, but not overly so," he said, and returned his attention to his own circuit board. "Certainly helps spread a little extra wealth around to Azras's poor."

"Right," Daulo muttered under his breath. "Obolo Nardin is just as noble as all creation."

"If I were you," Akim said coldly, "I'd try and forget my village prejudices and concentrate on the task at hand. Do you see anyone here who could be the woman in disguise?"

With a sigh, Daulo gave the room a careful scan, the image of Jin getting into Radig Nardin's car rising up to haunt him. "I don't think so."

"Keep an eye out," Akim told him. "They may occasionally rotate workers between groups."

Daulo nodded and turned back to his work.

It was perhaps an hour later when he suddenly noticed Akim had stopped working and was gazing straight ahead into space. "Something?" he asked.

Akim turned sharply to look at him. "Something's wrong," he whispered hoarsely. "There's—" he licked his lips, eyes darting all around him. "Don't you feel it?"

Daulo leaned close, fighting against the sudden dread rising in his throat. Akim's barely controlled panic was contagious. "I don't understand. What is it you're feeling?"

Akim drew a shuddering breath. "Treachery," he said, hands visibly trembling. "There's . . . treachery here. Don't you *feel* it?"

Daulo threw a quick look around the room. So far no one else seemed to have noticed them, but that wouldn't last long. "Come on," he said, getting to his feet and gripping Akim's arm. "Let's get out of here."

Akim shrugged off his hand. "I can manage myself," he snarled, standing up unsteadily.

"Whatever you want," Daulo gritted. The door they'd come in by was all the way at the back of the room; much closer was another exit near the front podium. Taking Akim's arm again as the other staggered slightly, he headed that way.

The instructor intercepted them as they got to the door. "Where are you going?" he demanded. "The exit is back that—"

"My friend is sick," Daulo cut him off. "Is there a lavette out there somewhere?"

The other seemed to draw back, and Daulo took advantage of his hesitation to push past. Outside was a corridor he hadn't seen on their way into the building, with a heavy-looking door at the far end. Halfway toward it was the lavette he'd hoped for; guiding Akim through the door, he all but pushed the other down onto a cushion in the lounge section.

For a long moment neither man spoke. Akim took several slow, deep breaths, checked his fingers for signs of trembling, and after a bit rose and studied his face in the mirror. Only then did he finally look Daulo in the eye. "You didn't feel it, did you?" he demanded. "You didn't feel anything in there?"

Daulo spread his hands, palm upwards. "You'll have to be more specific," he said.

"I wish I could." Akim leaned back toward the mirror, gazed deeply into his own eyes. "I felt—well, curse it all, I felt treason. There's no other way to put it; I felt *treason*. Whether it makes any sense of not."

It didn't; but it almost didn't matter. Whatever the reason, Akim had finally been jolted out of his indifference toward Mangus, and it was up to Daulo now to fan that flame. "I don't understand," he admitted, "but I trust your instincts."

Akim threw him a baleful glance. "Instincts be cursed," he ground out. "There's something wrong in this place, and I'm going to find out what it is."

He started toward the door. "You going back in there?" Daulo asked carefully. "I mean, considering what just happened—"

"I'm fully under control now," the other said stiffly. "As far as you're concerned, I just had a bad reaction to something I ate for breakfast. Understand?"

The instructor was watching from just outside the assembly-room door when they emerged from the lavette. He accepted Akim's suitably embarrassed explanation and escorted them back to the room and their tables. Returning to his work, Daulo stretched out his senses to the limit, trying as hard as he could to pick up the feeling Akim had described.

Nothing.

What was perhaps worse, Akim could apparently no longer sense it, either. Grim-faced, he sat at his table and worked on his circuit boards, without even a mild recurrence of his earlier reaction.

Which meant either that whatever it was had passed . . . or that it had never been there in the first place.

It was, Daulo decided, probably the oddest sunset he'd ever seen. Ahead, the sun was invisible below the level of Mangus's outer wall, while overhead it still sent multicolored light patterns across the shimmering canopy. "I wonder if that thing keeps the rain out," he commented, twisting his head to gaze upward out their window at it.

"Why else would it be there?" Akim growled from his bed.

To keep Jin's people from seeing in. But he couldn't tell Akim that. "You still bothered by what happened in the assembly room this afternoon?" he asked instead, keeping his eyes on the canopy.

"Wouldn't you be?" the other snapped. "I behaved like a fool in public, and then couldn't even discover why I'd done so."

Daulo pursed his lips. "Could it have been some chemical they use in the manufacturing process?" he suggested. "Something that might still have been evaporating from the circuit boards?"

"Then why didn't anyone else react? More to the point, why wasn't it still there when we came back into the room? And it *wasn't* still there."

Daulo chewed the inside of his cheek. "Well, then . . . maybe it was something meant for me, something you got caught in by accident."

Behind him, Akim snorted. "Back to your paranoia of Mangus wanting to keep villagers out, are we?"

"It fits the facts, doesn't it?" Daulo growled, turning to face the other. "A stream of gas, maybe, designed to make me feel frightened and leave on my own?"

"It wasn't fear I felt."

"Perhaps you're braver than I am. And then when *you* reacted instead of me, they may have panicked and shut it off."

Akim shook his head. "It doesn't make any sense. You're talking something far too sophisticated to be used in what amounts to a telephone assembly plant."

"And how do you know those *were* telephone circuit boards we were putting together?" Daulo countered.

Akim's forehead creased. "What else would they be?" he asked.

Daulo took a deep breath. "Weapons. Possibly missile components."

He'd expected at least a snort of disbelief and scorn. But Akim merely continued looking at him. "And what," the other said quietly, "would give you that impression?"

A cold shiver ran up Daulo's spine. *He knows*, was his first, horrible thought. *The Shahni are in this with Mangus—the cities really* are *preparing for war against the villages.* But it was too late to back out. "Rumors," he said through stiff lips. "Bits of information, pieced together over the months."

"As well as suggestions from the Aventinian spy?" Akim asked bluntly.

"I don't know what you mean," Daulo said as calmly as possible.

For a half dozen heartbeats the two men stared at each other. "You slide dangerously close to treason, Daulo Sammon," Akim said at last. "You and the entire Sammon household."

"The Sammon family is loyal to Qasama," Daulo said, fighting a trembling in his voice. "To *all* of Qasama."

"And I, as a city man, am not?" Akim's eyes flared. "Well, let me tell you something, Daulo Sammon: you may *think* you love Qasama, but any loyalty you possess pales against mine. We of the Shahni's investigators have been trained and treated to be totally fair in our dealings with Qasama's people. *Totally* fair. We cannot be corrupted or led astray from what we see as our duty. And we do *not* show prejudice, to *any*one on our world. If you remember only one thing about me, remember that."

Abruptly, he got to his feet, and Daulo took an involuntary step backward. But Akim merely walked past the two beds and seated himself at the writing desk. "So you think we've been assembling parts for missiles, do you?" he said over his shoulder as he picked up the phone and turned it over. "There ought to be one quick way to settle that."

Daulo stepped over and crouched down beside him as Akim pulled a compact tool kit from his pocket and selected a small screwdriver. There were, Daulo noted, about a dozen screws holding the bottom of the phone to the molded resin top. "Why so many fastenings?" he asked as Akim got to work.

"Who knows?" Akim grunted, getting the first one loose. "Maybe they don't want anyone messing around with his phone unless it really needs fixing."

Akim was working on the last screw when Daulo first noticed the odor. "What's that?" he asked, sniffing cautiously. "Smells like something's burning."

"Hmm. It does, doesn't it." Frowning, Akim lifted the phone to his nose. "—uh-oh."

"Did we ruin it?"

"Sure smells that way. Well . . . the damage is probably already done." He got the screw free and carefully pulled the bottom plate out.

Just inside the plate was a circuit board—the same board, Daulo saw immediately, that they'd been working on all day. All the same components, plus a tangle of connecting wires, plus—

"What are those things?" he asked, pointing to a row of slightly blackened components. "We didn't put those on our boards."

"No, we didn't," Akim agreed thoughtfully. He raised the board to his nose again. "Whatever they are, they're where the smell is coming from."

A knot began to form in the pit of Daulo's stomach. "You mean . . . we tried to take the phone apart, and they burned themselves out?"

Akim held the board closer, peering at it from different angles. "Take a look," he said, lifting a bundle of wires and pointing beneath it. "Right there. See it?"

Daulo tried to remember what that component was. "A capacitor?" he hazarded.

"Right. And *there*—" he pointed beneath it "—is what releases its stored current into that section of the circuit."

The knot in Daulo's stomach tightened an extra turn. "That's . . . right over one of the screw holes."

"Uh-huh," Akim nodded. "And now that we've got it open, it's clear that screw doesn't help hold the phone together at all." He looked up at Daulo. "It's a self-destruct mechanism," he said quietly.

Daulo had to work moisture into his mouth before he could speak. "Any way to find out what those burned-out components are supposed to do?"

"Not now. Not this set, anyway." Akim gazed at the board another moment, and then put it back into the phone and picked up one of the screws. "I'll have to find out where they finish this part of the assembly and get in there." He paused, a strange look flashing across his face. "You know . . . phones manufactured in Mangus have been the most advanced on Qasama for the last two or three years. They're very popular among top city officials."

"And the Shahni?" Daulo asked.

"And the Shahni," Akim nodded. "I've got one on my desk . . ." He took a deep breath. "I don't know what we've got here, Daulo Sammon, but whatever it is, I need to check it out, and quickly."

"Are you going to call for reinforcements?"

Akim gave him a sardonic look. "Over these phones?" he asked pointedly.

Daulo grimaced. "Oh. Right. Well . . . look, it probably wouldn't take more than an anonymous tip to the right person to get me thrown out. If you want to give me a message, I'll make sure to deliver it to Moffren Omnathi in person."

"Even if Radig Nardin decides to make sure you never try to enter Mangus again?" Akim asked.

Daulo licked his lips, remembering the toughs who'd attacked him and Jin. "And what do you suppose they'll do to us if they find out we know about their phones?" he countered.

Akim set the phone back on the table and stood up. "I'm a representative of the Shahni," he said flatly. "They wouldn't *dare* harm me."

There was no response Daulo could make to that. "Were you planning to try and find that extra assembly room tonight?" he asked instead.

Akim hesitated, looking out the window. "It's getting late . . . but I don't remember them saying anything about us being confined to quarters in the evenings." He turned back to Daulo. "I suppose you want to go, too?"

"If I may. Unless you don't trust me."

Akim looked at him steadily. "To be perfectly honest, no, I don't. I don't think you're the innocent bystander you try to appear, and until I figure out just what the game is you're playing I'm not going to like having you at my back." He snorted gently under his breath. "Unfortunately, if you're working against me I risk just as much by leaving you here where I can't watch you."

Daulo grimaced. "Is there anything I can say or do to convince you I don't oppose you?"

"Not really."

"Then I guess you'll have to make up your mind on your own. Bear in mind that I can't come with you and stay here at the same time."

Akim's lip twitched. "True." He inhaled deeply. "All right, then. Come on, let's go."

Chapter 37

It was something of a surprise to Jin to awake and find herself still alive.

She took a moment first to listen with her eyes closed. Silence, except for the hum of distant machinery or forced air venting. No sounds of breathing except her own.

Which meant that, along with leaving her alive, they'd left her alone.

Opening her eyes, she found herself in a small room, perhaps three meters by four, bare except for the thin mattress on which she was lying and a somewhat thicker sitting cushion in one corner. Set into the ceiling was an air vent, too small for anything larger than a cat to get through; on one wall was a metal door.

Carefully, she got to her feet. There was no dizziness, no pain except for a mild ache from the bruise where she'd allowed her head to hit the floor. *And no way to know how long the stuff had me under, either,* she reminded herself grimly, wishing she'd thought to start her clock circuit before going under. Stepping to the door, she pressed her ear against it and activated her audio enhancers.

The faint sound of cloth on skin came from outside, followed by a cough.

At least they thought enough of me to lock me up, she thought, feeling a little mollified. Even recognizing on an intellectual level that her supposed feminine weakness was greatly to her advantage, it still somehow rankled to be so casually treated by her opponents.

Whoever these opponents were.

She frowned as the memory of that last overheard conversation came back to her. Obolo Nardin had known about the shuttle crash—had known she was an offworlder and that she'd been staying with the Sammon family in Milika. Had the Shahni made that information public? Or was Mangus in fact a government operation? Neither option was especially attractive.

And yet . . . unless the drug they'd been blowing in her face had thoroughly scrambled her memory . . . hadn't they also been openly worried about the risk of having an agent of the Shahni in their midst?

Which implied they *were* hiding something from the Shahni. But how then did they know things only the Shahni were supposed to know?

Could Mangus be some kind of chip in an internal power struggle among the Shahni themselves? One side's jealously guarded effort, perhaps, to come up with a way to fight back against the Cobra Worlds?

Cobra Worlds. Cobras. Mangus. Mongoose . . .

God above.

For a long moment Jin just stood there, rooted by horror to the spot. *God above.* It'd been staring her right in the face the whole time, and she'd managed to completely miss it. *Mongoose . . .*

Angrily, she shook her head, the movement sending

a stab of pain through her bruise. It still wasn't too late to redeem her error . . . assuming that she could get out of this room. Gritting her teeth, she crouched down and examined the door's lock.

It was instantly obvious that the room hadn't originally been designed to hold prisoners. The door had been locked by the simple expediency of removing the inner knob mechanism and welding a metal plate over the resulting opening.

Moving back from the door, she gave the room a quick but careful scan. There were no hidden cameras that she could find, though there could still be subsurface microphones buried out of sight in the walls. Those could be dealt with, though. A more pressing problem would be to find something she could use to bend back the metal covering the lock. Pulling off one shoe, she experimented with the heel. Not ideal, but it would do. Taking a deep breath, she wedged the heel beneath the edge of the plate with one hand and activated her other hand's fingertip laser.

It was easier than she'd expected it to be; clearly, the man assigned the job of securing the door hadn't wanted to make a career of the task and had used a soft metal that he could spot-weld in place in a couple of minutes. It took Jin even less time than that to free three of its edges and soften the rest enough to pry it back from the hole. Waiting for it to cool was the hardest part, but the door itself was a fair heat sink, and within a few minutes she was able to get close enough to see into the opening.

Inside the door was the minor maze of wiring and equipment: an electronic lock. She knew a dozen quick ways of dealing with such a device, ranging from frying it with her arcthrower to slagging it with her antiarmor laser. Unfortunately, most of them tended to be extremely noisy, and the last thing she could afford right now was for the guard outside to hit whatever panic button he was equipped with.

Fortunately, there were more subtle approaches available to her. The solenoids and deadlock bolt of the actual mechanism were easy enough to locate; easing a finger into the hole, she found the bar that blocked the deadbolt in place when the lock was engaged. Pushing it out of the way with one finger, she teased the deadbolt back with two others . . .

There was no click, just a slight inward movement of the door as it was suddenly freed to swing on its hinges again. Straightening up, Jin slipped her shoe back on and licked her lips. This was it. Activating her omnidirectional sonic to interfere with any microphones that might be operating, she got her fingernails on the door edge and pulled it open.

The two guards standing with their backs to her probably weren't even aware the door behind them had opened before she dropped them where they stood with a blast from her sonic. Gripping the door jamb, her own head ringing from the sonic's backwash, Jin leaned out into the hallway and looked around. No one was in sight; and from the level of light coming in a window down the hall, it was already early evening out there. She'd slept the whole day away . . . Gritting her teeth, she bent to the task of disposing of the unconscious guards.

The next door down the hall turned out to be a small washroom, its size indicating it had been designed for use by one person at a time. Carrying the guards inside, she propped them up in such a way that they would help wedge the door once she closed it. Her trainers had warned them repeatedly that the duration of sonic-induced unconsciousness varied so wildly between people and situations that it couldn't be relied on, but with nothing around to secure them with, she would just have to hope that they wouldn't wake up too soon.

Her next stop was the window down the hall. The

sun was indeed well down past Mangus's western wall, though its light was still sending a rainbow of color across the canopy overhead. More importantly, the view outside told her that she was still in the building she'd first been brought to that morning.

Which gave her a very good idea of where she ought to start her investigation . . .

There were still a handful of people roaming around the building, but in the relative stillness their footsteps carried clearly to her enhanced hearing, and she found it an easy task to elude them. It took her several minutes and a few false turns, but eventually she made it to the hallway leading to the ornate door of Obolo Nardin's office-cum-throne room.

There hadn't been any guards outside the door when she'd been first brought before Obolo, and there weren't any now, either. Which implied either very good electronic security on the entrance itself, or else human guards waiting out of sight behind some of the hanging curtains inside. She was just starting around the corner to check out the door when another set of footsteps caught her ear and she ducked back.

It was Radig Nardin.

Jin gnawed at her lip. The messenger who'd taken her to Obolo earlier had announced their arrival on an intercom set beside the door and they'd been admitted by someone inside. But given Qasama's culture, it seemed unlikely that the son of Mangus's director would have to go through such a routine. On a sudden hunch, she clicked her optical enhancers to telescopic and focused on the door.

Radig stepped up to the panel, tapped six buttons on a keypad she hadn't noticed before, and opened the door.

Jin was gliding down the hallway toward the closing door before it occurred to her on a conscious level that sneaking into Obolo's office right on Radig's heels might be an unnecessarily stupid risk to take. But she kept going. Obolo presumably had a perfectly adequate communications system available in his office, and if he and Radig needed to speak in person, perhaps it would be worth listening in on.

She reached the door unseen and repeated Radig's code on the keypad. Too late, she wondered if the system might also be sensitive to fingertip pattern . . . but Obolo hadn't bothered with extra refinement, and with a quiet click the door unlocked.

She opened it just enough to slip through, closing it again behind her and moving immediately to the cover of the nearest hanging curtain. The room seemed hazy, and she nearly choked on her first breath. *Chemical smoke*, she realized, remembering the unnatural glow in Obolo's eyes earlier. Presumably one of those wonderful mind-stimulating drugs. Keying in her audio enhancers, she slid off her shoes and moved out cautiously in Radig's wake.

Two guards were near the door, hidden from view behind a pair of curtains. Pinpointing them by the sounds of their breathing, Jin moved silently past on her bare feet. Radig's footsteps were easy to follow, and she was within a single curtain of Obolo Nardin's cushion throne when they came to a halt. Squatting down behind the curtain, Jin held her breath.

"My son," Obolo's voice said, his tone oddly grating in Jin's ears—the vocal equivalent, perhaps, of the drug user's shining eyes.

"My father," Radig greeted the elder Nardin in turn. "I've brought you the manifest of the latest shipment. Unloading has already begun; transfer of the special components to the assembly building will begin as soon as it's dark and all the temporary workers are properly confined in their houses."

The familiar *shisss-click* of a magdisk into a reader

. . . Obolo grunted. "Good. Have they begun work on the second computer system yet?"

"They're still setting it up," Radig told him. "They estimate it'll be ready in about two days."

"Two and a quarter," Obolo said with casual certainty. "They consistently underestimate the actual time they'll need."

"Perhaps this time—" Radig stopped as a *ping* came from the work table.

"Obolo Nardin," Obolo said. Something inaudible even to Jin's enhanced hearing . . . "Command," he bit out angrily. "Specified recorder; last playback."

More inaudible speech . . . but even without visual cues, Jin could sense a sudden tension on the other side of the curtain.

As Radig clearly also did. "What is it?" he asked tautly when the voices had stopped.

Obolo took an audible breath. "The Shahni agent who came in with Daulo Sammon has found the key to the Mongoose Project."

"The Shahni—? You know for certain that's what he is?"

"If I hadn't already, his last conversation with Daulo Sammon confirmed it." Obolo's voice was settling down, drifting almost toward boredom. "His reaction this morning to the subliminals was actually all the proof I needed."

Radig seemed to be having trouble catching up. "You say he knows? How?"

"He was pushed into the discovery by Daulo Sammon, as it happens. There was some fantasy about missile production here, and it goaded the agent into disassembling the phone. Perhaps you were right; perhaps we should have removed the villager right at the beginning."

"But the phone's self-destruct—"

"Worked properly, of course. But you don't suppose

for a minute that that really helped, do you? Destroyed evidence is as intriguing to such people as undestroyed evidence."

Radig cursed. "We'd better get some guards to their complex right away."

"Why?"

"*Why?*" Radig echoed in disbelief. "Because if he gets that information to his superiors—"

"He can't." Obolo was almost glacially calm. "Mangus is sealed for the night, and I've had all outside phone contact except that from this building shut off since he betrayed his identity this morning. Quiet, now, my son, and let me think."

For a moment the painful thudding of her own heart was all Jin could hear. It had happened, her worst fear about this whole penetration: Daulo was in deadly danger. Her legs trembled with the urge to leap out of concealment, cut both Obolo and Radig in half with her antiarmor laser, and get herself and Daulo out of here . . .

"Yes," Obolo said abruptly. "Yes. You will assemble a small force, my son—four men—and take them to the assembly building. The agent's next step will be to try and find some of our special components in undamaged form to take out of Mangus with him."

"How will he know—"

"He'd have seen the final assembly room door this morning when he and the villager left their own area in reaction to the subliminals. He'll remember it and go there first."

"I understand. Do you wish them killed there, caught in an act of burglary?"

Jin's hands twitched involuntarily into combat position: little finger pointed straight out, thumb resting on ring-finger nails . . . "Of course not," Obolo snorted scornfully. "That would merely bring others from the Shahni to investigate why one of their preconditioned agents would stoop to simple thievery. No, my son, bring them back here, alive and unharmed."

"We *will* eventually kill them, though, won't we?" Radig asked, almost pleading. "A Shahni agent's training won't allow—"

"Of course we won't kill them," Obolo said evenly. "*We* will do nothing. It'll be the offworlder spy who'll handle that task for us."

Chapter 38

The door to the assembly building was locked, but an unusual-looking tool from Akim's kit took care of it in short order. "Now where?" Daulo whispered as they slipped inside.

"That room we saw when I—" Akim pursed his lips. "You remember—at the end of the hallway the instructor tried to keep us out of?"

"Right," Daulo nodded, glancing out the window beside the door. At Akim's insistence they'd taken a leisurely, roundabout route here from their housing complex, and the earlier twilight had faded now into deep dusk. "What do you want me to do?"

Akim stepped past him to relock the door. "You might as well stay here," he said, not sounding entirely happy with the decision. "This is the door any visitors would be most likely to use. If you see anyone coming, give a whistle."

"A whistle?" Daulo frowned.

"Whistles carry as well in a building as shouts do

311

with less chance of being heard from outside," Akim explained briefly. "Watch carefully."

And he was gone. Daulo listened as his footsteps faded down the hallway, trying to ignore the gnawing sensation in the pit of his stomach. So Jin had been wrong all along. It wasn't missiles . . . or was it? There was still that walled-off section of Mangus that none of their instructors had even referred to.

But then what was all this business with the phones?

The tap on the window barely ten centimeters from his face nearly threw him across the hall in reaction. *God above!* He staggered, trying to regain his balance—tried to shape unsteady lips for a whistle—

"Daulo!" The whisper was barely audible through the glass. His whole body trembling, Daulo moved back to the window.

It was Jin.

Taking a shuddering breath, Daulo stepped to the door and unlocked it. "Jin—God above, but you startled me—"

"Shut up and listen," she growled, brushing past him to peer out the window. "Obolo Nardin's on to you and your Shahni friend. Radig Nardin's gone to assemble a guard force to come here and pick both of you up."

Daulo felt his mouth drop open. "Over *here*? But how did they know we were coming here?"

"Obolo deduced it. He seems to be running on one of those mind-expanders you Qasamans are fond of." Jin turned back from the window. "No sign of them yet—Radig must figure there's no hurry. Where's your Shahni friend?"

"Miron Akim's down the hall." He pointed. "And he's not exactly a friend."

"Go get him anyway—he's dead too if Radig catches him here. If we can hide you somewhere until you can get out of Mangus—"

"Wait a second, we've got to talk first. I think you

were wrong about the missiles. They're playing some sort of game with the phone instead."

She hissed between her teeth. "It's no game, Daulo. My guess is that they're systematically planting bugged phones all over Qasama."

"Bugged?" Daulo frowned.

"Equipped with microphones. Listening devices."

"God above," Daulo murmured. *Phones manufactured in Mangus are very popular among top city officials*, Akim had said. And among the Shahni, as well. "But even with microphones in the phones . . . God above. The long-range phone system."

Jin nodded grimly. "That's it, all right. Your marvelous detection-proof underground waveguide has been turned against you. It's tailor-made for this sort of thing."

Daulo clenched his teeth hard enough to hurt. She was right. With virtually every phone in the Great Arc linked through the natural waveguide beneath the planet, it would be childishly simple for any phone conversation to be picked up, duplicated, and the copy routed via that same waveguide back here to Mangus.

With the villages west of Azras one of the few areas immune to that surveillance. One reason why they'd tried so hard to keep him out of Mangus? "Milika's in danger," he murmured.

"All of Qasama's in danger," Jin retorted. "Don't you get it, Daulo? Once this system's completed—if it isn't already—Mangus will have access to practically every communication and data transfer on the planet. And that kind of information translates directly into power."

Daulo shook his head, forehead tight with thought. "But only if they can sift out the specific information they're looking for. And the more microphones they've got planted, the more they'll have to sort through to get it."

Even in the dim light he saw something flicker across her face. "I've got an idea how they might be handling that," she said, her voice heavy with reluctance. "For the moment, though, there's a rather more immediate threat to us: I think they're trying to build themselves an army among their temporary workers. Did Miron Akim have some kind of reaction this morning? I heard Obolo Nardin mention it."

"Yes—said he felt treason in the assembly room. We left for a few minutes, and he was fine afterwards."

"Presumably because they turned the thing off. You ever heard of subliminals?"

Daulo gritted his teeth. *Treason* . . . "Yeah," he breathed. "If you mix a mild hypnotic gas with subaudible vocal messages, you're supposed to be able to create minor attitude changes in a person."

"We don't use anything like that on Aventine, but the theory's known well enough," Jin nodded. "Is it something common here?"

"I've only heard of it being used as a last-try method with chronic criminal types. It's not supposed to be all *that* effective." Abruptly, another piece of the puzzle fell into place. "Of course—the temporary workers. That's why they keep hiring new men; they're trying to run as many of Azras's people through their conditioning as they can."

"Azras and Purma both," Jin grunted. "On the way in this morning I saw some loaded busses heading back to Purma. They're rotating their work force between the two cities, maybe hoping neither city will notice what they're doing."

"Yeah. You think they've found a way to make subliminals powerful enough to force people into treason?"

"I don't know," Jin shook her head. "I hope all they're trying to do is sow discontent among the cities' poor. Given your current political climate, even that might be enough."

Daulo nodded, feeling cold all over. "God above. We've got to get this to the Shahni."

"No kidding—and may I suggest as a first step that you go collect your friend and we all get out of here?

Radig Nardin could arrive any minute now, and if he finds us we probably won't have any choice but to kill them." She stooped again to look out the window.

Daulo shivered. The way she just automatically assumed who would win such a faceoff . . . "Yeah. Okay, I'll go get—"

"Too late." Peering out the window, Jin hissed a curse between her teeth. "They're coming."

Stupid, Jin bit out silently at herself. *Yes*, it'd all been information the Shahni were going to need; and *yes*, Daulo was the best person to give it to them. But she still should have gotten him and Miron Akim out first.

Clenching her teeth, she looked around the entrance hallway. There was nothing here she could use to fight with; nothing that might realistically allow Daulo to defeat five alert men without killing them. And it *had* to be Daulo who did all the fighting; if Akim found out Daulo had been talking to her he would probably have the entire Sammon family up on treason charges.

Her eyes fell on an electric socket. *Unless*, she amended, *no one actually sees who it is fighting them . . .*

Radig's men were almost to the door now. "All right," she muttered to Daulo. "Get back there—across the hallway—and cover your eyes. Cover them *good.*"

"Then what?" Daulo asked, moving obediently to the spot she'd indicated and raising his forearm across his eyes.

"With luck, you'll grab their full attention when they come in and they won't have a chance to see me. So I wasn't here—you understand? If anyone asks, you took them all out by yourself." Her enhanced hearing was picking up footsteps outside now. "Get ready; here they come."

She flattened herself into the corner behind the door, keying her targeting lock to the electrical outlet and raising her right fingertip to the ready position . . .

And abruptly, the door was flung open.

"Well, well," Radig Nardin said sardonically, sauntering into the entrance hallway. "What have we here? —one of our trustworthy employees overanxious for tomorrow's work to begin? Put your stupid arm down, Daulo Sammon—"

And as the last of the guards stepped across the threshold, Jin squeezed her eyes shut and fired her arcthrower.

Even through closed eyelids the flash was dazzlingly bright. Someone gasped, someone else bit out an oath— and then Jin was in their midst.

It was no contest. Temporarily but totally blinded, facing a sighted opponent with Cobra servos behind her punches, the five men went down like randomly flailing target dummies.

The last *thud* of a falling body was still echoing in Jin's ears when she heard the gasp from Daulo's direction. "God above," he breathed. "Jin—you—"

"No; *you* did all this," she snapped at him. The door was still open; throwing a quick look outside, she caught its edge with the tip of her foot and swung it closed. "Don't forget that—it could cost you your life."

Daulo took a deep breath. "Right." He swallowed and tried another breath. "You'd better get going—Miron Akim's sure to have heard all of this."

"I know." Jin hesitated. There was so much more she needed to tell him, but for now they'd run out of time. "You and Miron Akim had better do the same. If you can get out of Mangus before they realize you haven't been captured, you ought to have a good chance."

"What about you? Aren't you leaving with us?"

"Don't worry, I'll be right on your tail," she assured him. "There's something else I have to check out first, but then I'll be heading for Azras with you. Or behind you, anyway—we don't want Miron Akim seeing me."

Daulo clenched his teeth. "Right. Good luck."

"You too. Remember not to use any of the phones in Azras." The faint sound of running footsteps could be heard from down the hallway now. "And be careful," she hissed. Opening the door, she took a quick look around and slipped outside.

Again, the nearby area was deserted. Moving around the corner, where she'd be out of sight when Daulo and Akim left, she crouched down against the building and made a more leisurely scan of the area. There was occasional movement near the center of the black wall dividing Mangus in half, as well as some quiet activity around the housing complex backed up to the wall. Otherwise, nothing. Keying her optical enhancers for telescopic, she focused on the wall.

It was too tall for her to jump—that much was quickly obvious. Half again as tall as the three-story housing complex near it, it was at least a meter beyond her leg servos' capabilities. She'd been taught a lot of climbing techniques, but all of them assumed some kind of hand and foot grips in the surface to be scaled, and a quick study of the wall didn't look especially promising.

Which left ladders, grappling hooks, or the armored gateway. The first two would require equipment she didn't have. The third, on the other hand . . .

It was the obvious way for her to get in, and for a long moment she seriously considered it. Radig Nardin had mentioned a transfer of material, and if they were going to open the gate anyway, all she had to do was properly disguise herself and walk on in.

Except that her disguise kit was twenty kilometers south of Azras in Daulo's abandoned car. And anyway, if her suspicions were right, Obolo Nardin would hardly have trusted the secret to more than a handful of his closest family members. A stranger—any stranger—would be caught instantly.

A movement from her right caught her eye: Daulo and his companion, walking with forced casualness in the general direction of the gateway she and Radig had entered Mangus by that morning. For a second she

wondered if she should perhaps sneak on ahead and
help clear the way.

But if and when their escape was discovered, the
evidence Jin needed to get could literally go up in
smoke. And besides, Daulo had a new protector now.
She could only hope that the Shahni picked competent
people for their agents.

Taking a deep breath, she headed at a crouching run
across the compound toward the wall.

Chapter 39

The courtyard of the housing complex was bustling with quiet activity, the intermix of voices including those of women and children as well as men. *Must be the permanent workers*, Jin decided as she crept carefully along the roof. Members of Obolo Nardin's family, if the Milika pattern held here; the trustworthy ones, who could be relied on to ignore odd sounds that might come from beyond the wall towering over them.

Though presumably they wouldn't ignore odd sounds coming from directly over their heads. No one seemed to have noticed any noise from her jump up to the roof, but now that she was silhouetted against the overhead canopy all anyone in the courtyard below had to do was look up . . . Gritting her teeth, Jin crouched down a little more and concentrated on keeping her footing.

But she reached the far side of the complex without incident, to find that she hadn't gained as much of an advantage as she'd hoped to. Her rangefinder put the top of the wall at eight meters away and six meters up, and from a standing start—on uncertain footing—it was going to be close. Stepping back a pace, she checked her balance and jumped.

She made it with scant centimeters to spare, her nanocomputer jackknifing her horizontally to let her absorb the impact with her legs as she slammed into the smooth ceramic. Her fingers lunged forward, locked hard over the edge, and for a few moments she hung there motionlessly, listening for any sign that she'd been seen. But the compound remained quiet. Pulling herself up into a prone position atop the wall, she looked down over the edge.

And found she'd been right.

A cold chill shivered its way up her back. *Mangus,* she thought to herself, bitterness at her stupidity bringing a knot to her stomach. *Mangus. Mongoose.* An utterly obvious and natural name for a group seeing itself as the Qasaman answer to the Cobra threat. She and Kruin Sammon had both caught the name's significance, even to the point of having an argument about it . . . and in all of that fuss both of them had still managed to miss one small fact.

The fact that no one on Qasama had any business naming such a group *mongoose* in the first place . . . because no one on Qasama had ever heard the hated demon warriors referred to as Cobras.

Until now.

The Troft ship below was only about half visible, its long neck disappearing into a Troft-style maintenance building while a squat siege-tower unloader partially blocked her view of the main drive nozzles at the aft end. But enough was showing for her to see that the usual inkblot/sunburst indicators of ownership and de-mesne identification were missing.

There were figures moving down there—mostly Trofts, but a handful of humans as well. If the Trofts hadn't bothered to remove the equivalent identity marks from their clothing . . . but a quick telescopic examination showed they had. Something on the oddly shaped residential building across the compound from the ship, then? She shifted her attention to it—

And without warning there was a hooting of alarms from behind her.

Reflexively, she flattened herself to the top of the wall, biting back a curse as the human half of Mangus seemed to explode with light. Her light-amps automatically shut off in the glare; clenching her jaw, she kicked in her audio enhancers to compensate. Her opponents had the edge in sheer numbers, but if she could spot their positions before they started shooting, she might be able to eliminate them before they could do her too much damage.

Trained responses took over from the momentary panic . . . and it was only then that she realized that the floodlights weren't being directed at her. In fact, the placement of many of them—fastened to the wall a meter below her—had actually wound up leaving her in relative shadow. Lifting her head a few centimeters, she keyed her optical enhancers to telescopic and scanned the compound for the focus of the commotion.

It wasn't hard to find. Daulo and Akim, the latter limping slightly, were being half dragged away from the outer gate by an escort of six armed men.

Jin ground her teeth savagely. *I should have gone with them*, she told herself bitterly. For a long minute she watched the group walk toward the administrative center, a hundred wild schemes for saving them rushing tornado-like through her mind. Then, with a shuddering breath, she forced her emotions aside. *All right, girl, knock it off. Calm down and think it out.*

Daulo and Akim had been captured. All right. Obolo Nardin would know soon that they were on to his secret; but then he'd already suspected that much,

anyway. Furthermore, since neither man had escaped
or otherwise breached Mangus's security, there was no
reason for Obolo to panic. Which meant that the inevitable interrogation would presumably be handled in a
relatively leisurely fashion, and also that the Troft ship
down there wouldn't be sent scurrying prematurely off
to space with its cargo only half unloaded.

Until, that was, Obolo discovered his offworlder spy
had escaped.

Damn.

Jin chewed at her lip, trying hard to come up with an
alternative . . . but there wasn't one. Not if she wanted
Daulo to live past the next hour or so. And the whole
idea wasn't as crazy as it looked at first glance, anyway.
Obolo was smart enough, but for all his chemically-
stimulated mental abilities, he still lacked one crucial
fact . . . and as long as he thought Jin was just an
ordinary Aventinian, she and Daulo would have a chance.

The floodlights bathing the compound were still on,
but the activity at the gate was dissipating now as the
prisoners and their escort marched down the road
toward the administrative center. Sliding along on her
belly, Jin eased forward until she was between two of
the wall-mounted lights. The ground directly below
wasn't exactly dark, but it was as good as she was going
to get. Taking a last look around, she slid off the wall to
hang for a second by her hands, and dropped.

And gasped in shock as the impact of landing sent a
stab of pain up through her left knee.

"Damn!" she hissed under her breath, rolling awkwardly over to a sitting position and clenching her leg
tightly. For a long and terrifying minute she was afraid
the vaunted Cobra equipment had failed her, that she'd
actually succeeded in spraining or even breaking the
joint. But finally the pain began to ease, and in another
minute she was able to scramble carefully to her feet
and start limping toward the administrative center.

She hadn't yet figured out how she was going to cover that much floodlit ground without being seen, but fortunately that problem solved itself. She'd taken only a few steps before the lights abruptly cut off, plunging the compound again into darkness. *Excitement's over, folks; go to bed*, she thought, increasing her speed to a sort of syncopated trot. Now if the freshly relaxed security extended to the doors of the administrative center . . .

Surprisingly, it did. Even more surprisingly, it also extended to the lower levels of the building where her cell was located; though once she thought about it it was obvious that any preliminary interrogation of their new prisoners would be taking place upstairs in Obolo's throne room. She hoped Daulo would remember to leave her out of whatever story he and Akim told them.

The guards she'd stunned were still lying unconscious in the washroom where she'd left them. Retrieving them, she treated each to another blast from her sonic as a precaution and then carried them back to their posts. A quick study of the cell door; then, raising her fingertip lasers, she burned a spectacular but shallow arc part of the way around the lock area. *Not too much*, she warned herself. *Your theoretical rescuer didn't get very far, remember*. When Obolo sent someone to check on her—as he eventually would—there had to be a plausible explanation as to why the guards had been knocked unconscious but Jin still a prisoner. Whatever conclusion Obolo came to, it ought to be possible to bend it to her own ends. She hoped.

A minute later she was back in her cell, relocking it behind her via the exposed mechanism. Replacing the metal plate over the opening was somewhat trickier, but by softening it first with her lasers she was able to smooth it back without leaving any major stress wrinkles to show it had once been off.

And after that there was nothing to do but wait. *We'll*

let the offworlder spy kill them for us, Obolo had told
his son. Jin had no idea how he planned to do it; but if
he wanted to do it properly he would need to at least
have Jin in the same room with Daulo and Akim before
they were killed.

She hoped to God that Obolo would want to do it
properly.

"In the name of the Shahni," Akim intoned formally,
"I hereby charge you with treason against Qasama. All
here are released of vows of loyalty to others and ordered to surrender to my authority."

A fine speech, Daulo thought; delivered with just the
right combination of command and righteous anger.

It would undoubtedly have sounded even better if he
and Akim hadn't been on their knees with their hands
manacled behind them.

Seated on his cushions, Obolo Nardin raised a bored
eyebrow. "You maintain your dignity well, Miron Akim,"
he said in a raspy voice. "So. You have said the required words. Now tell me the reason for which you
charge my household with treason."

Akim's lip twisted. "Or in other words, what do the
Shahni know about your treachery? Don't be foolish."

Obolo chuckled humorlessly. "Better and better. Now
you seek to plant doubt within me as to whether any of
my plans are known outside the walls of Mangus. Unfortunately, your attempts are useless. You forget that I
know exactly what the Shahni know of me . . . which is
nothing at all."

There was a flurry of movement behind them. Daulo
risked turning his head away from Obolo Nardin, received a slap from one of his guards for his trouble. But
not before he saw that it was an unsteady Radig Nardin
who was being helped into the room. He focused on
Obolo again, but if the other man was concerned over
his son's health, it wasn't visible. "Well, Radig Nardin?"

he asked. "You were sent to detain them. Why did you fail?"

Radig passed the two prisoners, throwing acid looks at them as he did so. "They ambushed me, my father. One of the guards who was with me may not survive the night."

"Indeed?" Obolo's voice was cold. "Were five then not enough against two?"

Radig refused to shrivel under his father's gaze. "No, my father. Not when they were armed with devices of offworld origin."

Daulo felt his stomach knot up. "Explain," Obolo ordered.

Radig nodded to one of his men, who stepped forward and made the sign of respect. "We found severe burns on and around an electrical socket in the hallway where Master Nardin was attacked," he told Obolo. "Clearly the source of the bright flash that was used against him."

"Indeed." Obolo shifted his eyes to another man standing by. "Bring the offworlder woman." The other nodded and hurried out.

Beside him, Daulo felt Akim stiffen. "What is this about an offworlder woman?" he asked cautiously.

"We have the Aventinian spy you've been seeking," Obolo told him calmly. "She's been our prisoner since morning."

Akim seemed to digest that. "Then perhaps your activities this evening can yet be overlooked," he suggested slowly. "The Shahni are very anxious to find and interrogate this spy. If you release her to me, I'm sure any other problems between you and the Shahni can be . . . worked out."

Daulo held his breath . . . but Obolo merely smiled. "You disappoint me, Miron Akim. The lie saturates both your face and your voice. However—" He raised a finger "—I'll grant you this much: you'll have your chance to interrogate the spy before we kill her."

Akim didn't reply.

"And you, Daulo Sammon," Obolo said, turning his eyes on Daulo. His *shining* eyes, Daulo noted, feeling a tightness in his throat. Jin had been right; the man was high on mind stimulants. "What is your interest in Mangus?"

Daulo considered fabricating a lie, decided it wasn't worth the effort. "The same interest any rational Qasaman would have in a nest of treason," he bit out. "I came to find out what you were doing here, and to stop you."

For a long moment Obolo continued to gaze at him. "You aren't yet defeated, are you, Daulo Sammon?" he said at last. Thoughtfully. "Your friend there is, though he hopes against hope for rescue. But you are not. Why? Is it simply that you don't realize what's at stake here?"

Daulo shook his head silently. "Answer!" Radig snarled, taking a threatening step toward him.

"Peace, my son," Obolo told him calmly. "Whatever secret Daulo Sammon thinks he possesses, it'll be ours soon enough." Abruptly, he leaned over toward his table and touched a button. "Yes?"

The voice was unintelligible from where Daulo knelt, but even so he could hear the nervous excitement in it. A tight smile tugged at Obolo's lips . . . "Interesting, though not entirely unexpected. Alert all guard posts and have a full sweep made of the grounds."

He leaned back into his cushions and glanced up at Radig. "As I said, my son, Daulo Sammon's secret is now ours. It seems the woman wasn't the sole survivor of her spacecraft's destruction."

Radig's hand strayed to the grip of the pistol belted at his side. "She's gone?"

"Her associate was fortunately not that competent," Obolo told him, eyes drifting to Daulo again. "Or perhaps he was sent on an errand. Did she tell him through the door that you needed aid?"

"If you're suggesting I would associate myself with an offworlder spy—" Daulo began.

"It hardly matters anymore," Obolo cut him off coldly. "Except possibly to you. You may be able to buy yourself a painless death if you can tell us where the other offworlder is."

A shiver ran up Daulo's spine. "I don't know what you're talking about," he growled.

Obolo shrugged. "As I said, it hardly matters."

For a minute the room was silent. Daulo concentrating on steady breathing, trying to stay calm. Could Jin have lied to him about being the only survivor? No, she wouldn't have done something like that. Whatever was going on—whatever evidence Obolo's men had found or thought they'd found—Jin was in control of the situation. His life, and Akim's, and possibly the entire future of Qasama—all of them were in her hands now.

It was a strangely comforting thought. More strange yet was the complete lack of resentment accompanying it.

There was the sound of an opening door back behind the curtains. This time he resisted the urge to look around at the approaching footsteps; and a minute later Jin and her escort came into his view.

Her appearance was a shock. Hunch-shouldered, almost visibly trembling as she was half led, half dragged toward Obolo, she looked like nothing more than a simple farming girl being hauled toward terrifying matters totally beyond her understanding. It was as if the Jin Moreau he'd come to know had never existed, and for a horrible moment he wondered if they'd gotten to her with one of their drugs.

And then he caught a glimpse of her eyes as she flinched back from Obolo . . .

Unfortunately, Obolo saw it, too. "Your act is amusing but useless, woman," he said, voice dripping with contempt. "I'm perfectly aware you're not a helpless

Qasaman female. You many start by telling me who you are."

Slowly, Jin straightened up, the aura of fear dropping away from her like a dark robe. "Not that it's any of your business," she said evenly, "but my name's Jasmine Moreau."

Beside him, Daulo felt Akim react. "You know her?" he murmured.

"We know her family," Akim muttered back. "They are . . . rather deadly."

Daulo glanced up at the guards towering over them. "Good," he murmured.

Akim snorted gently.

Obolo's eyes flicked to Akim, back to Jin. "I recognize the family name from our histories," he told her.

"The family name is important on Aventine, too," Jin returned. "Which means they'll eventually be coming to look for me."

"'Eventually' is a long time." Obolo's eyes suddenly narrowed. "Where's your accomplice?" he barked at her.

Jin remained unshaken. "Well beyond your reach," she said calmly. "Somewhere on his way to Azras by now, I'd imagine."

"Leaving you—a woman—to die?" Obolo snorted.

"Women die approximately as often as men do," Jin said icily. "Once per customer. I'm ready to take my turn at it if need be. How about you?"

Obolo seemed taken aback, and Daulo fought to hide a grim smile. Obolo's experience, his secret information network, his expanded mental abilities—none of it could have quite prepared him to face someone like Jin Moreau. Possibly for the first time in years, the man was actually flustered.

But he recovered quickly. "My turn at the cup of death will not be for some time," he snarled. "Yours, on the other hand, will be very soon now. If your

companion is lurking about Mangus, we'll root him
out quickly enough. If instead he's truly run away . . .
he'll return far too late to help you."

Abruptly, he turned to look at Daulo and Akim.
"Take them to the north chamber," he ordered their
guards. "Her as well," he said, gesturing back at Jin.
"Chain all three together, where they may share a last
half-hour together." His lips curled back in a sardonic
smile. "You see, Miron Akim, I keep my word. You will
have your chance to interrogate your prisoner. Before
she kills you."

Chapter 40

The north chamber turned out to be a cozy corner of the curtain-walled maze that was Obolo's throne room. "Quite a mouse track you have here," Jin commented to Radig as he supervised the chaining of her ankles to Daulo's and Akim's. "I'll bet someone who knew what he was doing could hide out for hours without being spotted."

Radig threw her a glower. "A feeble attempt, woman. Your companion isn't here."

"You sure?" she asked blandly. The more she could get them chasing each other in circles, the better.

But he just ignored her, and a moment later left with the other guards. *Well, it was worth a try*, Jin told herself, and turned her attention to Daulo.

To find him glaring bitterly at her. "So," he growled. "It seems Moffren Omnathi was right—you *did* come here to spy on us. We took you in and healed your wounds . . . and in return for our hospitality you lie to us."

The tirade was totally unexpected, and for an instant she stared at him in confusion. But only for an instant. In her peripherial vision, she could see Akim watching them closely . . . "I'm sorry, Daulo Sammon," she said with cool formality. "I regret having had to deceive your family. If it helps any, I never planned to involve you or anyone else on Qasama with my mission."

"That mission being . . . ?" Akim put in.

"I suppose it doesn't matter anymore if I tell you," she sighed, looking around the curtain walls surrounding them. No sounds of breathing; no body-sized hot spots showing on infrared. Which meant Obolo was relying on more sophisticated electronic methods of listening in on the private moments he'd so graciously granted his prisoners. Smiling grimly to herself, Jin activated her omnidirectional sonic. "My mission," she said quietly, turning back to Akim, "is essentially the same as yours: to stop Obolo Nardin and Mangus."

"Indeed," Akim said coldly. "So once again you reach down from the sky to interfere in matters that are ours alone."

"Can we forget politics for a minute and concentrate on the problem at hand?" Jin growled. "Or don't you understand just what Obolo Nardin's got going here?"

"He's tapping into Qasama's communications network," Akim shrugged.

Jin stared at him in disbelief. "And that doesn't *worry* you?"

"Of course it does," he said, eyes steady on her face. "But the scheme is self-limiting. Yes, he can listen into the Shahni's conversations, and that certainly must be dealt with. But you have to realize that the more communications he copies, the longer it's going to take him to find the ones he wants. At the rate he's making and distributing these phones, his entire system will eventually collapse under its own weight. If it hasn't already done so."

Jin shook her head. "I wish it were that simple, but

its not. You see, he doesn't need to sift all these conversations and data transfers by hand. He can do it with computers."

"With computers?" Daulo frowned. "How?"

"It's very simple. All he has to do is have the computers scan each conversation for preprogrammed words or names—"

"And he then has to listen personally only to the ones containing those words," Akim interrupted her. "Credit us with a little sophistication, offworlder—the method is well known. But for the scope you accuse Mangus of indulging in—" He shook his head. "Perhaps you don't realize just how much information is transferred around Qasama in a single day. It would take computers far more advanced than any available on Qasama to handle it all."

"I know," Jin said quietly. "But Obolo Nardin's computers didn't come from Qasama. They came from the Troft Assemblage."

For a half dozen heartbeats the others just looked at her, Daulo with his mouth hanging open, Akim only marginally less thunderstruck. Daulo found his voice first. "That's insane," he hissed.

"I wish it were," Jin said. "But it's not. There's a Troft ship parked right now in the other half of Mangus."

"Which you can't show us at the moment, of course," Daulo growled. "How convenient."

Jin flushed. Daulo was carrying this hostility act entirely too far. "I'll see what I can do later to remedy that—"

"And what," Akim interrupted her, "would the Trofts stand to gain from such a deal?"

Jin turned back to him. "I don't know how much you know about the Trofts, but they're not the monolithic structure you might think. The Assemblage is basically nothing more than a loose confederation of independent two- to three-system demesnes in constant economic and political rivalry with each other."

"Like the villages and cities of Qasama," Daulo muttered under his breath.

Jin glanced at him. "Something like that, yes. My guess is one of those demesnes has decided humans are more of a threat than we're worth, and is trying to do something about it."

"By helping Obolo Nardin gain political power?" Akim frowned.

"By uniting Qasama," Jin corrected quietly. "And then using your world as a war machine against us."

Akim's eyes flashed. "We don't need alien help to hate you, offworlder," he bit out. "But we don't make war under alien orders, either."

"If Obolo Nardin succeeds, you may not have much say in it." A sound caught Jin's ear. "Someone's coming," she hissed, shutting off her sonic.

A second later the curtain was pulled aside to reveal Radig and a handful of men. Radig looked rather annoyed, Jin noted; at a guess, his eavesdropping on their discussion had been something less than successful. "You—offworlder—put these on," he snarled, throwing her a tangle of male clothing. The same clothing, she saw, that she'd worn as a disguise that morning in Azras. "And then what?" she asked as one of the guards stepped forward to unshackle her.

He ignored the question. "That one—" he pointed at Akim "—will be coming with us to the assembly building. You, on the other hand—" he smiled chillingly at Daulo "—we'll keep alive a little longer. Though you probably won't like it."

"What's that supposed to mean?" Jin demanded.

"Get undressed!" Radig snapped.

"Tell me what you're going to do to Daulo Sammon."

One of the guards stepped forward, raised his hand to slap her—

"No!" Radig stopped him. "She's to remain unmarked." He glared at Jin as the guard reluctantly stepped back. "And you ought to be thankful my father doesn't want your body to show evidence of any *other* activities, either. Otherwise we would be postponing your execution by a few hours."

Jin glared right back at him. "You would have found it surprisingly unrewarding," she said evenly. "What are you going to do to Daulo Sammon?"

"Interrogate him, probably," Akim spoke up grimly from beside her. "They're still looking for your companion, remember?"

Jin glanced at Daulo's expression. "I've already said he's beyond your grasp," she told Radig.

"Get undressed," the other repeated coldly. "Before I allow my men to forget my father's orders. *All* of his orders."

For a long moment Jin seriously considered letting them try it. But this wasn't the time or the place for that kind of a confrontation. Swallowing her anger, she changed into the other set of clothes, doing her best to ignore the watching eyes.

It seemed darker, somehow, out in the compound, and it took Jin most of the short walk to the assembly building to realize that it was because the housing complexes were now completely dark. The timing was no doubt deliberate; whatever Obolo and his son had planned, they wouldn't want any witnesses around to see it.

The suspense didn't last long. "Let me explain what's going to happen," Radig said in a conversational tone as the two men holding Jin's arms positioned her in front of the building's entrance. "You, a spy and enemy of Qasama, were trying to steal our technology. Fortunately for Qasama, this alert Shahni agent—" he waved at Akim, held by two burly guards a few meters in front of her "—was here to stop you. Unfortunately for him, you were also armed." He nodded to one of Jin's guards and the man reached a gloved hand into his holster to produce a standard Qasaman projectile pistol. "He shot you, but you managed to kill him before you died. A pity."

"And you then put the gun in my hand to get my fingerprints on it?" Jin asked coldly, watching the pistol being held at her side. The second he raised it to shoot she would have to to act . . .

"Ah—something else you don't know about Qasama," Radig said sardonically. He nodded again, and to her surprise the man with the gun pressed the weapon into her hand, keeping his own gloved hand around hers in a firm controlling grip. "Our science is quite advanced in such matters—more so, obviously, than yours. Here it's possible to prove from a careful residue analysis that a specific shot was fired by a specific gun held in a specific hand. Therefore, each of you will have to fire the fatal shots yourselves. With our help, of course."

"Of course," Jin said sarcastically. A reddish haze seemed to be stealing across her vision, and for a second she wondered if they'd decided to risk drugging her after all. But it wasn't that kind of haze . . . and after a moment she realized what it was.

It was fury. Simple, cold-blooded fury.

A good Cobra is always self-controlled, the dictum ran through her mind . . . but at the moment none of those platitudes seemed worth a damn. Daulo had looked quietly horrified as he'd been led off for his interrogation; Radig's own self-satisfied expression here and now was in sharp contrast as he choreographed his double murder . . . and it occurred to Jin that up till now Mangus had been gaining all the benefits of treason without having to pay any of the costs.

It was time for the balance to be evened up a bit.

A third guard was moving up to Akim's side now, pressing his pistol into the other's clearly unwilling hand. Consciously unclenching her teeth, Jin activated her multiple targeting lock, keying for the centers of the three guards' foreheads. "I presume it's almost time," she said coldly, glancing at Radig before focusing on

Akim. "Tell me, Miron Akim: what's the penalty for attempted murder on Qasama?"

Radig snorted. "Don't try to scare us, woman—" he snarled, taking a step toward her.

"Miron Akim?"

"This is more than simple murder, Jasmine Moreau," Akim replied, his eyes on Radig. "It's murder combined with treason. For that the penalty is death."

"I see," she nodded. "I trust, then, you won't be too upset if I have to kill some of them?"

One of the guards snorted something contemptuous sounding. But Radig didn't even smile. Stepping to her side, he grabbed the barrel of the pistol in her hand and brought it up to point directly at Akim. "If you're waiting for your companion to save you, wait for him in hell," he snarled, eyes glittering with hatred. "In fact, I almost hope he's watching. Let him watch you die."

Jin glared straight back, twisted her right arm free of the hands holding it, and slammed the gun across the side of Radig's face.

He flopped over backwards onto the ground without a sound. The guard holding Jin's left arm spat a curse, but he'd gotten no farther than tightening his grip on her arm before she turned partly around in his direction to slam the pistol against his head. The grip abruptly loosened; and even as the guard to her right threw his arms around her shoulders, she twisted back that direction to swing the weapon into his face. Simultaneously, her left hand whipped up, swept across the group around Akim—

Her peripheral vision caught the triple sputter of light as her nanocomputer fired her fingertip laser, and she turned back just in time to see the three guards drop like empty sacks to the ground.

Leaving Akim standing among the carnage. The pistol they'd meant him to kill her with still gripped in his hand. Not quite pointed at her . . .

For a long moment they stared at each other. "It's all

over, Miron Akim," she called softly, the haze of fury
evaporating from her mind. The hand holding the pistol
was noticeably trembling now. "May I suggest we get
out of here before these men are missed?"

Slowly, the pistol sagged downward; and after a moment, Akim stooped and laid it on the ground, his eyes
on her the whole time. He flinched slightly as she
stepped toward him, but didn't back up. "It's all right,"
she assured him quietly. "As I said earlier, we're on the
same side here."

He licked his lips and seemed to finally find his
voice. "A demon warrior," he said. A shiver abruptly
ran through him. "A demon warrior. Now it finally
makes sense. God in heaven." He took a shuddering
breath. "On the same side, you say, Jasmine Moreau?"
he said with a hint of returning spirit.

"Yes—whether you believe it or not." She risked a
glance around the compound. He hadn't tried to jump
her by the time she looked back at him. "If for no
other reason than because Obolo Nardin wants both of
us dead. So which will it be?—you want to join forces,
or would you rather we tackle Obolo Nardin's private
army separately?"

Akim licked his lips again, glancing down at the three
dead men around his feet. "I don't really have much of
a choice," he said, looking her firmly in the eye. "Very
well, then, Jasmine Moreau: in the name of the Shahni
of Qasama, I accept your assistance in return for my
own. Do you have a plan for getting us out of Mangus?"

Jin breathed a quiet sigh of relief. "A plan of sorts,
yes. But first we're going to have to go back into the
administrative center. Or I have to, anyway."

He nodded with far too much understanding for her
taste. "To rescue Daulo Sammon?"

She gritted her teeth. "His family saved my life, long
before they knew who I was. No matter what Daulo
Sammon thinks of me now, I owe them his life in
return."

Akim looked back at the administrative center. "How did you plan to get him out? More of the same fire-power you just demonstrated?"

"Hopefully less of it." Jin grimaced, locating Radig's unmoving form. "I'd hoped to persuade Radig Nardin to tell me where they'd taken him. Unfortunately, it doesn't look like he'll be up to talking for a while."

"He'll be on the lowest level," Akim said thought-fully. "Probably in a corner room. An airtight one, if possible."

Jin frowned at him. "How do you know?"

He shrugged. "Historical precedent, coupled with the nature of the drugs used in the kind of interrogation they're probably doing. Drugs that are reported to be extremely unpleasant, incidentally. The sooner we get him out, the better for him."

Jin bit her lip. "I know. Unfortunately, there's some-thing else we have to do first."

"Such as?"

"Such as getting our escape route set up. Come on."

Chapter 41

The hard part wasn't taking the high road for the second time that night, jumping from ground to housing complex roof to the top of the wall. The hard part wasn't even inching along the wall on her stomach, leaning precariously down to cut the power cables linking the spotlights and splice them together into a makeshift rope.

The hard part was wondering the whole time whether Akim would still be waiting down below when she finally finished the chore.

But he was. Evidently, she decided as she carefully pulled him up, Shahni agents were not as fanatic as she'd feared they might be. A true fanatic would probably have preferred death to dealing with a perceived enemy of Qasama.

She got him up and spreadeagled in a safe if not entirely comfortable position atop the wall, and for a long minute he gazed in silence at the Troft ship below. "May God curse Obolo Nardin and his household," he spat at last. "So you were telling the truth after all."

"Keep your voice down, please. You know anything about Troft ships besides what they look like?"

He shook his head. "No."

"Me, neither. Which could be a problem . . . because that's where we're going to hide out for the next day or two."

He didn't fall off the wall, or even gasp in stunned astonishment. He just turned a rock-carved face to her. "We're *what*?"

She sighed. "I don't much like it either, but at the moment we're slightly low on options." She waved back toward the administrative center. "As soon as they find out we're gone, they'll turn their half of Mangus upside down looking for us. And since they're already scouring the countryside between here and civilization for my theoretical accomplice, going *out*side the wall isn't going to be any safer. What's left?"

"If we're discovered here, it will be Trofts we'll have to fight," Akim said pointedly. "Will you be as effective a warrior against them as you would be against Obolo Nardin's men?"

Jin snorted, the image of her father battling the target robots in the MacDonald Center's Danger Room flashing through her mind. "We were *designed* to fight the Trofts, Miron Akim," she told him grimly.

"I see." Akim exhaled a thoughtful hiss. "I suppose it really is our best chance, then. All right, I'm ready."

"Yes, well, I'm not. First I've got to go back and get Daulo Sammon, remember?"

"I thought perhaps you'd changed your mind." Visibly, Akim braced himself. "All right, then. Tell me what you want me to do."

He didn't think much of the idea—that much was evident from the play of emotions across his face as she explained it. But he didn't waste any time arguing the point. Unlike Daulo, Akim didn't seem particularly disturbed by the thought of taking orders from a woman. Perhaps he'd had experience with female agents of the

Shahni; perhaps it was simply that he knew better than to let pride get in the way of survival.

A moment later she was moving silently through the darkness toward the administrative center as, behind her, Akim pulled the cable back up. At least this time, Jin knew, she wouldn't have to worry about him leaving before she returned.

She hit the wall a little harder this time, rekindling the ache in her left knee. For a moment she hung by her fingertips, gritting her teeth tightly as she waited for the pain to subside.

"You all right?" Akim asked softly from half a meter in front of her.

"Yeah." Pulling herself up, she rolled onto her stomach facing Akim and took the end of the cable/rope from him. "Knee got hurt in the crash and hasn't totally recovered yet. How about you?"

"Fine. Any trouble?"

"Not really," Jin replied, trying not to pant. Even before that last leap over from the housing complex, the jog from Daulo's interrogation cell with the boy in fire-carry across her shoulder had worn her out far more than it should have. A bad sign; it implied she was getting too tired to give her servos as much of the load as they were capable of. "You were right about him being on the lowest level," she said as she began pulling Daulo up. "Obolo Nardin thoughtfully left a pair of guards outside his door to mark the spot for me."

"Did you kill them?"

Jin's cheek twitched. "I had to. One of them recognized me before I could get close enough."

Akim grunted. "They're all parties to treason. Don't forget that."

Jin swallowed. "Right. Anyway, I found Daulo Sammon strapped to a chair with a set of tubes in his arms and smoke curling around him from a censer under his chin."

"Was he alone?"

"No, but I was able to stun the interrogator without killing him. Okay, here he comes. I'll take his weight; you protect his head."

Between them, they got Daulo up on the wall, draping his limp body over it like a hunting trophy across an aircar rack. "Any idea what they might have used on him?" she asked, trying to keep the anxiety out of her voice as Akim peered closely at Daulo's slack face. The boy was so quiet . . .

Akim shook his head slowly. "There are too many possibilities." He took Daulo's wrist. "His heartbeat's slow, but it's steady enough. He should be able to simply sleep the drugs off."

"I hope you're right." Notching her light-amps to higher power, Jin gave the Troft side of the compound a quick scan. "Did you see any activity over there while I was gone?"

"No. Nor on the other side, either."

Jin nodded. "Hard to believe our escape still hasn't been noticed, but I suppose we should be grateful for small favors."

Akim snorted gently. "Perhaps Obolo Nardin expected his son to disobey the order about leaving you untouched."

"You're a cheery one," Jin growled, shivering. "Well, there's no point in postponing this. Watch his head again, will you, while I flip him over the side?"

A minute later Daulo was down, half lying and half slouching at the base of the wall. "Your turn," Jin told Akim. "Don't step on him."

"I won't. How will you get down?"

She felt her stomach tighten. "I'll have to jump," she said, trying not to think about what had happened the last time she'd tried that stunt. "Don't worry, I can manage it."

Akim's eyes were steady on her. "That last jump from the housing roof—you didn't make it by very much."

"I'm just getting a little tired. Look, we're wasting time."

He gazed at her another moment, then pursed his lips and nodded. Pulling a handkerchief from his pocket, he wrapped it around the cable and held on there with both hands. Rolling off the wall top, he slid down to the ground in a military-style controlled fall. Waving once to her, he knelt and began to untie Daulo from the cable.

This is it. Dropping her end of the cable to fall beside Akim, Jin lowered herself over the edge to hang by her fingertips. Knees slightly bent, she set her teeth and let go. The ground jumped up to meet her—

And she clamped down hard on her tongue as a hot spike jabbed up through her left knee.

"Jasmine Moreau!" Akim hissed, dropping to the ground beside her.

"I'm all right," she managed, blinking back tears of pain as she lay on her back clutching her knee. "Just give me a minute."

It was closer to three minutes, in fact, before she was finally able to get to her feet again. "Okay," she breathed. If she consciously turned over to her servos the job of keeping her upright . . . "I'm fine now."

"I'll carry Daulo Sammon," Akim said in a voice that allowed for no argument.

"Okay by me," Jin said, wincing as she eased back down to a sitting position. "I'll let you carry the cable, too, if you don't mind. But first we have to figure out how we're going to get into that ship."

Akim looked over at it. "Security systems?"

"Undoubtedly." Jin adjusted her enhancers to a combination telescopic/light-amp and made a slow sweep of the unloading tower nestled up to the ship's stern. "Looks like the twin horns of a sonic motion-detector over the doorway there," she told Akim. "As well as a—let me see—yes; there's also an infrared laser sweep covering the loading ramp and a fifteen-meter wedge of ground in front of it."

"What about that one?" Akim asked, pointing at the maintenance building. "The one the craft's nose is buried in."

"Probably something similar." Jin glanced back along the wall behind them. "More motion detectors and monitor cameras over the gateway to the other half of Mangus. A reasonably layered intruder defense."

"Can you defeat it?"

"If you mean can I destroy it, sure. But not without setting off a dozen alarms in the process."

"Well, then, what *can* you do?"

Jin gnawed at her lip. "It looks like our only chance will be to approach the ship from the side. If I can get on top of it, there'll probably be a way to get through the coupling between the unloading tower and the ship proper."

Akim considered that. "That almost sounds too easy. Except for a demon warrior, of course."

"No, their security wasn't planned with demon warriors in mind," Jin said dryly. "On the other hand, they haven't been totally stupid, either. You can't see it, but for about thirty meters out from the side of the ship there's a crisscross infrared laser pattern running a few centimeters off the ground."

"Can *you* see it well enough?"

"Seeing it isn't what I'm worried about. The problem is that the pattern of crisscrosses changes every few seconds."

Surprisingly, Akim chuckled. "What's so funny?" Jin growled.

"Your Trofts," he said, the chuckle becoming a snort of derision. "It's nice to know they're neither omniscient nor even very clever. That laser system is a Qasaman one."

"What?" Jin frowned.

"Yes indeed. Perhaps Obolo Nardin deliberately gave it to them to keep a little extra control over the bargain."

"Meaning there's a weakness in the system?" Jin asked, heart starting to beat a little faster.

"There is indeed." He pointed toward the ship. "The pattern changes randomly, as you noted; but there are between three and six one-meter-square places in every system of this sort where the lasers never touch."

"Really?" Jin looked back at the ship. "Doesn't that sort of negate the whole purpose?"

"There's a reason behind it," Akim said, a bit tartly. "It gives those using the system places to mount monitor cameras or remote weapons. The gaps are normally set far enough back from the edge to be useless to the average invader . . . but of course, you're hardly an average invader."

"Point." Bracing herself, Jin eased to her feet. A flicker of pain lanced through her knee as she did so; she tried hard to ignore it. "Okay. Wait here until you see me wave to you from the top of the tower ramp over there. *Don't* move until then, understand?—I don't want you wandering into range of the detectors by mistake before I figure out how to shut them down."

"Understood." Akim hesitated. "Good luck, Jasmine Moreau."

Akim had been right: the gaps were indeed there, though she had to spend a few tense minutes out in the open watching the lasers go through their paces before she had all four of the spots indentified. The pattern led like meandering steppingstones back toward the ship itself, with distances between them that under normal conditions would have been child's play for her. But with her knee the way it was, it wasn't going to be nearly that easy.

But then, it wasn't as if she had any real choice in the matter. Clenching her teeth, she jumped.

Akim had said the gaps would be a meter square each; to Jin they'd looked a lot smaller. But they were big enough. Pausing just long enough at each point to regain her balance and set up the next leap, she bounded like a drunken kangaroo through the detection field.

The second-to-last jump took her to within three meters of the ship's hull; the last took her to the top of the stubby swept-forward wing.

For a long minute she crouched there, watching and listening and waiting for her knee to stop throbbing. Then, standing up again, she made her way aft along the wing, passing over the blackened rim of the starboard drive nozzle to the forward edge of the unloading tower.

The tower, like the ship, was of Troft manufacture, and the two had clearly been designed to mate closely together. But "closely" was a relative term, and as she approached it Jin could see that the metal of the tower proper gave way to a flexible rubberine tunnel half a meter from the entryway cover. Rubberine was inexpensive, flexible, and weatherproof, but it had never been designed to withstand laser fire. A minute later, Jin had sliced a person-sized flap in the soft material; a minute after that, she was inside the tower.

Inside the tower . . . and standing on the threshold of a Troft ship.

The emotional shock of it hit her all at once, and her mouth was dry as she stepped through the vestibule-like airlock into the ship. *Inside a Troft ship*, she thought, a shiver running up her back as she paused in the center of the long alien corridor. *A Troft ship . . . with Trofts aboard?*

Her stomach tightened, and she held her breath, keying her auditory enhancers to full power. But the ship might have been a giant tomb for all the activity she could detect. *All of them ashore?* she wondered. It seemed foolish . . . but on the other hand, if Troft shipboard life was anything like what she'd experienced on the way to Qasama, the crew was unlikely to spend their nights here by choice. And if there were only two or three duty officers aboard, they'd probably be all the way forward in the command module.

It was a good theory, anyway, and for now it would

have to do. Returning to the airlock, she went back out into the loading tower.

She'd half feared the controls to the approach-detection system would have been routed to the command module, but it turned out the Trofts had elected convenience over extra security. All those long hours of catertalk classes were paying off now; scanning the labeled switches, she figured out the procedure and shut off the system.

Akim was on his feet against the wall, Daulo already hoisted onto his back, when she stepped out into the cool night air and waved. He headed toward her at a brisk jog, and a minute later had reached the ramp. "Is it clear?" he hissed as he started up.

"Far as I can tell," she whispered back. "Come on—I don't want the security system to be off any longer than it has to be."

A handful of heartbeats and he was beside her. "Where to now?" he puffed, pulling back from her attempt to take Daulo's weight from him.

"Forward, I think, at least a little ways," she told him. "We need to find an empty storeroom or something where we won't be getting any company."

"All right," he nodded. His eyes bored into hers. "And when we're settled and have time to talk, you can tell me exactly why you came to Qasama."

Chapter 42

The confrontation was fortunately postponed a few minutes by the necessity of covering their trail. Switching the motion detectors back on was the work of five seconds; trying to seal the hole Jin had made in the rubberine took considerably longer and with far less success. She was able to use her lasers to fuse the edges back together, but the procedure left shiny streaks that stood out all too well against the duller background material. Roughing up the shiny parts with her fingernails helped some, but not enough, and eventually she gave up the effort. As Akim pointed out, anyone coming in through the tunnel would probably be more concerned with his footing than with watching the walls, anyway.

The ship was still quiet as they started down the long central corridor. Jin had hoped to hide them in an empty storeroom where they could be assured of privacy, but it was quickly apparent that that plan would have to be altered. Most of the rooms they found along their way were locked down, and the few that were open still had a fair assortment of scancoded boxes guardwebbed to walls and floor. Akim pointed out at one stop that even with the boxes there was enough room for the three of them; Jin countered with the reminder that the Trofts would probably be coming in to continue their unloading in the morning.

So they kept going. Finally, in the forward part of the main cargo/engineering section, just aft of the ship's long neck, they found an unlocked pumping room with enough floor space for at least two of them to lie down comfortably at the same time. "This ought to do, at least for now," Jin decided, glancing around the vacant corridors one last time before shutting the door behind them. "Let me give you a hand with Daulo."

"I've got him," Akim said, lowering the youth to a limp sitting position against one wall. "Is there a light we can turn on?"

The glow filtering in from the corridor was enough for Jin's light-amps to work with. Locating the switch, she turned on the room's wall-mounted lights. "We shouldn't leave them on long," she warned Akim.

"I understand," Akim nodded, giving the room a quick once-over.

"Do you see anything we can use as a pillow?" Jin asked, lowering herself carefully to the deck beside Daulo.

Akim shook his head. "His shoes will do well enough, though." Stooping down, he removed Daulo's shoes and leaned awkwardly over the unconscious youth.

"I can do that," Jin offered, reaching over.

"I'm all right," Akim said tartly, avoiding her hands. The motion threw him off balance, and he had to drop one hand to the deck to catch himself.

"Miron Akim—"

"I said I was all right," he snapped.

"Fine," Jin snapped back, suddenly fed up with it all. Akim glared up at her as he slipped the shoes beneath Daulo's head. "You'd be advised to show more respect, offworlder," he growled, moving back and sitting down across the room from her.

"I save my respect for those who've earned it," Jin shot back.

For a long moment he and Jin eyed each other in brittle silence. Then Jin took a deep breath and sighed. "Look . . . I'm sorry, Miron Akim. I realize my personality grates against your sensibilities, but right now I'm just too tired to try and fit into the normal Qasaman mold."

Slowly the anger faded from Akim's face. "Our worlds would have been enemies even without the razorarms, wouldn't they?" he said quietly. "Our cultures are just too different for us to ever understand each other."

Jin closed her eyes briefly. "I'd like to think neither of our societies is *that* rigid. Just because we're not the best of friends doesn't mean we have to be enemies, you know."

"But we *are* enemies," Akim said grimly. "Our rulers have shown it in their words; your rulers have shown it in their actions." He hesitated. "Which makes it very hard for me to understand why you saved my life."

Jin eyed him. "Because you're not the Shahni and their thirty-year-old words, and I'm not the Aventinian Council and their thirty-year-old actions. You and I are right here—right now—facing a threat to Qasama that both of us want to stop. *We* are not enemies. Why shouldn't I save your life?"

Akim snorted. "That's a false argument. We're extensions of our rulers—no more, no less. If our rulers are at war, we are, too."

Jin chewed at her lip. "All right, then. If I'm such a threat to Qasama, why didn't you call Obolo Nardin's men while I was off rescuing Daulo Sammon?"

The question seemed to take Akim by surprise. "Because they would have killed me along with you, of course."

"So? Aren't you supposed to be willing to die for the good of your world? I am."

"But then—" Akim stopped.

"But then what?" Jin prompted him. "But then the threat Mangus represents would remain hidden?"

Akim's lip twisted. "You're subtler than I'd thought," he said. "You fight me with my own words."

"I'm not trying to fight you," Jin shook her head wearily. "Not verbally or any other way. I'm simply trying to point out that you're doing exactly what you're supposed to: you've evaluated the potential threats to Qasama, you've figured out which of those threats is the most immediate, and you're throwing every weapon you possess at it." She smiled wryly. "At the moment, I'm one of those weapons."

He smiled, too, almost unwillingly. "And I one of yours?" he countered.

She shrugged. "I could hardly stop Obolo Nardin on my own, even if I wanted to. Besides, he's one of your people. Dealing with him should be *your* business."

"True." Akim glanced around at the metal walls surrounding them. "Though dealing with him from here may prove difficult."

"Don't worry, we'll get out all right," Jin assured him. "Remember, Obolo Nardin seems to be very big on mind-expander drugs, which means he'll be thinking about this very logically. If we aren't in his half of Mangus—and he'll be able to confirm that pretty quickly—then he'll have to assume we got out somehow. It's a solid fifty kilometers back to Azras and we're on foot, so he knows we can't possibly be there before midday tomorrow—today, I mean. Then we either have to contact the Shahni by phone—"

"Which he would know about instantly."

"Right. And since he knows *we* know about his rigged phone system, he knows we'll have to try something else instead." And now came the crucial question. Jin braced herself, trying to keep her voice casual. "So. Are there any radio systems in use on Qasama? Big ones, I mean, not like the little short-range things the Sammon family uses inside their mine."

She held her breath; but if he noticed anything odd in her voice or face he didn't show it. "The SkyJo combat helicopters have radios," he said thoughtfully. "But the nearest ones we could get to are in Sollas."

Her heart skipped a beat. "There aren't any at Milika?" she asked carefully. "I'd assumed your people would come in by helicopter when you heard about the supply pod."

"We did, but those SkyJos have since been sent into the forest to guard your spacecraft's wreckage."

Jin began to breathe again. "I see. And of course, Obolo Nardin will know all that," she said, getting back on the logic of her argument. "So he'll know that we'll have to go all the way to Sollas to find any kind of assault force to hit him with. How far is that by car?"

"Several hours. And more time after that to assemble a force and get it back here, especially since we can't use the phone system. Yes, I see now where you're heading. You think Obolo Nardin will feel secure enough not to panic and begin destroying evidence of his treason?"

"Not for at least the next half day, no. Face it; he's got too much to lose if he cuts and runs when he doesn't have to. Not to mention the fact that if he pulls up stakes here he also loses his best chance of finding us before we can talk. I doubt he'd do that without a specific and imminent threat swooping down toward him." She shrugged. "Now, if another day goes by without him catching up with us, then he probably *will* start worrying. But by then his search parties ought to either be back home or spread out too thin to bother us. And Daulo Sammon will hopefully be back on his feet, too."

Akim looked down at Daulo. "I hate the thought of hiding here while Obolo Nardin has full freedom to operate," he admitted candidly. "The damage he could do to Qasama . . . but I also see nothing better for us to do."

"Well, if something occurs to you, please don't hesitate to speak up," Jin told him. "I might have more of this tactical military training than you do, but you know the planet far better than I ever will."

He grimaced. "Most of it, perhaps. But apparently not enough. Tell me, how did your people discover Obolo Nardin's treason?"

Jin snorted gently. "They didn't. They knew there was something wrong with Mangus, but they got their conclusions almost completely backwards."

She described the satellite blackouts and the missile-test theory the Qasama Monitor Center had come up with. "Interesting," Akim said when she'd finished. "I hope you aren't suggesting the Trofts have given Obolo Nardin advanced weapons, too."

"No, I don't think they'd do anything like that," Jin shook her head. "Trofts never give anything away for free, and certainly not to a human society that's still considered a threat. They'll be keeping a very tight control over what Obolo Nardin gets, and any technology that could conceivably be used against them won't be on the list."

"Hence the security around this ship," Akim nodded. There was an odd note of disappointment in his voice. "Yes, I suppose they would be careful about such things. I take it that it wasn't Obolo Nardin who was knocking out your satellites, then?"

"No, it was the Trofts playing games with them. Trivial to do, too, from close range. They probably sneaked up behind the one they needed to knock out and left a remote chase satellite slaved in orbit to it. That way they could remotely arrange blackouts to cover both landing and liftoff and still leave no hard evidence of tampering when our ships came by to pick up the recordings."

Akim snorted gently. "Yes, your ships. Odd. We've watched them come by for many years, Jasmine Moreau. In the early days we prepared for attack each time we spotted one, wondering if *this* would be the one that would bring warriors down to the surface. Then we discovered the satellites, and began correlating your ships' movements against them, and realized what you were actually doing. But still we watched . . . and two weeks ago, when the long-expected invasion actually came, we missed it entirely." He eyed her. "I trust you appreciate the irony of it."

Jin shivered. "I gave up on irony when my companions were killed."

His expression was almost sympathetic. "We didn't shoot your spacecraft down, Jasmine Moreau," he said quietly.

"I know."

"The Trofts?"

She nodded. "You appreciate irony, Miron Akim? Try this one: given that they never came out to investigate, I don't think they even knew who and what they'd hit."

He frowned. "They attacked without knowing what they were attacking?"

"It was probably some kind of automated hunter/ seeker missile patrolling the airspace, programmed to hit anything flying too close to Mangus. We must have just happened to arrive at the same time one of their ships was landing or lifting; they surely wouldn't have missiles flying around the area all the time."

"Uncontrolled weapons." Akim spat. "And they consider themselves civilized, no doubt."

Jin nodded. "There are things Trofts won't do . . . but some of the things they *will* do are pretty disgusting. We'll have to try and scramble the controls for launching the missiles before we leave the ship or any helicopters you send will be shot out of the sky before they get past Purma."

"Shall we go do that now?"

Jin glanced down at Daulo's slack face. "No. There'll probably be Trofts on duty on the bridge, and we don't want to risk starting anything right now. Tomorrow night, when Daulo Sammon's recovered and you and I have caught up on our sleep, we'll give it a try."

Akim stifled a yawn. "All right. Should one of us stand watch?"

Jin shook her head. "Just lie down against the door, if you don't mind. As long as we're alerted the second anyone tries to get in, I'll be able to deal with them."

"What about you?" Akim asked, sliding across the floor to parallel the door. "There's not really enough room for all of us to lie down."

"Don't worry about me," Jin yawned. "I used to sleep sitting up all the time when I was a girl. I should be able to recover the technique."

"Well . . . all right." Reaching to his feet, Akim pulled off his shoes and slid them beneath his head as he stretched out on his back against the door. "But if you have trouble sleeping, let me know and we can trade off partway through the night."

"I'll do that," Jin promised. "Thank you, Miron Akim. Goodnight."

For a moment his dark eyes bored into hers. "Goodnight, Jasmine Moreau."

Reaching up, Jin flicked off the light. The room fell silent, and for a long while she just sat there in the darkness, feeling utterly drained in body, mind, and spirit. *Two weeks*, Akim had said, since Jin's "invasion" had begun. Two weeks, now, she'd been marooned on this world.

And with an almost shocking suddenness, the end of it was upon her.

With an effort of will, Jin activated her optical enhancers and looked over at Akim. His eyes were closed, his body limp, his breathing slow and steady. Sleeping the sleep of the righteous. *And why not?* she thought, almost resentfully. After all, she'd done her best to convince him that there was nothing for them to do *but* sleep for the next half day or more. This was the eye of the storm, the lull before embarking on what he surely knew would be a long and perilous journey to Azras to sound the alarm.

Except that, with any luck at all, it wouldn't be.

Two weeks. Eight days for the *Southern Cross*, six days for the *Dewdrop*. Fourteen Aventinian days were . . . Briefly, she tried to make the conversion to Qasama days, but her brain wasn't up to it and she gave up the effort. It was close, though; the two planets' rotation periods didn't differ by more than an hour or so.

Which meant that the rescue team could be here almost any time.

We'll listen for your call at local sunrise, noon, sunset, and midnight, Captain Koja's supply pod message had said. *If you can't signal, we'll come down and find you.*

How long would they wait before landing and beginning a full-scale search? Not more than a day, surely. Especially once they confirmed that the shuttle's crash site was being guarded by military helicopters. Twelve hours in orbit, no more, and they'd be coming down.

And when they did . . .

Jin shivered. *We aren't enemies,* she'd told Akim. And she'd meant it. Whether he liked it or not, they really *were* allies in this battle to tear Obolo Nardin's sticky fingers off Qasama. The landing team, though, was unlikely to see things that way.

Which meant she had to get in touch with them before they landed. Probably within the next day. Almost certainly before it was safe for Akim and Daulo to leave.

Her stomach knotted at the thought. What would they think, she wondered uneasily, when she abandoned them here tomorrow evening and made her solitary escape from Mangus? Would they understand that all this really *hadn't* been a cold-blooded scheme to trap them here out of her way? Would they believe her when she repeated that this was still the safest place for them to wait for their own reinforcements to arrive?

And would either understand if she had to kill someone in order to get access to one of those helicopter radios out at the shuttle crash site?

Probably not. But ultimately, it didn't much matter. Whether they understood or not, it was something she had to do. As much for Qasama's safety as for her own.

With a sigh, she turned off her optical enhancers and tried to sink into the darkness surrounding her. Eventually, she succeeded.

Chapter 43

She woke abruptly, and for a moment just sat there in the darkness, heart thudding in her ears as her fogged brain tried to figure out what it was that had startled her so thoroughly out of a deep sleep. Then it clicked, and she surged to her feet, stifling a groan as pain lanced through sleep-stiffened joints and muscles.

"What is it?" Akim hissed.

"Trouble," Jin told him grimly, keying in her optical enhancers. Akim was sitting up now, a hand dabbing at his eyes as he grabbed his shoes; Daulo was still stretched out in sleep. "That deep drone you can hear sounds very much like a pre-flight engine test."

Akim's eyes widened. "A *what*?" he demanded, jamming his shoes on and scrambling to his feet.

"A pre-flight engine test," she repeated, squatting down beside Daulo and shaking his shoulder. "Daulo Sammon?—come on, wake *up*."

"What time is it, anyway?" Akim asked. His groping hand found her arm, squeezed with painful force.

"Take it easy," she growled, shrugging off his hand and checking her nanocomputer's clock circuit. The readout stunned her: they'd been aboard the ship barely seven hours. "Only about mid-morning," she said.

"Mid-*morning*? But you said—"

He was interrupted by a sudden gasp from Daulo. "Who is it?" he croaked.

"Shh!" Jin cautioned him. "Relax—it's Jasmine Moreau and Miron Akim. How do you feel?"

He paused, visibly working moisture into his mouth. "Strange. God above, but those were bad dreams."

"Some of them may not have been dreams," Jin told him. "Do you feel up to traveling?"

Clenching his teeth, Daulo pushed himself into a sitting position, a brief spasm flicking across his face. "I'm a little dizzy, but that's all. I think I'll be all right if we don't have to go too far or too fast. Where are we, anyway?"

"Inside the Troft ship." Jin turned to Akim, noting with relief that he seemed to have recovered his balance. "I'm going to make a fast reconnoiter outside," she told him. "See if I can figure out just what's happening."

"I'll come with you," the other said.

"It might be better if you stayed here with—"

"I said I'll come with you."

Grimacing, Jin nodded. "All right. Daulo, you stay here and get all the kinks out of your muscles. We'll be back in a couple of minutes."

The corridor directly outside the door was deserted, though the sounds of activity coming from all directions indicated that that was probably a very temporary condition. "Where to?" Akim hissed in her ear as she stepped out.

"This way," she whispered back, leading the way

back to the ship's central corridor. Glancing both ways
along it, she started forward at a fast jog. "We need to
find a room with a full-sweep monitor," she added as he
caught up and matched her pace, "and most of those'll
be in the neck and command module."

"You're certain?" he snarled. "As you were certain that Obolo Nardin wouldn't be reacting until
tomorrow?"

She glanced back over her shoulder at his tightly
hostile face. "So maybe I overestimated Obolo Nardin's
nerve," she growled. "Or maybe the Trofts decided the
odds of us getting recaptured weren't all that good and
decided to offload and run before your people caught
them here."

"Or maybe—"

And barely three meters ahead, a door slid open and
a Troft stepped into the corridor.

The alien was fast, all right. His hand went instantly
to the gun belted against his abdomen, closed on the
grip—

And Jin leaped across the gap, one hand grabbing the
gun to lock it in place as the other jabbed hard against
the Troft's throat.

The alien dropped with no sound but a muffled clang.
"Come on," Jin breathed to Akim, looking over at the
door the alien had emerged from. *Port drive monitor
station*, the catertalk symbols read. "Here we go," she
muttered to Akim, and jabbed at the touchplate. The
door slid open onto a roomful of flashing lights and
glowing displays and a second Troft seated in a swivel
chair in front of them.

The alien was just starting to turn around toward the
door as she took a long step forward. It was doubtful he
ever knew just what had hit him.

"Bring that other one in," Jin whispered to Akim,
glancing around to make sure there was no one else
in the room. Akim already had the unconscious Troft

halfway through the door, leaning over to throw one last look each way before he let the panel slide closed.

"Are they dead?" he asked, letting the limp form drop to the deck with a shudder.

"No," she assured him. "They'll be out of action for at least an hour, though. Better leave that alone," she added as Akim gingerly picked up the Troft's laser. "Those are extremely nasty weapons, and I don't have time to teach you how to use it properly. Right now you'd be as likely to damage yourself with it as shoot anyone else."

Reluctantly, he let the laser drop onto the Troft's torso, and Jin turned her attention to the control boards. Somewhere here had to be . . . there it was: *Monitor camera selection*. Now if she could find a camera that covered the rear loading hatchway, or even outside . . . there. "Here goes," she said, tentatively touching the switch.

The central display shifted to a fisheye view that seemed to be coming from somewhere near the starboard drive nozzle. At one edge was a corner of the loading tower's ramp; at the other was the gateway to the human half of the Mangus compound. In the center about a dozen people were running motorized load carriers both ways between the gateway and the ship.

Akim spotted it first. "They're not *un*loading," he said abruptly. "The carriers leaving the ship are empty— see?"

"Yeah," Jin agreed, stomach tightening into a hard knot. "Damn. Perhaps you were right after all, Miron Akim. Obolo Nardin's apparently packing his alien gadgetry onto the ship and deserting Mangus."

Akim swore under his breath. "We can't let him escape," he said. "With those alien computers he'll be able to set up somewhere else in the Great Arc and continue his treason."

"I know." For a half dozen heartbeats Jin watched

the display, trying to think. "All right," she said at last. "Wait here; I'm going back to get Daulo Sammon."

"And then what? Everyone out there is armed; and even if we could get past them all, there's still no way we could call for reinforcements in time."

"I know." Stepping to the door, she slid it open and glanced out. Again, no one was in sight. "We'll have to do something else. Like take over the ship."

Daulo was waiting when she reached the pumping room, pacing restlessly around the cramped space. "What's going on?" he demanded as she slipped back into the room.

"It looks like Obolo Nardin's preparing to leave," she told him, giving him a quick once-over. "How are you feeling?"

"I can make it. What do you mean, leaving?"

"Just what I said. He's got his people loading stuff onto this ship right now."

"And the aliens aren't stopping him?"

"Hardly. They're helping him. Shh!"

A double set of hurrying footsteps passed by out in the corridor. "But how are we going to get off before they leave?" Daulo hissed.

"We're not." The corridor was quiet again. Sliding it open a crack, Jin looked out. "Okay, looks clear. If we meet any Trofts, let me handle them."

They slipped out and headed forward. "Where are they all?" Daulo hissed, glancing around as they jogged.

"A lot of them are probably in the stern, helping with the loading," Jin murmured back. "Most of the rest will be busy back in the engineering rooms or up front in the command module."

The latter being where they were headed. It didn't seem a good idea to worry him with that.

They reached the port drive monitor station without incident, collected Akim, and continued on. "Stay at my sides," Jin warned the two men as they neared the end of the neck. "If I have to shoot it'll probably be straight ahead or behind, and I don't want you getting in the way."

They left the neck and entered the flat-steeple command module beyond it. Jin had been braced for an immediate battle; to her mild surprise, again there was no one in sight. "How many aliens are we going to be up against?" Akim muttered.

"Probably thirty to fifty in a ship this size," Jin told him, trying to remember what little she knew about Troft ship layouts. The bridge ought to be near the top of the command module, just below the sensor blister. A collision door slid open at their approach—

And they found themselves in a spacious monitor intersection.

It was a design, Jin remembered, peculiar to Troft ships. A circular area seemingly carved out of the intersection of two major corridors, its walls were covered by monitor screens and displays. In its center, a wide spiral stair led to the level above. "I think we're here," Jin murmured to the others. "Now stay behind me and—"

"Stop, humans!" a flat, mechanical voice shouted in Qasaman from behind them.

Jin spun around, dropping into a crouch at the base of the stairway and shoving Akim and Daulo to either side. A flash of light and heat sliced the air above her, and an instant later her nanocomputer had thrown her in a flat dive to the side. She rolled up onto her right hip, left leg sweeping toward the Troft as he swung his own weapon toward her. She won the race, barely, and the corridor lit up with the blaze of her antiarmor laser.

She was on her feet in an instant, sprinting back to the stairway. "Follow me up," she snapped at Akim and Daulo, leaping onto the stairs and starting up them five at a time. Whoever was up there couldn't possibly have missed hearing the ruckus, and she had to get to them before they sealed off the bridge.

And for one heart-stopping second it looked like she was going to be too late. Even as she came around the last turn of the staircase she looked up to see a heavy blast hatch starting to swing down over the opening.

Her knees straightened convulsively, hurling her in a desperate leap straight up. Her hands caught the rim of the opening, barely in time—

And she gasped with pain as the rubberine rim of the hatch slammed down on her fingers.

For a long second she hung there, vision wavering with the agony in her hands, mind frozen with the realization that she was completely and utterly helpless. The triggers to her fingertip lasers were out of reach, her sonics useless with a metal hatch blocking them, her antiarmor laser impossible for her to aim. Servo strength . . . Pressing upward with the back of one hand did nothing but send a fresh wave of pain through her fingers like an electric shock—

Electric shock!

Her mind seemed to catch gears again; and, gritting her teeth, she fired her arcthrower.

There was no way to tell if the random lightning bolt actually hit anything; but the thunder was still echoing in her ears when the pressure on her hands abruptly eased a little. Again she shoved upward, and this time it worked. Arm servos whining against the strain, the hatch swung open; simultaneously, she pulled down hard on her other hand, launching herself up and through the opening.

They were waiting for her—or, rather, those who hadn't been leaning on the hatch in the path of the arcthrower blast were waiting for her—but it was clear they didn't really understand what it was they were facing. Even as she shot out of the hatchway like a cork from a bottle, the room flashed with light as a crisscross of laser fire sliced through the air beneath her.

There were five of them in all, and they never got a chance to correct their aim. Jin reached the top of her arc, head coming perilously close to banging against the ceiling, and her left leg swung around in a tight crescent curve across the crouching Trofts, antiarmor laser spitting with deadly accuracy.

By the time she landed, stumbling, on the deck, it was all over.

For a moment she just sagged there, teeth clenched against the throbbing pain in her fingers. The ceramic-laminated bones were effectively unbreakable, but the skin covering them had no such protection, and it was already turning black and blue with massive bruising.

"Is it all right?" a muffled voice called tentatively from behind her.

She turned to see Akim poke his head cautiously over the level of the deck. "Yeah," she grunted. "Come on, hurry up. We've got to close this place off."

Akim came all the way in, followed closely by Daulo. "What happened to your hands?" Daulo asked sharply, stepping forward to take one of them.

"They tried to slam the door on us. Never mind that; you two get that hatch closed and sealed, all right?"

They moved to obey, and she moved past the line of smoldering Troft bodies to give the control boards a quick scan. A dull *thud* from behind her signalled the closing of the hatch, and a moment later Akim stepped to her side. "I don't hear anything that sounds like an alarm," he commented quietly. "Is it possible they didn't have time to call for help before they died?"

Jin frowned at one of the displays, which was showing the same outside scene she and Akim had watched earlier from the port drive monitor station. She wouldn't have thought it possible . . . but on the other hand, this craft was clearly built more along the lines of a small freighter than a warship. If there hadn't been laser alarms built into the corridors, perhaps there weren't any on the bridge, either. "It looks like they didn't," she agreed, gesturing to the display. "They're certainly not showing any signs of panic out there."

"Which means we have some time," Akim nodded. "That's something, at least."

"Only if we move fast," Jin said grimly. "I doubt that hatch will hold them for very long once they realize what's happened." A vague, half-formed plan was beginning to take shape in her mind . . . and unfortunately, she wasn't going to have enough time to work out all the details in advance. "You two stay here; I'll be back as soon as I can."

"Where are you going?" Akim frowned, his voice dark with suspicion.

"To try and put a wrench into Obolo Nardin's plans. Seal the hatch after me, and don't open it again until I signal—three knocks, two knocks, four knocks; got it?"

She turned back toward the hatch . . . paused at the odd expression on Daulo's face. "You all right?" she asked.

He tried twice before he got the words out. "You shot them down in cold blood."

She glanced down at the dead Trofts. "It was self defense, Daulo Sammon," she bit out. "Our lives or theirs, pure and simple."

But the words sounded strangely hollow in her ears; and even through the agony in her hands she could feel a twinge of guilt. Her grandfather, in very similar circumstances, had only destroyed his enemies' weapons . . . "And anyway," she snarled abruptly, turning her back on him, "whoever's running this operation needs a good object lesson. They're going to learn that fiddling around with human beings' lives is a damn costly proposition."

She stepped to the hatch and unsealed it. Or, rather, tried to. But her fingers seemed dead on her hands, and Daulo had to come over and do it for her. "Can you tell us what you're planning?" he asked quietly.

"I'm going to try and short-circuit Obolo Nardin's escape route." She paused for a moment, listening. If anyone was in the monitor intersection, he was keeping quiet about it. "I'll be back as soon as I can."

Chapter 44

The monitor intersection was still deserted, but Jin knew it wouldn't be that way for long. Slipping through the collision door, she left the command module and headed aft down the neck, taking long loping strides that gave adequate speed while still allowing her time between steps to listen.

She was about halfway down the neck when she heard approaching footsteps, and she risked taking another two strides before ducking into one of the rooms lining the corridor. Standing just inside, her ear pressed against the door, she listened as four Trofts hurried past. *Have they realized they've got intruders on their bridge?* she wondered uneasily. But it wasn't a question she could afford to dwell on. Daulo and Akim wouldn't have been any safer anywhere else . . . and anyway, the Trofts would surely try to get their bridge back intact before resorting to anything violent.

She waited until the footsteps had faded completely before opening the door and slipping out. Luck continued to be with her, and she reached the end of the neck without encountering any more Trofts. She stepped from of the neck into the large cargo/engineering section with a sigh of relief—here, at least, she would have room to maneuver if it came to a fight. And with many of the Trofts presumably working back here . . .

She paused as a sudden idea struck her. Interfering with the loading back there was all well and good . . . but if she could cut down the opposition at the same time . . .

She retraced her steps to the base of the ship's neck. Sure enough, the edge of a blast door was visible right where the cargo/engineering section began. The manual control for it had to be nearby . . . there. Hauling on the lever, she watched as the heavy metal disk slid silently across the corridor, cutting her off from the front of the ship. If the door was connected to an automatic alarm . . .

But no sirens or horns went off. *Must be tied into the decompression sensors instead,* she decided, looking for a way to seal the door. There was of course no lock; but she still seemed to be unobserved, and a two-second burst from her antiarmor laser did an adequate job of spot-welding it. The welds wouldn't hold longer than a half-hour or so, even if they were trying not to completely destroy the door in the process. But if she was lucky, a half-hour would be all they'd need.

She continued on into the cargo/engineering section, switching from the main corridor to a smaller—and hopefully less traveled—parallel one. Staying alert, she headed back toward the aft entryway and the loading tower there.

With voices and drones and clangings coming from all around her, her audio enhancers were all but useless; but even so, she heard the Trofts well before she saw them. They were talking, and with all the noise around them they were talking loudly, and for a moment Jin hung back behind a corner and listened.

[—*not* allow them to board yet,] one voice was saying. [The Commander, he does not want them aboard until all equipment has been loaded.]

[The isolation area, it is ready,] a second voice objected. [The humans, they would be out of our way if they were there.]

[More equipment, it must yet be brought to the ship,] the first said.

[The loading, we could handle it more efficiently alone.]

[The equipment to come, much of it is beyond the wall. Would you have the humans there see us?]

The second Troft gave a piercing, almost ultrasonic bray of laughter. [Why not? Their mythos, does it not allow for the existence of demons?]

The first alien didn't echo the laughter. [A risk, it is not worth taking,] he said sternly. [Return to your post. The humans, inform them that anything still beyond the wall in fifteen minutes will not be loaded.]

Jin licked her lips, setting her mind into full combat mode. Clearly, the Trofts weren't wildly enthusiastic about having their Qasaman clients aboard their ship, and while that was good for long-term plans, it did nothing for the upcoming near-term confrontation. The Troft outside the port drive monitor station had drawn on her without challenge or question; she had no intention of letting the ones back here do likewise. Setting her teeth, she stepped out from around the corner.

Just in time to see the two Trofts turn a corner of their own back toward the noise and commotion at the airlock.

She breathed a quiet sigh of relief and hurried after them . . . and was just two steps from the main corridor when the thin wail of an alarm abruptly split the air all around her.

The bridge? Or the welded blast door? She had no way of knowing which the Trofts had discovered . . . but it didn't much matter. Either way, her short grace period was over. Increasing her stride, she swung around the corner—

And skidded to a halt a bare three meters from a scene of chaos.

The rubberine tunnel she'd burned a flap in barely eight hours ago had become a bottleneck of activity, with a half dozen humans, an equal number of Trofts, and several equipment-laden load carriers all traffic-jammed together. The reason for at least part of the congestion was obvious: like a bucket brigade with a single node, the humans were bringing the equipment to the airlock and then passing it on to Trofts to haul into the ship proper.

And as she stopped every eye in the cramped space swung around to lock solidly onto her.

[You!—halt and identify yourself,] one of the nearer Trofts called toward her, his hand swinging toward his belted pistol. "You!" the Qasaman translation boomed from his translator pin an instant later. "Stop where—"

And the rest was swallowed up in the thundercap as her arcthrower hurled a lightning bolt into one of the boxes of equipment lying against the airlock wall.

Someone gave a choking scream; someone else cursed violently. Then all was silent, save for the wail of the alarm in the background.

The six Trofts were all armed, as were one or two of the Qasamans. But no one made any move toward a weapon. No one made any move at all, in fact . . . and as Jin gazed back into their frozen faces she realized why. They all finally understood what it was they were facing.

It would be easy to kill them all. A single swift crescent kick with her left leg, and her antiarmor laser would cut through them like a blazing knife. And it was surely the tactically intelligent thing to do. It would lower the number of opponents facing her, increase the odds of her and Akim and Daulo getting out alive.

You shot them down in cold blood.

She ground her teeth . . . but the memory of Daulo's quiet horror at her handiwork was too vivid to ignore.

And the Trofts on the bridge had fired first. These people hadn't even drawn their guns.

Damn them all. "You Qasamans will leave the ship," she grated. "Now."

No one tried to be a hero; no one tried to argue the point. Those farthest back on the ramp turned and fled, and the others followed immediately, abandoning their load carriers where they were.

Jin's eyes flicked across the Trofts, their arm membranes stretched wide with shock, fear, or anger. Or possibly all three. [Your hands, you will place them on your heads,] she ordered in catertalk.

One of the aliens looked around at the others, his arm membranes rippling for a second before going rigid again. [But you are a female,] he said, clearly bewildered. [A cobra-warrior, you cannot be that as well.]

[One of many things you don't know about cobra-warriors, consider this one of them,] Jin told him. [You and your companions, you will obey my order.]

Slowly, reluctantly, the Troft raised his hands away from his weapon and placed them on his head. After a long second, the others did likewise.

Jin stepped sideways to the edge of the airlock. [You will go into the ship now,] she instructed them. [The loading of equipment, it is now at an end.]

The first alien looked at his companions, gave the Troft equivalent of a nod. Carefully, they filed past Jin into the main corridor. [What about the humans?] the first Troft asked as he joined them.

[Your dealings with them are ended.] Carefully, Jin backed through the airlock toward the loading tower, trying to watch the Trofts and still keep an eye on the ramp behind her.

[A promise, our demesne made them.]

[The promise, it is broken.] At her side now was the control plate for the airlock, and her eyes flicked over to it. The large emergency button was, as she'd expected, easy to identify. Bracing herself, she set her feet, jabbed the button with her elbow, and simultaneously leaped back out of the lock onto the entryway platform.

The outer lock slid shut at high speed, just barely in front of her face. The *boom* of it echoed in the rubberine tunnel—

And a flash of laser fire sliced through the rubberine and metal behind her.

Instantly, she dropped to her belly, twisting over to face down the ramp. A handful of Trofts were visible below, loping cautiously toward the tunnel with lasers drawn. She targeted them, her hands automatically starting to curve into firing position—

She hissed a curse as a stab of pain shot through the injured fingers, belatedly reminding her that the triggers of her fingertip lasers were out of normal reach. Another laser blast sizzled the air above her head; swiveling on her hip and shoulder, she pivoted her feet around to point down the ramp and fired her antiarmor laser.

Her left leg seemed to jump of its own accord, the nanocomputer guiding the blasts with deadly accuracy, and the laser fire from below abruptly ceased.

Though presumably only for the moment. There would be other Trofts down there, as well as armed humans; but with luck, all such opposition would be concentrated on the ship's starboard side, between the Troft housing complex and the gateway to the human half of Mangus. Swinging her leg back toward the airlock, she repeated the welding procedure she'd used a few minutes earlier on the interior blast door. Then, shifting her aim, she lasered a chunk out of the rubberine tunnel. Rolling to her feet, she threw a last quick look down the ramp and leaped through the hole onto the ship's portside wing.

The heat rising from the drive nozzle hit her like something solid as she ran across and past it. Keeping low, she kept going, sprinting forward along the wing. Directly ahead loomed the maintanence building, a familiar-looking rubberine collar molding itself around the last few meters of the ship's neck. To her right, the upper deck of the engineering/cargo section hid her from most of Mangus. To her left—

To her left, a large section of the outer wall had vanished.

It was obvious, of course, once she thought about it. The overhead canopy that hid the Trofts' presence here so well also blocked all normal landing approaches. Building a sliding door into the wall was the most straightforward response.

And from her point of view, a highly useful one. It meant that if she and the others were able to get out of the ship, they wouldn't have any walls to climb.

She reached the rubberine collar without any shots or shouts being directed at her. Once there, however, she realized she had a new problem. There was no gap between collar and ship she could get through, and while her antiarmor laser would make short work of the rubberine it would do so spectacularly enough to alert any Trofts inside the building to her presence out here. But with her fingertip lasers out of commission . . .

Pursing her lips, she knelt down, bringing one knee up and resting the third finger of her right hand on top of it. Straightening the little finger, she mentally crossed her fingers and pressed down on the third-finger nail with her left thumb.

Somehow, she'd always thought that the triggering mechanism depended on having the finger of the appropriate hand curled. Apparently, that wasn't true. This way was awkward, but it worked; and within a few seconds she had a ragged flap burned through the rubberine. Taking one last look behind her, she ducked through into the building.

She'd seen a starship maintenance facility on Aventine once, and this one seemed built along similar lines. The ship's command module—a standard Troft flat-steeple design, as near as she could tell from her perch—stuck out into the center of a huge bay, with movable stairways and ramps leading to the entryways and equipment access areas. Scaffolds and boom cranes lined the bay's walls, all of them retracted away from the ship now in preparation for the imminent lift.

A dozen Trofts were also visible, standing on the ramps or milling about the bay floor. All had weapons drawn, and all were clearly agitated.

And none of them had yet noticed her.

Jin permitted herself a grim smile. They were rattled, all right; rattled and almost totally unsure of what they were doing. *But they're all armed*, she warned herself. *They're all armed, and there are a hell-and-crackling lot of them*.

The reminder sobered the wave of adrenaline-spurred cockiness. Crouching lower, she licked dry lips and considered her next move.

Below and to her left, leading to the rear/port side of the command module, she could see the lower end of one of the movable stairways. It seemed unlikely that it would still be against the ship unless there were an open entryway at its upper end. It was also unlikely that it would have been left unguarded.

But it was the best chance she had; and she had to take it quickly, before the Trofts outside figured out where she'd gone and alerted the rest. If she could get just another few meters along the neck and reach the rear edge of the command module before one of the aliens below happened to look up—

She'd made barely two meters of that distance when the bay suddenly echoed to the sound of excited catertalk.

Jin cursed under her breath, straightening and shifting from a crouch to a flat-out run. A laser split the air in front of her, sending a wash of heat and light over her. Automatically, she closed her eyes against the purple blob now floating in front of them and shifted to optical enhancers. She reached her target spot; skidding to a halt, she twisted forty-five degrees to the side and jumped.

And soared over the rear port corner of the command module to land squarely on the entryway stairs.

For a second she fought for balance, throwing her hands out to the sides and hooking her thumbs onto the railings in a desperate attempt to keep from falling backwards down the steps. For that second she was a sitting duck . . . but once again, the Trofts arrayed against her had been taken by surprise. The alien standing at the head of the stairs in front of the entryway simply stood there, frozen in shock; he was still standing like that when Jin's antiarmor laser all but cut him in half.

Another second was all she got before the weapons around the room opened up again; but it was all she needed. Regaining her balance, she took the remaining steps in a single leap, and an instant later was loping down what she hoped was the right corridor to get her to the bridge.

The corridor was deserted; and ten meters later, she reached the monitor intersection beneath the bridge to discover why. Nearly twenty Trofts filled the intersection, grouped around the circular stairway as they watched two more at the top working on the hatch with a laser torch. They turned en masse as she skidded to a halt, twenty lasers tracking toward her—

And with a *boom* that rattled her own skull, Jin fired her sonic disrupter.

A multiple flash of laser fire lit up the room as a wedge-shaped group of the Trofts collapsed into folded heaps, twitching hands firing almost at random as they went down. Again Jin fired, twisting her torso to a new firing angle; and again, and again, clenching her teeth tightly against the backwash from the sonic and the scorching near misses from lasers only marginally under their owners' control. By the time the first victims had ceased their spasmodic firing, the last group was collapsing to the deck; by the time the last group lay still Jin was on the stairs, pounding on the hatch with the heel of her hand in the three/two/four code she'd left with Akim.

She finished, and waited. And waited . . . and as some of the Trofts beneath her began stirring again there was the sound of released catches above her and the hatch suddenly swung open.

"Jin!" Daulo gasped, eyes wide as he stared down at her. "Are you—?"

"I'm fine," she grunted. "Get out of my way, will you?—they'll be able to fire again any second now."

He stepped back hastily, and she leaped up the last steps into the bridge. Akim was waiting to the side, and she'd barely cleared the rim before he slammed the hatch back down again. "You came back," he said, squatting down to seal the catches.

"Didn't you think I would?" Jin countered. Suddenly her knees were going all wobbly; staggering over to one of the chairs, she collapsed into it.

Akim stepped over to her, eyes flicking down her body. "We'd thought you might go for help."

"Help from where?" Jin countered. "Didn't we agree that we couldn't even reach any of your people for several hours?" Her foot touched something metallic; leaning back, she spotted a row of five laser pistols beneath the panel. "You making a collection?" she asked.

"We thought it would be good to have all the weapons together," Daulo told her. "For when . . . we weren't sure you were coming back, you know."

"Why *did* you return?" Akim demanded. "Let me be

honest: I don't want to share my death with an enemy of Qasama."

Jin took a deep breath, exhaled it raggedly. "With any luck, you won't have to. Has the Troft commander tried to communicate with you?"

"He wants us to surrender," Daulo put in from behind her, clearly fighting against a tremor in his voice. "He says we can't possibly win and that they don't want to kill us if they don't have to."

"I don't blame them," Jin nodded. "Especially since he'd probably wreck his bridge in the process." She leaned forward, studying the control panels before her.

Akim followed her gaze. "What exactly are you planning, Jasmine Moreau?" he asked. "Are you going to fly this spacecraft out of Mangus?"

Jin snorted. "Not a chance. I've never flown anything bigger than an aircar in my life, and this isn't the time to start." She paused, looking over her shoulder as a faint crackling sound wafted into the bridge. The sound was coming from the hatch. . . . "They're back again," she said, stomach tightening as she turned back to the controls. Somewhere here there had to be—

There it was. Taking a deep breath, Jin hunched forward and tentatively touched the switch. "What are you doing?" Akim demanded suspiciously.

"You remember, Miron Akim, how surprised we were that Obolo Nardin would panic this early?" she asked. The volume control . . . there. Microphone? . . . clipped to the wall over there. "We wondered why both he and the Trofts would throw away their listening ear when there couldn't possibly be any enemies on their way here yet?" she added, working the mike free of its clip and gripping it awkwardly between palm and thumb.

"I remember," Akim growled. "Are you leading up to giving us the answer?"

"I hope so." She took a deep breath. If she was wrong . . . Raising the mike to her lips, she touched the operating switch. "This is Jasmine Moreau," she said in Anglic. "Repeating, this is Jasmine Moreau. Please respond. This is Jasmine Moreau; please respond. This is Jasmine—"

And abruptly the board speaker boomed in reply. "This is Captain Koja; commanding the *Dewdrop*. We read you, Cobra Moreau, and we're ready to come down and pick you up."

Chapter 45

It took Jin three tries to relax her throat enough to speak again. "Understood, *Dewdrop*," she managed at last. "I—" she glanced up to see Akim gazing darkly at her. "Please tie in your Qasaman language translator."

There was a slight pause from the other end. "Why?"

"I have some Qasamans here with me," Jin explained, switching back to their language herself. "I think they ought to be in on the discussion."

"Who are you talking to?" Akim demanded.

"An Aventinian ship," Jin told him. "Here to rescue me. Captain, are you still in orbit?"

"Yes." The word was Qasaman, the voice the artificial one of a translator program. "Where are you?—wait a minute, the head of the rescue team wants to get in on the conversation."

"Jin?" a familiar voice said in accented Qasaman . . . a voice fairly dripping with relief. "Jin, it's Dad. Are you all right?"

Jin felt her mouth drop open. "Dad! Yes, yes, I'm fine. You—but—"

"What, you didn't think I'd drop everything to come get my daughter back? Oh, God, Jin—look, where are you?"

"In that covered compound west of Azras—Mangus, they call it. Wait a minute, though, you can't come down just yet."

"Why not?"

"You might run into a hunter/seeker missile. Courtesy of the Trofts whose ship I'm talking to you from."

There was a long pause. "We were wondering how you'd gotten on this frequency," the *Dewdrop* translator said at last. "What in blazes are Trofts doing there?"

"At the moment, trying to get us out of their bridge so that they can airlift some Qasaman allies to safety."

"*Allies*? You mean the Trofts and Qasamans have made an alliance?"

"No, no, it's not that bad. There's nothing official about this; it was a private deal with some Qasaman thugs making a power play."

"A power play which may yet succeed," Akim muttered.

Jin glanced up at him. "Yeah, right. The problem, Dad, is that we've got to find a safe passage out of here for the three of us and at the same time make sure Mangus's owners don't get away before the Qasaman rulers can deal with them."

"Now, wait a minute, Jin," Justin said cautiously. "We'll get you and your friends out, certainly, but the rest of it sounds like internal politics. Nothing we ought to get involved with."

Jin took a deep breath. "We're already involved, Dad, just by my presence here. Please just trust me on this one."

"Jin—"

"Cobra Moreau, this is Koja," the translator interrupted him. "Let's table this discussion until you're safe, all right? Now, you said you were on the bridge?"

"Yes, and we're sort of trapped—"

"Can you describe the ship? Is it a warship, or what?"

"From the way the crew fights, I doubt it. Let's see: the ship's got a large cargo/engineering section with sagging swept-forward wings over twin drive nacelles. The front section looked like a pretty standard flat-steeple command module, and there's a long neck connecting the two sections. No identification marks anywhere I could see."

"Okay. I'll see if we've got anything on this design on file."

"Jin?" Justin's voice came back on. "This is Dad. Now, you say you're trapped on the bridge?"

"Yeah, and they're trying to burn up to us through the emergency blast hatch. I can fight them if necessary, but I'd prefer it if we could find a way to convince the commander to just let us go."

"It's worth a try. Can you tie him in to us?"

Jin peered at the board again. "Hang on . . ."

[That will not be necessary,] a burst of catertalk cut in. [I have been listening.]

"I thought you might be," Jin said, only lying a little. "In Qasaman, please, Commander—as I told the *Dew-drop*, my companions need to hear all this, too."

There was a momentary pause. "Very well," the Troft's translator voice said. "I will listen, but you must realize that I cannot allow you to escape."

"Why not?" Justin asked.

"Our demesne-lord's agreement with the Qasaman Obolo Nardin will come to nothing if his plan is ruined."

"The plan's already ruined," Jin told him. "How are you going to get your allies into your ship for transport, now that I've sealed off the cargo section? And where are they going to stay during the ride?"

"Foolish human! How many other ways into our ship do you think there are?"

"Several," Jin agreed. "But you really don't want to let them see the areas you'd have to take them through. True?"

"The Qasamans can learn nothing from a casual glimpse of our equipment."

"Maybe. But if you're wrong, the Qasamans might advance a little too quickly . . . possibly quickly enough to break your grip on them before you have a strong enough puppet government in place. Is your demesne-lord willing to take that chance?"

"It is a negligible risk," the Troft insisted.

"Perhaps," the *Dewdrop*'s translator put in. "Let's put it another way, then. Would your demesne-lord be willing to let an entire Crane-class starcarrier fall into Qasaman hands?"

For a long moment there was silence; and in that hiatus, a keen awareness of her body's condition seemed to flood into Jin's consciousness. Awareness of the throbbing ache in the stiff fingers of both hands—of the burning sensation in her left ankle from excessive use of her antiarmor laser—of an even more painful burning along her ribcage where one of the laser shots fired earlier must have come closer than she'd realized. Her eyes drifted around the bridge, and she realized for the first time just how much equipment was really here. Would she have the ability and stamina to systematically destroy all of it if she had to? Because that was the only realistic threat they had to bargain with.

And the Troft commander clearly knew it. "Our ship can be flown without the use of the bridge," he said at last.

"Oh, certainly," the *Dewdrop* agreed. "Most ships can. But not very easily. Besides which, the bridge isn't the only thing in danger here. There's a sensor bubble directly over her head, for one thing—it wouldn't take all that much for her to punch through to that. Oh, now *there's* an interesting idea," Koja interrupted his own thought. "If your ship follows standard design, there should be parallel connections between all your sensors for making synchronity checks. A good jolt of high voltage along that connector cable might just take out every navigation sensor you have on the ship."

"Ridiculous," the Troft snorted.

"Maybe. There's one sure way to find out."

Again the Troft was silent. "You may have the Cobra," he said at last. "If she will leave the ship now, she will be allowed safe passage away from here. The Qasamans with her may not leave, though."

"Jin?" Justin asked.

"No," she said firmly. "My companions leave with me, or I wreck the ship. But I'm ready to make you a counter offer."

"I am listening."

"Okay. You let the *Dewdrop* land—safely—and allow the three of us to leave here, and there'll be no further damage to your ship."

"And . . . ?"

"No ands. We'll leave Qasama, you'll leave Qasama, and it'll all be over."

Akim snorted and turned away from her. Jin frowned over at his stiff shoulders, then turned back to the panel. "Face reality, Commander; your demesne-lord's scheme has failed, and all you can do is cut his losses."

"The scheme has not failed until the Qasaman authorities have been made aware of Mangus's true purpose," the Troft countered.

"Then your ship is dead," the *Dewdrop* said flatly. "Not just the bridge and sensors, Commander, but the entire ship. If Jin wrecks the bridge, it'll be hours before you can fly—you know it and we know it. Long before then we'll be there, even if we have to drop down outside your hunter/seekers' patrol range and come in on foot. And we have thirteen Cobras aboard."

A movement caught Jin's eye, and she looked up as Daulo stepped over to the spot at her side that Akim had just vacated. "Do you think he'll accept?" he asked in a whisper.

"He'd be a fool not to," Jin murmured back. "He has to have some idea of what a ship full of Cobras could do to him. Even just by myself, I could have killed half his crew if I'd wanted to."

"You should have done so," Akim growled from behind her.

"I'd like to end this mess with as little bloodshed as possible," she shot back over her shoulder. "It's enough that we chase the Trofts off Qasama; we don't have to kill them all just to underline the point. Unless the commander insists on that kind of lesson, of course."

"I do not so insist," the Troft commander said with something that sounded almost like a sigh. "Very well, Cobra: I agree to your terms. To your left is a keypad. Enter the following words."

Jin swiveled to the keypad as the Troft shifted into catertalk and gave a series of commands. "What's he telling you?" Daulo asked.

"Looks like the procedure for recalling the roving hunter/seeker missiles to the ship," she told him. A display above the keypad came alive. "Yes," she confirmed, studying it. "The missiles have been deactivated . . . they're on their way back to the ship."

"We're ready to break orbit, then, Jin," the *Dewdrop* said. "Shall we land near Mangus?"

"Better not—the Qasaman military may track your path in." She paused, thinking. Presumably the Qasamans weren't listening in . . . but Akim was, and she didn't want Qasaman helicopters getting to the *Dewdrop* before she did. On the other hand, if she shifted back to Anglic now, both Akim and Daulo might worry that she was giving the ship secret instructions.

And that bothered her. For reasons that weren't clear even to her, it had become very important to her to show that Qasama and the Cobra Worlds could trust each other at least this once. "Okay, here's how we'll do it," she said at last. "Picture Qasama as Aventine, with Mangus where Capitalia would be. Get down low where they can't track you and then take a circumspect route to Watermix. You get that?"

"Got it," the *Dewdrop* came back immediately. "You ready to head out to meet us?"

Jin looked at the hunter/seeker readout. If she was interpreting it correctly, the missiles were within fifteen minutes of reaching Mangus. "Yes, we're ready," she said into the mike.

"No, we're not," Akim said.

Beside her, Daulo turned and inhaled sharply. Slowly, carefully, Jin swiveled around in her seat, to find Akim standing against the opposite side of the bridge, a small device in his hand pointed at her. "What do you mean by this, Miron Akim?" she asked quietly.

"Exactly as I said," he replied, equally quietly. "We're not leaving yet. I'm claiming this ship for the Shahni of Qasama . . . and I intend to make certain it won't escape us."

Chapter 46

For several heartbeats Jin and Akim just gazed at each other. "I wondered why you went along with me on all this," Jin asked at last. "Now I know. You want the stardrive in this ship, don't you?"

"The stardrive?" Akim snorted. "You think too small, Jasmine Moreau—or perhaps too big." He waved his free hand around him, keeping the other pointed at her. "There's literally nothing aboard this ship we won't be able to use. The stardrive, the computer systems, the powerplants—even the crew's personal effects will give us information about these new enemies we face." He nodded his head slightly toward the lasers behind her under the panel. "Daulo Sammon and I had time in your absence to learn how to use those hand weapons. You were right; they are indeed powerful. All by themselves they will be worth a ransom."

Jin's eyes flicked to his hand. "Weapons mean a lot to you, don't they? That's, what, a breakapart palm-mate dart pistol?"

387

Akim nodded. "Designed from the one Decker York used on our people thirty years ago. We learned a great deal from your last invasion; we'll learn even more from this one. Get up, now, and go over to the hatch."

"Why?" she asked, not moving from her seat.

"I want one of those lasers behind you. This ship is staying here, and your people were kind enough to tell me how to keep it from leaving."

I can stop him, she thought. *My sonic—*

Would be slow enough to leave Akim time for a reflexive shot. And if the poison they'd coated the darts with was anything like the ones the original model used . . . *Okay, okay, don't panic girl*, Jin told herself firmly. *You're still in control here.* With a flick of her eyes her nanocomputer's autotarget capability was locked onto the palm-mate in Akim's hand; and with a casual curving of her hands—

She inhaled sharply as a fresh wave of agony lanced through her injured fingers. Once again, she'd forgotten about her hands.

And it left her only the antiarmor laser and arcthrower to use against the palm-mate. The first of which would vaporize Akim's hand in the process . . . the second of which would kill him outright.

A hard knot began to form in Jin's stomach. *I won't kill him*, she told herself firmly. *I won't.* "Miron Akim, listen to me—"

"I said *get up!*"

"No!" Jin snapped back. "Not until you hear me out."

Akim took a deep breath, and Jin could see the knuckles on his gun hand tighten momentarily. "I don't intend to break our truce, Jasmine Moreau," he grated. "You've been of great help to us, and I won't kill you unless I have to. But I mean to have this ship."

Jin was suddenly aware of the mike still in her hand, and of the total silence from the speaker behind her. Both the *Dewdrop* and the Troft commander were waiting. Listening. "Miron Akim, listen to me," she said, fighting hard against the trembling in her voice as she reached behind her to set the mike down on the panel. "You don't want this ship. Qasama isn't ready for it yet."

He spat. "And you of Aventine are omniscient enough to know that, are you?"

"How are you going to control it?" Jin persisted. "You've seen how Obolo Nardin used the computers he was given—how are you going to keep someone else from doing something similar?"

"The Shahni will control the technology. They'll make sure it's used properly."

"Used by whom? Are the Shahni going to become a technocratic oligarchy, then?—doling out new technology to those they deem fit?" She shook her head. "Don't you see, Miron Akim, how something like that would change the whole texture of Qasaman society? I've seen how you do things here, the way your cities and villages each have their own unique political balance, independent from that of the next town over. Your people take great pride in this, and well they should; it's one of your society's greatest strengths. For that matter, search your records and legends—it was to escape from an overly centralized government that your ancestors left the Dominion of Man in the first place."

"Then perhaps it's time we grew up," Akim said stubbornly. "Would you have us hold onto petty quarrels and pride at the cost of civil war?"

"Civil *war*?" Jin snarled. "God above—you worry about civil war, and you want to add new *weapons* to the mixture?"

"The weapons will be controlled by the Shahni—"

"For how long? Months? Days? And what do you think will happen once a single village or city gets hold of one of them?"

Akim clenched his teeth. "I'm an agent of the Shahni," he grated out. "I'm charged to obey their orders, and to do that which benefits Qasama as a whole. It's not my place to make these larger policy decisions."

"Why not?" she countered. "For that matter, you've already made a policy decision. If standing orders are all that count, why haven't you killed me?"

"If keeping Qasama defenseless is all that counts to *you*," he countered, "why haven't *you* killed *me*?"

She sighed. "Because ultimately it doesn't matter. No matter what you do, Qasama won't get this ship. If the Trofts can't get it off the planet, they'll destroy it."

"Even damaged, it'll be worth—"

"Not *damaged—destroyed*," Jin snapped. "They'll turn the engines into a minor fusion bomb and blow the ship, themselves, and Mangus into dust and scatter it into the upper atmosphere. You heard me talking to the Troft commander—they're scared to even let Obolo Nardin's people get a glimpse at their readout displays. You think he'll let you take his crew alive and his ship intact?"

For a long moment the only sound in the room was the muffled hiss of the laser torch coming from the direction of the hatch. Jin kept her eyes on Akim, acutely aware of the targeting lock on the other's weapon . . . acutely aware, too, of Daulo's stiff presence a meter to her left. She wished she could see his face, try and get some feeling as to which side of this confrontation he was on. But she didn't dare look away.

"No," Akim said suddenly. His face was rigid, eyes almost unfocused, and Jin felt a sympathetic ache for him. But the other's voice was firm, with no hesitation left for her to work against. "No, my duty is clear. Even if it doesn't seem that I can win, I still have to try." He took a deep breath. "Stand up, Jasmine Moreau, and move over to the hatch."

Slowly, Jin stood up. "I beg you to reconsider, Miron Akim."

"Move over to the hatch," he repeated stiffly.

Licking her lips, her eyes still on Akim, Jin took a sidling step to her left toward the lock—

And gasped as her left knee collapsed beneath her.

Perhaps Akim had been expecting a trick; perhaps he merely reacted reflexively to her sudden movement. Even as Jin's hands snapped out toward Daulo's chest, she heard the faint *snap* of the palm-mate, and the hoarse whisper of the poisoned dart piercing the air bare centimeters from her right arm. She could almost sense her nanocomputer assessing the situation; could feel it preparing to take control of her servos and launch her into a defensive counterattack that would leave Akim burned to ashes—

And at the last instant before her outstretched hands reached Daulo's chest, she flipped her left hand over, curving the palm inward, and jammed the heel of her right hand against the left's fingertips. The fingernails slammed into Daulo's breastbone with the full force of her right hand behind it—

And with a flash of heat against her right wrist her left-hand fingertip laser fired.

Akim jumped violently to the side, swearing viciously as the blackened remains of his palm-mate went spinning to the deck. With a curse, he leaped toward Jin, hands curving into talons.

Jin waited, feet braced against the deck; and as his arms curved toward her shoulders she jabbed her arms out, the heels of her hands slamming hard into his upper chest. The impact stopped him dead in his tracks; sliding one hand around each of his shoulders, Jin twisted him around and shoved him hard into the chair she'd just been sitting in.

For a moment he just sat there, looking up at her in dazed astonishment as he caught his breath. "All right," she told him, taking deep breaths herself as the pain in her fingers slowly retreated again to a dull ache. "Let's get out of here before the Trofts get nervous and blow the ship regardless."

"Jin!" The *Dewdrop*'s translator called faintly from the speaker. "What's happening? Are you all right?"

"I'm fine," she called back. "All of us are. Commander, call your men off and we'll open up the bridge."

"Understood," the Troft translator said. "You will not be harmed."

Slowly, Akim got to his feet and faced Jin. "Someday," he said bitterly, eyes boring into hers, "we will repay you in full for all you have done to us."

She met his gaze without flinching. "Perhaps. At least now you'll have a chance of surviving to do so."

Silently, he moved toward the hatch. She followed, keeping her attention on him . . . and because of that they were halfway there before she suddenly realized Daulo wasn't following. "Come on, Daulo Sammon," she called over her shoulder. "Time to leave."

"Not quite yet," he said quietly.

Frowning, she threw him a quick glance . . . and then looked again.

Daulo was standing well back from her, pressed against the communications board. In his hand was one of the captured lasers. "Daulo Sammon?" she asked carefully.

"Thanks to you, your world is now safe from us," Daulo said tautly. His face was pale, but the gun was steady. "At least for now. But *you*, Jasmine Moreau, aren't nearly so safe . . . and the repayment Miron Akim spoke of can begin with you."

"Hold it!" Justin shouted. "You—whoever you are—if you harm her, you'll never get off that ship alive."

"You'll have to catch us first," Daulo called to the mike. "And by that time, we'll have figured out just what to do with her."

"Damn you! If you so much as—"

Stepping to one side, Daulo shifted his aim and fired a long burst into the communications board.

The *Dewdrop*'s voice was suddenly cut off . . . and the clatter of Daulo's laser as he tossed it casually to the deck again was almost shattering in the taut silence.

"Daulo . . . ?" Jin asked, feeling her eyebrows come together in bewilderment.

Daulo looked at her, took a deep breath. "*Now* we can leave," he said quietly. "And we'd better go quickly. Before, as you said, the Trofts get nervous."

Beside Jin, Akim took a step toward Daulo. "Would you mind explaining," he grated, "just what in God's name *that* was supposed to prove?"

Daulo gestured upward. "Her father is up there," he said simply.

For a long second the two men eyed each other . . . and then a smile tugged at Akim's lips and he snorted gently. "Clever. Very clever. Or it will be if it works."

"I think it will," Daulo nodded. "Like a good Qasaman family, they are very close." He looked at Jin. "Well, come on, Jasmine Moreau," he said briskly. "Let's get out of here."

The walk down the corridor was a nerve-wracking one. Jin had rather expected a large escort to tag along to make sure they actually left Mangus, but to her uneasy surprise they rated only a single Troft to lead them out of the ship, and he abandoned them just beyond the portside entryway where Jin had earlier shot her way back into the ship. "I don't like this," Akim muttered as they hurried down the steps into the now deserted maintanence bay. "Obolo Nardin's men may be waiting to gun us down out there."

"If Obolo Nardin's got any brains, he'll have his people behind their own wall by now," Jin said as they ran across the bay toward an exit door that would let them out of the maintenance building near the gap in the outer wall. "The Trofts seem to be in a flat-out hurry— that drive rumble is getting louder, and I wouldn't want to be on this side of Mangus when they fire up the engines for real."

The words were barely out of her mouth when, abruptly, the rumble swelled to a roar and a piercing ultrasonic whine rose to accompany it. "It's moving!" Daulo shouted over the noise, waving back at the ship.

Jin glanced over her shoulder. *My God, he's right,* she thought, stunned, as she watched the command module sliding smoothly back through the now retracted rubberine collar along the reddish haze of the ship's gravity lifts. "Run!" she shouted to the others. "Outside, to whatever cover you can find."

They needed no urging. Flinging open the building door, they sprinted out across a short patch of bare ground to the wall. Even here the air was becoming noticeably warmer; if they were anywhere near the nozzles when the Trofts kicked the drive to full power, Jin knew, they would stand a good chance of being charred on their feet.

They passed the edge of the wall at a dead run, and it took only a glance to see that there was nothing anywhere that could possibly serve as cover. "That way!" Akim shouted into the din, waving his arm to the right as he turned to run that direction. "Around the corner of the wall!"

It was the best they were going to get. Akim in the lead, they tore along the wall toward the south-east point of the Mangus diamond-shape a hundred meters away. Jin's left knee flashed stabs of pain with each step; gritting her teeth against the agony, she forced herself to keep going. Behind and to her side, she heard Daulo panting with the effort—sensed him stumble—

"Daulo!" She skidded to a halt and grabbed for his arm, gasping with pain as she reflexively tried to close her hand.

"No!" he panted, waving her forward. "Just go—never mind me—"

The rest of his protest was swallowed up in a sudden blast of sound from beyond the wall. Jin didn't hesitate; throwing one arm across Daulo's back and the other behind his knees, she lifted him bodily and ran.

She nearly made it. Akim was around the corner, and she and Daulo were within five paces, when the landscape in front of them abruptly flared with light and an incredible wave of heat washed over them from behind. In her arms Daulo cried out; blinking back tears, Jin fought to keep her balance against the hurricane windstorm behind them. She reached the corner—tried to turn—

And from seemingly out of nowhere Akim's arm darted out, grabbing Jin's just above the elbow and spinning both her and Daulo around the corner to sprawl to the ground.

For a few seconds Jin couldn't speak . . . but then, for that same time neither of the others would have been able to hear her, anyway. The roar from the Troft ship was deafening—far louder than she would have expected it to be—and seemed to go on forever. Finally— finally—it began to ease, and within a few seconds had faded to a whine in the distance.

Leaving behind it the crackling of fire.

"God in heaven—they've set Mangus on fire!" Akim snarled suddenly, leaping up and disappearing around the corner in the direction of the wall opening.

Jin scrambled to her feet and took a few steps back from the wall. Sure enough, the overhead canopy was flickering with reflected light from the flames beneath it. On the ground in front of her, Daulo said something under his breath. "What?" she asked, stepping closer.

"I said they were fools." Gingerly, Daulo propped himself up on an elbow, took a deep breath. "If they'd wanted to destroy their half of Mangus properly, they should have had a self-destruct set up ahead of time. Now they're always going to wonder what they left behind we might be able to use."

"Good," Jin said grimly. "Maybe that fear will keep them from coming back and trying this again. Odd that they'd panic like that, though; once they were rid of us,

they really had all the time they needed to do their
cleanup properly."

Daulo chuckled. "No, they didn't." He squinted
toward the sky. "Take a look."

Frowning, Jin peered skyward . . . and felt her throat
tighten.

Above them, a dark shape ringed with red haze was
dropping swiftly toward the ground. "The *Dewdrop?*
But . . . I told them not to land here."

"Of course you did. And I expect your father had a
very sharp argument with the others about that after I
threatened you and then destroyed your link with them."

Jin looked back down at him, suddenly understanding. "Is *that* why you did it? To get the *Dewdrop* down
here faster?"

"Not faster, really. Just more directly."

"More—?" Jin clamped her mouth shut. "Oh. Sure.
Wherever they track the *Dewdrop,* that's where they'll
send the helicopters. Perfectly obvious."

His eyes were steady on her. "I had no choice, Jin.
Even if you'd been willing to take us directly to Azras,
we still might not have gotten the military here before
Obolo Nardin covered his trail and cleared out."

"Agreed," Jin nodded. "Very clever, as Miron Akim
said. I wish I'd thought of it myself." The *Dewdrop* was
showing a recognizable shape now. Lying down on her
back, Jin raised her left leg and sent three antiarmor
laser bursts in the ship's direction. "That should let
them know I'm all right," she explained.

Daulo slid over to sit next to her. "I'd rather . . .
hoped we'd have a little more time together once this
was over," he said, almost shyly. "Before you had to
leave."

Jin reached over to touch his hand with her fingertips. "I did, too," she said, and was mildly surprised to
find how much she really meant it. "But I don't think
we can afford to stay. Miron Akim told me there were
two of those SkyJo helicopters based near my shuttle; if

they get the tracking data fast enough, they won't be more than a few minutes behind us."

Daulo nodded, and for a moment they watched the *Dewdrop* dropping through the sky toward them. Then, with a grunt that was half sigh and half groan, Daulo climbed to his feet. "Speaking of Miron Akim, I'd better go and track him down. Make sure he hasn't found some weapon and is lying in wait for your ship with it."

Jin got up too, conscience nagging uncomfortably. "Daulo . . . look, I . . . well, I want you to know that I really *did* plan to fulfill my half of our bargain."

He frowned at her. "What are you talking about? You don't think that my finding the way to capture Obolo Nardin and Mangus isn't going to raise my family's status?"

"But that was all *your* doing, not—"

"Could I have done it without you?"

"Well . . . *no*, not really. But—"

"Jin." He stepped close to her, put his hands on her shoulders. "The bargain is satisfied. Really."

Over the plain behind him, the *Dewdrop* was sweeping down toward Mangus. "Okay," Jin sighed. "Well, then . . . I guess there's nothing to say but goodbye. Thank you for everything, Daulo."

Leaning forward, Daulo kissed her gently. "Goodbye, Jin," he said, smiling at her. "I hope this will let your uncle keep his power among your people."

Jin had almost forgotten about that. "He will," she nodded. "There's no way even his enemies can twist what's happened into failure."

"Good." He smiled again, this time with a touch of mischievousness. "Then perhaps he can talk them into letting you visit Qasama again."

She smiled back. "If I can, I will—that's a promise. If I can't . . . you'll be getting back into space again someday. You can come visit me."

The background whine that had been growing steadily louder over the past few minutes suddenly shifted pitch. Looking over Daulo's shoulder, Jin saw the *Dewdrop* had landed. "I've got to go," she said, disengaging herself and stepping away from him. "Goodbye, and thank your father for me."

There were five men crouching in a loose arc around the *Dewdrop*'s entryway before she was halfway there— Cobras, all of them, by their stances—but she didn't pay any real attention to them. Silhouetted against the hazy glow from the gravity lifts, another man was running toward her. Moving with the slightly arthritic gait she knew so well. "Dad!" she shouted to him. "It's all right—no one shoot!"

A moment later she was in his arms. A minute after that, they were aboard the *Dewdrop*, heading for space.

Chapter 47

". . . it is therefore the opinion of the undersigned members of the Directorate that the Mangus mission in general, and the actions of Cobra Jasmine Moreau in particular, be considered a success."

Corwin sat down, letting the end of the joint opinion—and its four signatures—linger on the syndics' displays for another moment before blanking it and pulling the magcard from his reader. At the center of the speakers' table, Governor-General Chandler stood up. "Thank you, Governor Moreau," he said, eyes flicking once to Corwin before turning away. "One might expect that, with virtually none of the facts or testimony from the Mangus mission in dispute, it would be a straightforward matter for this body to come to a conclusion as to its success or failure. However, as will soon become apparent, it's often possible to interpret things in more than one way. You've heard Governor Moreau's interpretation, and that of his co-signers; I yield the floor now to Governor Priesly and a different point of view."

Priesly stood up, his eyes fairly flashing with righteous fervor as he inserted a magcard in his reader . . . and Corwin braced himself.

It was even worse than he expected.

" . . . and so let me now summarize the main points:

"Cobra Moreau failed to keep her identity as an Aventinian spy hidden from the Qasamans, in clear violation of her orders.

"Cobra Moreau furthermore failed to keep her identity as a Cobra hidden from those same Qasamans, spoiling any future chance we might have of taking them by surprise with a similar ruse.

"Cobra Moreau voluntarily spent a great deal of time in close proximity to a member of the official Qasaman government. She spoke at length with him, cooperated with him, and—even more damaging—repeatedly demonstrated her Cobra weaponry in his presence.

"Cobra Moreau deliberately allowed the Troft meddlers to escape, thereby ruining any chance we might have of identifying them and making sure any threat of this alliance between them and Qasama is at an end.

"And finally, as a direct result of her actions, Cobra Moreau permitted the other mission members' bodies to fall into Qasaman hands, allowing the Qasamans to examine them and denying us the opportunity to give them decent and proper burials.

"It is therefore the opinion of the undersigned members of the Directorate that the Mangus mission in general, and the actions of Cobra Jasmine Moreau in particular, be considered a failure."

Jin was sitting by the window of her room, curled up into her old loveseat and staring outside at the waning light of sunset, when the tap came on the door. "Jin, it's Dad and Uncle Corwin," her father's voice said quietly. "May we come in?"

"Sure," she said, not turning around. "I've already heard, if that's what you want. It hit the net a couple of hours ago."

"I'm sorry," Corwin said, pulling up a chair to just inside her peripheral vision and sinking tiredly into it.

"May I?" her father asked, stepping to her side and waving at the loveseat. Jin nodded, shifting her legs off the seat to make room for him and wincing as her knee protested the action. The injury was probably going to lead to early arthritis in the joint, the doctors had told her; earlier even than the usual Cobra average. Just one more little sacrifice for the Mangus mission.

One more sacrifice for nothing.

Justin sat carefully down beside her. "How do you feel?" he asked.

"How *should* I feel?" she countered.

He sighed. "Probably about the same way we do."

She nodded. "Probably."

For a few moments the room was silent. "Look, Jin," Corwin said at last, "you really shouldn't be taking any of this personally. *I* was Priesly's target, not you. You just happened to be the most convenient conduit for the attack he had in mind."

"Oh, I was convenient, all right," she said bitterly. "Everything I did—everything I said—he just twisted all of it into knots like a snake pretzel. And everyone just rolled over and believed him."

Corwin and Justin exchanged looks. "Well, now, that may be open to debate," Corwin said. "I take it you stopped reading after the opinion reports and final vote came on?"

"I'd already seen how Priesly mangled what really happened," she said, blinking back tears of frustration. "I didn't need to see what the public would do with it."

"Oh, then, you missed a real treat," Justin said. Jin

frowned over at him, to find a smile quirking at his lips. "It seems that about fifteen minutes after the vote came out an anonymous transcription hit the net: purportedly, that of discussions in the upper ranks of the Ject camp over the past couple of days. It shows several men, including Priesly himself, deciding how best to distort what happened on Qasama to their own political benefit."

Jin stared at him. "But who would . . . you two?"

"Who, us?" Corwin asked, radiating wide-eyed innocence. "As a matter of fact, no, we had nothing to do with it. Apparently it was some unidentified Ject of Justin's acquaintance who decided that perhaps Priesly was going a bit too far on this one."

Jin took a deep breath. For one brief moment it had felt better . . . "But it really doesn't help any. Does it?"

Corwin shrugged. "Depends on whether you're talking short-term or long-term results. Yes, I've resigned my governorship, so as far as that goes Priesly's won; and yes, your supposed failure will probably make it difficult, if not impossible, for other women to be accepted into the Cobras."

Jin snorted. "So what are all the big long-term gains? The fact that Qasama is temporarily safe from Troft meddling?"

"Don't sell that one short," Justin chided her gently. "Mangus was indeed as great a threat as we'd thought all along, just not quite as immediate a one. *That* part of your mission was a complete and resounding success—and everyone on the Council knows it, whether they admit it publicly or not."

"And we've made at least two other long-term gains, as well," Corwin told her. "First of all, Priesly may not yet realize it, but in kicking me out of the Directorate he's shot himself in the foot."

"How?" Jin asked. "Because it makes him look like a bully?"

"More or less. Never underestimate the power of a sympathy backlash, Jin, especially when it involves a name as historically revered as ours." Corwin smiled wryly. "In fact, I've been preparing a campaign for the past few days to try and guide the expected public reaction straight down Priesly's throat. Now, with all this other stuff coming out, I don't think I'll have to bother."

Jin closed her eyes. "So the Jects lose power, and all it costs is your career," she sighed. "Standard definition of a Pyrrhic victory."

"Oh, I don't know," Corwin shrugged. "Depends on whether I was tired of politics anyway, doesn't it?" Gently, he reached over to take one of her bandaged hands. "Times change, Jin, and we have to change with them. Our family's had more than its fair share of political power over the past few decades; perhaps it's time for us to move on."

"Move on to what?" she asked.

"Move on from politics to statesmanship," Corwin said. "Because we've now got the one thing neither Priesly nor anyone else in the Cobra Worlds can take away from us." He lifted a finger and leveled it at her. "We've got *you.*"

Jin blinked. "Me?"

"Uh-huh. You, and the first ever genuinely positive contact with the people of Qasama."

"Oh, sure." Jin snorted. "Some contact. The twenty-year-old niece of an ousted political leader and the nineteen-year-old heir to a minor village mining industry."

Her father made an odd sort of sound, and Jin turned her head to look at him. "What's so funny?" she demanded.

"Oh, nothing," Justin said, making a clearly half-hearted effort to erase his amused smile. "It's just that . . . well, you never can tell where something like that will lead."

He took a deep breath; and suddenly the amusement in his smile vanished, to be replaced by a smile of pride and love. "No, you never know, Jasmine Moreau, my most excellent daughter. Tell me, have you ever heard the story—the *full* story, that is—of your grandfather's path from Cobra guardian of a minor frontier village to governor and statesman of Aventine?"

She had; but it was worth hearing again. Together, the three of them talked long into the night.

Here is an excerpt from Farside Cannon *by Roger MacBride Allen, coming in 1988 from Baen Books . . .*

The governor's aide smiled nervously and knit his hands together. "Governor, before you hurry back to your guests, allow me to suggest that you haven't quite absorbed the significance—and the urgency—of what's happened concerning the laser system on the Far Side. Let me take a moment or two more of your time."

The Governor of the Lunar Colony glared at his subordinate and snorted loudly—an impressive performance, thanks to his patrician face and aquiline nose. "Make it quick, for God's sake. This nonsense has taken up enough of my time already. I have reputation as a host to maintain."

The weasely-looking aide hurried around behind the console, sat, and set his hands on the controls of the display. "Let me go over the situation once again." The keyboard chuckled as he rattled in a series of commands. "I just want to show what that laser actually *did* to the comet during that so-called experiment. Here's the light curve off Comet Holmes. Luminosity over time." The governor had just about the technical proficiency to operate his wristwatch, the aide thought, but perhaps even *he* could understand this. A graph-grid sprung up on the big wall screen.

A line started to draw itself across the bottom of the grid, moving left to right, then suddenly turning almost ninety degrees, shooting nearly straight up. "This is the point where the 'fluorescing experiment' began," the aide explained. "Bear in mind that this is a logarithmic scale—each horizontal line represents a power-of-ten increase in luminosity. As you can see, Comet Holmes went from a

10th-magnitude object, far too dim to be seen with the naked eye, right up to negative 20th magnitude, about as bright as a full moon seen from Earth—over a period of *hours.*"

The aide shifted the controls again, and the image of the comet itself burst onto the screen, a phantasamagoric sprawl of light, a twisting, whirling starburst of reds and oranges, three separate tails writhing, undulating, out from the core. The governor and his aide both stared at the display in silence for a long time, as awestruck by the recording as they had been by the event itself.

As they watched, a bright flash of light swelled up from the center of the comet head and then vanished. "Outgassing," said the aide. "Violent outgassing. To put it another way, you're seeing the comet start to boil. An ice ball ten kilometers across, and they set it to *boiling.*" A note of hysteria started to creep into his voice. "After this point, the comet vaporized altogether in less than a day. It's now nothing more than a large and somewhat diffuse patch of gas and dust, not much denser than a low-grade vacuum, sailing through space about twenty million kilometers out starward from the moon." The aide pulled out his handkerchief and wiped a thin film of nervous sweat from his brow.

"After their cheerful little press release," he went on, "we now know that the comet was irradiated by the Farside Laser Relay, which is supposed to be a comm-laser system of relatively low power, with nowhere near the capacity to do this. *Nothing* is supposed to have this sort of capacity. However, it was a fairly straightforward matter to calculate the amount of energy Comet Holmes absorbed, and from there to back into an estimate of the Relay's *actual* power. We estimated that, instead of 50 laser units slaved together, the Array now has five to ten thousand laser units, each powered by its own solar collector."

The aide stood up and walked in front of the screen, a

short, spindly figure silhouetted by the glorious, glowing riot of color on the screen behind him.

"There isn't a single Free-Flier Settlement it couldn't destroy. There isn't a domed Settlement on any planet whose environmental system it couldn't wreck within hours, simply by heating the whole dome past safety limits. There isn't a ship in space that could get within twenty million kilometers of it that it couldn't incapacitate in ten seconds, or wreck altogether in under a minute.

"But the powr output of this laser isn't the most frightening thing about it. I'd like to remind the Secretary who, exactly, is in *control* of this little toy.

"Did you *read* the press release from Farside Station? No? Pity. I had it in your terminal the moment it arrived. You really ought to read more, sir. It's really most broadening." The aide smiled, a wild, alarming leer that flashed on and off in a moment, an eyeblink view of the madness of panic. "It's almost a truism that every malcontent intellectual and alarmist scientist in the whole Solar System ends up at Farside Station sooner or later. One of these malcontents, a gentleman by the name of Dr. Garrison Morrow—who can thank this office, and you *personally,* sir, for being stuck in the most isolated spot in the Inner System. Dr. Morrow has been declared the 'mayor' of Farside, whatever exactly that may mean. He, apparently, conducted this 'experiment.'

"*He* is now in charge of an impregnable weapon of immense power, whose elements are either well dispersed or well dug into the lunar surface, a weapon capable of tracking and destroying any ship, bomb, or missile that could be launched against it. I have given you some idea of what he could do with this laser cannon—but no one has the slightest idea what he *intends* to do with it. I think we can safely ignore their pronouncements about defending humankind—but you didn't read them anyway, did you? Again, a pity.

"At any rate, I respectfully ask the governor to consider the political ramifications of such a dangerous weapon being on the Far Side of the Moon—a point from which it can strike, and destroy any point in the inhabited Solar System. Every point except one: Earth.

"None of the other inhabited worlds can possibly tolerate its existence. They may be out-gunned and out-manned by Earth, but they can't possibly let that weapon exist. They will demand it be shut down, or better still, destroyed.

"Except, of course, that there is no way for them—or us—to destroy it, or even get near it, though we ourselves do not control it. Of course, I doubt the Settlement worlds will believe *that,* since it is on our territory—and the entire staff of Farside Station is on the Colonial government's payroll. All in all, it represents an interesting problem. Wouldn't you agree, sir?

"The Security Council will be convening in about fifteen minutes. Perhaps the governor would reconsider, and let his dinner guests fend for themselves just this once?"